Maeve Haran shot to fame with .... *Having It All*. Since then she has .... successful novels, including *Scenes From The Sex War*, *It Takes Two*, *A Family Affair*, *All That She Wants*, *Soft Touch* and *Baby Come Back*. She has twice been shortlisted for the Romantic Novel of the Year Award, in 1993 for *Having It All* and in 1999 for *All That She Wants*. A former journalist and producer, she is now a full-time writer and lives in north London with her husband and their three children.

Also by Maeve Haran

The Farmer Wants a Wife

MAEVE HARAN

timewarner
paperbacks

A *Time Warner* Paperback

First published in Great Britain in 2001
by Little, Brown and Company
This edition published by Time Warner Paperbacks in 2002

A CIP catalogue record for this book
is available from the British Library.

ISBN 0 7515 3284 3

Typeset in Berkeley by M Rules
Printed and bound in Great Britain by Clays Ltd, St Ives plc

Time Warner Paperbacks
An imprint of
Time Warner Books UK
Brettenham House
Lancaster Place
London WC2E 7EN

www.TimeWarnerBooks.co.uk

For my darling daughter,
Georgia, for her passion
and perceptiveness

Chapter 1

Flora Parker closed her eyes, struggling with a nagging sense that she'd done something really bad last night.

Not her usual level of bad: winding up pompous City types in wine bars or racing prats with big cars who thought they had willies to match. Something told her this was worse.

A lot worse.

A voice she dimly recognized as her conscience was whispering that last night involved a Major Sin, certainly a Major Mistake.

Error number one had been the whiskey. Why oh why had she developed a sudden taste for Irish whiskey? Normally she loathed all spirits, but Miles had been insistent. Blackmills Whiskey was launching its trendy new label, designed to appeal to hip young people, and Flo was one of the hip young people they'd invited to help the launch. So naturally she'd had to drink the stuff, but not, perhaps, in such large quantities. But then Flo never did anything by halves, good or bad.

She tried to climb out of bed but her head felt as if a jet engine had landed inside it and gone into reverse thrust.

Error number two was in bed with her.

Between her and the wall was a large lump under the duvet. If God still existed and he hadn't already hardened his heart against Flo because of her previous bad behaviour, the lump would turn out to be a giant cuddly toy, even one of those really repulsive ones full of stuffing you won on piers. Flo glanced round the room nervously, her eyes alighting on a pair of black and white ponyskin boots.

She groaned. Only one person in London, or probably the universe, was insensitive enough to wear those boots. What was she doing in bed with Miles? Miles was the leading light of Flo's glitzy set. An East End boy who'd started in Walthamstow and ended up in a smart house in the King's Road, Miles did a little bit of this and a little bit of that and somehow made an awful lot of money. He also knew everyone who was even remotely fashionable or useful and could persuade them to turn up at parties to add glamour and sparkle. Which was how Flo had come to be hired to promote Blackmills whiskey. Even the mention of the word now made her feel queasy.

Miles had been pursuing Flo for as long as she could remember but until last night she'd always resisted his advances. He was good-looking in an overblown kind of way and could be funny and acerbic. His painfully accurate yet horribly mean descriptions of people they both knew often had her in fits, even if they did leave a guilty

aftertaste. But there was something about Miles she
didn't trust. His darkly sensual looks made you think of
the young Elvis – the same full pouty lips, and the same
extra coating of flesh on his handsome face – yet there
was nothing soft about his personality. No detail ever
passed Miles by.

Flo shuddered at the thought of what they might
have got up to last night. Someone more gentlemanly
than Miles might not have taken advantage of the situation, but Miles was no gentleman.

But then you're no lady, Flo reminded herself sternly.

Still, she did have her standards even if they weren't
those of Mother Teresa. It was fine in Flo's book to sleep
with twenty men (not at once, of course, though that
had possibilities) provided you actually wanted to. The
worst sin was to sleep with even one that you didn't.

She tried to remind herself that most women had
slept with *someone* they regretted. Either they couldn't
find a way of saying no, or felt sorry for the guy, or even
(shameful to admit) couldn't be bothered to get a mini-
cab back to Clapham. Sex ought to be a garden of
delight but sometimes it was more of a convenient patio.

Flo had none of these excuses. She was in her own
home, under her own duvet, and was supposed to be
strong, feisty and one hundred per cent her own person.

If she was so strong and feisty, asked a nasty little
voice, how come she'd drunk half a bottle of whiskey
and gone to bed with Miles?

A hot blush of shame and anger spread across her
skin. Being your own person did not mean going to bed
with someone who reminded you of a boa constrictor

contemplating lunch. And now he'd had lunch. And she'd been it.

She could just picture Miles's leering expression when he woke up, not to mention his enthusiasm to take up wherever they'd left off last night. A cheering thought hit her; maybe Miles had drunk as much as she had and she'd been rescued from her fate by Blackmills Droop – though being Miles he probably had his own personal store of Viagra.

Next to her the duvet stirred. Miles's face emerged, a knowing smile lighting up his clever, calculating eyes.

'Good morning, gorgeous. At last you succumbed. And, I have to admit,' he leaned towards her possessively, 'you were well worth the wait.'

Flo had to restrain herself from whacking him. The creep even thought she'd be flattered by this revelation.

Miles pulled himself up and sat back on her personal pillows. His skin was pale and hairless, a stark contrast to his almost-black hair. Most women in her set fancied him rotten. Miles's particular brand of ravaged sophistication spiced with a hint of rough trade gave them orgasms on the spot. But Flo wasn't one of them.

She jumped out of bed, grateful that her messy blonde hair (it defied any hairdresser to make it look chic) almost covered her boobs and that at least she'd kept on leopardskin bikini briefs. 'We're out of milk,' she announced by way of explanation.

Miles smiled seductively. 'I'm prepared to make the sacrifice.'

'But I'm not,' Flo insisted. She needed to get away. To think. To come up with an excuse that would get rid of him without offending him totally. Miles wasn't the type you'd want as your enemy even if you didn't want him as a lover. Besides, she owed him some shred of dignity.

She found one of her five-inch Jimmy Choo stilettoes under the bed and hopped about looking for the other.

'Love the shoes. You look like a high-class stripper,' Miles approved, 'or a dancer at the Crazy Horse Saloon. I can just see you in tassels.'

'Sorry, chum.' Flo pulled off the shoe since she couldn't find its pair, and wasn't going to give Miles the satisfaction of seeing her stick her bum in the air as she searched for it. God alone knew what low desire that would stimulate. 'You'll have to settle for a mac and trainers.'

When she opened her bedroom door a small white ball of fur hurled itself at her, covering her ankles with slobbery kisses. Flo bent down and tickled her little terrier's ears. 'Hello, Snowy. Who's a brave guard dog, then?'

The abject adoration turned to a snarl when Snowy caught sight of Miles in her mistress's bed. Snowy had been a present from a previous incumbent who'd insisted that if Flo wouldn't keep his heart, she could at least keep his dog. No doubt Snowy saw Miles as the enemy.

'Come on, good dog,' Flo enticed, 'come and get some milk with me.' Snowy, who was always given bars of chocolate by Mr Sanjay who ran the corner shop, yapped in enthusiasm.

Outside the flat Flo could breathe again. Miles's

pervasive presence had caught at her throat like asthma.

The lugubrious Mr Sanjay smiled at her approach and even turned down his radio, an unusual honour. 'Top of morning to you, Miss Parker,' he greeted her.

Mr Sanjay's range of greetings was always colourful.

Was it Flo's imagination or was he looking at her oddly this morning? She glanced in the mirror Mr Sanjay kept hidden amongst the packets of Rothmans and Marlboros, like a little shrine, to see if she had a huge spot, another side-effect of too much Blackmills. But no, her usual features stared back at her: untidy blonde hair, wide hazel eyes for once not smudged with three days' worth of mascara, a strong nose, as her mother had called it, and jawline to match. Not beautiful but somehow all the sexier for it.

'Very nice photo,' Mr Sanjay offered, staring not at Flo but into the middle distance behind her. 'Very lively and gay.'

Snowy, wanting her usual treat, was standing comically on her back legs.

'What's a very nice picture?' Flo asked, selecting a pint of milk from the chill-cabinet.

'Of you.' Mr Sanjay gestured towards the day's paper, trying not to grin disrespectfully. 'In newspaper.'

Flo followed the direction of Mr Sanjay's finger. There she was, on the front page of the *Daily Post*, stripped to her Wonderbra, holding a bottle of Blackmills whiskey towards the camera. HELLO BOYS, read the headline, FANCY A DOUBLE?

A hot wave of shame flooded over Flo, making her feel sick and shaky. It all began to come back to her. The

Blackmills, which seemed so innocent to someone who'd never touched whiskey before, the blaze of flash-bulbs. Why could she never bloody resist it? She picked up the paper wondering if her father would get to see this. Maybe the *Post* wasn't exported to America.

But isn't that what you really want? asked a voice inside her.

Weren't half the scrapes she got into at least partly because her father didn't seem to care if she were on the same planet? Even obscurely seemed to blame her for her mother's death.

'Oh, cut the self-pity, Flora,' she told herself merci-lessly. 'You screwed up, end of story.'

In that instant Flo knew she had to get away. Away from Miles and from the ludicrous freeloading world they inhabited, where image was all, and where drunk-enly taking your top off made you some kind of sleazy celebrity.

But where could she go to? If only she had a brother or sister. For the millionth time Flo longed for a happy family, for a family like they'd once been before her mother got ill. Since her mother died there'd been no one. No loving relatives to tease her for her outra-geousness and forgive her anything. Instead she had a bulging address book full of so-called friends, but apart from Miranda, her ally and friend since school days, no one would really care whether they heard from her again.

A distant memory seeped into her mind of a family holiday at her aunt's home in the country. It had seemed a happy house, bathed in the golden sunlight of her memory, full of mud and dogs, shabby yet comfortable. That had been before everything changed. Maybe she could go there now? But how would her straight-laced uncle react to having his wayward niece, currently flaunting herself all over the tabloids, suddenly arrive and fling herself into the bosom of his family?

As she tried to leave the shop, with Snowy behind her, she found herself doing an embarrassing little dance with a man who was trying to get in. Finally Flo stood aside and let him go first. The man's eyes flickered from Flo to the newspaper, displayed prominently on its wire rack. 'Bloody hell,' he mumbled, 'aren't you her, I mean . . .?'

Flo grabbed Snowy and ran back towards the flat. Surely her mother's only sister wouldn't turn her down even though she hadn't been in touch, apart from Christmas cards, for all these years?

The thought of her mother brought a stab of sudden pain. She'd never got over missing her, not for a single day. All the pain of losing her mother and of her father's rejection flooded back, choking Flo with unshed tears.

Her ancient Beetle was outside the flat. She couldn't bring herself to go in and face Miles. On the opposite corner of her street the flower seller called her a greeting. He was an old friend. She bought a bunch of roses from him every week and when she was broke, which was quite often, he gave them to her cheap saying a lovely girl like her had to have lovely flowers, considering all the old boots who bought thirty-quid bouquets from him.

'Terry, could you do me a favour?' she asked.

'Whatchoo been up to now then?' Terry greatly enjoyed hearing about Flo's latest antics.

She ignored his implication. He'd find out soon enough. She picked up a bunch of red roses. 'Could you take these to the gentleman in my flat? Tell him I've had to go away suddenly.'

'And fank him for last night? Ain't that what the bloke's supposed to do?'

'I'm not sure I'd go that far. He might thump you.'

She and Snowy leaped into the Beetle and drove round the corner. She parked behind a van where she could just still see her flat, and looked back over her shoulder.

The flower seller finished wrapping the flowers, took them over the road to her door and rang the bell. A minute or two later Miles appeared, wearing her bathrobe. His sly smile of expectation vanished when he saw Terry. It was replaced by a look of such pure dislike that it made her shiver. Miles took the flowers and flung them viciously into the well of her neighbour's basement.

'Oh shit, Snowy,' Flo confided. 'That didn't go too well, did it? He obviously hates me.' And as she drove away, slightly too fast, with Snowy's head sticking out of the side window, Flo felt she couldn't honestly blame him. 'After all, I've pretty well cocked up my life so far, haven't I?'

Chapter 2

'Hello, is that Aunt Prue?' Flo had to shout because the phone booth was at a service station in the middle of the motorway with lorries thundering past. 'This is Flo here, Flora Parker. Your niece.'

The astonished silence told her that her aunt was indeed staggered to hear from Flo after so long a silence.

'I know this is probably rather a shock, but I wondered if I could possibly come and stay with you for a little while? I'm having a bit of a crisis.'

She realized as she uttered those words that she wasn't exactly selling herself as an ideal house guest. A nutty niece phoning out of the blue wasn't top of every aunt's wish list. Nevertheless, this time there was no hesitation before her aunt's reply.

Prue Rawlings believed that blood was considerably thicker than any other substance. Indeed, she'd wanted to offer Flo a home with them when the awful business happened with Mary, but her husband Francis wouldn't hear of it. 'We've already got enough girls to feed and educate, all of them probably so thick they'll have to go to private schools. What do we want with another? It's not as if there's any money in it. If it were a boy he could at least help on the farm.'

'There speaks a mean, small-minded farmer,' Prue had thought at the time. But as usual she'd said nothing. A lot went through Prue's mind that would have taken her husband by surprise. For instance, sometimes she dreamed he'd fall under his own combine and be turned into neat bales of hay.

'Of course you can come, dear. What time?'

Flo had run away so fast that she was actually less than an hour away, but she suspected Aunt Prue might need a little while to deal with the shock of her black sheep relative descending into her midst.

'About four?' she suggested.

'That would be fine. I'll have finished the dreaded school run by then. Look forward to seeing you, dear.'

Flo replaced the receiver and wondered what to do for the next five hours. The tempting aroma of Burger King assaulted her nostrils. Why was it that fat was so bad for you, yet smelled so good? Just like everything else in life. She resisted a double Whopper in favour of pancakes and maple syrup and wondered if Miles had got dressed and gone home. Was he the type to trash her flat, slash her duvet, sew kippers in her curtains? She suspected he was, but not in that obvious way. Miles was too calculating for that. His revenge would be served cold, and would be far more effective.

She filled up with unleaded petrol, ate a Mars bar and realized she was desperate for the loo. It was only after she'd got the key from the cashier, avoiding his eyes in case he recognized her from the paper, and had picked her way through the piles of old magazines, dangerous-looking cleaning chemicals and vats of Screenwash, that she realized what a pickle she'd left herself in. It was all very well to make spur-of-the-moment life-changing decisions, she was always doing that, but this time she'd done it with no clothes under her mac apart from the bikini briefs. This was taking travelling light to unhealthy lengths. What if she were stopped on the motorway? They'd suspect her of being a female flasher, bent on luring motorists to their deaths, like a modern day Scylla, or was it Charybdis? She'd heard news reports of women driving their BMWs stark naked in the fast lane of the M25, but hadn't expected to feature in one.

She'd have to stop off in a town on the way and buy something suitable to wear until her friend Miranda could be persuaded to raid the flat and pack a bag for her.

The trouble was, there weren't any towns. She'd already passed Swindon and the next one of any size marked on the map was miles beyond Maiden Moreton, where Aunt Prue lived. She'd have to settle for some-where called Witch Beauchamp. Curious name. She wondered if they burned witches there and hoped they weren't eager for fresh blood. Witch Beauchamp was only five miles from Maiden Moreton but it looked quite big on the map. After all, she didn't need much. A tooth-brush, nightie, jeans, a jumper. Oh, and some wellies. Even Flo knew you needed wellies in the country.

Just before Witch Beauchamp, Snowy started to yowl. She knew that sound of old. Five more minutes and there'd be a puddle on the seat. 'Why didn't you go at the service station? Don't you know what the Queen Mum always says? Never pass a loo when you get the opportunity. Though in your case, I suppose, it's never pass a postbox or a pair of really expensive shoes.'

She pulled in to the side of the road. It was a glorious spring day with the clouds scooting across the sky leaving patterns of sun and shadow on the hills in front of her. 'Mad March wind', John Masefield had called it, with such phonetic perfection it stuck in your brain forever. She'd loved poetry when she was a teenager. What if she'd gone to university after all? Her mother had desperately wanted her to, but the cancer that killed her had arrived half way through Flo's A-level studies and from then on Shakespearean sonnets and the works of George Eliot had always seemed beside the point. Amazingly enough, she'd been offered a place at university all the same. But she was so angry with her father for thinking he had a monopoly on grief that she accepted a rather different offer. Being a cigarette-girl at Mezzo. She liked the costume, she told her father brazenly, and the pay was better. He'd been disgusted at her rebellion, and taken it as permission to disappear to America to live, telling her he'd always be there if she needed him. If it weren't, that is, for the small matter of three thousand miles.

Snowy finished squatting by a blackberry bush, but just as Flo was about to order her back into the car the little dog made a mad dash for the nearest field.

'Snowy! Come back, you horrible hound!' bellowed Flo. If dogs could put a thumb to their noses Snowy did so. Ignoring her owner's cries, she gambolled off deeper into the field.

Flo contemplated the stretch of land, separated from the road by thick barbed wire. It seemed to be a large pasture with cows peacefully grazing in a Constable-ish manner. But God knows what the beasts would do when they saw Snowy. Bolt probably, and start a stampede so all their milk would turn sour and the farmer would shoot Snowy as an example. At first Flo couldn't find a way through the hedge but on closer inspection the field turned out to have a five-bar gate. Flo climbed over. There was a haystack in the middle of the field which Snowy was sniffing eagerly. Perhaps she detected a rat or a harmless harvest mouse shivering inside it. Whatever it was, Flo blessed it, since it was keeping Snowy riveted to the spot and Flo could sneak up quietly behind her.

She had almost caught up with the wretched dog, and was feeling rather proud of her stalking techniques, when she heard the sound of heavy breathing just behind her left shoulder. Just her luck to bump into the local serial rapist out on a recce. Everyone knew the country was full of weirdos.

From her years in London, Flo knew there was only one way to deal with a weirdo, and that was to shout as loudly as you could to scare them off. She turned round to face her assailant but it wasn't a rapist, or even a dirty old man. A large group of cows had followed her and Snowy, and were moving in closer and closer like a scene out of *Rosemary's Baby*. Worse than that, Flo's heart beat wildly, these cows didn't have any udders! In fact, it became increasingly apparent, they weren't cows

at all. Only she, Flora Parker, failure, could find herself
on her first day in the country marooned in a field of
mad bulls.

It was then that inspiration struck her – some atavis-
tic memory from man's hunter-gatherer days. Faced with
the choice of fight or flee, she fled. With the bulls' hot
breath only millimetres behind her she hared at Olympic
speed towards the haystack in the middle of the pasture,
grabbed Snowy, and scrambled up it. The bulls, still
snorting and padding with bloodlust, followed her and
stationed themselves at its base. Probably they'd been
brainwashed by their Spanish cousins, and blamed her,
singlehandedly, for the cruel sport of bullfighting.

Flo tried not to panic, asking herself what a country
dweller would do at this juncture. The trouble was, she
had no idea. Instead she took the townie option and
reached for her mobile phone. In her panic the only
person she could think of calling was her friend
Miranda. Miranda had at least grown up in the country
before she abandoned it at the age of eighteen with a
heartfelt promise never to return.

Miranda, sitting in her smart office overlooking the
lock in urban Camden Town, took in the situation with
admirable aplomb. 'These bulls. Can you describe them
to me? Big, small, black and white?'

'Miranda.' Flo tried to dampen her fear with sarcasm.
'Of course they're not black and white. Even I know the
black and white ones are cows. These are all one colour,
sort of shit colour, one or two all-black. And they're
absolutely enormous!'

'Okay, do they have pricks?'

'Really, Miranda,' Flo despaired, 'how the hell should I know? I'm not Catherine the Great looking for a quickie. I'm up here and they're down there snorting at me. Do you want me to ask them?'

'How big are they?'

Flo was beginning to lose patience with her friend. Miranda didn't seem to appreciate the urgency of the situation. 'Look, Miranda, I'd love to chat but this isn't getting anywhere. I think I'll just dial 999.'

'No, really, Flo. I mean are they huge like bulls in bullfighting posters or are they more like very large calves?'

Flo surveyed the twenty or thirty beasts still surrounding her. 'I suppose they're not *absolutely* huge,' conceded Flo. 'But there are an awful lot of them.'

'In that case,' Miranda pronounced, 'I think they're probably . . .'

'Bullocks!' cut in a laughing masculine voice some feet behind her. Flo swivelled round precariously, phone still glued to her ear, to find two young men surveying her from the far side of the haystack. One was blond-haired, green-eyed and incredibly handsome, like a model from one of those rugged outdoor-wear catalogues – only whereas their models looked like gay schoolteachers, there was absolutely nothing gay-looking about the vision of gleaming manhood that was laughing up at her. The other was dark-haired, wearing a crisp cotton shirt and jeans.

'How dare you take the piss out of my situation,' Flo glared. As if in endorsement of this Snowy began yapping loudly.

'I think what my brother means,' explained the dark-haired one, whom she'd hardly noticed, so eclipsed was he by his golden twin, 'is that these animals aren't bulls, they're bullocks. They're not dangerous, just inquisitive.' Flo considered him critically. He might not be as dazzling as his brother, dark and blue-eyed, as opposed to his brother's fallen angel perfection, but you still wouldn't kick him out of bed on a cold winter's night. Unless his name was Miles, Flo thought guiltily, wondering whether he'd got over his humiliation yet or was in the act of shredding her undies.

Flo remembered her dignity. She'd come here to get away from her shallow life, not sign up for some rural dating agency. 'Well, they look like bulls to me.'

'Flo! Flo, what's happening?' bellowed a disembodied voice from the phone in her hand. Flo had forgotten all about Miranda.

'It's all right, Miranda. The farmer's arrived, or rather two of them, to round up these out-of-control cattle.'

'You think you'll survive un-gored then?' Her friend laughed. 'That's a relief. I'll catch you later. I've got a meeting.' The phone clicked.

'Shall I take the dog?' offered Fallen Angel. 'I think he's frightening the out-of-control cattle.'

Flo, who'd been on the point of softening, glared again. 'I hope you're not blaming *me* for the behaviour of your animals.'

'Heaven forbid!' he countered, his green eyes twinkling. 'In fact, we'll have all these bulls slaughtered at once, won't we, Hugo?' He reached up for Snowy but the dog unaccountably bared its teeth.

'You take it, Hugo. My brother Hugo has a way with animals.'

Hugo reached up for the dog who, to Flo's amazement, went into his arms like a lamb. 'Whereas my brother Adam has a way with . . .'

'Thank you, Hugo,' cut in the blond Adonis. He clapped his hands and the beasts scattered to the four corners of the field. 'Let me help you down.' Adam stretched up his arms to catch her and Flo attempted to slide gracefully into them. As she did so the mac she was wearing gaped suddenly, revealing the one thing Flo, in her panic and anger, had forgotten. That all she was wearing underneath it were trainers and leopardskin briefs.

Adam simply grinned. Hugo looked away discreetly and patted Snowy. He caught his brother's eye. 'I expect they dress differently in London.'

Flo decided the only course open to her was to pretend that her outfit was perfectly normal. 'What makes you assume I come from London?' she demanded.

Hugo offered a hand to help her over a cowpat as big as the Ritz. 'Just a wild guess,' he shrugged. 'It's just that most of the girls round here wear clothes.'

'Hugo, where are your manners?' Adam chided suddenly. 'We ought to introduce ourselves. 'I'm Adam Moreton and this is my sensible brother Hugo. We farm with our uncle in Maiden Moreton. This field's up for sale. We were just inspecting it.'

'Like every other farmer for miles around,' Hugo pointed out.

'And will you buy it?'

'Maybe,' Adam smiled enticingly, his green eyes lighting up. 'It will remind us of you.'

'An expensive memory,' reminded Hugo. Flo wasn't sure she liked him. There was something dismissive in his manner. Perhaps he resented his brother's dazzling good looks. 'The owner wants double what it's worth.'

'Hugo always knows the price of everything,' Adam's voice sharpened almost indistinguishably, 'as well as the rate of return the year after next.'

The sudden flare-up of tension between them intrigued Flo.

'Somebody has to,' Hugo said softly. Flo detected a hint of steel beneath the calm exterior. 'Uncle Kingsley certainly doesn't.'

'Our uncle,' confided Adam, steering her through the thistles and the rabbit holes, 'is charming but eccentric. He doesn't approve of modern farming methods, which is why we've got the prettiest farm for miles around.'

'And the least profitable,' pointed out Hugo.

'There have been Moretons at Maiden Moreton for four hundred years. Uncle Kingsley believes they'll be there for the next four hundred.'

'Let's hope he's right,' Hugo muttered grimly, 'or the next ten anyway.'

They'd arrived back at Flo's car. 'You didn't say who you were,' pressed Adam, opening the door for her with a flourish. He really was stunningly fanciable.

'My name's Flora Parker and I'm on my way to stay with my aunt and uncle. You probably know them. Prue and Francis Rawlings. They live somewhere called Hunting Farm.'

Hugo grinned at his brother. 'We certainly do. At least Adam certainly does. Their daughter Veronica has a soft spot for him. But then so does half the county, don't they Adam? It's hell having a brother who looks like Michelangelo's David in rugger shorts.'

'Who was he when he was at home?' demanded Adam.

Flo wasn't sure if he was joking or not, but with looks like his who was complaining?

'Do you want to follow us to your aunt's house?' Adam offered, his green eyes inviting her not to Maiden Moreton but to heaven. 'We go that way anyway, don't we Huge?'

Flo's fantasy dented slightly. Could she fall for a man who called his brother Huge?

'Thanks.' Flo didn't want to have to get into some long explanation about why she wasn't arriving for two more hours, 'Actually I need to stop in a town to buy some . . .'

She hesitated, not wanting to give them the satisfaction of embarrassing her.

'. . . Clothes?' offered Hugo, his face deadpan.

'Flowers for my aunt,' she finished frostily.

'And I'd get a lead for the dog, too, if I were you.' Even though she'd been thinking this herself, Flo still minded when Hugo suggested it. She'd met his type before. They saw a cloud behind every silver lining. 'If she runs around without a lead like she did today she'll end up getting shot by some angry farmer. Probably Uncle Kingsley,' he added ominously.

'I must say, your uncle sounds absolutely charming,' Flo said sarcastically. 'I can't wait to meet him.'

'I'm sure you will soon,' Adam pointed out. 'He can spot a pretty face from ten miles off.'

Hugo pushed a reluctant Adam in the direction of their old blue Land Rover. 'As you can see it runs in the family.'

Flo waved them away, holding her mac tightly against her body. What had started as a sunny spring day in London had turned bitter down here in deepest Westshire. The blue sky of earlier had changed to solid grey. But at least there was one piece of good news. Apparently neither Adam nor Hugo Moreton read the *Daily Post*.

'Well, Snowy, what do you think? Are those two going to liven up our stay at Auntie Prue's? Mind you,' she added, scooping up the little dog and putting her in her favourite warm place in the well by the front seat, 'don't fancy yours.' But Flo didn't divulge, and Snowy couldn't ask, which hers was.

The small market town of Witch Beauchamp turned out to be quite a pleasant surprise. A row of weaver's cottages took up one side of the High Street and five or six splendid Georgian houses the other, with a small line of colonnaded shops at the far end opposite a market cross. A small herd of disconsolate cows stood in a pen constructed from three-foot metal barriers opposite a pub called 'The Sign of the Angel'. Obviously they still had cattle markets in Witch Beauchamp.

Flo, although she'd hardly set foot in the countryside for years, still felt obscurely comforted that cows got auctioned instead of despatched straight to Tesco's meat department. At least there was a chance for them to see the world before turning into tournedos or brisket.

She parked the Beetle in the car park behind the pub and headed back towards the shops. She found two serviceable cream sweaters in a wonderful Ladies Outfitters' of the type she'd never dreamed still existed, plus two long-sleeved vests – the country was clearly *freezing* – though she drew the line at long johns. Her lower half was more of a problem (isn't it always?). Country ladies favoured the skirt, in a hideous array of tweed, denim or even polyester. The only things in the shop with two legs were hideous tartan trews for the lady golfer. Flo suddenly yearned for the jumble of skintight DKNY jeans on the floor of her cupboard. She'd never appreciated them, would apologize to them when she got back to London and promise to treat them with more respect. In the end she was saved from the tartan travesties by the Oxfam shop tucked at the end of the colonnade, where she picked up two pairs of jeans, one fashionably (well, fashionably in the sense of only about ten years out of date, which was probably still pretty current here) torn at the knee. She swapped her black Nikes with the silver flash for a pair of walking boots which looked surprisingly stylish, the great outdoors being the latest 'Big Thing' in the fashion world, even though none of them actually went there.

Thanks to the Oxfam shop, she hadn't spent much on her country wardrobe. All the same, if she was staying long in Westshire she'd have to rent out her flat. It was one thing to turn her back on her shallow and meaningless life, but it also meant turning her back on her shallow and meaningless income, which was a lot tougher.

She was half way back to the Beetle when it struck her she'd forgotten the one thing a girl really needed round here: wellies. Right at the end of the colonnade of shops she noticed a tiny shopfront with a saddle outside, offering 'Finest Saddlery and Footwear'. But was that footwear for people or horses?

Flo thought about asking the rather unusual-looking man who was opening the door of the shop for a bit of advice but stopped just in time. She'd already made enough of a fool of herself for one day. The man, who was holding open the door, had spotted her already. 'After you,' he said with a flourish and bowed like Puss in Boots. He was much older than she'd thought at first, with a distinguished brow, large nose, moustache, and copious white hair. But it was his outfit that registered most. The old man sported a tweed shooting jacket with shirt and cravat, teamed not with the more conventional plus fours, but a pair of jeans and hi-tech trainers. The effect was slightly shocking, rather like Patrick Moore advertising Guess Jeans.

Inside, the shop was tiny and Dickensian, furnished from floor to ceiling with countless shoe boxes, broken up by the occasional display of riding boots, children's shoes and fluffy slippers. The two elderly assistants blinked at their arrival and exchanged weary glances. The old man, whoever he was, was clearly a regular and not entirely welcome customer. 'I'll fetch Miss Little,' announced the younger of the two assistants.

'Can I help you, miss?' asked the other.

Flo sat down, grateful for being at least decent if not exactly trendy.

'Yes, thanks, I'd like to buy some wellington boots.'

'Of course. Dunlop, Hunters or Lady Northampton?'

Flo had less idea about What Gumboot? than she did about how to pack for the Amazon rainforest. 'What's the difference?'

'Cost mainly. You look like a Lady Northampton to me.'

'I'll take your word for it.'

The boot, when it returned, was amazingly stylish for a wellie.

'These are fine.' Flo gave them to the assistant to wrap just as an attractive woman in her late fifties emerged from behind the curtain. She wore a smart lavender skirt and toning blouse. Even her hair had a tinge of lavender in it. Flo assumed she didn't make a habit of standing in front of lavender bushes or she'd become invisible.

'Hello, Kingsley,' she asked the newcomer brightly, 'what brings you in here again today?'

Flo noted that there was affection rather than irritation in the older woman's voice.

Flo looked sneakily over her shoulder. So this was the famous Uncle Kingsley.

'Will there be anything else, young lady?' asked the assistant.

Flo wasn't leaving now, it was too fascinating. 'Slippers,' she announced, 'I need new slippers.'

While the assistant fetched an armful, Flo discreetly eavesdropped.

'Well, Joan,' Uncle Kingsley pulled a supplement from

Runner's World out of his pocket with a flourish as if it were crucial evidence in a trial that had somehow been kept from him, 'you didn't tell me about these. New Balance 853s. Just out.'

'I didn't tell you because you've only had the 852s a few weeks. Besides, we haven't got any and anyway they're a ludicrous price as well as being quite unsuitable for a farmer. White! How long will they last in the muckspreading season?'

'Ah, but Joan, remember, my muckspreading days are over. I have nephews to spread the muck.'

'And how *are* your muckspreading nephews? Worried that you're squandering their inheritance on unnecessary Nikes? They ought to be.'

Kingsley snorted. There was no other word to describe it. 'Bloody useless. Still as single as the day they were born. Who am I going to hand the farm on to, if they won't find themselves a nice wife with childbearing hips to sort me out an heir?' He patted Joan's discreetly elegant rump. 'If I were younger, I'd do it myself.'

'I'm sure you would, Kingsley.'

Suddenly the old man laughed. It wasn't a chortle or a discreet giggle, but a belly laugh that seemed to shake him to his innermost being. 'Just wait,' he began, his eyes beginning to stream with delight, 'just you wait till those nephews of mine find out about my little surprise!'

'Kingsley,' Joan counselled, knowing him very well of old, 'what the devil are you up to? You mustn't go and do anything you'll regret, now.'

'Of course I won't. Besides, I've already done it. Saw

the solicitor only this morning. Mind you order me those trainers now.'

After he'd left, still grinning manically, Joan turned to the two assistants while Flo pretended to mull over a pair of hideous maroon fluffy mules.

'Those poor nephews of his,' Joan tutted. 'I adore Kingsley Moreton but when it suits him he can be a complete bastard.'

'What's he going to do?' asked the first assistant, dying of curiosity.

'I'm not sure,' Joan replied, 'but if his happy mood's anything to go by, it's something really diabolical.'

Joan switched her lavender-coloured focus to Flo. 'Hello. My name's Joan Little. This is my shop. It's very rude of me to ask, but you seem awfully familiar. I was wondering if perhaps we'd met.'

Flo scanned the older woman's face. She didn't look like a *Daily Post* reader. On the other hand she might have glimpsed Flo's picture adorning a news stand. But the smile that accompanied the question was warm and genuine rather than sarcastically inquisitive.

'Perhaps we have. My aunt lives near here and I used to sometimes visit her as a child.' She didn't add that she hadn't been for ten years, ever since her mother died.

'Really, who's that?'

'Prue Rawlings at Hunting Farm.'

'Prue!' There was surprise and affection in the woman's voice. 'I didn't know she had a niece.'

'I'm sort of the black sheep of the family.' Flo could see the two assistants pretending to tidy up the shoe boxes they'd just straightened up a moment ago. 'Always getting into trouble.'

Joan smiled again; her smile really was lovely. The wide mouth curved up in a perfect arc and her eyes sparkled, while hundreds of tiny wrinkles spread around her eyes and mouth. She reminded Flo of very precious china whose tiny imperfections only made it more beautiful. She hoped she looked like Joan in thirty years' time.

'So, are you staying with Prue?' She noticed the two eavesdropping assistants. 'Rose. Sally. Could you both go to the stockroom and bring up some more slippers? We need to get them all sold by May or they'll clutter up the shelves till next year.'

'Yes,' Flo nodded, 'I'm on my way there now.'

'How lovely for Prue. She needs all the moral support she can get.'

'But I thought she had three children and a husband.'

'Husband!' snorted Joan fierily. 'Millstone more like! And Vile Veronica's no help.'

Dismay spread like a stain through Flo's vision of a rural idyll. 'Who on earth's Vile Veronica?'

'Her eldest. Obsessed with husband-hunting. And Mattie, the next one down's a sweet child, but withdrawn, Prue says. She spends her life reading in the airing cupboard. And as for that brat of a youngest . . . ! Not to mention that the whole farm's on a knife-edge and poor Prue's terrified it'll go down the plughole any time now, taking the family with it.'

Flo picked up her wellingtons and held them close to her chest. So much for her memories of happy families.

Maybe the truth was, whether President Bush liked it or not, most families *were* more like the Simpsons than the Waltons. And she'd had no inkling of the farm's financial problems.

'Anyway,' Joan continued, oblivious to the storm of doubt she'd stirred up in Flo, 'it'll be interesting for all of us having a stunning girl like you around. Spice things up a bit. You get very insular in rural areas. We'll have to find you a nice young man.'

'I've just come for a rest, actually. My life in London's pretty hectic. I don't think I'm interested in men, nice or otherwise.'

Joan held the shop door open for Flo and watched her walk across the square. The girl wasn't the country type at all, far too blonde and stylish, but there was something touching about her, and Joan, who didn't like people easily, had warmed to her at once. Maybe it was the vulnerability that showed through the surface gloss. And the fighting spirit she glimpsed in Flo that reminded Joan of herself a long time ago. She guessed that life hadn't been as kind to Flo as her looks suggested. Joan certainly knew how that felt. Loving a man who didn't seem to love you back wasn't an easy option.

She felt the tiniest twinge of excitement. Something told her that the arrival in their midst of Flora Parker was going to shake things up. And Joan Little liked a bit of excitement. The country could be so dull.

Flo waved goodbye. It was the funniest feeling since she'd only been in the area five minutes, but she felt she knew quite a lot about the locals already.

*

It was almost four by the time Flo turned into her aunt's driveway.

The sign to Hunting Farm led between two over-grown elder hedges with trees hanging down almost to the gravel on either side. The effect was like driving through a tunnel. The place had a still and neglected air as if you were entering a fairytale halfway through a long sleep.

Just next to the house a topiary shape suggested that it might once have been a peacock, but was now a leafy mess. Clearly Uncle Francis wasn't a man for clipped hedges and manicured lawns.

The house itself was slightly better – an old, square, red-brick building with twisty gables and elaborate eaves, and even a little tower with a weather vane. It could have been charming if it didn't look quite so stark. The farmyard seemed to be round the back. A friendly duck appeared, caught sight of Snowy and beat a hasty retreat.

Even more disconcerting was how quiet the place seemed. Somehow she'd imagined sunlight and laughter, toys on the lawn or perhaps a rug, dogs barking; at the very least someone to meet her other than a duck. Remembering Joan's words, Flo had a sudden urge to leave, to drive quickly back to London and take up her old life where she'd left off instead of chasing a fantasy here. Then the thought of Miles and the newspaper came back to her with a hot flush of shame.

She rang the bell. At the second ring she heard a man's voice shout for someone to answer the bloody door and a fair-haired owlish child of about ten appeared, surveying her evenly from behind round glasses, her hair plaited in two immaculately even plaits. 'Yes? Can I help you?'

'Hello. Is Aunt Prue in? I'm your cousin Flora.'

'Oh God, Daddy,' the child shouted to her father inside, 'Mummy's screwed up again.'

Flo's heart creased up for her Aunt Prue. What had she done to deserve such a patronizing little brat for a daughter? 'She thought you were coming by train,' the child elaborated. 'She's gone to meet you at the station. Typical. She always gets my lunch wrong too.'

Behind the plaited brat, another face appeared. It was a girl in her early twenties with shoulder-length blonde hair, a blue velvet hairband, steely blue eyes in a plump face above a piecrust frilled shirt and blue appliquéd sweater. 'Come in. I'm Veronica and this is my sister India-Jane. You must be Flora.'

The words were friendly enough but the look that accompanied them could have removed varnish from a polished surface. Vile Veronica, Flo could see, was not best pleased at this cousinly invasion. Maybe she thought it would up the ante in the husband stakes. Flo would have to assure her that one thing she was *not* looking for during her stay here was a spouse.

'Yes, hello. I'm sorry about Auntie Prue. I probably didn't make it very clear I was driving. I hope she didn't have to go far.'

'Oh, probably all the way to Brittenham knowing Ma. The train'll be in by now so she'll be back in an hour. Have you got any luggage?'

Flo could hardly confess that all she'd brought was

two pairs of second-hand jeans, a couple of jumpers and a pair of already-worn leopardskin briefs. 'Oh, not much. I'll bring it in later.' *Under cover of darkness preferably.*

'Righto. You'd better come in. Fancy a cup of tea?'

Vile Veronica's briskness softened a tad at the realization that with so little luggage, Flo's visit would probably be brief.

The hallway, which had been bathed in spring sunshine as they made their introductions, was suddenly plunged into darkness when the door closed. Veronica flicked a switch and a dim light went on.

The hall was a classic of its kind. A huge Chinese vase of dried blue hydrangeas adorned the marble-topped table with its Egyptian claw feet. The table, if its flaky gilding were ever restored, was probably worth a fortune. Instead it was the resting place for piles of newspapers, old letters and seed catalogues. A pair of gardening gloves peeped out from behind the hydrangeas. Dog leads, presumably from generations of ex-dogs, festooned the wall like the strings of a maypole. Underneath it piles of wellies fought for space with ski boots, tennis racquets and golf clubs. It was the kind of room that Ralph Lauren would have had an orgasm over. And proceeded to smarten up beyond recognition. Eat your heart out, Ralph, thought Flo, this is the real thing.

'Is Uncle Francis around?' Flo asked.

'He's chopping wood,' supplied India-Jane. 'He always goes and chops wood when guests arrive. Then he doesn't have to talk to them.'

Veronica gave her a quelling glance. 'Ivy!' she shouted, putting her head round the door of the kitchen where an elderly woman in a nylon apron was sitting at the table with her feet up, reading the paper. 'Where's Flora been put?'

'In the primrose room. I've just made the bed up. Bloomin' inconvenient, visitors arriving out of the blue like that. I hope she's not a bloomin' vegetarian.'

Flo wondered when to break the news that it wasn't just her who would be staying, but Snowy too.

Veronica surveyed her cousin keenly. She didn't look like a vegetarian. In fact, Veronica decided, red meat probably wouldn't satisfy her. Flora Parker probably ate men for breakfast.

In the end, Flo didn't have to explain about Snowy. Uncle Francis noticed her escaping from the Beetle and heading for the field where his prize cows were quietly grazing. 'In God's name,' he bellowed, his already rubicund nose looking as if it might explode with fury, 'who the hell does that damned animal belong to?'

So Flo spent the next half-hour chasing through thistles and cowpats in pursuit of her West Highland terrier for the second time that day, watched by Uncle Francis, India-Jane and Vile Veronica, none of whom offered to help. Even Ivy had emerged from the kitchen and was considering Flo with a particularly beady eye. 'There's something about that girl . . .' she confided to no one in particular.

Snowy thought it was a grand game, and only agreed to surrender when her fur got caught in the barbed wire.

Flo tenderly unhooked her. 'You're a bad, bad dog.

This isn't London where you can chase traffic wardens, it's the country.'

She glanced up to a window at the top of the house where a lone figure was leaning out, watching. This had to be the reclusive Mattie, who apparently spent most of her life reading in the airing cupboard. Flo could see her point. Sometimes she felt like retreating to a warm, safe place too. The only trouble was, she'd been hoping this was it.

She turned to find all eyes fixed accusingly not on her but a small blue car which was speeding up the drive, showering gravel and making the cows, who had just settled down after their ordeal by terrier, start to skitter off again.

The car finally screeched to a stop and a harassed-looking woman with an uncompromisingly awful hair cut and an apologetic smile looked out. 'Hello, Flora love. How nice to see you. Silly old me. I thought you were coming by train. I must have got the wrong end of the stick.'

'When do you ever get the right end?' mumbled her husband.

Flo fought the temptation to kick her uncle or get Snowy to bite his ankles. Instead she opened the car door and her dishevelled aunt climbed out.

For a few seconds they held each other in a tight embrace. Sudden tears pricked at the back of Flo's eyes. This was the closest she'd ever get to being held by her own mother.

'It's lovely to see you too,' Flo replied shakily, banging self-pity firmly back into its box. 'I'm sorry it's been so many years.'

'The main thing is, you're here now. And for a good long stay I hope.'

India-Jane and Vile Veronica exchanged glances.

'Right,' Ivy announced. 'I'll be getting back to my kitchen. Alf'll be coming in for his cuppa soon.'

'Ivy's husband Alf does our garden for us,' Aunt Prue explained. If this were the case, Flo decided, then they were being robbed. The garden looked a mess. 'He works on the Moretons' farm too,' Prue continued, as if reading her mind.

'I met the uncle this afternoon.' Flo decided against admitting to the nephews just yet. It could wait till later. The story was too embarrassing.

'Did you? Wherever was that?'

'The shoe shop in Witch Beauchamp. I was buying wellies.'

'And what did you think of him?'

'He's not your average farmer, is he? Actually, something really odd happened. He told the lady in the shop that he'd just been to see his solicitor and that he was about to tell his nephews something that would really shake them up.'

Vile Veronica perked up at once. 'What kind of announcement would that be?' She had her sights firmly set on Adam Moreton and if his uncle was finally going to retire and hand over the farm, then Adam would be needing a wife. And she was the perfect candidate.

'I don't know, but the shoe shop lady said it sounded like trouble.'

To Flo's eternal gratitude they all trooped back inside. It was starting to freeze. Too much to hope for a log fire, she supposed. The Rawlingses seemed to make a habit of not living up to her fantasies.

'Supper at seven?' enquired Ivy.

No one bothered to answer. Uncle Francis was a stickler for punctuality and insisted they ate at precisely the same time every night.

'Could we have some tea first, Ivy dear? And some of your home-made scones?'

Ivy's scones would have been useful in medieval warfare had they run out of bricks or rocks, but at least they were better than her terrible trifle. That would come later.

Everyone expected Ivy to complain. But for once she didn't. She wanted five minutes to herself before Alf came and reclaimed his newspaper. In fact, she wanted to take a good look at the front page. Back in the kitchen, Ivy grinned to herself maliciously. She'd just worked out where she'd seen Flo's picture before.

And it hadn't been in no family album neither.

Chapter 3

It was agreed by everyone, some with admiration, most with envy – or if they were estate agents, with greed and longing – that Moreton House was the loveliest property in the whole of Westshire. A perfect Queen Anne gem, a doll's house you could actually live in.

It was built of mellow honey-coloured stone with proportions never quite achieved again in English architecture. Moreton House seemed to have been designed by angels rather than lesser mortals such as Inigo Jones or Robert Adam. It even had a blissful orangery, its own chapel, a stable block complete with clock tower and an ornamental lake added by Humphry Repton.

It had been built, almost four hundred years ago, by the first of the Moretons, Rupert, who rather despised farming even though it provided his income, and left most of the work to his tenant in the next combe. Thus it was that Moreton was a farmhouse that didn't look like a farmhouse. It was now worth millions; or at least it would be if the family abandoned the hard drudge of farming and sold it off to a rich commuter.

Kingsley Moreton poured himself a pint of the home-brewed beer he made himself from hops he had specially sent from Kent. It was strong stuff. So strong it kept exploding in the boiler room where he left it to ferment, almost giving guests a heart attack in the middle of the night.

With his silver pint mug in one hand and a cigar clenched firmly between his teeth, he started on his daily tour of the property. He loved this place with the passionate ardour he had never felt for a woman, which perhaps explained why he'd never married. That and the fact that his divorced sister Pamela, Adam and Hugo's mother, was the most efficient housekeeper any man could hope for, and a lot less demanding than a wife. There was one person he'd thought of tying the knot with, but every time he came close to asking her he'd lost his nerve.

The advantage of this, Kingsley reflected, was that he had been able to lead an exceedingly pleasant life brewing beer, breeding pheasants and collecting rare running shoes. It had only one major drawback as far as he could see and that was the odd twinge of loneliness.

Until now, that is. He needed to be absolutely sure that Moreton House stayed in the family. And so far, despite endless hints, neither of his two nephews showed any sign of settling down and creating an heir.

Which was why he had been driven to drastic action. He had summoned Adam and Hugo here, together with their mother, for his little announcement.

'Evening, Alf.' Ivy's husband appeared out of the

herbaceous border, looking like a weatherbeaten pixie. 'Damn fine show of narcissi up by the wood.'

'Thank you, sorr,' acknowledged the gardener.

'Come on, Kingsley,' Pamela shouted to her brother rattily from the front door, 'we're all in here waiting for this big revelation of yours.'

'Must dash, Alf. I'd appreciate a bunch of daffs for the library. No hyacinths. The pong always reminds me of funerals.'

'Certainly, sorr.'

Alf made no move towards the banks of glorious spring flowers. Instead he waited until Mr Kingsley had gone inside then walked quietly and purposefully to the flower bed in front of the drawing room. One of the six graceful windows was open a few inches and if he strained his ears he might just hear what this important announcement consisted of. For all he knew it might affect his job. And if you waited for the gentry to keep you informed, you'd be there till pigs could fly.

After a few minutes Alf crept closer to the window and peered discreetly in.

Adam and Hugo sat either side of the elegant fireplace, with their mother opposite on a gilded French sofa. She was still an attractive woman, with high cheekbones and wide arching eyebrows, and would have been beautiful if not for the deep lines of disappointment at either side of her mouth.

'Come on, Kingsley,' she said waspishly. 'Do you always have to be so bloody dramatic? We're all starving and this pantomime's keeping us from dinner.'

'All right, Pamela dear. I'll come to the point. You all

know how much the farm and this house mean to me. We're the thirteenth generation of Moretons living here. We go back, unbroken, to nearly 1600. I know times are changing and women are changing and everyone's getting married later, but I have to think of the future.' He turned to Adam. 'As the oldest son you may be expecting to get the farm and the house, and if you act intelligently you still might. But I'm tired of waiting for you boys to settle down. So I went to see my solicitor in Witch Beauchamp this morning and drew up a document.'

Adam was looking shocked, Hugo impassive. They both loved the place almost as much as their uncle, but they'd grown up knowing only one of them would inherit it. Farms were rarely if ever shared, that was the ancient rule.

'Come on, Kingsley, get on with it, for God's sake.' Pamela had already had her first gin of the evening and was eager for her second. 'You're not Laurence Olivier doing *Henry V*. Spit it out.'

She leaned forward.

Adam leaned forward too.

Outside in the herbaceous border, Alf leaned forward.

Only Hugo didn't. He wasn't giving his uncle the pleasure of seeing how much he cared.

'What I've done is this. It's five months till Michaelmas and Michaelmas is the start of the farming year. So, whichever one of you two, Adam or Hugo, gets married by Michaelmas will inherit the farm, the house, everything. But if neither of you ties the knot, I'm selling up.'

'You wouldn't!' accused Pamela. 'You've just said how much you love it here.'

'I do, but I'm too old to face uncertainty about the future. It's giving me an ulcer. I need to know where I stand. By Michaelmas, that's giving you five months. Plenty of time. You could find a wife in five days, or five hours even, if you wanted to enough.'

'Kingsley, this is blackmail!' accused his sister.

'Yes,' agreed Uncle Kingsley cheerfully, looking from one nephew's stunned face to the other. 'I can't wait for ever, you know. We need an heir.'

'Bloody hell!' said Adam. 'But I'm the eldest. Surely that makes a difference?'

'It might if you were my son, but since I'm childless I can leave the place to Alf the gardener if I feel like it.'

'Well, I'll be blowed,' muttered Alf so loudly that if Adam's chair hadn't squeaked at that precise moment everyone in the room would have heard him.

'I hope you realize what you're doing, Uncle Kingsley,' Adam challenged. 'I mean, farming isn't really Hugo's thing.' It had always rankled with Adam that his brother had buggered off to university and studied economics, and that even now he worked part-time as a consultant specializing in agriculture, while Adam did all the hard grind. Adam smiled his most winning smile at his brother. 'Hugo's more interested in the money markets than the cattle markets, aren't you, Huge? Farming's more of a hobby with him.'

'And no bad thing, either,' Uncle Kingsley cut in firmly before Hugo could answer. 'You can't swan around being Tom Jones any more, seducing maidens and expecting peasants to touch their forelocks. Understanding money helps.'

No one in the room pointed out that Uncle Kingsley behaved more like Squire Weston himself. In the tense silence, Hugo noticed his mother's shocked expression. 'It wouldn't affect you, you know Ma,' he said quietly. 'Whether it was Adam or I who ended up with the house, you'd still go on living here.'

Pamela looked stricken. 'Thank you, darling, but I'm not sure your wife-to-be, whoever she is, would fancy a resident mother-in-law in her love nest. But, Kingsley, if you give this house to Adam or Hugo where will you live?'

'At Home Farm.' Home Farm was a much more modest property at the far end of the estate. 'You can come too. You'll be nice and handy for when we hear the patter of tiny feet.'

'And work as your unpaid housekeeper as I do here? No, Kingsley, I may have to reconsider my position.'

For the first time, Kingsley looked shocked.

'I think I need a drink after that,' Adam announced. 'Anyone joining me?'

Outside in the herbaceous border, Alf very nearly volunteered. Instead he hugged Uncle Kingsley's news to himself and headed for home. It wasn't often he knew something before Ivy. Maybe he'd insist on some outrageous sexual demands before he told her.

Alf always enjoyed the short walk between Moreton House and Hunting Farm where Ivy worked for Mr and Mrs Rawlings. As Mr Kingsley's gardener he was entitled to a tied cottage somewhere in the village, but

Ivy preferred the lodge at the bottom of the Rawlings's drive. It gave a better view of all the comings and goings in the village and Ivy enjoyed that. 'What do I want to look at bloomin' fields for?' she'd whispered when Mr Kingsley had shown them the cottage he was offering. It was pretty and thatched and had probably the most spectacular views in the county. It was the kind of cottage London city-dwellers would die for. 'I've been looking at blessed fields all me life.'

Unusually, since it was after seven, Ivy was still up at Hunting Farm. Alf peered in through the top half of the stable-style kitchen door, thinking to himself that they ought to replace it with a nice modern one, but Mrs Rawlings liked to lean on it and look out at the garden.

'I've got big news,' he informed Ivy smugly.

'Sez who?' Ivy demanded. She'd been thrown by Flo's arrival. The Rawlingses didn't have many guests, and although she professed not to care, she secretly wanted to impress the newcomer with her cuisine. That was why she'd pulled out all the stops and made her terrible trifle.

'Sez I,' Alf announced, his smugness level zinging off the scale. 'You guess.'

'The ewes busted out and got themselves impregnated by that randy ram?'

'Nope.'

'That hussy up at the Angel got herself impregnated by the Artificial Insemination man?'

'Nope. You're obsessed with sex, you are.' Except doing it, he thought gloomily, remembering the readers' wives surveys in Dickey's men's magazine; *they* seemed up for anything.

'All right.' Ivy thought for a moment. 'I know. Mr Kingsley finally came out of the wardrobe.'

'*Closet* you means. Anyway, Mr Kingsley ain't one of them hom-o-sexuals just because he ha'n't got married.'

'All right.' Ivy added the coup de grace to her trifle – green and orange angelica. 'I s'pose you'd better tell me then.'

Neither of them had noticed Vile Veronica arriving to check on the progress of the pudding. Not that she wanted any herself – Ivy's trifle induced instant bulimia – but cousin Flora wasn't to know that, was she?

'Mr Kingsley called everyone in all formal-like,' Alf was enjoying his role as Shakespearean messenger. 'Mrs Pamela and the two lads, said he had something big to tell 'em.'

Veronica paused and hid herself behind the pantry door. This must have been what Flora was talking about earlier.

'Well, spit it out, Alf Leach, I haven't got all night. This trifle wants eating this century.'

'He told them lads he were fed up with waiting for 'em to get wed. He needed a young 'un to keep the farm going. He said he were damn fed up wi' waiting.'

Veronica gasped and leaned forward.

'So, he sez unless one of 'em gets hitched by Michaelmas he's going to sell up the big house and go and live in Barrrrrbuda.'

This last part wasn't strictly true, but Alf had read about the place, once Princess Diana's favourite and the acme of new moneyed aspiration, and felt it an acceptable piece of embroidery.

'Michaelmas!' For once he had his wife's full attention. 'That be only five months away. The lasses better
get movin' then. Horseface in the hairband's got her eye
on one of 'em.' She nodded towards the dining room.
'Which one do you reckon'll do it?'

'Mr Adam's ahead, I'd say, but Mr Hugo's a dark
horse.'

Veronica emerged, her face the colour of an overripe
tomato, from behind the Welsh dresser. 'Thank you, Ivy,
I'll relieve you of the trifle.' She turned on her heel without another word.

'That girl,' Ivy confided loudly, 'ought to be relieved of
her cherry. She'd be a lot nicer-tempered for a start. By
the way,' Ivy remembered that she had a little revelation
up her apron too, 'that niece of theirs, the one that's just
arrived from London. The one I was sure as eggs is eggs
I'd seen before.'

Alf remembered none of these things, but after nearly
fifty years together he had the sense not to admit it. 'Aye.'

'Take a look at this.' She removed the copy of the
Daily Post that she'd spirited away behind the breadbin.
' 'Oo do you reckon this is, then?'

Since Alf hadn't had the pleasure of meeting Flo yet,
he was still at a loss. 'Gawd alone knows, but it certainly bain't Snow White, I'll grant you that.'

'It's only *her*, isn't it? The fast piece.'

Alf studied the paper for rather longer than was
strictly necessary. 'I has to say, she's got a lovely—'

'—Thank you, Alf. She may have the twin pyramids
of Egypt on her chest but she's no call to flash 'em all
over the newspaper.'

'. . . smile, I was going to say,' Alf finished limply.

Ivy ignored him. 'The thing is, Alf Leach, am I going to tell the master and mistress?'

'Maybe you should send it over to Moreton House, like. It might speed things up a bit.'

'Alfred Leach, shame on you. Men don't *marry* girls who behave like that. There's only one thing they do with girls like that.'

Alf sighed, briefly allowing himself to dwell on what that might be.

'Best to stay out of family matters, I always say. People don't thank you for interfering.' Ivy looked like a dog whose prize bone had been confiscated. 'Why don't you just leave it somewhere they'll see? The downstairs lav, p'raps, then it won't be your fault if they comes across it.'

'That's a damn good idea.' Ivy sounded surprised. 'I'll put it there now while they're still in the dining room. Then we'd be best getting home. They can do their own washing up.'

In the dining room, everyone was moving Ivy's terrible trifle around on their plates.

'God, this is awful.' Uncle Francis pushed his away in disgust.

'It's because she uses artificial cream,' announced India-Jane. 'Ma buys the proper whipped stuff but Ivy just puts it in her coffee instead.'

Flo made a mental note not to let this awful brat see any of *her* secret weakspots. They'd be dining table conversation in no time.

'Right, girls,' Prue announced brightly, 'all hands to the washing up. It won't take a moment if we all help.'

Veronica's face took on a pained expression. It was time she was rescued from all this domestic squalor and had a place of her own. Her mother was so hopeless at it. She was sure when it was her turn she would be different. Effortlessly in charge.

As she swept the crumbs off the tablecloth with the special silver brush, Veronica allowed herself to imagine life in her own establishment, which bore a startling resemblance to Moreton House. There would be flower arranging to be done and servants to be briefed (Pamela seemed to manage with only one daily plus occasional help from Ivy which was, in Vee's view, understaffing to a woeful degree and most unfair to the local unemployment rate), in addition to all those magazine articles with herself starring as the farmer's wife – no, make that the Lady of the Manor.

'Veronica's looking very pleased with herself tonight,' pointed out India-Jane, who seemed to have X-ray vision as well the perception of a post-Freudian psycho-analyst.

Veronica shot her a quelling look. 'Actually, I heard some interesting news today.' Veronica refrained from mentioning the fact that she'd been eavesdropping on the kitchen staff to get it. 'Apparently Kingsley Moreton's dropped rather a bombshell.'

Flo found herself paying sudden attention. This must have been what Joan in the shoe shop was talking about. 'What did he do?' she asked, fascinated, even though she'd only been in Maiden Moreton for five minutes.

'Oh, nothing much. Just said that he's fed up with

neither of the boys settling down and is giving the house and the farm to whichever of them gets married by Michaelmas.'

'Good God,' spluttered Uncle Francis, 'the man's mad. They'll only end up in the divorce courts and they'll lose the damn farm altogether.'

'My heavens!' said Auntie Prue, looking slyly at Veronica in her sensible country clothes. 'That'll cause some fluttering in the winebars of Westshire. Adam's a bit of a local Lothario, isn't he?'

'Only because he hasn't met the right woman,' Veronica announced in saintly tones.

'And Vee's convinced that's her,' slipped in India-Jane.

'When is Michaelmas exactly?' asked Flo. 'I'm afraid I'm right out of touch with my Saints' days.'

'The end of September,' informed India-Jane.

'Five months to find a wife. Do you think he really means it?'

'Knowing Kingsley, very probably,' huffed Uncle Francis. 'The man's a crackpot. Refuses to use fertilizers, sticks to mixed farming because it makes the landscape look prettier, and even plants bloody wildflowers in his set-aside. He's a complete fruitcake, even if he is our neighbour, Prue.' He made this, like everything else that went wrong in the world from losing his cufflinks to the breakup of the former Soviet Union, sound faintly his wife's fault. Poor Auntie Prue, how could she stand the man?

'How are you going to catch him, Vee?' India-Jane trilled. 'Seduce him in the hayfield in your winceyette pyjamas or lure him with your minced lamb patties?'

Veronica had recently been on a cookery course at the Young Farmers' Guild.

'Go away and empty this in the bin,' Veronica scowled, handing her younger sister the dish of crumbs. 'By the way, Ma, where's Mattie? Not *still* in the airing cupboard. You ought to put a padlock on it. It isn't natural.'

'I know,' admitted Prue ruefully. 'But at least she's incredibly well-read. I'll take her a sandwich.'

'That's hardly the point. She'll lose the power of speech if she's not careful.'

'I'll just skip off and empty these crumbs then, while Vee plots her conquest,' said India-Jane.

Veronica looked at her vengefully. Maybe losing the power of speech wasn't such a bad thing.

India-Jane dutifully took the tray of crumbs out to the kitchen. She was a world expert in avoiding the washing up. 'Won't be a minute, Mum,' she trilled when she came back. 'Just nipping into the loo.'

This was one excuse no one could argue with. She reached for her copy of *The Worst Witch*, which she kept secreted behind the fading damask curtain, and as she did so her eye fell on the folded newspaper Ivy had tucked into the box of magazines they kept as lavvy literature. It wasn't the dull paper they usually ordered, full of tedious foreign news. Maybe this would have some hideous crimes written up in glorious detail or gory stories about child prostitutes in Bangkok.

At first India-Jane didn't notice who was featured in the photo on the front page, and when she did it was to stare mesmerised at the sheer miraculous uplift of Flo's cleavage. India-Jane's own bosoms showed no sign whatsoever of sprouting. Then she registered the face above.

'Well . . . well . . . well!' she purred to herself. 'If it isn't our long-lost cousin Flora! So that's why she appeared in the . . . er . . . bosom . . . of our family so suddenly.'

India-Jane stared at the photo one more time then tucked it inside *The Worst Witch*. At ten she had already made an important adult discovery. Knowledge was power. It was all a question of how you chose to use it.

Once the washing up was done, Auntie Prue sat down next to Flo with a basket of mending. The ghastly India-Jane started ostentatiously flicking through the *Children's Encyclopedia* before watching a worthy documentary on preserving the world's water supply. There was no mention of bedtime, Flo noticed. The elusive Mattie made no appearance. Uncle Francis fell asleep and Veronica studied *Delia Smith's Summer Collection*, no doubt searching out 'Recipes to Seduce Young Farmers By'.

Flo decided it was time Snowy had a walk. Outside the night was clear and cold, with a million stars in the sky and a sense of space and silence Flo had forgotten existed. She tried to fight off her disappointment that the Rawlingses weren't the loving family she'd remembered from those happy holidays long ago. Maybe they never had been, or something had gone wrong in their family just as it had in hers.

She looked up into the stars and thought of her mother and father. 'Are you up there somewhere, Mum?' She felt a sudden urge to ring her father, to say, 'Look,

Dad, it isn't too late. I loved her as much as you did. She wouldn't want this rift between us and neither do I.' But it would be business hours in America and her father would probably be angry at being interrupted.

Instead Flo got out her mobile and phoned Miranda.

Inevitably, since it was between six and midnight and there was no electrical storm raging, no taxi strike to keep her at home nor an unexpected attack of bubonic plague, Miranda was out.

'It's me, Randa.' Flo left a message. 'Call me tomorrow if you can. The country's not nearly as dull as I expected.'

And she realized it was true. She'd run away expecting placid cows, comforting country peace and big English breakfasts. Instead she'd found family feuding, an oppressed auntie and a farmer who needed a wife by Michaelmas. It was all rather promising.

Chapter 4

'Do you think the old sod's serious?'

Adam tried to contain his irritation as he and his brother walked up to Long Meadow to inspect the new shoots. Adam adored women but he didn't want to get married to one. Not just at the moment, anyway. 'I mean, it's a bloody daft idea. How are we supposed to find someone we want to spend the rest of our lives with in five months? What does he expect us to do? Buy a bride via mail order?'

'You'd hardly need to resort to that. You always seem rather spoilt for choice.' Hugo's dark hair, in need of a visit to the barber, fell into one eye. 'Remember, we didn't take him seriously about leaving the poppies in the wheat field. Or about planting wild flowers in the set-aside. But he did it.'

'Do *you* want to get married?' Adam asked. He picked a blade of grass and started chewing it. 'I mean, you're such a mystery, Huge. You might have a stable of fiancées up in town just waiting to get your ring on their fingers.'

'I might, mightn't I? On the other hand maybe I prefer the celibate life. You have enough sex for both of us.'

Adam laughed. His brother might be mysterious, but he doubted if he were celibate. Hugo's apparent lack of interest in women piqued them almost as much as Adam's marked enthusiasm. Not quite, though, Adam reassured himself. If it came to notches on the bedpost, Adam prided himself that he was well in the lead.

They walked through the meadow in silence with Rory, their uncle's mad red setter, at their heels. 'What do you think of the new girl? The Rawlingses' cousin?'

Hugo looked away, his attention suddenly caught by a heron that had swooped down above them and landed in the shallows by the stream just beyond the meadow. 'She won't last. Two weeks at the outside before she misses the nightlife. She's party girl incarnate, according to Ma. Can't see her taking to the farming life.'

'Or being married to a farmer? You won't be proposing to her then, in time for Michaelmas?'

'For God's sake, Adam. I'm not asking someone to marry me just to get Moreton!' Hugo sounded far angrier than Adam expected.

'Oh, I don't know. Maybe I'll have a crack then. I think she'd look lovely in a pinny.' He shot a sly glance at his brother. 'Preferably with nothing underneath. She seems to specialize in that.'

Hugo made a conscious effort not to dwell on the image, but the glimpse he'd had of Flora Parker, her mackintosh parting to reveal two perfect breasts, was a hard one to shake. Why had she been dressed like that, for God's sake, in the middle of the day? Try as he might to dismiss it, the image persisted.

'Come on, boy.' Hugo threw Rory's stick and watched the wild setter launch through five feet of thin air and catch it. 'Women are beyond the understanding of mere men. We'd better get back. There's more silage needed up on the end field.'

'And I'd better make sure Dickey's okay,' Adam agreed. 'He's out with the hedge trimmer and that can be lethal. Uncle Kingsley asked him to trim the "edges" yesterday and Dickey thought he meant "hedges" so took down the whole bloody lot. The birds won't find anywhere to nest till kingdom come!'

By some unspoken agreement neither brother talked on the way back. Hugo went on throwing Rory's stick and Adam planned his activities for that night. If Uncle Kingsley really was serious, he'd have to review his marital options. The thought of Flo stuck in the haystack suddenly invaded his mind. Adam smiled slowly. Perhaps marriage didn't have to be dull and dutiful after all.

When they got back the sun was just dipping down behind the hills and Moreton House was bathed in golden light. It looked eerily beautiful, unreal, almost like a house in a film. Would Uncle Kingsley really sell it, Hugo wondered, or was this some elaborate spoof?

At that precise moment their uncle wandered out from behind the neatly clipped hedge, accompanied by a man in a suit who was speaking into a mouthpiece attached to a mobile phone. The man, overweight and beaming, appeared to think he'd died and gone to heaven. 'I never thought I'd get the chance to put Moreton House on the market,' he muttered orgasmically.

'Come on, man, stop faffing about,' Uncle Kingsley berated him. 'It may never happen if my nephews do their duty but how much do you reckon it's worth?'

'Well, I . . .'

'Come on, man. Or I'll get your rivals in.'

'With or without the farm?'

'With, of course. Who'd want a damn fool loss-making farm to run? Besides, no one in my family's ever sold land on. Houses, however beautiful, are a different proposition.'

'About two million. Maybe more if you find a buyer from the City.'

Hugo breathed in. There were exactly two million reasons for his uncle to be very serious indeed.

'Do you think he really means it?' Flo asked her Aunt Prue the next morning in the pleasant fug of the morning room. Flo had discovered, like a cat who finds the warm spots, that this was the only cosy room in the house.

'Means what, dear?'

'Uncle Kingsley. About one of his nephews having to get married by Michaelmas.'

Auntie Prue smiled wickedly. It was such a rare sight in her harassed aunt that Flo had to smile too. 'India certainly thinks so. She's written the odds for Adam's choice on her blackboard just to annoy Veronica. Vee comes in at twenty-to-one, behind the vicar's daughter at sixteen-to-one and the barmaid at the Angel at ten-to-one. I wouldn't be surprised if you don't feature too.'

'Me? I'm not in the running to marry Adam Moreton. I've only just met him.'

'You've got more chance than Vee, poor thing, I suspect she's too dull for Adam.'

'Unlike me?'

Auntie Prue considered her niece. Flo was wearing her Oxfam jeans with a hole in the knee, a cheap ribbed jumper and thick socks. With no make-up and her hair scraped back she still made Veronica look like a heavy heifer next to a prize calf. Still, Veronica did have some sterling qualities highly suitable to a farmer's wife. She was a good plain cook, had childbearing hips and limited imagination. All these, especially the last, Prue reminded herself ruefully, were a positive asset to a farming wife.

'Miranda!' Flo suddenly exclaimed, interrupting her aunt's thoughts. 'Of course! She'd be absolutely perfect for Adam!'

'Who's Miranda?'

'She's my best friend from London. Adam would fall totally in love with her. She grew up on a farm! She even knows one end of a bull from the other.'

'What a good idea. I know, why don't you ask her down to lunch next Sunday?'

It struck Prue, after issuing the offer, that her own daughter might not appreciate the competition. Another reason for Veronica to resent her mother on what seemed to be an already long list of grievances.

Prue sighed. There was only so much you could do

for your children, as she constantly tried to remind herself. In the end their happiness wasn't her responsibility. If only she believed it.

There was also the question of the cost of having a lunch party. Francis would kill her. Even if they used their own lamb and vegetables from the garden there was still the expense of the wine. For just a millisecond, Prue allowed herself to think about the life she'd dreamed of when she first got married. Collecting bantam eggs with her rosy-cheeked children, feeding motherless lambs and cooking delicious meals for tired men. Unfortunately the truth had turned out rather differently. They'd started out happily enough, but then, ten years ago, farm prices had started to tumble and Francis had got more and more sullen and secretive.

Flo watched her aunt as she sat lost in thought across the other side of the breakfast table. There was something so endearing about her. She was loving and giving, and yet her horrible family didn't begin to appreciate her. Would she, Flo, have behaved as Vile Veronica did towards her own mother if Mary had lived? Seen her as a form of talking laundry-cum-taxi service to be relied on without ever being appreciated? Flo wished there were some way she could get them all, Francis included, to see what a gem their mother was. That they were bloody lucky to have a mother at all.

She'd have to work on that one.

Meanwhile, here she was in the country, actually on a farm, and it was time, if she was to be the slightest help to anyone, that she got to grips with their way of life. If things really were that tough at Hunting Farm maybe she could actually try and help. She was glad Miranda wasn't here yet to laugh or remind her of the incident with the bullocks. She had a long way to go.

'Is there anyone who could show me around?' Flo asked, hoping she wasn't being a nuisance. 'Give me an idiot's guide and not mind when I ask really silly questions?'

'I will, if you like,' said a voice behind her.

Flo almost choked on her coffee in surprise. It was Mattie of the Airing Cupboard.

'Hello, stranger,' Prue greeted her. 'Fancy some toast?' The tenderness in Aunt Prue's voice brought a stupid tear to Flo's eye. This was obviously her favourite child, perhaps because she seemed the most problematic.

'Hello, Flora,' said the small, serious, wispy-haired child as she took her hand and shook it solemnly. 'I'm Matilda. I like your car.'

Flo almost made some reference to the airing cupboard but saved herself in the nick of time. She hadn't much experience of children but something told her one mention of it would send Mattie scuttling back there.

'Would you like to see the farm now?' Mattie offered shyly.

'I'd love to. Don't you have to go to school though?'

'Not on a Saturday,' Prue pointed out. 'Put on your wellies, Matt, and for heaven's sake have some toast.' The child never seemed to eat.

Flo grabbed her coat and followed her twelve-year-old guide. She was tempted to try and bring Snowy but thought better of it. She'd bought the dog a lead but so far Snowy just dug her paws in every time she saw it and refused to budge.

It was cold and clear outside, with a wintry edge to the wind. Mattie led her across the cobbled yard behind the house to the group of barns and sheds. In the field beyond, black-and-white cows were grazing peacefully.

'Those are ours. Friesians. We have one hundred and fifty of them.'

'What on earth's that noise?' From inside the barn Flo could hear the most heart-rending sound of cows bellowing in a high-pitched, piteous tone.

Mattie smiled. 'That's because they've just calved and their calves have been taken away.'

'Why? Isn't that incredibly cruel?' The sound made her think of refugees torn away from their children.

'They won't produce the milk otherwise. The milk they provide is really for their calves, not our cornflakes.'

Flo stopped in her tracks. To think she'd taken milk so much for granted without ever thinking where it came from. Now every time she had some on her Weetabix it would feel like breast milk!

Mattie eyed her sympathetically. 'I know what you mean, but the cows wouldn't be bred at all if it wasn't for their milk.'

A powerful pong assaulted Flo's nostrils. 'That's the milking shed. They get milked twice a day, at five-thirty in the morning and three in the afternoon.'

'What, all by hand?' She had visions of rows of rosy milkmaids, all on little stools, like in *Tess of the D'Urbervilles* – each trying to sit next to the dishy but difficult Angel Clare.

'No,' laughed Mattie. 'By machine. But the cups have to be put on by hand.' Putting cups on cows' udders, Flo decided, would lack the seductive charm of the milking scene in *Tess*. Ah well. She was beginning to see that the modern countryside was practical rather than romantic.

They rounded the corner of the farmyard and walked across a large pasture. Beyond that was an even bigger field with a tractor to-ing and fro-ing in immaculately straight lines. 'That's probably Adam Moreton drilling linseed.'

'I thought drilling was what you did to roads.'

Mattie laughed. 'Not in the country. It means planting the seeds. Some people say it's the most important bit of farming. Even more important than harvesting.'

On the other side of the field, Adam executed a perfect turn. When he caught sight of them he waved and mimed that he was coming over.

'It'll take him twenty minutes to get here. He can't just drive over. He has to keep the lines straight.'

'What do you think of the Moreton brothers?' Flo realized that though Mattie was only twelve and spent most of her time in the airing cupboard, her opinion was worth listening to.

'You mean this silly bet of their uncle's? I think it's absolutely scandalous. Farms are too important to risk on some stupid whim.'

'And what about Adam and Hugo?' Flo realized she was more interested in the brothers than she'd pretended. 'Which one would you marry if you really had to choose?'

'Neither. I'm going to have my own farm and be a

lady farmer in my own right. But I like them both. Adam's my favourite, though. Ivy prefers Hugo. She says he's got wisdom inside his trousers.'

'What a curious place to keep it,' Flo commented.

'I like Adam because he often gives me a ride on his quad bike.'

'Whatever's a quad bike?' Flo envisaged a push-bike with four seats on it.

'A sort of mini-tractor. They're fantastic fun, go right across fields and streams.' She reverted to her user's guide to the Moreton brothers. 'Hugo's quieter. He spends ages in the farm office running some kind of business. I'm not sure he's really a farmer like Adam.'

By now Adam was finally approaching their corner. Flo stood watching him, feeling unexpectedly moved. There was something elemental about one man alone in a huge field, pitted against the vast blue sky.

'Nice ploughing,' Flo congratulated.

'Drilling,' Adam corrected with a jaunty smile. 'Got to get your terms right if you're going to be a country girl, hasn't she Mattie?' He leaned forward and scooped Mattie up as if she were a thistledown. 'This one'll tell you. She knows more about farming than any of us.'

Mattie grinned delightedly, the brace on her teeth glinting in the sunlight. Suddenly she no longer looked gawky and pale but sparklingly pretty. If Adam Moreton had this effect on all women, from twelve to eighty, he deserved his reputation. Somehow she couldn't imagine him scooping Vile Veronica up like that, or Vee looking half as pretty as Mattie did. She fairly glowed with pleasure and Flo found herself responding too.

'Room for another one if you'd like a ride,' Adam offered, with the air of a bucolic buccaneer.

'All right,' Flo said tentatively, embarrassed at the strength of her response to Adam Moreton.

Mattie grinned and scrambled to one side, leaving the only available space on Adam's knee. Flo could have killed her, but it was too embarrassing to back off now.

Flo jumped off the stile and started to climb up into the tractor.

Adam laughed down at her. 'What's that in your hair?' he asked, a look of puzzlement in his gorgeous green eyes.

Flo patted her head and gasped. It was her leopard-skin briefs, which she'd used to tie up her hair in the shower because she didn't have a scrunchie or a shower cap and promptly forgotten all about.

'It's not a pair of . . .?' Adam began.

'. . . knickers!' supplied Mattie helpfully.

Flo could feel her face going red with embarrassment. She dragged the briefs out of her hair and stuffed them in her pocket.

'Fine.' Adam and Mattie exchanged a conspiratorial glance. 'We'll say no more about it.'

It was almost lunch by the time they'd had their ride and trudged back home across the muddy fields and Flo's head was full of facts and figures about milk quotas and EC subsidies, not to mention hygiene regulations for the proper management of milking parlours. There was more to the country, Flo was finding, than nice green fields and pretty cottages. Things were only there at all if they had a sound financial explanation. Adam had been impressively knowledgeable.

As soon as she got in she retired to her room, lay exhausted on her bed and phoned Miranda. 'Randa, you've *got* to come down this weekend. There's the most fabulous farmer next door called Adam and he has to find a wife by Michaelmas or he'll lose his farm, and you'd be so absolutely *perfect* for him!'

Miranda sounded decidedly unkeen. 'Number one, I'm a farmer's daughter and it's a known fact that farmers' daughters can't wait to run away to the drug-crazed overcrowded squalor of the city. Number two, I hate the country; it's dull and it smells and everyone goes to bed at nine o'clock. Number three . . . I can't think of number three, but what have you done to Miles? He keeps ringing me and asking me where you are in the kind of tone that implies he's booking a hit-man rather than phoning Interflora.'

'He probably is. Now, are you coming this weekend? *Please!* I need your moral support and a breath of your cigarette-soaked London air.'

To Flo's delight, Miranda finally agreed. 'Only because I want to get a blow-by-blow account of what you did to the gorgeous Miles.'

'I promise. Just come.'

'Anyway, how are you surviving in the benighted sticks? I can't see you yomping across fields in your Jimmy Choos.'

'That reminds me. Could you pack me a bag? I left rather on the spur of the moment.'

'Okay. What *did* you take?'

'Nothing.'

'What do you mean, nothing?'

'This is rather embarrassing to admit. *Really* nothing. A mac, briefs, trainers.'

'God, you did leave Miles in the lurch then.'

'Under the duvet, actually.'

Flo heard a gong booming down in the hall. 'My God, I'm being summoned by the Rank Organization.'

'That'll be lunch,' Miranda pointed out. 'They do things early in the country. Early breakfast. Early lunch. Early supper. Early bed. And not even early death to relieve you of the boredom. Awful. Are you sure it's all right for me to come at the weekend?'

'Absolutely. I'll tell the cook. She seems to be in charge.'

'They always are.'

Downstairs, everyone except Veronica was sitting round the table. 'She's gone to do the church flowers,' Auntie Prue explained. 'It's my turn today, but Vee kindly offered.'

'She just wants to impress Adam with her Lady of the Manor potential,' commented India-Jane. 'She'd be better off learning to down a yard of ale. Adam goes to the Angel every Sunday, and I don't mean the one in church.'

'Ah,' pointed out Auntie Prue cannily, 'but his *mother* goes to church, doesn't she? And Adam Moreton's devoted to his mother.'

'Only because she dotes on him obscenely,' said India-Jane. 'It's positively Oedipal.'

'India,' her mother asked, stunned. 'How on earth do you know about Oedipus?'

'We did him at school. He killed his father and

married his mother. Though I can't see Adam wanting to actually *marry* his mother. She does all his ironing already.'

Her father suddenly perked up from the far end of the table. 'What *is* all this nonsense they teach them at school nowadays? I blame the National Curriculum.'

'Anyway,' Auntie Prue continued serving Ivy's revolting shepherd's pie, 'if she wants to impress Adam she should take over running the Brownies. Show him how good she is with children. They desperately need a Brown Owl. All the mums work now and no one can spare the time. The pack might have to fold after fifty years.'

'One small problem,' India-Jane pointed out sweetly, 'Vee hates children. She'd like to send them all to concentration camps.' She fished a lump of un-defrosted mince from her pie. 'Mum, you really ought to sack Ivy before one of us dies of food poisoning. Her cooking is catastrophic.'

'I know dear, but in the country you don't sack people who've been with you for ever and ever, you just hope one day they'll sack you.'

'Don't tell Uncle Kingsley about Vee not liking children,' offered Mattie. Everyone stared at her. She hardly ever joined them at the table and when she did she rarely spoke. 'After all, it's an heir they really want, not a bride. I think it's positively medieval.'

After lunch, Flo and Mattie offered to clear the table.

'You two seem to be getting on famously,' Aunt Prue whispered. 'Maybe you can find out why she keeps running off upstairs. I can't get a peep out of her on the subject.'

When they'd finished, Flo put the table mats of Constable's Hay Wain and the view from Flatford Mill back in their place in the dining room dresser. It was now twenty past one, supper would be at seven sharp, and tea, if they were lucky, at four-thirty. There was an order and a structure about life at Hunting Farm which Flo found oddly comforting, even though it seemed to disguise so many swirling tensions.

'Tell you what,' Flo whispered to Mattie, 'this house is awfully crowded. I really came here to get some peace and quiet. You don't happen to know where we might get some?'

Mattie looked intrigued. It was nice to know adults ran away too sometimes.

'I suppose there's always the airing cupboard,' Flo suggested finally. 'It's very quiet there.'

Mattie laughed at the absurdity of it. Adults didn't hide in airing cupboards. But then Flo wasn't like any adult she knew. She certainly wasn't like Vee. Flo actually listened and seemed interested.

'All right,' Mattie conceded, 'but you have to bring a book.'

'I'll do better than that,' Flo promised, 'I'll bring a treat. Frosties Cereal Bars. I've just discovered them. They're *Scrrrumptious*!' Flo's pathetic imitation of Tony the Tiger made Mattie hide her head in her enormous jumper, but she was smiling when she came out.

Flo was crackers.

'See you in ten mins,' Flo tapped her nose, 'loaded down with comforting calories and escapist reading matter.'

Mattie tapped her nose in acknowledgement.

The description 'airing cupboard' was a bit of an understatement. Mattie's hiding place was actually more of a large closet containing a vast hot water cylinder and capacious shelves piled with fresh linen. The cylinder itself was festooned with Uncle Francis's shirts, brought inside in case they got soaked by an April shower. Mattie had lined the floor with old feather pillows.

There was something about the fresh, laundry-smelling warmth that brought a lump to Flo's throat. Suddenly the memory flashed back, as clear as a photograph, of Flo helping her mother put away the laundry in a big Provencal cupboard. It had been one of her mother's favourite jobs and Flo, standing on the upturned laundry basket, always helped her.

Flo felt a small hand creeping into hers and sensed the pressure of reassuring fingers. She opened her arms and Mattie pressed herself tight against Flo's body. 'It must have been awful for you,' Mattie said softly, 'to have your mother die so young. Do you miss her very much?'

Flo was taken aback. 'How did you know I was thinking about my mother?'

'Because you cried. I cry sometimes when I think of my mum. Dad's so horrid to her these days and she just takes it. He used to be really good fun. He'd take me out on the tractor to put hay out for the sheep and round up the ewes who'd wandered off. At lambing time he said I was always his number one helper. I remember one Christmas morning hearing someone singing carols and I thought it was Santa, but it was Dad, coming back from the lambing shed. It was frosty and completely silent. It felt like there was just him and me in all the world. He called me down and gave me a newborn lamb to feed.'

She hadn't imagined the happiness this house had once held, then. Mattie remembered it too. Mattie sniffed and buried her head in Flo's shoulder. It was a heartrending sound. The sniff of a child trying not to be weak. 'That was before everything started going wrong on the farm. Now Dad just shouts at everyone. Or he goes to the pub.'

Flo had had no idea how serious their financial problems really were. 'What's gone wrong on the farm then?'

'Dad always loved sheep. But he had to get rid of them. They were only worth a pound each, not even what it costs to feed them, and he just couldn't bear looking at them. And I can see Mum's worried sick too. I used to hear them talking to each other when we'd gone to bed. But the awful thing is, Flo, now they've stopped. They hardly talk at all any more.'

Flo hugged Mattie tighter. Her own father had stopped talking to her when her mother had got really ill. Maybe, like Uncle Francis, he didn't know how to share his pain; perhaps he thought it'd look weak. Or maybe, just like Uncle Francis, he'd been so damn angry he *couldn't* talk about it and instead of going to the pub he'd gone to America.

Flo closed her eyes. She couldn't let what had happened to her repeat itself with Mattie. Mattie was too vulnerable.

'Is that why you come up here? To get away from all that?'

Mattie nodded. 'It feels safe here, somehow.' She pushed a wispy strand of mouse-brown hair from her eyes. 'It won't be, though, if we have to sell up and move.'

Flo patted the child's hair. 'Surely it won't come to that?' To think she'd bowled up here, imposing herself on the Rawlings family without a thought, expecting them to feed and house her because of her own stupid fantasy about this being a happy home. And all the time this was going on.

'Thanks for confiding in me, Mattie. It's really useful and helpful. Together you and I are going to try and sort it out and I'll need a lot of advice from you about how to do it. There's just one condition.'

'What's that?' Mattie's face looked fearful again, like a child who's been given too much responsibility and isn't sure how to use it.

'That you stay out of the airing cupboard and help me.'

Mattie grinned, her thin, serious little face lit up with pleasure and relief. 'Okay. It's a deal. But how on earth are we going to do it?'

It was a good question. How did Flora Parker, party girl, who'd already made a botch-up of her own life, have a hope in hell of sorting out anyone else's?

Chapter 5

Flo's London friends, Miles in particular, would have creased up with laughter at the sight of Flora Parker, Harvey Nicks *habituée*, in a flannelette nightie. She was curled up under a patchwork quilt with her uncle's copy of *Fream's Agriculture*, a weighty tome designed to refresh farmers' memories on such edifying topics as animal artificial insemination, deep-litter systems and the use of winter brassicas, as well as to appeal to 'the interested general reader'. Flo could not imagine the kind of general reader who would settle down with a cappuccino and a copy of *Fream's Agriculture*.

She was half way through the chapter on 'Sheep Production Systems', having read, if not entirely digested, the one on 'The Changing Face of Agriculture', when there was a knock on the door. Flo stuffed the book under the bedclothes quicker than a convent girl hiding *Lady Chatterley's Lover*.

Vile Veronica appeared at the end of her bed in a hideous pink dressing gown with little flowers appliquéd on it.

'I was just wondering,' began Veronica with a tinny smile, 'how long you planned to stay with us?'

'What Vee really means,' translated the high-pitched voice of India-Jane from behind her, 'is that she's having a drinks do after church this Sunday to impress Adam with her skills as a hostess, and she'd rather you weren't around as competition.'

Flo tried not to giggle. 'Sorry, Vee, but I'll still be here on Sunday. Aunt Prue said I could invite a friend down from London.' Flo sat up on her pillows and pursed her lips primly. 'As a matter of fact,' she added wickedly, 'I thought she might be perfect for Adam. As well as being stunningly chic and witty, she's a farmer's daughter.'

Veronica looked as if she might explode and shower the room with bits of quilted cotton. She flounced out.

'That's put a spanner in her works,' approved India-Jane, 'she's spent all morning planning ham and pineapple canapés.'

'Then we'll have to hope she thinks again.' Flo pushed her copy of *Fream's Agriculture* further under the covers, away from India's X-ray eyes.

'What's that you're reading?' The all-seeing India had noted the gesture and leapt round the other side of the bed, faster than a whirling dervish, and dragged back the quilt.

Her eyes widened like two saucers of cream when she saw the book's title. 'Mmmmmm . . . mmmm. We are taking this husband-hunting seriously. I thought it was just Vee who was falling over herself to be the farmer's wife, but you're at it too. Which one are you after, cousin Flora, hunky Adam or strong and silent Hugo? If it's Adam, you'd better watch out.' She produced her notebook from her jeans pocket with a flourish. 'The competition's hotting up. Daddy saw Adam chatting up Donna the barmaid in Witch Beauchamp. And they weren't discussing milk yields.' She winked at Flo in a manner highly unsuitable for a ten-year-old. 'Not from cows anyway.'

Flo disappeared under the patchwork quilt. She had been about to insist that the news meant nothing to her. But the truth was, she was a little piqued.

'You look quite different in real life,' India commented slyly to the lump under the bedclothes.

Flo decided India couldn't mean what Flo feared she meant. She was getting paranoid.

'Different from what?' Flo asked evenly, emerging tentatively from the covers.

'From your photo in the paper, of course. Wearing the Wonderbra. Can I try it on?' India thrust her small breasts in Flo's direction like two tiny artillery shells. In another couple of years they'd be just as lethal. 'I can't wait to have a bra of my own. If you let me try on yours, I promise I won't tell on you.'

'Why would I mind if you did tell on me?' bluffed Flo. 'I've nothing to be ashamed of.'

'It's not so much *if* I told on you, more *when*. Timing is so important, isn't it?'

Flo threw her copy of *Fream's* at the ghastly brat. If Mata Hari had needed a deputy, India-Jane Rawlings would have made the ideal candidate.

When India had finally disappeared to torture someone else, Flo wondered how many more people knew about the photo. There was only one thing for it; if she really wanted people to stop saying 'Wasn't that you I saw in the paper?' she'd have to change her appearance.

The next morning Flo went out for a brisk walk over the fields, breathing in the fresh air, listening to the skylarks swooping above her. Their wonderful liquid song would cheer anyone up. It would be May in a few days and Flo defied anyone to be miserable in an English country springtime. Except perhaps Uncle Francis.

She was no nearer to seeing a way of sorting things out at Hunting Farm, but she was certainly learning a lot about sheep. After school Mattie had promised her a visit to a rare breeds centre about an hour's drive away. But first Flo had something important to do.

The hairdresser, nestling in the colonnade of shops next to the saddlery cum shoe shop in Witch Beauchamp, was hardly Nicky Clarke, but it would have to do.

There were two stylists. The male one was busy washing a client's hair in the alcove round the corner while a young redhead lounged against the counter, yakking on the phone to a friend. She looked annoyed at Flo's unscheduled interruption.

'I'm Elaine,' she said when eventually she put down the phone. 'What would you like done today? Nice shampoo and a blow-dry?'

'Actually,' Flo replied, 'I'd like something a bit more radical.'

The girl cheered up. Her usual Thursdays were taken up with 'Perms for Pensioners' at £6.50, so at least Flo represented a change.

'Sun-kissed tips and streaks? Brass and copper low lights?'

'No, thanks. I want to go back to my natural colour.'

'And what's that?'

'Unadulterated mouse.'

'That *is* radical.'

She surveyed Flo's messy long blonde hair. 'Are you sure about this? Only I spend half of my time trying to make other people's hair look like yours. Rather than the other way around.'

'Yes, I'm sure. I like to swim against the tide, or in this case the peroxide. How long will it take?'

'I'll have to strip out the bleach,' Elaine mused doubtfully, 'but that'll leave it looking the colour of a dead rat, rather than mouse, so I'll have to lift it with a rinse.'

'Right. Fire away.'

The girl covered Flo's hair in an evil-looking blue solution that smelled as if it had been purchased from Dyno-Rod. It could clear drains, Flo wagered, from a hundred yards. She'd probably end up less mouse than bald.

Flo closed her eyes and tried to ignore the intense desire to scratch that this foul stuff was inducing.

'Tsk tsk,' a teasing voice interrupted her thoughts. She hadn't noticed someone being seated at the basin next to hers. 'We men are so naive. Somehow I imagined you were a natural blonde.'

She looked over into the sceptical eyes of Hugo Moreton, his abundant dark hair hanging wetly across his forehead.

Tony, Hugo's stylist, a young man clearly trying to

compensate for his receding hairline with a droopy moustache that resembled a tarantula, began to blow-dry Hugo's hair.

'I wouldn't mind hair like this myself,' confided Tony, as Hugo's locks sprang into shining life under his fingers. 'Dries in minutes. Do you condition regularly?'

'Almost never,' replied Hugo. 'How about a drink when you've finished here?'

Tony looked as if it were payday. 'Love to. Six o'clock at the Angel?'

'He doesn't mean *you*, pillock,' Elaine pointed out. 'He's talking to my client.'

Tony surveyed the blue-hued Flora. 'Suit yourself. Looking at the state of her she'll be *hours*.'

'Will you?' Hugo enquired. 'Only I'm seeing the feed merchant at four.'

'You *do* know how to charm a girl, don't you?' Tony commented.

Flo looked at her watch. 'I'll see you in the pub at three. This can't take any longer than that.'

But Flo was wrong. Having your hair bleached might take hours wrapped up in tiny pieces of foil, but getting *un*bleached took even longer. Days seemed to have passed by the time Elaine was ready to start the cut.

'Right. Just a couple of inches, is it?'

The vast majority of Elaine's clients came up with the unchanging litany 'Just a little trim, thanks.'

Flo surveyed her long, newly brown hair. 'Chop it all off,' she commanded. 'Give me something short and feathery.'

'You're sure about this?'

'One hundred per cent.'

Half an hour later she stood back to take a long look at the new Flo. 'Even your mother wouldn't recognize you now.'

'Do you have any make-up remover?' Flo asked.

'Just the stuff we wipe off colour with when it runs.' Tony handed her some cotton wool balls and Flo removed her mascara for the first time, she had to admit, in several days. Eventually her face was glowing clean and bare of any make-up.

'Blimey,' commented Tony, 'are you joining a nunnery? If so, leave us your boyfriend. It'd be a pity to waste him.'

Flo was about to explain that Hugo Moreton certainly wasn't her boyfriend when Elaine interrupted.

'You haven't even looked at yourself,' she pointed out, fascinated by the change in Flo.

'I'm sure it's fine.' Flo grabbed her bag. 'Thanks for all your help. How much do I owe you?'

The amount wouldn't have paid for the conditioner in her usual stylist's.

'Well,' said Elaine after Flo had left, 'I've had plenty of ugly girls coming in and saying, "Elaine, make me beautiful, please," but that's the first time I've had someone gorgeous asking to look plain.'

'Maybe she's screwed up big time and come here to start a new life?' Tony commented, without the slightest idea of how near the mark he was.

'To Witch Beauchamp?' said Elaine.

'Nah,' they chorused. 'Nothing interesting ever happens in Witch Beauchamp.'

Flo ran across the small market square, past the saddlery, past the medieval cross, to the whitewashed pub beyond. To her relief Hugo wasn't there yet.

She ordered a white wine, even though it was three in the afternoon. Some London habits died slowly.

Behind the bar a sexy-looking girl with slanted green eyes and almost-black hair, wearing skintight DKNY jeans just like the ones Flo had left behind, and a fringed black crop-top, watched her curiously.

When Hugo arrived moments later, he walked straight past Flo.

'Hello there,' she laughed, tickled at the effectiveness of her transformation.

'Good God,' Hugo stuttered. 'Is it really Flora?'

Donna, the slant-eyed barmaid, watched with satisfaction. Flo, she'd been told, would be stiff competition where Adam was concerned – a blonde hussy from London who flashed her boobs and drank men under the table. They must have been dreaming. This one looked like a campaigner for Greenpeace.

'It's me all right,' said Flo. 'Can I buy you a drink?' The old Flora would have waited to be bought one.

'Good heavens,' Hugo studied her from every angle, 'you look like a *real* girl now.'

'I'm not quite sure how to take that. What did I look like before? A blow-up-doll?'

Hugo grinned. His eyes, Flo noticed, crinkled up at the corners rather engagingly. 'Well, you'd certainly have stood out at a point to point, shall we say?'

'But I won't now I've gone native. I'll look just like all the other county gels.'

'I'm not sure you *could* look like a county gel even if you wore boots and a Barbour.'

'What about a nice velvet hairband?'

'Nope.'

'A frilly piecrust blouse like Veronica's?' Flo was enjoying herself.

'Especially not a frilly piecrust blouse.'

'There's no hope for me, then? Branded an incurable townie for ever and ever?'

'I'm afraid so.'

'Actually, I may be about to surprise you all.' She produced her uncle's copy of *Fream's Agriculture* from the backpack at her feet.

'Good God!' Hugo marvelled. 'I haven't seen one of those since I was at Agricultural College. Why on earth are you reading it? Don't tell me, you're another one looking for a shortcut to Adam's hand, heart, and fabulous Queen Anne farmhouse?'

Flo felt a flash of resentment. Why did everyone treat Adam like first prize in a raffle? 'Personally, I doubt the way to Adam's heart is by mugging up on beet harvesting. I suspect he's more of a frilly suspenders man, don't you?'

Hugo looked away. The image of Flo in her mac and briefs already kept lodging itself in his mind with quite unsuitable frequency. He didn't think he could cope with suspenders.

Flo considered him. Adam was the more flashily attractive, but there was something about Hugo she rather trusted. She leaned forward, her eyes losing their flirtatious gleam. 'Actually, I want to try and help my uncle out. Mattie tells me Hunting Farm is in real trouble.'

'Is it? I'd heard rumours but Francis doesn't say much. Though given the state of things it's not surprising. Hardly anyone can make a living at the moment and Hunting Farm's pretty small scale. If you want to see how bad it is, look at this.'

He handed Flo a copy of *Farmer's Weekly* with the headline 'How to Spot the Warning Signs of Suicide'. Flo read it, appalled.

'I had no idea things had got so bad.'

'I don't suppose it's a hot topic in Daphne's or the Met Bar.'

Flo looked away, not wanting him to see how hurt she felt. His tone didn't need to be so dismissive.

She decided to fight back with some sarcasm of her own. 'You seem very well up on London's smart watering holes.'

'For a hick from the sticks, you mean? We don't all ride cows and sing Oooh-aar like the Ambrosia ad. As a matter of fact, I work in town a couple of days a week. One of the reasons Adam feels the farm should be his.'

'Why can't you both run it?'

'Recipe for disaster, Uncle Kingsley thinks. He's probably got a point.'

'So Mattie's not imagining it, that Hunting Farm could go under?'

'Unfortunately not. No one's safe these days, especially the smaller farms. Perhaps Uncle Kingsley's right to think of selling up and moving somewhere warm.'

'You don't mean that,' she insisted sternly. Adam, Flo

felt instinctively, would never joke about something so important.

'I ought to mean it if I had any sense. How do you think you can help Hunting Farm?'

She looked at him through narrowed eyes to make sure he wasn't laughing at her. 'I'm not sure yet. I'm working on it. You're supposed to be the financial whiz. What would you do if you were my uncle?'

Hugo looked grim. 'You probably won't want to hear the answer and neither will he. His best bet would probably be to sell his milk quota and get a job.'

'At fifty-five? Doing what? Stacking shelves in Tesco?'

'Point taken. Is there anything they can sell? Barns for conversion? Cottages? Land that could have caravans on it?'

'I'm not sure my uncle has the temperament to deal with campers. All the same, he loves Hunting Farm. He'd feel a terrible failure if he had to leave.'

'Maybe it won't come to that. I'll see what I can find out.' Hugo stood up. 'I'm sorry this has been so short. The feed merchant beckons.' He picked up her copy of *Fream's Agriculture* and opened it at the page for 'Protein Concentrates for Animal Consumption'. 'There you are. A little light reading for you.'

Flo studied him, her cool hazel eyes considering his clear blue ones. Was his tone patronizing or friendly? She didn't know him well enough to tell.

'Excuse me.' The sexy girl behind the bar was smiling at her. It was a sly smile with a touch of superiority. 'If you're looking for your uncle, he's in the snug.'

Flo was amazed that the girl even knew who she was.

Had she been listening to their conversation? Flo picked up her backpack and followed in the direction the girl had pointed.

Off to the right of the blackened and beamy bar was a much smaller room. It was dark even at this time of day, lit by a small coal fire, and seemed to be entirely empty. Flo turned, an unexpected relief flooding through her. The barmaid must have got it wrong. There was no one in here. Behind her a whiskey glass fell to the floor and shattered, making her jump. Flo peered into the corner where the sound came from.

Sitting alone, a pint of Guinness in one hand and a row of empty whiskey glasses in front of him, Uncle Francis had passed out on the table.

'Oh shit,' Flo didn't realize she was speaking out loud, 'how the hell am I going to get him home?'

'A bit the worse for wear, is he? He comes in here most Thursdays as a matter of fact. Sad when someone can't take their drink, isn't it?'

Flo disliked the girl intensely. She was pretty enough but there was no warmth or sympathy about her, merely a kind of cold curiosity.

'I'll just bring my car round.' Thank God the pub was empty. Everyone else had gone back to work in office or field. Except Uncle Francis. Should she phone her aunt? She didn't even know if Aunt Prue was aware of her husband's drinking habits.

She fetched the car and pulled it up on the kerb outside the Angel, as near as she could get to the side entrance. Fortunately, Uncle Francis wasn't the aggressive kind of drunk and she managed to half-drag him into the passenger seat without attracting too much attention. The barmaid, Flo noticed, didn't offer to help.

What if Hugo had still been around? Would he have helped or watched, like the girl, in silent disapproval?

Flo told herself it was a damn stupid question and drove off, with her uncle strapped into the seat next to her. How was she going to handle getting him into the house? Should she summon Aunt Prue or make an attempt to sneak him in without her knowing?

It had turned into a glorious afternoon, warm and bright, but her feeling of happiness and optimism that she could actually be of help evaporated. Instead she felt gloomy and absolutely alone. What was the point of dreaming up schemes to save the farm if her uncle was an alcoholic?

At the bottom of the drive she could see Mattie, smiling and waving, leaning on the gate waiting for her. Damn! She'd forgotten her promise to take Mattie to the Sheep Centre. She'd have to suggest they went tomorrow instead.

She parked the car at some distance from the house so that Mattie couldn't see its occupant and ran the rest of the way.

'Hi, Flora,' Mattie greeted her. 'I'm all ready. I've brought my special baby bottle so we can feed the lambs.'

Mattie was looking happier than Flo had ever seen her and Flo hated imagining how disappointed she'd be. Now she'd see Flo as another unreliable adult. But it was better that she resented Flo than saw her father in that condition. 'Mattie, love, I'm afraid something urgent's come up. I won't be able to take you this afternoon but I wondered if we could go at the weekend instead?'

Mattie's face collapsed in on itself, the smile imploding with disappointment. 'Don't worry,' she replied in a tight voice. 'I didn't think you were really interested. Let's just forget the whole thing. I wish I hadn't told you about the farm's problems. What's it to you anyway? You'll only get bored and go back to London.' She turned away. Flo could guess where she was headed. Shit and blast!

Flo followed her inside the house. Where was Aunt Prue?

'Gorn out,' Ivy answered the question for her. 'Gorn out to shop for the weekend.'

Flo sighed and turned back to cope with Uncle Francis alone. Carrying him out of the pub was relatively easy compared to the challenge of supporting him down the drive. Maybe she should move the car right down close to the house as she'd done at the pub.

In the end she had to do neither. When she got back to the car she found the passenger door wide open. Uncle Francis had completely disappeared.

Back in the house the only sign of activity was in the kitchen, where Veronica and Ivy battled for control of the work tops and the cooker as fiercely as armies facing each other across No Man's Land.

'I'll remind you, young lady, that I've got the supper to do and your father'll kill me if it's a second past seven.'

'I've got to put these vol-au-vents in *now*,' Veronica hissed, 'or we'll never be ready for the party on Sunday. My hair appointment's in half an hour.' She pushed past

Ivy and triumphantly wrenched open the door of the Aga. 'They'll only be fifteen minutes. Would you be an angel and take them out?'

'No, I would not,' snapped Ivy. 'They're the devil's food, they are, designed to seduce Mr Adam into falling for you. But I happen to know,' Ivy paused dramatically before producing her trump card, 'he don't even like prawns, anyhow.'

Flo decided to intervene before they moved on to mortal combat with egg slices. 'I'll take them out if you like,' she offered.

'Thanks, Flora. That's good of you. I'd better dash.' Veronica took off her apron and stared at Flo as if seeing her for the first time. 'Good heavens, what have you done to your hair? You look like Joan of Arc.'

'Better than Pamela Anderson, perhaps,' Flo replied.

'Who's Pamela Anderson?' Veronica asked.

'Blonde piece with falsies and a tattoo,' offered Ivy disdainfully. 'Got married in a bikini.'

'I suppose that does sound a bit like you.'

'Thanks a lot. How long for the vol-au-vents did you say?'

'I wonder where the master's got to?' Ivy complained. 'Normally he comes in for his tea and a bit of cake after he's done the milking.'

A sudden panic gripped Flo. What if he'd fallen face-down in the slurry pit and she was the only person who knew about his condition? 'I'll just have a quick look for him, shall I?'

Inside the milking parlour there was the reassuring in-out of the machines, like a giant animal breathing somewhere in the background. The cows were ranged peacefully in their positions, but there was no evidence of her uncle. He must have recovered by now to have remembered to milk the cows at all.

'Flora.' A voice made her turn. Uncle Francis's head appeared from the far side of a cow's behind. 'Thanks for bringing me back. I don't do it often.' His face had deepened from stern to haggard, reminding her of a gargoyle on Witch Beauchamp church. 'I'd just been offered less for my sheep than it actually costs to rear them.'

'That's outrageous!'

'I know. But it's reality. Flora?'

'Yes?'

'I'd rather you didn't mention this afternoon to Prue. She's got enough on her plate.'

'All right.'

'Thanks.' And then he added, as if even so small a sign of emotion was too difficult, 'She's very glad you came, you know. You've given her back memories of her sister. The last few years have been hard for her too.'

'I know.' Flo wanted to squeeze his hand but her uncle seemed to have a protective wall round him. Still, this was a start, a small chink in the brickwork. 'Thank you for telling me.'

Flo remembered the vol-au-vents and dashed back to the kitchen where India-Jane had removed them from the Aga in the nick of time. Ivy, Flo noticed, had made no attempt to do so.

'So 'oo's coming to this so-called party of hers anyway?' Ivy enquired.

'Adam and Hugo, obviously, their mother Pamela, Uncle Kingsley, Joan from the shoe shop, probably the vicar, all of us and Flo's friend from London.'

'And 'oo's staying for lunch?'

Only the English county set, Flo decided, could invent a sadistic system whereby some drinks guests were invited to lunch and others weren't, and neither set knew which was which. It was designed to lead to acute embarrassment and nearly always succeeded.

If Flo's hair resembled that of Joan of Arc, Veronica's, when she got back from the hairdresser, looked like Joan of Arc's helmet. It had a solid, immovable quality that made it seem as if fashioned from PVC resin. 'Are the vol-au-vents all right?' she asked as soon as she came in the door. Flo, on her way back upstairs to phone Miranda, stopped to listen.

'Yes,' India-Jane said modestly, 'and no thanks to Flora. I had to rescue them from the Aga while she was out admiring the moo-cows.'

'Typical,' Veronica remarked acidly. 'She'll have to get over this Marie Antoinette-ish view of the country. Farm animals are only there because of their usefulness to man, not to look pretty. Just as well she's not planning to marry a farmer. She wouldn't last five minutes.'

'Whereas you're the perfect candidate?' India-Jane asked in tones of purest aspartame. 'Pity Adam doesn't think so. I suspect he rather likes Flo. Though I've a feeling she was more his type with the blonde hair and the Wonderbra.'

'What are you drivelling on about now?' demanded Vee. 'If Flora's got a Wonderbra, Adam couldn't possibly have seen it. Even Adam Moreton isn't *that* fast a worker.'

'I wouldn't be too sure.' India was enjoying herself. 'Quite a lot of people have seen Flo's Wonderbra. Thousands. Millions even.'

'Come on, India, Flora might be a bit of a floozy but I'm sure she has *some* standards. After all, she is our cousin.'

Thanks a lot, Veronica, Flo longed to shout.

'You'd be surprised,' India smiled slyly. 'And one day I might show you the evidence.'

But Vee was too carried away with the catering to pick up the hint.

'Now,' Vee began to bustle about, 'who's seen those pretty serviettes I bought for the party?'

'Do we *have* to go to church?' moaned India-Jane on Sunday morning. 'My teacher says religion is a form of organized repression and people ought to think for themselves.'

'You can tell your bloody teacher you think for your-self too much already,' bellowed Uncle Francis, a touch of pride tempering his annoyance. 'Now get your coat on. We're going to be late. As usual.'

Going to church, like meals being served on the dot, Flo suspected, were ways in which her uncle hung on to some tentative idea that life at Hunting Farm was secure and predictable.

Flo thought about making her excuses and staying in bed but Veronica would only seek her out and leave her in charge of more revolting canapés, so she reluctantly joined the others.

Maiden Moreton church turned out to be a delight. It was tiny – more of a chapel really – with ancient knights, no doubt Moretons to a man, carved in stone in every alcove. The flowers, Veronica's handiwork, were glorious. White tulips and pale pink roses, bound together with swathes of honeysuckle. Flo hadn't suspected Vee had so much originality. The arrangements on the altar and the font, it struck her, had a faintly bridal air. Perhaps, Flo thought meanly, she was planting a subliminal message for Adam.

If so, Adam had clearly failed to pick it up. He sat with his mother and Hugo in the front rows reserved exclusively for the Moretons. He ignored Vee and turned instead to greet Flo with a broad wink. Much to Veronica's annoyance, he then came out of his pew to make sure she had a hymn book. His mother, Pamela, looked firmly ahead, but Flo suspected she was taking in every detail with photographic recall. She was a tall, elegant woman, dressed in a subtle but stylish silk suit. She reminded Flo of the headmistress of an expensive finishing school, more interested in manners than brains or individuality. She had none of the warmth of Auntie Prue. In fact, Flo decided, she looked like the kind of mother-in-law who would perpetually make you feel you were using the wrong knife. She wished Veronica joy of her. Fortunately, Vee had the skin of a rhinoceros, a quality she might find very useful if she ever finally hooked Adam. Joan was seated just behind Flo, a wry smile brightening her usual lavender tones. 'People pretend to worship God,' she whispered to Flo, 'but actually they come to eye up the talent just as they always did.'

The feel of the service was astonishingly feudal. Harry and Bill, the Rawlingses' farmworkers, sat at the back with their equivalents, Dickey and Ted, from Moreton Farm; Ivy and Alf, higher up the social scale by dint of Ivy being Hunting Farm's cook, sat two rows further forward; the Hunting Farm contingent took up the next few rows, then the doctor's family and a few enthusiastic incomers, leaving the front two rows to the Moretons themselves. Uncle Kingsley read the lesson and Pamela delivered the epistle.

Hugo Moreton was in charge of the collection plate. Flo realized with horror that he was coming towards her and she hadn't got any change. She searched her bag and pockets, but nothing jingled in response.

India-Jane offered to lend her ten pence. There was no choice for it but to resort to her wallet. Typically, Witch Beauchamp's cash machine, clearly in league with the Church, had only dispensed twenty-pound notes. Reluctantly, she handed one over.

Hugo raised an eyebrow. 'I'm sure the Farmers' Benevolent Fund will be grateful.'

Why was it, Flo asked herself, that while Adam treated her with unashamed admiration, to Hugo she always seemed the cause of faint amusement, as if she were a sideshow or an entertaining freak?

After church Veronica wrung the vicar's hand and departed with unseemly haste to take the cling-film off the canapés while the others followed, chatting, down the narrow country lane that divided the church from Hunting Farm.

Flo found herself glancing round for Hugo, but it was

Adam who appeared at her side. Hugo was still by the church gate, deep in conversation with the vicar.

'Hello, Flora.' Adam looked extraordinarily attractive in a suit, Flo noted, his lean and tanned frame could easily have been snapped up by Hugo Boss. 'What do you think of us all? Dull as one of the vicar's sermons? A bit different from the people you meet in your rackety London life, I expect.'

Flo shook her head. 'My friends aren't that exciting. Stories about my life have been greatly exaggerated.'

Adam looked disappointed. Flo considered him for a moment. He really was exceptionally handsome. His fair hair was going even blonder in the surprisingly strong midday sun, and the skin in the hollow of his neck was beginning to bronze.

'You're getting a tan,' she pointed out.

'That's the tractor. Better than Marbella for sun-bathing.'

'I'll take your word for it.'

'Hugo tells me you're reading up on farming methods.'

Flo glanced at Adam sharply. Had Hugo taken the piss out of her to his brother? 'I suppose he thought it was hilarious. The girl who couldn't tell a raging bull from a harmless bullock boning up on agriculture?'

'He was quite impressed actually. It was Ma who wondered why you'd taken such a sudden interest.' Adam's face was earnest and eager-to-please, but Flo could imagine Pamela's sarcastic tone. Pamela, no doubt, would have a very straightforward theory. She'd probably ask, ever so sweetly, if Flo had got to the chapter on

'How to Harvest a Husband'. Suddenly Flo longed for her louche London set, who didn't all behave as if they were in a Jane Austen novel.

'Flo! Over here!' bellowed a voice from the other side of the hedge. A yard ahead, dressed in white parachute silk combats, a matching gilet and dark glasses, Miranda waved, a wonderfully welcome refugee from Flo's old life.

'God, I've missed you!' Flo enveloped her in big hug of delight.

'Fuck me, you look different!' Miranda marvelled, fixing her friend with a meaningful stare. 'And speaking of surprises, have I got one for you . . .'

Behind her, casually strolling across the wooden bridge over the ha-ha, a tall, dark-haired man appeared, wearing a purple suit, ponyskin boots and a dangerous smile.

'Hello, everyone,' Miranda chipped in, 'I'm Miranda Stapleton and this is Flo's old friend, Miles.'

Chapter 6

'Hello Flora, how's country life treating you?'

Miles attempted a friendly tone which unfortunately came out more Big Bad Wolf than Little Red Riding Hood. 'I love the new image. Misleadingly vulnerable.'

Flo was torn between wanting to run away and the desire to hit him. How could Miranda, her best friend in the world, do this to her?

'Fine, thank you, Miles. As a matter of fact, I'm loving it.'

'Strange,' Miles's eyes glittered maliciously. 'You always said you were glad the country was there, but you never wanted to actually visit it.'

'That's because I was extremely ignorant.' Flo could feel India-Jane's eyes boring a hole in her back. No detail would escape the brat. 'Let me introduce you to everyone.' Flo led Miles and Miranda through the garden and on to the terrace behind the house where Vee had laid a table with a white tablecloth and drinks and canapés. 'This is my Aunt, Prue Rawlings, Uncle Francis, India-Jane, my cousin . . .' Fortunately neither Adam nor Hugo had arrived yet and no further embarrassing introductions were necessary. Except for Vee, who was eyeing Miles as if he were a caviare blini amongst a plate of Spam fritters. 'And this is my cousin, Veronica Rawlings.'

Miles took her hand. 'What delicious-looking canapés.'

To Flo's amazement, Veronica actually blushed.

Miranda scanned the drinks selection. 'God, is that Pimms? How fab, I'm absolutely gasping. I wanted to stop for a coffee but Miles couldn't wait to get down here and see you again.' Miranda helped herself to a large Pimms. 'And then we went and got lost. We tried the wrong house. An absolutely glorious place just down the road, the loveliest house I think I've ever seen. It was just like the doll's house I had when I was a kid, only huge.'

'That's Moreton House,' India explained. 'It belongs to Uncle Kingsley. He's going to give it to whichever of his nephews gets married by Michaelmas.'

'Is he now,' Miles drawled dangerously, looking at Flo. 'Now I wonder if that's got anything to do this sudden conversion to the countryside?'

'Lucky nephew!' Miranda sighed. 'It must be worth millions. Maybe I ought to throw my cap in myself.'

'Here's your chance,' Flo said tartly, ignoring Miles's question. 'Adam and Hugo are just about to arrive.'

Miranda fiddled with her fringe, which was so long it kept catching in her mascara'd eyelashes, and gave her full attention to the two young men who were walking through the garden towards them, accompanied by a chic middle-aged woman and an odd-looking type wearing tweeds and trainers, a sort of Salvador Dali in running shoes.

'Miranda and Miles, I'd like you to meet Pamela Moreton and her brother Kingsley Moreton, who live at Moreton House, and Pamela's sons, Adam and Hugo. I'm afraid Miranda's fallen in love with your house, Mr Moreton.'

'Call me Kingsley,' he twinkled. 'Has she now? Well, you'll have to get one of these two young chaps to propose to you, then you can have it all to yourself.'

Flo witnessed the unheard of sight of Miranda reddening. 'Flo was telling us about the bet. It's not serious, is it?'

'One hundred per cent serious. The estate agent fella can't wait to get his hands on it if these two let me down. He's sitting there in Witch Beauchamp rubbing his hands and crossing off the days till Michaelmas.'

'When is Michaelmas exactly?' Miranda asked. Being a farmer's daughter she'd known once but had wiped it from her memory along with tractor parts in the kitchen, no summer holidays because it was harvesttime, and being permanently broke.

'September twenty-ninth,' reassured Uncle Kingsley. 'That still gives you five months. A lovely young lady like you shouldn't have too much trouble snaring Adam or Hugo in that time. I can't tell you which is the better bet. Adam's the looker, and Hugo's got the brains. No idea what either of them are like in bed.'

'Well, that's a relief!' Miranda giggled. 'We've heard what you country people get up to on cold winter's nights.'

Uncle Kingsley guffawed with laughter. 'I stick to sheep, m'dear. They don't ask for presents and there's no paternity suits. Though last year there was a nice little blackfaced lamb . . .' He guffawed again at his own wit. 'Maybe that's who I should hand Moreton House over to.'

'Really, Kingsley,' Pamela interrupted. 'Stop all this vulgar nonsense and get me a drink.'

'Absolutely,' Uncle Kingsley looked completely unabashed, 'nice dry sherry, was it?'

While they were talking, Flo kept as far away as possible from Miles. She wanted to kill Miranda for bringing him. But Miles still managed to ease his way in her direction. Eventually she felt him take her elbow, with such a tight grip that it was painful, and steer her a few yards away from the rest.

'Miles,' she jerked hard, trying to force his hand away, 'that hurts.'

'Good. It was supposed to.' Miles's clever eyes glinted not just with malice but a spark of pleasure at the thought he was causing actual pain. 'It hurt me, too, when you left me in the lurch, and sent some fucking flower seller to make your excuses.'

'I'm sorry. I know I behaved badly.'

'So why did you do it?' He dropped his voice so the others couldn't hear.

'I had to get away. I felt cheap. I'd got drunk and gone to bed with you. Then I saw the photographs in the paper and I couldn't even remember taking my blouse off, and I just had to escape.'

'So you cut your hair and put on sackcloth and ashes

and buried yourself in the sticks. Did it ever occur to you that you might have hurt me too?'

Flo felt the familiar shame and regret burn up through her lungs like acid. 'Yes, it did. I'm sorry, Miles.'

'Both personally and professionally. Blackmills were thrilled with all the publicity. They wanted you to do more stuff for them, but no one could bloody find you. Not even me.'

Flo felt relieved. Miles's wounds were more to his image than any more delicate part. 'That was supposed to be the idea. Call it a crisis of the soul, or a mini-breakdown if you prefer, but I just had to get away.'

'Another drink, you two?' Adam appeared by their side holding a jug.

Next to Miles's pale skin and black looks, the glow-ingly healthy Adam, his blond hair gleaming in the sun, seemed like the archangel Gabriel next to wicked Lucifer – though whether Gabriel ever offered Lucifer a Pimms was, Flo realized, on the fanciful side. 'What do you think of the new, revamped Flora?' Adam asked.

'You mean the new un-vamped Flora,' corrected Miles, his voice velvety with possessiveness. 'Lovely as ever, with a certain scrubbed and nun-like appeal. More of a challenge, perhaps, which is always exciting.'

'You mean I used to look like a tart.'

'Ah, but, like all men, I have rather a weakness for tarts.'

'Just as well I didn't do it for your sake then,' smiled Flo, her tone deadly. Behind Miles's shoulder she caught sight of Hugo, talking to Joan from the shoe shop. She had the distinct impression he was listening to every word they said.

'Psst!' Miranda hissed suddenly from behind the hedge. Flo excused herself and went to join her, leaving the two men watching each other like suspicious jungle animals. At least hidden here behind the elder hedge she could strangle her ex-friend in private.

'Miranda, what the hell were you thinking of—' she began.

Miranda put a finger to her lips. 'I know, believe me, I know! I knew you'd kill me, chop me up into little pieces and sauté me, but I couldn't help it. He just showed up and when he guessed where I was going, he insisted on coming. I was actually rather scared. I thought maybe he'd grab the wheel and hurtle us into the path of a lorry just to teach you a lesson!'

'Come on, he isn't *that* sinister.'

'Isn't he? There's something about Miles that freaks me out. He's no little pussy cat. I must say, Flo, you chose a strange bloke to totally humiliate.'

'I didn't set out to humiliate him. It's just that waking up in bed with Miles, and then finding out I'd stripped off in public the night before, made me hate myself and my life. I needed a blast of normality before I really went off the rails.'

'And have you found it?'

'I'm not sure yet. The funny thing is, I came here because I remembered this as a happy house, and for all sorts of reasons it isn't any longer.'

'So why don't you come back to London?'

Flo shrugged. 'Maybe I feel an obligation to make it happier again. For my sake as well as theirs.'

'Sounds dangerous. You're not about to start

interfering in other people's lives, by any chance, are you?'

'Who, me?' Flo asked innocently. 'I'm a walking disaster area. An emotional black hole. I can't even get my own life sorted. Anyway, enough about me. What do you think of Adam? My cousin Veronica's after him, but I thought you'd be a far better Lady of the Manor. You'd know how to boss the servants about and terrify the gardener, not to mention Pamela, the frosty mother-in-law. She scares the pants off me.'

'There's just one problem, you know, in your little fairy tale.' Miranda threaded her arm through Flo's. 'I was watching the way he looks at you – as if he'd like to have you on toast. You're the one he's fallen for, Flo. I wouldn't have a cat in hell's chance.' She guided Flo out from behind the hedge towards the group gathered on the patio. 'But tell me about the other brother, the dark quiet one. Much more intriguing. He dresses like the English country gent but something tells me that's the last thing he is underneath.'

'The country bit or the gent bit?'

'Maybe I'd better find out.' Miranda gave her friend an appraising look. 'At least he isn't totally besotted with you.'

Flo struggled not to feel irritated. This wasn't going according to her plan at all. Miranda was supposed to fancy Adam, not Hugo. 'I wouldn't have thought he was your type. Serious and disapproving. Thinks Londoners should be sprayed with DDT and left for dead.'

'I quite agree with him. Now take me over and introduce me.'

'Right, everyone,' Veronica's Valkyrie tones commanded before Flo got the chance, 'time for lunch.'

She led them, leaving them no time to protest or grab another drink, into the dining room where the table had been laid so elaborately the Prince Regent would have felt at home.

'At least Vee looks happy,' commented Flo to India-Jane, who'd sidled up behind her as they shuffled in.

'Not for long,' winked India. 'She spent all morning organizing the seating plan so that she'd sit next to Adam, but I'm afraid she's in for a bit of a shock.'

'India, you haven't!' Flo giggled. 'You wouldn't . . .'

'Adam bribed me with a Toblerone to put him next to you. He tried a Mars Bar but I upped the stakes.'

'Right. Everyone sit where you've been put,' beamed Veronica. Her face fell with such comic speed when she realized the settings had been changed that Flo took pity on her and discreetly swapped them back.

'Right,' Adam grinned at Flo, not realizing she'd switched the place-cards back. 'I think I'm sitting here.'

'How lovely,' Miles drawled, 'right next to me.'

The lunch, once Veronica had claimed her rightful place next to Adam, was a big success. Veronica's cookbook on 'How to Be a Perfect Country Hostess' had counselled simplicity, and she had stuck to salmon with watercress sauce followed by summer pudding.

'How clever of you!' congratulated Miranda as she finished the last spoonful of her dessert. 'Your summer pudding's red all over. Whenever I do it there's always one little patch that's still white.'

'There was with this,' offered India-Jane helpfully. 'Vee

painted it with the vinegar from the pickled beetroot.'

Miranda almost choked.

'So,' asked Joan, trying to change the subject. 'Who's going to the Young Farmers' Ball this summer? I hope none of you are intending to miss Witch Beauchamp's major social event.'

'I'm on for a start,' Adam said enthusiastically. 'As a matter of fact, I was going to ask if you'd come with me, Flora. I know it sounds dire, but they're really quite good fun.'

Flo didn't dare even look at Veronica. 'I'm really not sure it's my kind of thing. I don't even have a ball-gown.'

'I'll lend you one,' said Miranda archly. 'Especially if Hugo could be persuaded to invite me as well.'

Hugo half-smiled back at her.

Later, when they were all drinking their coffee out in the garden, Joan leaned across and whispered to Kingsley, 'You've certainly put the fox in the henhouse with this mad scheme of yours. Veronica's determined to get Adam up the aisle even if she has to drag him.'

'I know, but I doubt she'll do it. Flora, on the other hand . . .' Uncle Kingsley winked broadly.

'You like her, don't you?' Joan prompted.

'I always like bad girls. Veronica hasn't the imagination to behave badly.'

'I'd always understood that was a good thing in a wife,' Joan countered archly.

'Only if the husband's got no imagination either.'

'Why did you never marry, Kingsley?'

'Because I only met one bad girl and she wouldn't

have me.' Under the cover of the tablecloth he slipped a hand on to Joan's knee.

'Perhaps you didn't try hard enough. Given that your family didn't approve of her.'

From her chair under the lilac tree, his sister Pamela looked in their direction. 'I'd like to go home soon, Kingsley,' she called in pained yet commanding tones. 'I'm afraid I'm getting one of my migraines.'

Joan shrugged. For as long as she'd known her, Pamela Moreton always had extremely convenient ailments. Especially if Kingsley was showing particular attention to Joan. But then, at his age, why did Kingsley put up with them unless it suited him?

Flo was amazed to find it was already four o'clock. 'Is there a loo anywhere?' Miranda asked suddenly, grabbing Flo by the arm. She had either come down with an acute attack of the runs or had something private to impart.

As soon as they were upstairs she locked the door and leaned on it conspiratorially. 'I want you to tell me every single thing you know about Hugo Moreton. He's absolutely five hundred per cent gorgeous. I think I'm in love!'

Flo raised an eyebrow. She knew Miranda. With Miranda everything was five hundred per cent wonderful.

'Well, I'm not sure I know him that well. He's the younger brother, the planner of the two, and he seems to have some kind of part-time consultancy job advising banks about farming.' She didn't add that he had a wry way of dealing with bra-free strangers who got stuck on haystacks. 'He's a little bit in his brother's shadow, Adam being the glamour boy.'

'Preferring Adam to him would be like putting Coca Cola above claret.'

'My God, he has made an impression on you!'

'Look, Flo, there was one other thing.' Miranda stopped applying killer red lipstick and studied her friend in the bathroom mirror. 'Hugo told me the Rawlingses are in real trouble financially.'

'*I* told him that,' Flo commented waspishly.

'Real edge of bankruptcy stuff, he says.'

'I know. Their daughter Mattie filled me in. She's really worried about them all, especially her father.'

'Well, then, sorry to be a party pooper, but do you think it's really fair of you to arrive on their doorstep with a suitcase and Snowy and expect them to put you up indefinitely?'

This unexpected empathy on behalf of Miranda for Flo's exploited aunt and uncle didn't quite ring true. 'Personally I think you should stop imposing on their kindness and get yourself back to London.'

'Leaving a fairer playing field for you and Hugo?' Flo teased. 'Don't worry. Love's the last thing I've come here looking for. And now that you mention it, I've been intending to talk to Auntie Prue about ways I could make myself useful. Pay my way.'

'Nice thought, but what possible use could a Londoner who doesn't know hay from grass and thinks drilling's something you do at the dentist going to be?'

The question hit home. There was an obvious truth in it that Flo found hard to deny. Maybe she was just in the way, making things harder for the family by being there, adding another burden to their already heavy load.

Downstairs everyone was getting ready to go. Mattie, who had been rather withdrawn but at least present during the lunch, catapulted herself into Flo's arms. 'Can we go to the Sheep Centre now? You promised, Flo. You said you couldn't take me yesterday but we could go today!'

'But what about all the clearing up?' Flo asked. 'We've got to help your mother.'

'It's all right,' Auntie Prue beamed. 'It's a weight off my mind actually,' she added in a low voice, 'to see Mattie looking so happy. You've really helped that child.'

Flo hoped Miranda had overheard. It might convince her that Flo wasn't just a hopeless sponger.

'Come back to London soon,' Miles pressed Flo's hand rather too hard as he kissed her goodbye. 'Blackmills really want to use you again. Money no object. You've got just the image they're after, apparently.'

'What, loud, exhibitionist and drunk?'

Miles smiled lazily. 'Glad to see you've still got an acid tongue. We wouldn't want you turning into a quiet little country mouse, would we?'

'Goodbye, you two,' Veronica gushed like a geyser in Laura Ashley. She'd been getting on with Miles surprisingly well, Flo had noted. 'And don't forget to pop down any time you feel like a bit of R&R.'

'I might just do that,' Miles drawled, raising Flora's unwilling hand to his lips. 'I'm intrigued to know how far Flora's clean new image goes. Would it survive half a bottle of whiskey and the temptation of a lot of lovely money?'

'Goodbye, Miles,' Flo said firmly, refusing to be drawn. 'Mattie and I are off to the Sheep Centre.'

'Have fun,' Miles said pointedly. 'And save me a pretty one. With you burying yourself down here I might need it.'

Flo flushed like a Tequila Sunrise. No one could have missed the deliberate innuendo in Miles's voice. Even a five-year-old couldn't have missed it. India-Jane was probably printing up copies at this very moment.

'Don't forget to call me when you come to town,' Miranda reminded Hugo for the tenth time. She was, Flo noticed, in full temptress mode – flicking her hair, pursing soft pouty lips, her body language playing Easy To Get. And it seemed to be working extremely effectively.

'I'll be up on Wednesday as a matter of fact,' Hugo replied, helping Miranda with her coat with, in Flo's view, quite unnecessary enthusiasm. 'Why don't we have a drink then?'

Jesus, he wasn't even making her sit by the phone and wait.

'Fine,' Miranda purred. 'Make it seven o'clock at Bluebird.'

Miranda had never been confident and decisive like this with Flo. It was always 'Oh shit, where the hell shall we meet?' when it was girls together.

Flo was beginning to wonder about Miranda.

'Well, that was a big success,' Flo said to Mattie as they drove to the Sheep Centre.

'Yes. Ma was terrified about how much it'd cost but Mr Dawson from the fish farm gave us the salmon in exchange for some of our lamb, and the wine merchant wanted some pheasant, so Ma did a swap.'

'Like barter, you mean?'

'That's how things are done round here. No one in farming's got any actual money, so they swap services instead. It only works with little things though. No one would let Ma and Dad barter for their farm rent.'

'When's it due?'

'When *was* it due you mean. Lady Day.' Mattie's face took on a pinched, carrying all the responsibilities of the world, expression.

'And when's that – sorry, was that?' Flo was getting used to these weird occasions in the country calendar. Lammastide. Michaelmas. Lady Day.

'March. They've been given ninety days' grace. I heard them talking last night.' There was a catch in Mattie's voice as she looked out of the window to hide her fears. 'Dad thinks we might be evicted.'

My God, Flo thought, and I imagined the countryside full of flowers and happy peasants. Just like Marie Antoinette had.

She had to think of some way of helping her aunt and uncle out.

'Here's the Sheep Centre,' Mattie pointed out excitedly.

Flo had to admit the location of the place was staggering. In a gentle dip of the downland hills, with wild dramatic views to the sea a mile away, the centre was based around a farmhouse with a lovely old flint barn to one side and a range of wattle lambing pens down the other. A sign promised 'The greatest range of rare breeds in Britain'.

'Can I feed one of the newborn lambs?' Mattie begged.

'Do they still have any? I thought lambs were born earlier than this.'

'Not here they're not,' explained a gruff iron-haired lady in a shapeless hat, tattered corduroy jacket and riding boots. 'Ours are born right through to the end of June. We kid them into ovulating when we want them to, so we can extend the lambing season for all you lucky visitors.'

'How do you manage that?' asked Flo, suspecting she might regret raising this question.

'We put this chap in. Rowley the Ram. Known throughout five counties.' She pointed to a huge beast with enormous black horns and a knowing glint in his eye. 'Go on, have a proper look.'

Flo, even more sure she was going to regret this, bent down and inspected his undercarriage. 'Fuck me!' she exclaimed involuntarily.

'That's exactly what he'd do, given half a chance,' agreed his owner. 'I'm afraid he isn't very discriminating.'

'Thanks a lot,' Flo replied.

'I mean he isn't even species-specific.'

The ram moved meaningfully in Flo's direction. Flo grabbed Mattie's hand and dragged her towards one of the pens where, to their absolute delight, a lamb was just being born.

'That's a Greyfaced Dartmoor,' confided the owner, who had come to join them. 'Lovely breed.'

'What an amazing place you've got here,' Flo marvelled. 'Children must love it.'

'They do. The schools come here from miles around. We're very good at tying it in to the National Curriculum.'

'Don't tell me. The ram comes under Biology.'

The iron-grey lady laughed and unbent a little. 'He'd be an excellent teacher. It's just such a pity we've got to close. You don't know anyone who'd give a home to forty-seven different rare breeds, do you? They aren't worth a ha'penny on the market. Poor beasts, I hope they won't literally end up as lambs to the slaughter. Still, Rowley's had a full and active life. Made quite a contribution to the gene pool, you might say.'

'I'll bet he has.' For some reason she found herself thinking of Adam. 'Why are you closing down? Are you too seasonal?'

'Not at all. We have events all year. The commercial aspect's fine – not a fortune but enough to tick over nicely. Better than conventional farming anyway. But my children all have good jobs in London. You wouldn't catch them mucking out a sheep pen and I'm too old, so I'm having to sell up. Probably at a rock bottom price.' Flo sensed the emotion behind the old lady's words, which her country stoicisim didn't quite camouflage. 'Otherwise it's the abbatoir for all of them.'

'How sad for you. I'll help out if you need volunteers,' offered Mattie. Flo had rarely seen her so talkative. 'I'm sure my father would too. He's always saying sheep have been his life. He went into dairy because he was told there was more money in it, but the bottom's dropped out of that too.'

Flo didn't point out that Mattie's father probably had more on his mind than volunteering at a sheep centre.

'Time to shut up shop. This lamb's going to need feeding twice in the night.' The owner smiled wearily, her weatherbeaten face breaking into a thousand cracks, like a lump of clay that had dried out too quickly. 'Worse than babies, lambs. At least you can give babies dummies. Nice meeting you.'

On the way home Mattie's happiness seemed to evaporate and the old, withdrawn child reappeared.

'What's up, Matilda? You've gone all quiet.'

'I was thinking of what the lady said. All those lovely sheep having to be slaughtered.' A small sob escaped her. 'Even Rowley the Ram. Do you think Dad would let us take some home?' she perked up.

'Your father's got quite a lot to think about, hasn't he, without feeding extra mouths,' Flo said gently.

'I suppose. Yes, I was being selfish.' Flo was infinitely touched by the child's reply. At twelve she'd already learned that life was tough. At least Flo had been allowed another few years before she'd found out that harsh truth.

Back at Hunting Farm everything was restored to order. Ivy was moaning. Veronica looked smug. India-Jane was watching out jealously for their return. Flo went to look for her aunt in the kitchen.

'Let me make you a cup of tea,' Flo offered. 'You're looking whacked out.'

Aunt Prue smiled gratefully and sat down at the vast kitchen table. The room reminded Flo of their own kitchen when she was a small child. One day she'd caught the spicy whiff of cinnamon and apples and rushed down, eager to help, like her friends did their mothers. But her mother was sitting down, reading and looking tired, while the daily woman prepared the pie. And the daily certainly hadn't wanted her help.

From behind the vast table her aunt watched her. 'I haven't told you, Flora, how much you remind me of Mary now that you've changed your hairstyle.'

'Do I?' Flo hadn't heard the longing in her own voice, but her aunt did.

'It's quite striking. I hadn't seen it under the blonde mane, but now the bone structure's visible, it took my breath away. She loved you so much, you know. You were her one true achievement, she said.'

'Not much of an achievement.'

Prue was startled at the depth of her niece's self-loathing. It seemed tragic that such a lovely girl should dislike herself so much. 'That isn't what she thought. Having you meant her life hadn't been wasted. It got her through her illness.'

'And turned my father against me.'

'Your father didn't know how to cope with pain. He'd never felt it before. He was a successful businessman. He thought he could control everything, but he couldn't control your mother's cancer. Or his own feelings.'

'So he ran away.'

'Yes. Or rather he was offered a job in America and he took it. And you didn't want to go.'

'Everything I knew was here. My friends. Mum's grave. I didn't feel strong enough to start all over again. But I needed him. He just didn't need me.'

Aunt Prue reached across the table and took Flo's hand. 'You poor girl. I'm so glad you came, even if it was a very long while afterwards.'

'But it's such a difficult time for you. I was so thoughtless, just turning up out of the blue, not even finding out how things were with you first.'

'If you had, you might not have come. And that would have been our loss.'

The tenderness in her aunt's voice was too much for Flo. The tears began to blur her vision until she could hardly see her aunt, only feel the comforting pressure of her hand. For a split second Flo closed her eyes and pretended this was her mother's hand. Eventually the tide of emotion stilled and she turned away to collect herself.

'Sorry about that. It's just that Mattie told me how tough things are for you and Uncle Francis.'

'Yes. Though you wouldn't think so with Vee giving lunch parties, even if we did swap most of it.' Prue sighed. 'And there's Ivy and Alf and Harry and Bill on the farm. We ought to let them go, but they're all older than us. None of them would find work easily. The countryside's changing so much – one hundred cows used to be enough to survive but now you need two hundred and fifty and we can't afford them. To be honest, I'm not sure how much longer we can carry on.'

This time it was her aunt's turn to try and hide her worry. 'The farm's been in the family for three hundred years. If we go it'll be sold to some stockbroker who'll put in a sauna.'

'Is there anything you could sell off? A barn that could be converted? A field or two?'

'We've done it already. Long Meadow paid the school fees. The cottage where Alf and Ivy live went years ago to buy farm equipment. I'm afraid there's nothing left now except the farm and this house. Flo, I'm really worried about Francis.'

Flo wondered if this was the moment to reveal her uncle's trips to the Angel, but what good would it do? He probably just needed some release from his worries.

If only there was something she could do to help. She'd never felt more like a useless onlooker. The only talent she seemed to possess was getting drunk and taking her clothes off.

Then it struck her. There was something. She could get out of their hair and stop adding her keep to their mounting bills. 'Aunt Prue, you've been incredibly generous to me and I've had a wonderful time this past week, but I think I ought to be getting back to London.'

'Ought you?' The sadness in her aunt's voice tore at her. 'Of course you should, you can't bury yourself down here. It must be incredibly dull for you. It's just that it's so lovely having you. Veronica's about as much help as a pedigree poodle, only interested in finding a husband, and India's not as tough as she seems. Mattie's blossomed so much since you arrived . . .'

'You mean you actually like having me here?' The incredulity in Flo's tone made her aunt want to hug her niece like a little child. Flo was so unused to being valued for herself, it was heartbreaking.

'Flora Parker, you mad child! Of course we do. You're a breath of fresh air. Twice as helpful as my children. And it's hard to explain, but it's almost like having Mary back.'

Relief flooded through Flo. She was wanted. Useful even. 'Is there anything I can do to help? I insist on paying rent for starters.'

'A drop in the ocean,' her aunt smiled palely, but at least it was a smile. 'But do so by all means if it makes you feel better. Though really the best thing is being friends with Mattie and perhaps looking after her when school finishes. That really would take a weight off my mind.'

'It'd be a pleasure. I'll meet her from school tomorrow.'

Flo jumped up to make her aunt that cup of tea. No matter what Miranda said, she was wanted here. For the first time since childhood she felt she was part of a family.

The next day was so beautiful that Flo couldn't resist spending it outside. She took the roof down on the Beetle and drove Mattie to school, a delirious Snowy hanging her head over the side. On the way back she stopped for a walk down by the river. The sky was a clear dazzling blue, the sun already hot even though it was early and a mist hung over the valley like the smoke from some exotic Turkish cigarette. Flo sat down on the small wooden bridge and sighed. Across the river she could just make out the shape of a white horse carved in the chalk hillside. These drawings of white horses were everywhere in Westshire, no one knew why, and they gave the place a sense of timelessness, of life being about more than survival but a lifting of the spirit. She wished Uncle Francis could feel that. It seemed impossible to be depressed on a day like today. A few fields away, on the Moretons' land, a distant figure on a tractor was cutting down grass for silage. My God, thought Flo, with a surge of satisfaction, I actually knew that without anyone telling me.

Flo beamed to herself that after the short time she'd been here she was actually beginning to understand a little about the countryside and how it worked. She wouldn't have to climb a haystack now because she couldn't tell a bull from a bullock. She wondered who was on the tractor, Adam or Hugo or one of their workers.

Why should you care anyway, she asked herself, but failed to answer. Instead she lay back in the tickling grass and felt the sun on her face. High above a distant bird sang as it swooped and dived, always just out of sight. A skylark. Again she felt the pleasure of continuity and of the timeless beauty of the landscape, but since yesterday there was something else. A sense of belonging.

And then reality flooded back. Behind the beauty was a harsher truth. Her aunt was worried sick and her uncle was getting blind drunk to forget the fact that they might be on the point of losing the farm, and with it their whole livelihood.

At three-thirty she drove to Mattie's school. The child came out alone, Flo noticed, while the others were in giggling groups, shouting 'Goodbyes' and 'See you tomorrows' to each other.

She beamed at the unexpected sight of Flo waiting for her. 'Any homework?' Flo asked as Mattie climbed into the car.

Mattie took in the envious glances from her classmates. They were all supposed to be old enough to get home on their own but it was a treat when you were met. Especially by someone who looked as much fun as Flo.

'No. I think the weather got to Miss Prescott. She didn't set any. And it should have been decimal fractions.'

'What do you want to do then?' Flo asked as they sped up the drive to Hunting Farm. India-Jane was already peering out of the open sitting room window, flute in hand.

'She's supposed to be practising. She's doing Grade six. She'll be revolting if she passes.'

'What,' Flo whispered, 'even more revolting than she is now?' They giggled, making India stare at them furiously. Behind them the roar of an engine made them turn.

'Oooh,' Mattie yelled delightedly. 'It's Adam on the quad bike.'

Adam waved. His blond hair had grown over his collar, Flo noted, and his tan was deepening daily. He really was quite a specimen.

'Come on, young lady,' he shouted to Mattie, 'the weather's been so good we're doing some early haymaking. Want to come?'

Mattie threw her school bag in through the open window. 'It's not you he cares about,' India hissed at her meanly. 'It's Flo he's trying to impress.'

'He's got good taste then!' called Mattie, the train tracks on her teeth flashing as she smiled.

'Can we bring Snowy with us?'

'Why not,' Adam shrugged good-naturedly, 'she can chase rabbits.'

'What's the difference between haymaking and harvesting?' Flo shouted to Adam over the noise of the engine, as they sped over the fields back towards Moreton Farm.

'Haymaking's much earlier. Not many farmers do it any more, they use silage instead. We're cutting grass instead of corn.' There was no sarcasm in his tone, as there might have been in Hugo's had she asked the same question. No suggestion of *Bloody townies trying to play 'Let's Understand the Pretty Countryside'*.

There was a tractor standing ready in the big meadow beyond Moreton House, with just enough room for the three of them. It was hot and dusty work. Three quarters of the way through, Adam stopped and turned to Flo and Mattie. 'Do you girls mind if I take my top off?'

Mattie looked at Flo and giggled. Flo felt as if she'd wandered on to the set of the Coca Cola ad where the women workers gather to watch the hunky window cleaner. Except that Adam had an even better body. Lean and long and glowing like a toffee that had just been unwrapped.

Flo felt a sudden pinprick of desire and looked away, shocked. There was no denying that Adam Moreton was a perfect piece of manhood. And on this beautiful sunny day, in this golden, inviting landscape, there was something about his lack of complexity that strongly appealed to her. She still felt bruised from her disaster with the devious Miles. With Adam, what you saw was what you got, and frankly, Flo decided as she stole a glance at his lean golden frame, that was quite a lot.

As if by extra-sensory perception Adam returned her glance. That was when Flo noticed the telltale bulge in his safari shorts. It was just as well Mattie was around as chaperone or Flo might not be able to answer for herself.

'Flora!' Adam broke into her lustful thoughts. 'Could you open the gate, do you think?'

Grateful that at least women didn't demonstrate their erotic arousal in quite the same way as men did, or Rowley the Ram for that matter, Flo jumped down.

Adam parked the tractor in the farmyard, next to the haybarn, then whispered something to Mattie. Mattie promptly jumped down and tore off with Snowy in the direction of Home Farm.

'Come in here a minute. I've got something to show you.'

Flo glanced nervously round at her rapidly departing chaperone, but Mattie and Snowy had already disappeared round the corner. Flo was quite alone.

Feeling a sudden heat that had nothing to do with the weather, Flo followed Adam inside.

Chapter 7

Inside the barn it was dim and sweet-smelling and stunningly hot.

Adam seemed to have disappeared. Flo had visions of him stripped to the waist, already lying lasciviously in the hay like something out of *Tom Jones*.

'Up here,' invited his voice. 'There's a ladder.'

Gingerly, wondering with every step whether she was going to regret this, Flo climbed up the rungs. 'Look, Adam, I'm not sure this is a good idea . . .' she began, trying to sound stern.

'Ssshhh!' Adam whispered. 'Look up there.'

Flo felt a disconcerting stab of disappointment. He really was going to show her something, and not the something she'd imagined.

'It's a fledgling barn owl roosting in the rafters,' he said leaning towards her. 'Just a baby. Probably only a few days old.'

She could feel his hot breath on her neck as he bent down to whisper in her ear and she shuddered, hoping he hadn't noticed. People said only men felt pure unadulterated lust, but Flo had no other explanation for her reaction to Adam's glisteningly perfect body.

'I'll try and get it for you,' he offered and before she could stop him he'd stretched up towards the lowest beam.

'Owwwww!' he yelped suddenly, clutching his side, 'I think I must have pulled a muscle.'

Flo rushed towards him, concerned, and reached out a hand to explore the affected spot. Instead Adam grabbed it and guided it expertly downwards. 'Forget my side,' he said, pulling her against him so quickly she didn't have time to argue, 'that's where the ache is. And it's been there from the first moment I saw you, up that haystack in just a raincoat and no knickers.'

'No bra,' Flo corrected him breathily, trying to hold on to the few brain cells that hadn't been melted by Adam's devastating animal attraction. 'I had perfectly respectable knickers.'

'There's only one cure for an ache like this,' Adam insisted, his voice rusty with desire.

'Is that so?' Flo tried to list all the reasons why this wasn't a good idea, starting with the possible return of Mattie and Snowy, and ending with all the disastrous relationships she'd already been through. But it was no good, nature triumphed.

Together they fell in a crumpled heap while Adam undid her buttons with alarming efficiency.

'You've done this before,' Flo accused, biting his ear.

'What else can a farmer do on a long winter's night?'

It was no good. Her mind might be resisting but her nipples were already shamelessly erect and wasn't that a groan of pleasure escaping her lips? Aaaaaaaah . . . Even to her own ears that hardly sounded like a plea to stop.

After that Flo stopped thinking about anything but the blissful sensations of Adam's lips and fingers. It seemed years since she'd felt like this.

A sudden commotion below made her sit upright. 'My God! Mattie! What are we thinking of?'

'It's all right,' Adam reassured. 'I sent Mattie on an errand. It's probably just Dickey back from drilling. He'll go away.'

But it wasn't Dickey.

Flo, hastily coming to her senses and trying to do up the buttons that had been so expertly undone moments before, peered over the edge and found herself staring into the irate face of Hugo Moreton.

'I just came to tell you,' Hugo's tone was suddenly as uncompromising as the steely blue of his eyes, 'that your terrier has just shamelessly seduced our mother's prize dachshund.' He paused contemptuously. 'But I see it's simply imitating its owner.'

A hot flush of embarrassment sizzled over Flo's face, swiftly followed by a blast of anger. 'Is the dachshund enjoying it?' she demanded rudely, giving a push to the ladder he was standing on, which toppled backwards in comical slow motion. 'Then maybe you'd better let nature take its course.'

'That was telling him.' The tone of sibling satisfaction in Adam's voice was unmistakable.

'Come on, you,' Flo pulled him up unceremoniously. 'We must have been off our heads anyway.'

'All good things, or even bad things, come to those

who wait.' He gave Flo his most fallen angel smile and slowly began doing up his shorts.

'You seem to be having trouble with that zip,' Flo replied unsentimentally, not knowing who she was angrier with, herself or holier-than-thou Hugo. 'Here, let me help.'

'Owwwwww!' Adam yelped for the second time that afternoon. 'Watch out. That's what we call a mutual investment down there.' He laughed at his own joke, tenderly massaging his damaged manhood. 'Though Hugo's the one who usually knows about all that stuff.'

'You've lost me.' Flo hopped up and down looking for her shoe which had lodged itself behind a bale of straw.

'Investments. He spends half his week on the computer, studying the stock market.'

'Well, bully for him. Shouldn't he be out ploughing furrows straighter than dies, whatever they are.'

The sound of Snowy's feverish barks informed them that she'd finished whatever shameless activity she'd been engaging in and that she and Mattie were back. Flo found her missing shoe and then realized that because she'd kicked down the ladder with Hugo on it they couldn't get down either. It was seven or eight feet to the barn floor. 'Mattie!' she yelled. 'Could you stick the ladder up here?'

Mattie stared up into the hayloft, her eyes on stalks. 'How on earth did you get up there?'

'Adam was showing me a baby barn owl.'

A small smile stole across Mattie's serious little face. 'As long as he wasn't behaving like Fritz.'

'Don't tell me. Fritz is the prize dachshund.' Flo

choked suddenly. 'Hugo said Snowy was the one who started it.'

'Yes, but Fritz didn't have to be so Germanic and thorough. There's bound to be puppies, you know. Can I have one?' She fetched the ladder and pushed it up to the trap door. 'By the way,' Mattie asked, not entirely innocently, 'what was the matter with Hugo? I've never seen him so cross.'

'Don't worry about him,' Adam winked. 'He just thinks I got a bigger present from Santa than he did.'

Before Adam could say any more, Flo slid down the ladder Mattie had rescued, and then removed it. 'I wouldn't count on it,' she shouted up, nearly as cross with him as she was with his brother for his knowing arrogance, 'it's a long time till Christmas.'

Mattie, mystified but admiring, trotted along behind her as they headed back to Hunting Farm. 'Gosh, Flo,' Mattie congratulated, 'you certainly know how to keep men in their place!'

Yes, thought Flo furiously, *only usually it's lying on top of me.*

'And as for you . . .' she turned to Snowy, who immediately rolled over and rubbed herself outrageously on the ground, 'you're a bad example to bitches everywhere.'

· 'Just like her owner then,' said a sarcastic voice behind them.

Hugo, his dignity restored apart from a piece of straw sticking from above one ear, was about to climb in to his car. 'Can I offer you a lift?' he added with exaggerated politeness.

'I'd rather be driven by a poisonous tarantula.'

'Tarantulas aren't poisonous,' Hugo said pompously.

'Oh yes they are,' contradicted Mattie. 'That's why they're supposed to cause all that gypsy dancing.'

'Well,' said Hugo, trying to retrieve himself and secretly cursing that he ever thought he'd know more than Mattie, 'they certainly can't drive.'

But Flo, dragging Mattie in her wake, wasn't listening. She'd had enough of the Moreton brothers for one day. So, ignoring both Hugo's as well as Adam's cries, she set off at breakneck speed down the farm track.

As Hugo stood watching them, a sudden sound made him turn. Adam had leapt gracefully down from the hayloft, or at least as gracefully as anyone can leap eight feet.

'So, little bruv,' Adam asked, ostentatiously doing up the top button of his shorts, 'How're you doing in the marriage stakes?'

'Oh for God's sake, Adam,' Hugo fought the sudden desire to punch his brother's smugly handsome face, 'the whole thing's a farce.'

'Is it?' Lazily, Adam shook the straw out of his blond hair. 'Only I think I may just have made the first move.'

At Hunting Farm, Aunt Prue was watching out for them. 'You've got a visitor. She's in the kitchen talking to Ivy.'

The lady from the Sheep Centre, still wearing her ancient Barbour even though she was only inches away from the sweltering Aga, sat in a newspaper-covered armchair with a cup of tea and a plate of Ivy's terrible scones.

'Delicious,' pronounced the visitor untruthfully.

Mattie giggled. Ivy's scones, as the family well knew, had the quality and texture of shrapnel.

'Mattie! Miss Parker!' The visitor gratefully abandoned her plate and jumped to her feet. 'I wondered if I could have a word in private? By the way, my name's Dorothy Williams.'

Ivy, deprived of the meat of the conversation, banged around in the kitchen planning a particularly gruesome supper.

'You seemed so interested in the Sheep Centre when you visited,' Mrs Williams began as soon as they were out of Ivy's earshot, 'and you mentioned your uncle was a farmer, so I came to ask you, would he consider taking on my flock? I'd give it to him free, of course,' she hastened to add. 'And throw in Rowley the Ram too. I had a look at your farm outbuildings and in my view you could easily set up pens here, and there's ample parking for visitors.' She gestured towards the views of lush rolling farmland under the shadow of Firmingham Beacon. 'It's the most blessed spot.' Mrs Williams took in the uncertainty on Flo's face.

'My flock will have to be slaughtered otherwise. They're worthless on the market. Even Rowley's past his prime – except that nobody's told him that yet. And the Sheep Centre is a going concern. It won't make your uncle rich but in these days when farming's so tough, at least it's an alternative.'

'Oh, Flo, do let's!' begged Mattie.

'Mattie, be serious. It's your parents' farm. They'll probably think the idea's daft.'

'Mum won't. She'd adore it. She's brilliant with people. And Ivy would love to make the scones.'

Flo and the sheep lady exchanged nervous glances.

'We'll talk to your parents, I promise,' Flo agreed.

'The only thing is,' continued their visitor, 'I hate to be pushy but there isn't that long to decide. My son has already found a buyer for the land.'

'No time like the present then,' Flo reassured her. 'I'll go and find my aunt now.'

Mattie was right. Her mother did love the idea.

'It'd be perfect for Francis,' Aunt Prue enthused, the anxiety that seemed an almost permanent fixture lifting from her face like a lovely landscape emerging from the mist. 'It'd be much less strain for him. He loves sheep and we could all help out.' The mist settled again. 'But surely starting a Sheep Centre would cost a lot of money? And who would even lend us any?'

'I don't know.' Flo wished she could be more positive. 'Hugo mentioned something about selling the milk quota.' The mention of Hugo made her flush guiltily. 'But would Uncle Francis get enough from that to start a Sheep Centre?'

'He never talks to me about the business side of things. I'm ashamed to say I have no idea.'

Flo was shocked. As a farmer's wife, Aunt Prue worked just as hard for the farm as her husband did. It was inconceivable to Flo that Prue wasn't even consulted about how to run it.

'Hugo would know what it was worth,' Mattie supplied helpfully. 'He's the business brain at Moreton. Adam's always saying so. Why don't you ask him?'

Flo shot her a quelling look. The last person she wanted to discuss anything with was Hugo.

'Flora, darling,' Flo couldn't bear seeing the brief flare of optimism fade from her aunt's eyes. 'I think it's a brilliant scheme but we need a few more facts if we're going to tackle Francis. Do you think you could possibly ask Hugo's advice?'

There was nothing else for it. Flo knew when she was beaten. This whole thing wasn't to do with her but her aunt and uncle. Flo made herself swallow her pride.

On Wednesday she walked across to Moreton House.

As she strolled through the grounds in search of Hugo, Flo was struck for the first time by quite how perfect it was. No wonder Miranda had fallen in love with it. It reminded Flo of one of those samplers laboured over by seventeenth-century ladies. Eight windows across the top, eight across the middle and six across the bottom, and a white stuccoed arch complete with globe above the white-painted front door in the middle. She half-expected a ghost in satin and ringlets to appear.

Instead, a very much alive Pamela emerged, carrying a flower basket, with her precious dachshund trotting behind her. 'I hope you haven't brought your disgraceful little dog with you,' she shouted testily to Flo. 'You really ought to lock her up when she's in season, or at least cover her rear end. Poor Fritz didn't know where to put himself.'

'From what I heard,' Flo replied frostily, 'he soon worked that one out.' She had meant to apologize but Pamela's tone was so haughty and *grande dame*-ish.

Besides it was she, Flo, who would be left holding the puppies.

'Are you looking for Adam?' News obviously travelled fast in the farmyard.

'No. Hugo actually.'

Pamela raised her perfectly plucked eyebrow. 'It's his consultancy day in London.'

'When will he be back, do you know?'

Pamela's smile melted into smugness. 'Not until late. Or possibly not at all. He's meeting your friend Miranda for a drink and dinner. I thought she was a frightfully pretty girl.'

Flo repressed a stab of annoyance. Pamela seemed remarkably well-informed about her son's movements. Maybe she was one of those ghastly mothers who brought her sons and their paramours a cup of tea in bed after they'd spent the night noisily bonking.

Besides, no one in their right mind would call Miranda 'frightfully pretty'. Frightfully stylish perhaps, or frightfully thin. Disapproval of Flo was obviously producing rose-coloured spectacles.

After she'd bid Pamela a brief and not very polite goodbye, Flo punched Miranda's number into her mobile but got a hideously superior-sounding message telling her Miranda was tied up.

'Probably by Hugo,' Flo muttered darkly to herself and decided to see if she could persuade Adam to come to lunch.

She found him ploughing more of his incredibly straight furrows in the ten acre field under the shadow of the Beacon.

'What are you doing up here?' he shouted, smiling sexily. 'Can't keep away from me, eh?'

'Actually,' Flo said loftily, 'I was looking for Hugo but he's gone to London.'

'Why Hugo?' Adam looked touchingly crestfallen, like a baby bird who isn't going to get a worm.

Flo took pity on him. He was so easy to read. 'I just need some business advice for a scheme I'm trying to talk Uncle Francis into.'

'Try me instead,' offered Adam, looking as if his mind were on anything but business.

'I thought seeing as you're a ploughman, you might like a ploughman's lunch,' Flo suggested.

'Just let me finish here. Twenty minutes then we'll go into the Angel. They do the best ploughman's in the county.'

Flo leaned against the gate, waiting for Adam and feeling the sun warming her face. It was so hot for early May that she stripped down to her vest top. After ten minutes she could feel her skin begin to redden and glow.

'Look at you, Rudolph.' Adam's lips skimmed the end of her nose then slipped to the little crater at the base of her neck, where the sweat had gathered. His lizard's tongue licked it up. The effect was electric. Flo had to force her consciousness back to the job in hand.

The good weather had gone to everyone's heads and the tables outside the pub were already full, under their green and white Heineken umbrellas.

'It looks like we'll have to go inside.' Adam pushed her gently towards the gloom within. 'Rather a pity on a day like this. On the other hand another ten minutes and you'd be peeling.' He leaned her up against the empty bar. 'Seems like we've got the place to ourselves.' He slipped one hand inside her top. Flo gasped at the erotic charge.

'Don't mind me, folks,' drawled a ripe Westshire voice, sweet and sharp like the best apples, 'I'm just part of the furniture.'

Flo narrowed her eyes and made out Donna, the cat-eyed barmaid, hidden in the gloom polishing a glass. 'In the old days,' Donna went on, 'they used to have rooms where a couple could slake their thirst in private.' Her voice implied no connection with drink. 'Pity they stopped. Beds are so boring, I think. Though there's always the haybarn. Has he taken you there yet, Flora?'

Flo was so angry she forgot all about the ploughman's lunch. 'Let's go, Adam. There's a nasty chill in here.'

'How's your uncle?' Donna called after her, maliciously. 'Still getting rat-arsed every Thursday?'

Donna grabbed Adam's arm as he tried to run after Flo. Her hand was cold and he shivered involuntarily. 'You know what they say,' Donna whispered, 'cold hands, warm clit. I bet her hands are warm as coal.' She pulled him against her body, her nipples pressing into him. Adam groaned.

'Spoiled for choice, aren't you then Adam?' her voice bubbled over with invitation. 'And why not? There's nothing wrong with sowing your wild oats. As long as none of them take seed, that is. I should watch that Flora Parker. I reckon it's not just your body she's after.'

*

'Why don't you come in and have a look round?' Miranda's smile was pure sugared almonds. 'They say someone's home tells you all about them. This is my little boudoir.'

Hugo looked about him in amazement. He'd never seen anything quite like Miranda's flat in his life. The sitting room was dominated by a fuchsia velvet sofa with extraordinary white wrought iron legs, with a matching white iron and glass coffee table. They looked as if they might have come from some Romanian gypsy's veranda. The walls were subtler but still pink, adorned, incongruously, with a set of black-and-white photographs of haughty 1940s *Vogue* models.

'It's very . . .' Hugo for once found himself lost for words.

'Kitsch? Girlie? I know. I'm just a girl who can't say no to pink.'

'So I see.'

His eye was drawn with relief to the one ordinary object in the room, a small framed photograph of two teenage girls in stripey swimsuits. It was Miranda with Flo. 'How long have you known each other?'

'It seems like for ever. But actually since we were twelve. Flo's father and my parents found the idea of actually having their children home for the summer pretty terrifying so we ended up at Camp Cerne. Flo and I teamed up on the first day and spent the next six weeks trying to avoid ever going outdoors, except to sunbathe on the flat roof above the gym. You could get an all-over suntan there without any of the geeks knowing.'

'Has she changed much?'

'Not really. Flo was always a bit of a wild child. She discovered boys while I was still stuck into *Swallows and Amazons*.'

'I can well imagine,' Hugo said wryly. 'And she's perfected her studies ever since.'

The truth was rather different, but Miranda decided Hugo didn't need to know that. In fact it had been Miranda who was the wild child and Flo who'd preferred books.

'She wasn't that academic, then, our Flo?'

'Far too dizzy.' Miranda patted the sofa next to her invitingly. 'She just wanted to leave school and get on with life with a capital "L".'

A very small pang of guilt assailed Miranda. Flo had been quite a high-flyer, with potentially brilliant A-levels and a glittering career at university predicted. Then her mother had died, she'd fallen out with her father and left school overnight.

But then all was fair in war and seduction. Besides, ever since that photo had been taken, Flo had had all the men. There had always been something about Flo that spelt sex, and boys, from nine to nineteen, had instantly known it. Even now Flo had both Adam and Miles dangling.

'What sort of jobs did she go for?'

'*Jobs?*' Miranda already felt they'd been talking about Flo for far too long. 'Oh, Flo's never really had a job. She just flits from here to there. Parties. Yachts. Men. Her boyfriend Miles had wonderful contacts.'

Miranda was vaguely aware that she made Flo sound like a high-class hooker with Miles as her pimp.

'I didn't know Miles was her boyfriend.'

'Oh yes. It was Miles who set up the newspaper thing for Blackmills Whiskey that caused all the stir.'

'What newspaper thing was that?'

Miranda couldn't believe her luck. 'You mean you've never seen it?' She had a feeling Hugo didn't select his girlfriends from the front page of the *Daily Post*. More like the front page of *Tatler* or *Harpers & Queen*.

Miranda rifled through her kidney-shaped dressing table, with its pink flounced skirt, and pulled out the offending newspaper. 'Actually, it made Flo quite a star.'

Hugo stared. There, across most of the front page, was Flora, clutching a bottle of whiskey and wearing a minuscule platform bra from which her breasts boiled voluptuously over, so that even the areola of the nipple was clearly visible.

He stared at it for perhaps longer than was strictly necessary. 'She looks as if she's having a good time.'

Miranda might have said, 'As a matter of fact she was so ashamed she ran away to Westshire.' Instead she shrugged and said, 'That's our Flo for you. Always the Party Girl.' Miranda decided it was high time they stopped talking about Flo. Flo already had Adam the Hunk and the mysterious Miles to choose from. Miranda was damned if she was going to get Hugo as well.

'Right.' Miranda forgot for a microsecond that she was supposed to be the shy, book-loving one. 'Shall we go? What about the K Bar first and then on to Coast?' Hugo's beat of silence told her perhaps she was being a tad too sophisticated. After all, he was a farmer up from Westshire. 'Or we could hop on an open-topped bus and see the sights if you like. Buck House, Tower of London, and end up in a riverside pub.' Maybe this was more his level.

'As a matter of fact,' Hugo's smile was swift and sudden, 'I've already made a booking. Le Pont de la Tour at nine-fifteen.'

Le Pont de la Tour, one of Terence Conran's lavish ventures, was expensive and so packed with media types from Canary Wharf it was hard to get a booking. 'If I'm going to gawp at the Tower of London I'd rather do it with a glass of champagne in my hand than from the top of a tourist bus.'

Miranda, so used to being in the driving seat she'd hardly paused to listen, actually blushed for the first time she could ever remember.

It was the first night since she'd been at her aunt's that Flo actually missed London. Ivy's supper had been gruesome in the extreme. Jugged hare with shot still left in the poor creature, so that Veronica chipped her tooth and loudly insisted that if her mother and father were too soft to sack Ivy, they should at least give her early retirement. 'Alf and she have a perfectly nice cottage over on Moreton Farm. They could go and live there instead.'

'But, Vee,' India-Jane pointed out sweetly, 'if you did get to be Lady of the Manor she'd be much nearer to you then, wouldn't she?'

Veronica sniffed. 'As a matter of fact, I don't think Adam Moreton's the marrying kind. He doesn't need to be, with women spreading their legs for him like . . .' Veronica paused, unable to find the appropriate simile.

'Bitches on heat?' offered Mattie innocently.

Mattie's parents gawped at her. Mattie never made jokes. Especially risqué ones.

'Exactly.'

'Really, Veronica,' Aunt Prue chided, 'I hardly think that's a fit subject for the dinner table, especially in front of your younger sisters.'

'Anyway,' Mattie jumped in, trying to defend her heroine, 'Flo wasn't spreading her legs as you so charmingly put it. Adam only took her to the hayloft to show her a baby barn owl.'

Vee turned to Flo like a kestrel eyeing a fieldmouse. This was obviously the first she'd heard of Flo's encounter with Adam. 'I didn't know you were a bird-lover, Flora,' she said acidly.

'Oh yes,' Flo replied. 'And he's a wonderful teacher. There's not much Adam Moreton doesn't know about the birds and the bees.'

'From what I hear,' Ivy had returned with the pudding, 'that Donna from the Angel's been giving him a few lessons. Lemon meringue pie.' She banged it down so hard in front of Veronica that it jumped off the plate. 'Just the thing for sourpusses.'

'Father,' Vee demanded, 'you're not going to let Ivy speak to me like that, are you?'

But Uncle Francis had disappeared behind a thick grey cloud of worry that only someone as insensitive as Vee would have tried to penetrate.

The next day when Flo tried to reach Hugo again she had more luck. She found him in a converted outhouse, sitting in front of a computer screen, his dark hair flopping over one eye so that Flo was surprised he could see out from under it.

'Hello there,' he said, not removing his gaze from the screen. 'Looking for Adam?'

Flo didn't know what irritated her more. The fact that everyone seemed to think she and Adam were joined at the hip (as well as somewhere else more intimate), or that Pamela had omitted to mention that it was Hugo she'd been trying to find.

'Actually, it's you I'm looking for.'

'Ah.' He looked at her for the first time, trying not to remember the image from the paper. She certainly looked different now, but not entirely unrecognizable. It was as if Pamela Anderson were auditioning to be Maria in *The Sound of Music*. It didn't quite convince, but it was a touching idea anyway. 'What can I do for you?'

Flo looked around her. Although the office they were in must once have been a barn, it was hard to imagine sheep lambing in it now. Blond wood and tasteful brickwork, plus air conditioning to keep out extremes of temperature, made it seem more like an expensive tourist agency. 'How much did it cost you to do all this?' she asked bluntly.

'Why do you want to know?'

'Mrs Williams from the Sheep Centre at Firmingham's just offered my uncle her flock, with a ram thrown in. He loves sheep much more than dairy, and anyway the dairy herd's not breaking even. I need a rough idea of what it'd cost to convert their outbuildings into a Visitor Centre.'

Hugo fought off the temptation to laugh. Francis Rawlings usually hated the public. He couldn't quite see him in the role of Old Farmer Giles.

Flo got there before him. 'It'd be Aunt Prue who dealt with the visitors,' she said quickly.

'Why don't you sit down? You're making me nervous standing there like a baby owl contemplating flight.'

Flo flushed slightly. Was this a dig at the other day with Adam?

'There's an adage I learned at business school . . .' he began.

'I didn't know you went to business school.' Flo hadn't meant to sound quite so surprised. 'I mean, I thought business school was for corporate high-flyers . . .'

'. . . and not hicks from the sticks? I did it as a post-grad course after Agricultural College. Do you want to hear the saying or not?'

'Certainly.' This wasn't going terribly well.

'Where the public are concerned you have to give them three things: something to see, something to eat and something to buy.'

'And something to steal.' Adam had materialized from one of the outhouses and slipped his arm possessively round Flo. 'Everyone loves a freebie, be it ashtray or bathrobe or even a box of matches from the Plough & Ferret.'

'Adam, we're talking about a Sheep Centre, not a Hilton hotel,' Hugo said testily.

'Anyway,' Flo went on. 'Say we did all that. Had a tea-room and a shop and lambing pens, plus perhaps some other attractions through the rest of the year. And loos. I suppose we'd need those. Have you any idea what it might cost?'

'Forty thousand or so? It's hard to say exactly without a proper business plan. Perhaps less if the family run it instead of hired labour.'

Flo's spirits drooped. There was no way her aunt and uncle would be able to afford that. She brightened momentarily. 'What about selling the milk quota?'

'Peanuts, I'm afraid,' Adam chipped in.

'You might get a few grants,' Hugo tried to cheer her, 'but you'd have to match them with your own money.'

'Would anyone lend to Uncle Francis do you think?'

Hugo shrugged, not wanting to disappoint her. 'I don't think so.'

'That's why it's all such tosh,' Adam cut in, 'the Government refusing to bail farmers out and telling them to diversify. What *with*?' Flo seemed so cast down that he squeezed her arm comfortingly. She looked pretty and vulnerable, Adam's two favourite qualities in a woman. 'Come on, I'll give you a lift back.'

Flo summoned up her strength. 'It's all right. I've got the Beetle. Aunt Prue will be waiting to hear. I'd better go and break the news.'

But it wasn't her aunt who stood outside Hunting Farm, lounging against the flint wall in ponyskin boots and a purple suit, waiting for her.

'Hello, Flora,' Miles smiled wolfishly. 'I bet you're surprised to see me.'

'Surprised isn't the word I'd choose.' Flo wondered what the hell he was doing here. 'Suspicious would be more appropriate. You aren't the type to drive a hundred miles unless you're hoping to get something out of it.'

'Terrible to hear such cynicism in one so young. Actually, I've got a very interesting proposition to put to you. A very interesting proposition indeed.'

Flo glanced up at her bedroom window to find India-Jane sitting at Flo's window-seat, apparently engrossed in cross-stitch, but actually earwigging every word.

'India. Do you mind going and doing that in someone else's room?'

'Why?' the child demanded crossly. 'This is the best bedroom and you don't even pay any rent.'

Flo would happily have throttled India with her own embroidery thread.

'Out of the mouths of babes,' commented Miles smugly.

'What crap,' Flo replied, nettled. 'I've offered my aunt money more often than a Tory minister does a hooker.'

'Don't be so sensitive,' soothed Miles, with all the reassuring sibilance of the serpent in the Garden of Eden. 'If you accept my proposition you could buy them the house. Well, put up the deposit anyway.'

Normally she would have told him to get lost, but this wasn't a normal day. 'You and I had better go for a drive.' She glanced up at the window. India, she suspected, was still there but in hiding.

They drove to another village pub, four miles away. She avoided the Angel with Donna lurking in the gloom, no doubt with a split-crotch thong under her DKNY jeans to lure the unwary. At the White Horse Flo noted with relief that not a single face was familiar.

'So, what's this famous proposition then?'

'It's Blackmills. They tried to recruit someone else to front their new ad campaign, but they can't find the right face. Even the ones that look like you are wrong, apparently.'

'But Miles, wake up and smell the coffee. Even *I* don't look like me any more. The girl in the paper had long blonde hair.' She pointed to her dark elfin cut.

'No problem. You could wear a blonde wig. I'd hire a stylist. The It girl formerly known as Flora Parker would be back in no time.'

'Except for one reason.'

Miles took a large swig of claret. 'And what's that?'

'I'm not doing it. I came here to get away from all that stuff. I never meant to flash my boobs at the camera in the first place and I'm certainly not doing it again. Deliberately. For money.'

Miles smiled foxily. 'You don't know how much they're offering yet.'

'How much?'

'If you're prepared to be the face, or rather the tits, of Blackmills Whiskey for the duration of their campaign, fifty thousand quid.'

Flo gasped and began to feel faint. It would more than cover the sum her aunt and uncle needed to start the Sheep Centre.

Chapter 8

As she trudged up the front path towards Hunting Farm she wished she'd never asked Miles about the money. Part of her mind was saying *Why not? You've done plenty of cheap, stupid things before. This is one cheap stupid thing that could have some benefit.*

But that was before she'd come to Maiden Moreton. In the time she'd been here, she'd begun to feel like a different person. Cutting her hair had just been part of it. For the first time in her life she felt accepted. By Aunt Prue. By Mattie. Even by Uncle Kingsley. They'd stopped thinking of her, at least she hoped they had, as a silly party-goer with about as much depth as a weather girl. She was becoming one of them. This advertising campaign, and the publicity it generated, would rebuild the wall between her and normal people. She'd stop being helpful, ordinary Flo and be dizzy drunk Flo who couldn't keep her top on again.

It was early evening and Aunt Prue was shelling peas on the veranda. Mattie was beside her, her nose in a book, while India-Jane sat on the grass making daisy chains. If you didn't know about the crippling financial problems the farm was burdened with, it looked like an idyllic family scene.

'Hello, Flora darling,' Aunt Prue said in the kind of tightly controlled voice that told Flo her aunt had been thinking of their money worries all day. 'What did Hugo have to say?'

Flo glanced round in case Uncle Francis was lurking nearby. She knew Aunt Prue didn't want to build his hopes up if they couldn't get the money to do it.

'Don't worry,' reassured Prue, 'I decided to come clean with him. And the thing is,' Prue glowed with excitement, 'he's incredibly keen. He thinks it might be the answer to a lot of our problems. He'd just heard that dairy prices are down again and spent the afternoon in the pub.'

Flo touched her aunt's arm. So Prue did know about her husband's drinking. 'It was because he was going to have to shoot the calves this afternoon,' Prue added, defending her husband. 'He hates doing that so much.'

Flo was appalled. 'Why would you shoot calves?'

'The male ones have no value now that beef's fallen through the floor. Abattoir costs are so high we actually *lose* money if we send them there. So farmers have to shoot the calves themselves, sometimes after they've been up all night helping at their births. It feels like murdering babies, I know. I can't tell you how much Francis hates doing it, and now perhaps he won't have to.'

Uncle Francis appeared with a tray and glasses. He was actually happy for the first time since Flo had arrived, his usually furrowed face had smoothed out into something approaching a smile. There was even a hint of boyish enthusiasm about him which stunned Flo. She could see, for the first time, why Aunt Prue might once have fallen for him.

'I'm sorry I've been so bad-tempered and curmudgeonly since you've arrived,' her uncle apologized. 'It was unforgivable. It'd be self-pitying of me to say it was just the worry, but the worry has been quite something. This farm's belonged to my family for generations and it looked as if I was going to be the one to lose it.' He put down the tray and began opening a bottle. 'This scheme of yours might just tide us over. We aren't asking to be rich, after all, just to stay on the land.' He handed her a glass. 'Here, have some of Kingsley's elderflower champagne. It's not often we feel like celebrating. Here's to Hunting Farm Sheep Centre.'

Flo wanted to run away. She couldn't bear to tell them that Hugo had said they'd need forty thousand pounds to go ahead and that they had no way of raising it.

She didn't need to. The hideous India-Jane had already noticed her hesitation. 'What's the matter, cousin Flo? Did Hugo pour cold water on the idea? I think it's stupid, anyway. I wouldn't want to go and look at a load of stinky smelly sheep, and I'm your target market.'

If anyone ought to have been shot at birth, Flo wanted to shout, it wasn't the calves but India-Jane.

'As a matter of fact,' Flo said quietly, 'he thought the idea was an excellent one. It's just that he reckoned it would cost a bit to make a go of it. You see, to really make it work it'd need a tea-room and a shop, and loos for the visitors because of the health regulations.'

She felt Mattie's anxious gaze scorching into her and wished she'd never suggested the idea at all.

'How much does Hugo think we'd need?' Prue asked.

Flo hesitated, knowing she was about to throw a blanket over her aunt and uncle's new-found excitement. 'About forty thousand pounds, I'm afraid.'

Aunt Prue visibly drooped. 'Oh, Francis, where would we get that kind of money?'

Uncle Francis froze, his glass halfway to his lips, like a deer trapped in the headlights of his wife's disappointment. 'We couldn't. We already owe twenty to the bank. They won't lend us any more.' He put his glass back on the tray and straightened his shoulders. The visible effort at self-control touched Flo to the core. 'I think I'll go and deal with the calves now. No point in putting it off just because it's unpleasant.'

He turned away, gently brushing off Aunt Prue's hand as she tried to comfort him. 'Supper's in half an hour,' she reminded him gently. 'Lancashire hot pot, your favourite.'

Uncle Francis answered her with a tight smile and went back into the house, just as Veronica, who'd been washing her hair in the shower till it squeaked for mercy, emerged. 'What on earth's the matter with Dad?' she asked worriedly. 'He looks like he's been invited to his own funeral.'

After the meal was over and they'd cleared it up, Uncle Francis disappeared outside again. 'I won't be long,' he announced, avoiding their anxious gaze. Flo and her aunt both heard the sound of a car door banging followed by an engine starting up.

'Oh God,' Prue muttered, 'he's not going to the calving shed. He's going to the Angel.'

'Will he be all right?' Flo asked, knowing the answer already.

'I very much doubt it. Unless they refuse to serve him, which isn't likely, is it? Poor Francis, he's obsessed with being the one who loses the farm. I'm sorry, Flo, we jumped on your suggestion far too quickly. It's our own fault.' Flo reached out her hand and squeezed her aunt's. 'We had such high hopes when we started out,' Prue said quietly. 'We love the way of life. It's not just about money. If you farm well you feel you're putting something back, that you're a custodian, not an owner. Oh, Flora, there's nothing for it. We'll have to sell up no matter how hard it is on Francis. There really isn't any alternative.'

Behind them they heard a sudden sniff from Mattie as she dashed out of the room and tore up the stairs. They both knew where she was heading. 'Poor child. You've been so good for her, you know. She's changed since you've been here.'

'So have I,' Flo smiled.

It was two hours before they heard the sound of the car returning. Flo and Prue sat, ramrod stiff, waiting and listening. But Francis didn't come back in.

Moments later, just as Flo was about to offer to go and search, a series of bangs echoed from the barns on the other side of the farmyard. Her aunt clutched Flo's hand, frozen with horror. Vee's comment earlier about

Uncle Francis being invited to his own funeral sliced into her mind.

'I'll go.' Flo jumped up and ran out of the dining room and across the yard.

The scene in the dairy complex was horrific. Five or six golden brown calves lay slaughtered on the floor, another kicked piteously. Blood drenched the antiseptic whiteness of the walls.

Uncle Francis's shotgun was propped up inside the handle of a garden spade, with another supporting it, a length of baler twine attached to the trigger. The safety catch was off and it faced directly at his forehead.

Both his eyes were closed.

Chapter 9

Flo kicked the garden spade as hard as she could, so that the whole contraption collapsed, but not before one bullet ricocheted out, hitting the wall behind them. Flo felt the air cool as it passed and almost threw up.

'Daddy!' shrieked a high-pitched voice behind them. Mattie flung her tiny body against her father's and clung on to him as if he were the child and she the grown-up who could protect him.

'I'm sorry, darling,' Francis sobbed at last. 'I just felt I couldn't go on any longer. It was very wrong of me.'

Flo watched the pair of them clinging to the wreckage of their life at Hunting Farm, and made up her mind. She would get them the money to start the Sheep Centre.

After all, what would it really cost her? And it would give the Rawlingses a last chance for the happiness she so desperately wanted them to find again; but whether for their sake or for her own, she wouldn't have liked to answer.

'Do we have to tell Prue?' Francis asked eventually, his eyes still haggard in his pale face.

'Yes,' Flo said gently, putting a hand on his arm to guide him back towards the farmhouse. 'She would hate us for hiding it from her. She loves you, Uncle Francis, and Aunt Prue's the kind of wife who really wants to share your burdens.'

'But it's my job to protect her from worries about money. She expected a secure life when she married me.'

'Aunt Prue isn't some fragile bloom who needs sheltering from reality. She's stronger than you think. Her worst fear isn't losing the farm, it's feeling isolated from you. She told me the other day that she wished you'd tell her more of your worries.'

'Flo's right, Dad.' The brave tone in Mattie's voice wrenched at Flo's heart. Mattie was having to face things she shouldn't even know about at twelve.

'My poor little Mattie,' mumbled Francis, almost as if he were noticing his daughter for the first time. 'You've been so unhappy you hide away all the time.'

'I won't any more. If you'll promise not to do that again.' She took his hand. 'We all love you, you know.'

Francis choked at the undeserved tenderness in Mattie's tone. 'But I've failed you all.'

'It isn't your fault, Uncle Francis,' Flo said gently. 'You've really tried. Your whole family knows that.'

Prue was waiting in the kitchen, her face rigid and blank with worry. One glance at her husband's face told her everything. 'Francis! You look like a ghost! What on earth's happened?'

'Oh my God, Prue, I've been so bloody stupid.' Her uncle's almost naval bearing crumpled before their eyes. 'I was out there with the shotgun, and it all seemed so pointless going on . . .' He trailed off and sat down heavily on one of the oak kitchen chairs. 'Fortunately Flora came out and . . .'

'. . . Stopped you doing something very foolish indeed,' her aunt supplied, shooting a grateful glance at Flo.

It was as if this jolt to their life had uncoiled all Aunt Prue's battened down unhappiness and despair. 'We need you, Francis. The only mistake you've made is to think you could get through this on your own.'

'But I've let you all down. As a husband. As a father. Even as a bloody farmer!'

'It wasn't your fault dairy prices plummeted. Or beef cattle got BSE. You're a good man and you've done your best. No wife could ask for more than that. Now promise me that whatever we do, however we try and get out of this hole, we'll do it together.'

'You know, Prue,' Francis reached out his arms and Aunt Prue ran into them, 'I don't deserve your loyalty. I've been a selfish sod of a husband. But you've no idea how comforting that sounds.'

Mattie and Flo exchanged glances weighed down with relief and crept upstairs. 'Not going back to the airing cupboard?' Flo whispered to her small companion.

'Not now I've promised Dad. Not now you're back.' And then a look of fresh anxiety darted across the small pale features. 'You're not going again, are you?'

'Try and make me. Though I may have to disappear up to London at some point to sort something out.'

'As long as you promise to come back. Do you think Dad will be all right now?'

Flo hugged her. The tiny birdlike frame felt so fragile, as if it might snap under the slightest pressure. 'You know what, Mattie, there's something really funny about life, but sometimes when it looks really awful that's the moment it starts to get better. That's what tonight was all about. Before today your mum and dad were feeling a long way from each other. Now they're back together.'

'I just wish,' Mattie produced the lopsided, old-before-her-years look Flo had come to recognize, 'he didn't have to nearly shoot himself to do it.'

Flo laughed and hugged her even harder. 'You're a wonderful kid, do you know that?'

'Goodnight Flo.' Mattie released herself from Flo's arms.

'Sure you're okay? You can sleep in with me if you like.'

'No thanks. You snore.'

'Excuse *me* . . .' Flo protested.

'I'll tape you one day,' Mattie threatened, laughing. '. . . Er, Flo?'

'What now? Don't tell me. I grind my teeth and fart as well?'

'I was just going to say . . . things are much better since you came.'

Flo waved and headed for her own bedroom, biting back the emotion that threatened to swamp her. By some miracle, she'd started to feel part of the Rawlings family. She was useful here, they actually needed and wanted her. 'By the way,' she added, hoping this was the right thing to say, 'maybe we shouldn't mention tonight to Veronica or India-Jane.'

'No,' Mattie winked, 'I think you're probably right. Not unless we want the entire county to hear.'

'Hello, Miles.' Flo tried to keep her voice light and friendly. She didn't want Miles prying into the real reason for her change of heart. 'Are you tied up all day?' The words came out before she realized their double entendre. 'Only I thought I might hop up to London and take you out to lunch otherwise.'

'I see,' Miles drawled, his voice dripping with sarcasm. 'You might hop up, drive for two and a half hours, deserting all those skylarks and Morris dancers you love so much, battle through London traffic and risk getting clamped, just for the pleasure of seeing me? I call that rather touching. Perhaps now that I've rekindled your interest, I should demand we spend the day in bed together and take up where we left off.'

'Sorry, Miles, this is about work, not pleasure.'

'It is possible to combine the two, you know. I've made a living out of it.'

'The thing is, if the deal is right, I've decided to go for Blackmills.'

Miles sat up and stopped twirling the two little silver balls of his executive toy. 'I thought a few weeks thinking about it would change your mind. Fifty grand is too tempting even for a convert to the simple life.' His tone infuriated her. It overflowed with pleasure at this evidence that Flo was as bribable as he was.

'Let's just say I've had a change of heart. Julie's Restaurant at one? There's a little room at the side where we won't be overheard.'

'I'll live for the moment.'

It struck Flo that she hadn't really thought about her appearance for weeks. Instead of the painstaking ritual of hairwashing, conditioning, exfoliation, toenail painting (even if it was electric blue), eyelining and general maintenance that had been her daily routine in London, she now just wore lipbalm and hoped for the best. Admittedly, in her old life she had left her mascara on for days thus acquiring a Bardotesque smoulder others could only aim for, but even her slutty look had required a certain effort. Her current appearance required none at all.

Flo trawled under the bed for the pair of cargo pants she'd acquired in Etam summer sale, a khaki cardigan which looked as if it were made for Mattie and a red and white spotted bargee scarf which she tied round her neck. Her mud-splattered trainers gave the finishing touch to her Cowshed Chic. Maybe someone from Storm would spot her and she'd start a trend.

Mattie watched Flo anxiously as she wolfed her breakfast. 'You will be back later, won't you?'

'Absolutely.'

'No need to rush,' Veronica cooed. 'You won't miss anything, seeing as nothing ever happens here anyway.'

It was a fabulous day and Flo found, as she raced along the narrow road from Maiden Moreton with the roof of the Beetle down, that she really begrudged going back to London. She glanced briefly in her driving mirror to see how she looked, forgetting that since she was still in the country it was possible that a farm vehicle might appear from the opposite direction.

Which is precisely what happened. Flo bowled round the final corner before the turn-off to the main road, REM blaring on the radio, and found herself yards from an oncoming tractor.

She swerved to the right, cursing, and just made it off the road and into the entrance to a field, avoiding the tractor by inches.

'What the bloody hell do you think you're doing!' shouted the driver, whipping off his earphones and striding towards her. Thank you, God, it would have to be Hugo. 'You could have killed us both,' he thundered.

'I'm really sorry. I should have been concentrating. I'm afraid my mind was on a meeting I'm going to in London.' For a mad moment she was tempted to confide in him about last night. She had a feeling he'd sympathize.

'What's the interview for,' he asked, surveying the four or so inches of tanned stomach visible between Flo's cardi and her cargo pants, 'table dancing?'

Flo's temper soared. To think, moments ago she'd had him down as sympathetic. Who the hell did he think he was?

'Look, I know you think I'm one rung up from a hooker, but actually it's about something quite important. And I'll never make it unless you kindly get that tractor out of the road.'

With exceptionally bad grace Hugo stomped back to the vehicle and reversed it ostentatiously and, in Flo's view, at considerable risk to anyone who might be behind him, ten yards up the lane to a passing place.

Then he leaned out of the cab and doffed his hat. 'Just call me Mellors, my lady. At your service any time.'

'If I were Lady Chatterley,' Flo shouted back as haughtily as was possible when you were bellowing, 'I'd find myself a new gamekeeper. The present candidate is rather lacking in the necessary equipment.' And then the devil came and perched on her shoulder and, unforgivably, she added, 'Unlike his brother,' and sped off, leaving Hugo seething on the sidelines, wondering what it was that came over him every time he was in the presence of Flora Parker.

The traffic heading in to west London was surprisingly thin and Flo, once she'd put her encounter with Hugo out of her mind, had a pleasant journey. She even found a parking space outside Julie's.

Most people opted to eat in the busy brasserie and so the restaurant on the first floor was virtually deserted apart from one other couple, who seemed so wrapped up in each other Flo wondered if they would climb under the table and get down to it. Probably Hugo thought she'd be doing the same thing only with a great dane, given his estimation of her morals.

'What a nice surprise,' drawled a familiar voice and she swivelled her eyes away from the almost-copulating couple. Miles, wearing a subtle bright red suit with matching tie and his trademark ponyskin boots, followed the direction of her stare. 'Something you're not getting enough of in the country?' he asked sweetly. 'That's easily remedied.'

'Tell me,' she asked wearily, actually eager for enlightment, 'what is it about me that even when I shave my hair off and go round in a sack, men still want to get me on to my back? Is it an odour I give off? Because if so maybe I should be marketing it to people who actually want it. Unlike me.'

'Flora, Flora, don't be so pompous. Nine tenths of the women in England would like to have your problem. Call it sex appeal or animal attractiveness, but when men look at you – even nice, intelligent wimpy men that are, thank God, nothing like me – they go "Phooaarrrr!"'

Miles caught the waitress's eye and ordered champagne. 'Why else do you think Blackmills are offering you all this fucking money? Because you look like Mary Poppins? It's a cross you'll just have to bear.'

Flo sipped her champagne. He was right. She was being pompous. 'I suppose I'll just have to live with being a universal lust object then. I guess there are worse things.' She surveyed him through narrowed eyes. 'You're being very charming. Why? I thought you wanted to kill me.'

'I do. But I'm almost as keen on money as I am on sex, so for once our interests converge. Besides,' he smiled silkily, 'I can always kill you later.' He picked up his glass of champagne. 'So, last time we met you seemed pretty adamant you didn't want to be the face of Blackmills. What changed your mind?'

'I need the money.' This was an argument Miles would sympathize with. 'In fact, I need it now.'

Miles's eyebrow rose fractionally. 'Why is that? Not buying a house in the outback? Bit of a waste of time if you're in the running for Lady of the Manor. Anyway, cloud cuckoo land, darling. They might give you half when you sign the contract, but first we'll have to go and win them over. After all,' he sipped his drink, his eyes ranging over her body, 'maybe they will have gone off the idea. Found someone who actually likes the idea of half the nation wanting to screw her. Tell you what, why don't I give them a call now?'

'Doesn't that sound a bit too keen?'

'If we hang about, they may find some other unique icon of our times.' Miles got out his mobile and hit the buttons. Five minutes later the first meeting was fixed.

'Tomorrow afternoon. It just looks as if you might have to stay over. Why not make it at my place and we can run through a few ideas.'

'And I can just imagine what those will be. Miranda's arranged a sublet for my flat but I can always stay with her. What time do they want us?'

'Three-thirty at their ad agency. They stressed this was just a preliminary meeting to see how we all get on.'

'And what do you think they'll make of my slightly altered image? They're thinking *Baywatch* babe and I look like Demi Moore in *GI Jane*.'

'Now you do, but by tomorrow afternoon the old Flo will be back from the grave.'

After lunch Miles took them to an extraordinary shop called The Phoenix in deepest North Kensington. It was a discreet little place full of row after row of spangled Eartha Kitt frocks and bras with falsies. An enormous sheeny Ethiopian with a voice several ranges below Paul Robeson's let them in. Flo tried not to be disconcerted by the blue satin basque and lacy suspenders he was wearing, or by his obvious familiarity with Miles. 'Come in, man,' he beckoned, 'have you finally seen the light? I can just see you in this scarlet silk sheath dress.'

'Sorry, Deirdre,' Miles drawled, overlooking the loudness of the suit he was actually wearing, 'but I hate bright colours.' He pushed Flo into the middle of the shop. 'I'd like a blonde wig for my friend here. None of your flash trash now, it's got to look convincing.'

Deirdre disappeared into the backroom, leaving Flo to wonder at the rows of size-thirteen stilettoes and XXXXL sparkling thongs. She didn't even want to think about what the riding crops and jewel-encrusted hammers were for.

A few minutes later Deirdre came back with three wigs. One made Flo look like Dolly Parton on a bad hair day, another bore a startling resemblance to Dusty Springfield, but the third was perfect. It was quite strange to be transformed from novice nun to redlight resident in a matter of seconds. 'Fabulous,' congratulated Miles, seeing the old Flo miraculously restored, 'Deirdre, you're delicious.'

'You can come and eat me up any time.'

'Thank you so much,' Miles handed over his credit card, 'but I'm afraid I'm sickeningly straight.'

'You don't know what you're missing,' Deirdre chided. 'Everyone looks the same in the dark.'

'But they don't feel the same.' He ran a hand over Flo's rounded bottom. Flo glared. 'Somehow I don't feel the same temptation to sink my teeth into male flesh.'

'What about clothes?' Miles enquired on the

pavement outside The Phoenix. 'You're not intending coming like that, I hope.'

'Miranda will lend me something. We're the same size.'

The thought of Mattie's anxious little face invaded her mind and she almost decided to drive back now, but it would be great to see Miranda, and she'd be going back tomorrow. She decided to give Mattie a quick call instead.

Mattie had just arrived home from school.

'I just wanted to let you know I'm staying the night in town, but I'll be back tomorrow evening.'

'Promise?' Mattie tried not to let the depth of her anxiety show. 'I keep thinking, once you get back to the fleshpots of London you won't come home to us.'

Flo glanced at Miles. Fleshpot was such a perfect name for him that it made her giggle. 'Don't worry. I can resist. Promise.'

'What was that all about?' Miles's eyes had taken on a nasty narrowed gleam. 'How come you're the one woman on this planet who takes the piss out of me?'

'Now Miles,' Flo tried to lighten the atmosphere, 'I'm sure I must have *some* competition.'

'As a matter of fact,' Miles corrected her, 'you were the first woman to have ever turned me down.'

'I doubt that. Are you sure you didn't just get the signals wrong with the others?'

Miles took her wrist and bent it backwards as he stared stonily into her eyes. 'Believe me, I never get the signals wrong. That's how I know, even though you don't, that you enjoyed going to bed with me.'

'Miles,' Flo insisted coldly, 'I don't even *remember* going to bed with you. Now please let go of my wrist or I might have to scream. Being arrested might not impress Blackmills at this stage of the negotiations.'

The crazy thing, it struck Flo, as she pulled her arm away, was that Blackmills might actually like it. Notoriety was a desirable commodity in the mixed-up world they both inhabited. That was one reason why she'd wanted to get out.

'Flora!' shrieked Miranda when Flo arrived on her doorstep, 'I knew you'd finally get fed up with playing Marie Antoinette in Maiden Wotsit. Welcome back to Real Life!'

'Actually,' Flo unwrapped herself from Miranda's bony embrace, 'I'm just here for a night. I've got a meeting Miles has arranged.'

'How intriguing.' Miranda removed a pile of glossy mags from the sofa so that Flo had room to sit down. Nail varnish, cotton wool buds and a curious lilac gadget made of foam surrounded her. Flo didn't ask what it was, in case it came from the Ann Summers catalogue.

'I thought you wanted a barge pole between you and Miles on all occasions?' Miranda demanded. 'The words "How dare you bring him here, you bloody insensitive cow," seem to spring to mind. So what's changed?'

'Blackmills want me as their "face" for their advertising campaign, and as it happens I need the money. Miles set it all up.'

Miranda's dark eyebrow raised a fraction. 'I thought

the born-again Flora wanted to put all that behind
her?'

'Was I that pompous about it?'

'Just a tad. You did remind me just a teeny bit of the
old slapper who walks up the aisle and becomes a pillar
of disapproving morality before you can say "wedding
ring".'

Flo giggled. 'Sorry. I must watch out for that. Actually,
the truth is my aunt and uncle have some money problems. They want to get out of dairy farming and start a
Sheep Centre but they can't get hold of any cash and I
can, courtesy of Blackmills. At least I hope I can. They
may have changed their mind and signed up someone
deep and serious like Zoe Ball. Incidentally, can I borrow
something to wear?'

'My wardrobe is your wardrobe. Although I'm not
sure I have anything vintage Flora Parker. Snakeskin
leather dresses and vinyl boob-tubes aren't really my
scene. My style is more . . .' She paused, searching for
the word that would encapsulate her personal fashion
vision.

'Pink?' suggested Flo. 'I'm sure we'll find something.
Can I have a peek?'

'Help yourself. Just lay off my new Joseph jeans. They
may look cheap but that's because they were very, very
expensive.'

Miranda's bedroom was, like Miranda, totally over
the top. In her fuchsia boudoir clothes streamed from
the wardrobe on to the floor like a brightly coloured
river, and piles of discarded high heels laid traps for the
unwary.

By the side of her bed two Betty Boop mugs announced recent double occupancy. Flo refused to imagine who the other guest might be.

Eventually Flo found something halfway suitable – a black leather biker jacket and extremely tight miniskirt – so she and Miranda were able to retire to the sofa with a bottle.

'So,' Miranda demanded, 'how's the hunky farmer? Any nearer to putting a ring on your finger?'

'Miranda, get one thing straight. I'm not interested in becoming the Lady of the Manor. For a start there's an occupant already and she's pretty well dug in. Anyone who marries Adam or Hugo will have their mother Pamela to contend with. Anyway,' Flo confessed, grinning, 'I'm not sure it's marriage Adam's got in mind.'

'Has he been trying to drag you into the cornfield to have his wicked way?'

'Not the cornfield, no. But he did show me something interesting in the haybarn. And the thing is, he looked so sexy and golden all covered in dust and sweat that I almost fell for it. If Hugo hadn't appeared at the eleventh hour I'd be another notch on his tractor.'

Miranda's expression changed slightly at the mention of Hugo but Flo, still reeling from the memory of their recent encounter, didn't notice.

'I don't think tractors have notches,' Miranda pointed out. 'Anyway, isn't that a rather old-fashioned way of thinking about it? I'd have thought you were beyond that stage.'

'Things are different in the country. Everyone knows what you're doing, not to mention who you're screwing, before you've even had time to crawl apart. Besides,' Flo sat up primly, 'I haven't slept with *that* many people.'

'Only half the telephone directory,' corrected Miranda.

Flo choked on her wine. 'A-D maybe. And you've slept with the rest.'

The next few hours passed in a pleasant blur of wine and gossip. Miranda arranged a vast pile of cushions on the floor for Flo to sleep on. 'By the way,' her tone changed from slightly slurred to knife sharp, 'Adam or no Adam, you're sure you're not interested in the other one?'

'What, Uncle Kingsley?' Flo teased. 'He's a confirmed bachelor. Though he does have an eye for a pretty girl, I'm told.'

'You know who I mean. Hugo.'

'Oh, *Hugo*. No. Hugo disapproves of me. He thinks I'm flighty.'

'What can have given him that idea?'

'You, I expect.'

'Nothing to do with you appearing in your underwear on the front page of the *Post*?'

'As a matter of fact, I don't think he's even seen it. He's hardly a *Post* reader, is he?'

Miranda fiddled uncomfortably. 'No. *The Economist* is more his line. Did you know he advises City banks on agricultural investment?'

Flo snorted in a highly unladylike manner. 'That can't be very time consuming. The City wouldn't dream of investing in farms, and neither would anyone else. Farmers are closing down right, left and centre – family farms that have belonged to them for generations.' Briefly she considered confiding about Uncle Francis' suicide attempt, but it would seem like a betrayal. 'The Government's telling farmers to diversify. But what with? Diversification needs money. It's ludicrous that I can get more money in a week than Uncle Francis can make in a year, just by posing for some stupid drink campaign.'

'My, we are becoming a philosopher out in the sticks. The most you used to worry about was where your next free lunch was coming from. And as you know, there's no such thing as one of those. I expect there'll be a catch in your stupid drink campaign, don't worry.'

'Yes. They'll have found someone else. Oh God, I hope they haven't! I couldn't bear it if I had to let Uncle Francis down again.'

'You really care about this sheep thing, don't you?' Miranda asked curiously.

'Yes, I do.' She looked away suddenly; Miranda wouldn't understand the reason why.

'Better get some beauty sleep then,' her friend said more kindly. 'Or you'll scare off the nice men from marketing.'

Next morning Flo got up even before the alarm. She had a bit of resurrecting to do.

By the time Miranda appeared there was a long-legged, black leather-clad blonde siren sitting across the breakfast bar from her, who was unrecognizable from the Flo of the night before.

'Wow!' Miranda congratulated. 'You look amazing. Let's hope Donatella Versace meets Honor Blackman is what they're looking for.'

Flo sipped the black coffee which was all her jangling nerves would allow her. It was curious. Normally she would have found the whole thing either ludicrous or funny, but now there was something at stake she just felt sick with anxiety that for some reason it wouldn't work out.

She knew she mustn't let on. 'Screw you' was the style they'd responded to, not 'Please give me the job.'

Miles was waiting for her in the Cafe Italia across the road from Blackmills' advertising agency, looking his most overdressed.

'Very Oscar Wilde,' she commented, taking in Miles's fur coat over an eyecatching purple suit, 'but isn't it a bit hot for June?'

'I'm a cold-blooded bastard, as you have reason to know. This keeps me warm.' He returned the compliment after studying her appearance. 'Very Reeperbahn hooker. Shall we go?'

They were taken to a space-age lift which shot them to the top of the building, reinforcing Flo's feeling that she was in some elaborate charade.

A sleek secretary met them, dressed in head to foot greige, so similar to the colour of the carpet that if she'd lain down you could have walked all over her without noticing.

She led them to a small boardroom, dazzling with light, where the welcoming smell of fresh coffee greeted them. They were obviously the first to come.

'Negotiation tactics,' Miles murmured. 'They're showing us who calls the shots.'

A few moments later four people filed in and sat

down at the table opposite them. 'Let me introduce us all,' offered a keen young man in a sharp suit. 'I'm Jack, the Account Director from the agency and this is my creative colleague, Buzz Henderson.' The woman smiled a rather restrained smile. 'And this is Peter Harrison, Blackmills' Marketing Director, and Tony Williams, his deputy. Right. Coffee everyone? Carolyn.' He turned to the greige secretary. 'Could you, do you think?'

The secretary and Buzz exchanged glances. Flo studied Buzz. She was older than the men, late thirties probably, in a brown linen trouser suit with an expensive sheen to it which managed to look stylish without shrieking designer label. Her hair was blonde and short, tucked behind her ears with a long fringe she flicked back from time to time. In the lapel of her suit a brooch made of tin foil and paperclips winked in the sunlight.

'Did your daughter make you that?' Flo asked as she accepted her second black coffee of the morning.

Buzz looked stunned. 'How did you know? Everyone thinks it's by some expensive jewellery genius, not Year Five's Craft lesson.'

'My cousin Mattie made me one like it, then charged me a fiver.'

Buzz laughed. 'Mercenary little buggers, aren't they?'

Flo realized that all eyes were on them and that she wasn't projecting the raunchy good-time girl image they were expecting. She slouched in her chair and reached for her sunglasses.

'Right.' The man from the agency took control. 'Maybe you'd like to kick the meeting off, as Blackmills' marketing supremo, Peter.'

'Certainly. We asked Flo to help with our product launch a few months back for a particular reason. Blackmills and whiskey generally have a rather stuffy image. A male image. Either gentleman's clubs or young bankers in Dallas. We wanted to be modern. Reckless. To show that you could drink Blackmills and still cock a snook. You did that brilliantly, Flora. That's why we wanted to capitalize on the splash you made in the papers. We couldn't have bought that publicity.'

It was on the tip of Flo's tongue to quip, 'So it's lager louts from Essex you're trying to attract to your product, is it?' Instead she buttoned her lip and tried to think of the Sheep Centre.

'That's why,' chipped in his deputy breathlessly, 'we wanted to talk about making you the Face of Blackmills and building a whole campaign around you.'

'We want appeal to women, not just men. Whiskey's always been the drink of the power elite, and now women have joined that power elite. We want them to prove it by drinking Blackmills.'

'So what kind of women are you trying to appeal to?' Flo's words slipped out despite a quelling look from Miles. He'd obviously rather she kept her mouth shut and looked decorative. 'Career types? Girls who like Rum 'n' Coke? I'd have thought they were different markets.'

Buzz sat up and leaned her elbows on the table. The others turned to her nervously. Obviously her view counted for something. 'Flora's put her finger on it,' Buzz agreed. 'I think we are confused. Are we trying to say that whiskey is chic and sophisticated or bold and brash?'

'Bold and brash, obviously,' chipped in the deputy

marketing director, eyeing Flo longingly. Clearly he had a weakness for cheap blondes in leather.

'Yet your research indicates, said Buzz, 'that it's the chic career girl end of the market who's prepared to try – and pay for – your product. The ones who want to be better than the boys and show it.'

'So what you're saying,' the marketing director repeated in a loud, nervous voice, 'is that Flo flashing her bra in the newspaper wasn't the right image for Blackmills anyway?'

'That's crazy,' Miles chipped in, looking furious. 'No one under forty had even heard of Blackmills before Flo publicized it. You got the best coverage you've ever had. You said it yourself.'

'It got a lot of publicity,' Buzz conceded doubtfully, 'but not with the right people.'

Silence bounced off the walls, stunning everyone but Buzz and Flo herself. It was typical that here was a company directing its advertising at women, and yet pandering to male fantasies.

Flo closed her eyes for a fraction of a second, fighting back the bitter taste of disappointment. It had all been crazy, too good to be true. How could she have thought she could scrape together enough to start the sheep centre so easily? Miranda had been right about the catch being in the small print. Suddenly she wanted to get away, back to Maiden Moreton, to Mattie and Aunt Prue, to the clear skies and the ringing air. She stood up, biting back the sense of failure that she couldn't, after all, be the saviour of Hunting Farm and her aunt and uncle's future.

'Thank you all for asking me here. I can see I'm not actually what you were looking for.' With a swift gesture of impatience she pulled off the itchy blonde wig, threw it down on the table and ran her fingers through her short brown hair. 'To be honest, it wasn't really me. This is what I'm like now.' As the assembled group gasped in horror, Flo treated her stunned audience to a wicked smile. 'Not what you're after at all.'

For a moment she thought Miles was going to pick up the wig and throw it at her. His eyes were dark with venom that once again she'd made a fool of him, and this time in public.

'Hang on a moment,' Buzz ordered, cutting through the shocked silence in excited, commanding tones. 'Do that again.'

'Do what?' Flo asked.

'Take the wig off, like that, in that sweeping gesture, and then grin.'

As confused as the rest of them, Flo did as she was told.

'Gentlemen.' This time it was Buzz who was grinning from ear to ear. 'I think we may have your campaign. And it'll appeal to both kinds of women *and* cock a snook at male society. Our Blackmills girl goes into some crappy male environment – packed pub, rugger club, the Reform, you name it – looking like a stripper someone's ordered by mistake. They all leer and cheer. She asks for a Blackmills, sweeps off the wig, and there she is, today's woman, chic, reckless and totally in charge of her life! Don't you see, it reverses expectations. Instead of the librarian who turns out to be a sexpot, it's the sexpot who turns out to be her own woman!'

The marketing director of Blackmills Whiskey uncrossed his arms and looked at his deputy. 'You know, Tony, it might just work.'

'*It might just work*,' echoed Buzz with all the scorn of today's woman faced with slow, incompetent yesterday's man. 'It'll be absolutely fucking brilliant!'

Chapter 10

'I suppose I ought to congratulate you on that little performance,' Miles said in a low voice as they were shown out at the end of the meeting. 'You're full of surprises, aren't you? But then I of all people ought to know that.'

'Yes,' Flo replied lightly. 'But it was as much of a shock to me as you that they went for it. I was just getting up to go.'

'The woman liked you,' Miles conceded grudgingly. 'The men will need more convincing.'

'Then I'm sure she'll convince them.'

Miles hailed a cab, and with a certain misgiving, Flo joined him. The one drawback to all this was that Miles was still involved in it.

Once they were inside the cab she felt Miles's body suddenly pinion hers against the sticky plastic of the seats. Without warning he plunged his hand inside her jacket and grabbed at her breasts. 'Come back with me now,' he said thickly, his florid face already flushed with heat and excitement. 'After all, you've been to bed with every other man in London. Why should I be the exception?'

Flo pushed him away so violently that the taximan glanced over his shoulder. 'Or maybe you prefer women?' Miles asked nastily. 'You seemed to think a lot of that castrating bitch up there.'

'Oh for Christ's sake, Miles. You're pathetic!' Flo pulled Miranda's coat round her, noticing a red weal on her neck where she'd pulled his hands off. 'Please stop here!' she commanded the cabdriver. She flung a fiver at Miles even though her share of the fare was nothing like that. 'I'm ringing Blackmills when I get home and asking them to deal with me in future or I'm not interested. I never want to see your fat face again!'

'We'll see about that,' yelled Miles. 'I got you this deal. I'm damned if you're cutting me out just like that.'

'Just watch me.'

'You need my contacts. It was me who got you the publicity in the first place.'

'I'm a big girl now. I think I'll manage.'

Miles watched her, eyes narrowed into angry slits in his overblown face. He wasn't letting her get away with this. She'd cheated him in bed and now she thought she could do the same in business. Well, she'd soon find what a mistake that was. He'd make sure of that.

'My God, Flo!' squealed Miranda, when Flo told her about Blackmills' proposal. 'A TV commercial! You'll be famous like what's-her-face who did Boddington's!'

'Well, if I get so famous people like you can't remember my name, I'd better really start worrying.'

'When are they going to shoot it?'

'As soon as possible. Three or four weeks' time.' Flo had been relieved to hear this as it meant she'd get her hands on the money when she needed it.

'Wow! Do you think they need a stylist? Someone to advise you on your image?'

'If they do, I expect they'll find one,' Flo said gently. 'But I'd rather it wasn't you – even though you're the most stylish person I know—' Miranda looked ludicrously disappointed. 'The thing is, Miles already wants to kill me because I've said I won't do it if he continues being involved. No more friends.'

'But he set it all up.'

'I know. And I'll make sure he gets his cut. I'm not trying to rob him, but the shit tried to jump me in the taxi. Look.' She pulled down her jumper, revealing the livid red scratch. 'And that was in broad daylight in a London cab. I was right to dump him. He's dangerous.'

'Of course he is. That's why all the little debby girls like him. He doesn't say please when he wants something. Especially if it's them.'

'Call me old fashioned but I prefer sex to be voluntary.'

'Oh, I don't know . . .'

'Careful, Miranda, I'll report you to the Committee for Political Correctness.'

She felt a sudden longing to get back to Hunting Farm, a long way from Miles. The Sheep Centre could go ahead. She couldn't wait to tell Aunt Prue, though she had to think carefully about how to do so tactfully. Uncle Francis was a proud man.

'You're going to be a busy girl. First this and then don't forget the Young Farmers' dance Thingummy.'

'I hope *Jennifer's Diary* knows about it.'

'Hugo's invited me to stay at the Manor afterwards.'

'Has he now? How cosy. You'd better start sucking up to Pamela then. She'll certainly prefer you to me. Since Snowy seduced her dachshund she thinks I'm on about the same level.'

When Flo arrived home Mattie was standing at the end of the drive with the disgraced Snowy. Home. The word had slipped so easily into her consciousness. Both of them hurled themselves at her as she climbed out of the Beetle. 'Flo! Flo! You've come back!'

'Of course I've come back, silly.' Flo held the little girl tightly, touched to the core about how much Mattie seemed to have missed her. 'London's horrible. Filthy and full of beggars and they all seem to have the same dog. Maybe they pass him round or perhaps he goes with the pitch.' She petted Snowy's soft white ears. 'And the dog's always asleep. Maybe it's stuffed.'

'Snowy's missed you too.'

'I doubt it. I bet she's been sleeping on your bed.'

Mattie smiled shyly. 'She kept crying and keeping everyone awake. And Adam said the best place for her was in bed. Like her mistress.'

'Did he indeed? What was Adam doing here?'

'He came round to see you.' She grinned impishly, her thin little face lighting up, all trace of the anxious child from the airing cupboard wiped away. 'Don't worry. Vee looked after him.'

'I'll bet she did. How long before he managed to escape?'

'Oh, *hours*. She cooked him dinner. Steak and kidney pudding.'

'But doesn't it take ages?'

'She's had one on the hob ever since you left. Just in case he dropped round. So she could impress him with her homely skills.'

'And was he impressed?'

'He couldn't move afterwards, if you call that impressed.'

Flo slipped her arm into Mattie's and together they walked through the sunny front garden towards the farmhouse. It was hot and fragrant and the bees were buzzing in and out of the Canterbury bells. Suddenly she couldn't wait to shrug off her city clothes and get into her old jeans. Then she'd look for her aunt and uncle to tell them the good news.

Veronica was in the hall, artfully arranging a jug of shop-bought carnations. They were a particularly hideous shade of blue. It seemed crazy to Flo that anyone could go out and buy carnations when the garden was bursting with roses, honeysuckle and cottage lilies which would have made the most glorious display. Tactfully she restrained herself from saying so.

'As a matter of fact,' cackled Ivy, peering out from the kitchen like a gnome in a pinny, following her line of thought, 'they're for you. From Mr Adam. He said they were original like you are and not to forget about the Young Farmers' Ball coming up. Isn't that right, Miss Veronica?'

Veronica almost spat when she finished arranging the carnations.

'Gosh, Flo,' Mattie giggled, ignoring her older sister's stony face, 'that's pretty lyrical coming from Adam. You must bring the poetry out in him.'

Veronica jammed in the last of the blooms and stomped up to her room.

'As long as it's just the poetry you bring out,' Ivy smirked.

Aunt Prue emerged behind her, with a basket full of bantam eggs. 'Hello, Flora love, I didn't know you were back. How was town?'

'Horrible. Hot and sticky and hellish compared to how totally glorious it is here. I can't understand how anyone lives in London.'

'I expect they feel the same about the country. Just like you did till five minutes ago. What's the matter with Veronica?'

'Jealous,' supplied Mattie instantly. 'Adam brought Flo some flowers.'

'But they're hideous,' shuddered Prue. 'For such a handsome young man he's got terrible taste.'

'Except in girls,' supplied Mattie loyally.

'I don't know about that.' India-Jane appeared, flute in hand. 'Donna the barmaid looks like trailer-trash and he's pretty keen on her according to Joan from the shoe shop.'

'What do you know about trailer-trash?' demanded Auntie Prue, stunned.

'I don't. It's what Joan said. I was looking at Winnie the Pooh slippers and I overheard her. She said if Adam ended up with that trailer-trash it would serve Uncle Kingsley right.'

'But it's Flo that Adam likes.' Mattie was puzzled by the possibility of such adult duplicity.

'Mr Adam just likes women,' Ivy threw in darkly. 'All shapes and sizes. But he don't usually buy 'em flowers.' She smirked again and added in a low voice: 'Mind you, that ain't generally what they come for. Even when he were fourteen years old, that maidservant Lucy used to tell me . . .'

'Thank you, Ivy.' Aunt Prue came to her senses before there were any further revelations about the youthful Adam's precocious sexuality. 'It's time the best silver came out for a polish.'

'Why's that? Not planning a wedding are you? Still three months till Michaelmas. A lot can happen in three months.'

'Aunt Prue,' Flo said quietly, making sure she was well out of Ivy's earshot. 'I've had rather an amazing stroke of luck. I've been hired to promote some whiskey and they're paying me a ludicrous amount of money and I really don't know what to do with it. So I wondered if you and Uncle Francis would let me invest it in your Sheep Centre?'

Prue's eyes crackled with sudden hope, then died down to their usual solemn grey. 'Flo, darling, we couldn't let you. The Sheep Centre will never make much of a profit. You'd find much better investments.'

'Not one that would save Rowley the Ram. And I couldn't bear to see those woolly Southdowns go like lambs to the slaughter, if you'll pardon the pun. And

Mattie's desperate for a lamb of her own, and as you said, she's so much better than she was and . . .'

'All right, Flora,' smiled her aunt, 'I get the message. You want to lend us the money and you're trying to find a way of persuading us that saves our dignity.'

Flo's shoulders sagged. 'A bit,' she admitted. 'But I also mean it about Rowley, and Mattie. Please, Aunt Prue. I couldn't bear to see you and Uncle Francis lose the farm. The happiest memories of my childhood were here. I've lost all the others. And recently I've glimpsed Hunting Farm as a happy house again.'

Her aunt smiled at Flo, her eyes alight with gratitude. 'It's all thanks to you, Flora. It's you who's opened the shutters again.' She suddenly felt wildly and furiously angry with her brother-in-law Martin, Flo's father, for disappearing and leaving this lovely girl alone, no matter how bad his own wounds had been. No wonder she'd led a rackety life, always wanting to be the centre of attention, looking for love in people's beds instead of their hearts. Martin had a lot to answer for.

Prue wondered where his high-powered escape had taken him now. It couldn't be that hard to find out if she were a little devious. 'All right,' she finally conceded. 'We'll let you invest in us, and we'll do our damnedest to make it work. On one condition. You leave it to me to persuade Francis.'

She disappeared, humming, with a new spring to her step, out into the farmyard.

Flo grabbed her keys and headed out the front door to the Beetle. 'Where are you going?' demanded India-Jane, grateful for another excuse to put down her flute.

'Into Witch Beauchamp. To buy some champagne. I think we may have something to celebrate tonight.'

As luck would have it, by the time Flo's tyres screeched into Witch Beauchamp Victoria Wine had just closed. 'Damn!' she swore. Then she remembered the pub. It would cost the earth but at least they might have a bottle there.

'Do you have any Lanson Black Label?' she asked the landlord, not noticing the stir that such an unusual request caused in the public bar of the Angel, where the more usual tipple was a pint of Old Red Hen.

He shook his head.

'Moët & Chandon?'

'Nope.'

'Any champagne at all?'

'We do have this,' said a familiar voice, followed swiftly by a black lacy vest top with a push-you-up bra underneath it, from which peered two dizzying globes. 'It be Krug. And I'm afraid it's vintage.'

Flora bristled. 'How much is it?'

'Sixty pounds.'

Flo tried not to gasp. It wasn't, after all, any more than you'd spend on a bottle of champagne in a crappy London nightclub. 'Fine. If that's all you've got, I suppose I'll have to take it.'

When Flo had gone, followed by the curious stares of everyone in the pub, the landlord's wife turned to Donna, whom she thought a lazy slut. 'Why didn't you offer her the Mumm? It's only twenty-two pounds.'

Donna smiled slowly. The Krug had been in the pub's cellar so long that with luck it would have lost its fizz and taste of very expensive vinegar. 'I wonder,' Donna put one hand on each hip and stuck out the precipice of her breasts still further, 'what she's prepared to spend sixty quid on celebrating?'

'Perhaps it's an engagement,' suggested the landlady nastily. 'That'd serve you right, wouldn't it?'

Donna turned away and silently, invisibly, pulled in the muscles deep down in her vagina. Other women might get their man by attacking their double chin and flabby waist, but Donna knew better. Your pelvic muscles were the key to a satisfied lover. And Donna's pelvic muscles were so toned they could pick up fluff like a Hoover.

The next day Flo rang Buzz at the advertising agency and told her to forget Miles, that she'd be representing herself in future.

'Great,' Buzz endorsed, 'Miles struck me as a sleaze-ball. I thought it was mad having him taking a cut, but you'd be amazed how the most stunning models come in here with some ten-cent Svengali called their "manager" and he's often the lover too. He wasn't yours, was he?'

'Absolutely not,' replied Flo, refusing to acknowledge her disastrous one-night stand.

'I suspect they feed on these girls' insecurity. The whole world thinks they're beautiful except for one creep and they fall for him. So much for Girlpower. Anyway, good for you, I'll tell our contracts people to deal with you direct.' She paused a moment. 'Is he going to be trouble?'

'Don't worry,' Flo hoped she sounded more optimistic than she felt, 'I'll handle him.'

'Good. We've already started setting up the shoot. We've found this great place that looks just like a gentleman's club, full of green baize and old fogeys who think women should be pregnant and in the kitchen, preferably with their mouths taped up. We're looking at about three to four weeks' time. Would you be up for that?'

The sooner Flo got her hands on the money, the better. 'Absolutely.' And she felt an instinctive trust for Buzz.

'I'll get a contract out to you. Have you done any acting, as a matter of fact, even at school?'

'Only acting up, I'm afraid. At school I was branded a bad girl and never considered worthy of the play.'

'You'll be fine,' Buzz reassured her. 'It's something you've either got or you haven't, and no amount of coaching really helps. I'd lay money that you've got it.'

'Because I'm a shameless, loudmouth extrovert who can't hold her drink or keep a relationship going more than five minutes?'

'It's a well-known industry saying,' Buzz endorsed. 'Shameless loudmouth extroverts who can't hold their drink make the best actors.'

Flo was about to put the phone down, but she felt at ease enough with Buzz to ask the next question. 'I know this sounds weird, but how soon do you think I'll get some money?'

'Why?' Buzz's voice became faintly wary. 'You don't have a drug habit, do you? Or a vast bill at The Priory?'

'As a matter of fact I don't do drugs, and despite appearances to the contrary I'm reasonably sane.' Flo laughed nervously. 'I'm not sure you'll believe the answer. I'm buying a flock of sheep.'

'Like Little Bo Peep?'

'They're for my uncle. He's starting a Sheep Centre and he hasn't got a lot of cash. The sheep are going to be slaughtered unless we can take them on.'

'I'll see what I can do. It's better than white powder or gambling boyfriends, I suppose.'

To Flo's eternal gratitude, Buzz was as good as her word. A contract arrived next day followed by a cheque for ten thousand pounds with a note from Buzz saying they didn't usually pay anything in advance but the thought of all those lamb chops had been on her conscience.

Flo had never seen Uncle Francis so happy. Over the next few weeks he'd sold on his milk quota and the dairy herd had gone, relieving him from the chore of twice-daily milking and the raft of hygiene regulations that had taken up all his waking hours. He, Harry and occasionally even Alf, on loan from Moreton House, were clearing out the milking parlour and erecting sheep pens instead.

India-Jane and Mattie were dragging bales of straw almost as big as they were from the trailer, Aunt Prue was stacking yellow bags of concentrates to feed the new arrivals, and Vee was sketching a rough outline of where the tea-room would go.

There was such happy chaos that no one noticed the arrival of Adam and Hugo on their tractor.

'What's going on?' Adam asked.

Flo left it for her uncle to reply; after all this was his venture, not hers. To her delight he laughed, a sound so unfamiliar that Harry and Alf stopped working in amazement. 'We're diversifying,' grinned Francis. 'Just like good farmers should according to the Government, when they can't squeeze a brass farthing out of conventional farming.'

'We're opening a Sheep Centre,' sang Mattie, 'and I'm going to help deliver baby lambs.'

'Bloody hell,' Adam swore. 'What brought all this on?'

There was a brief moment of tension. 'It was either a radical change of direction or topping myself,' Uncle Francis said, with a surreptitious wink at Flo. 'With a little help, I decided a change of direction might be preferable. And certainly less final.'

Fortunately, the truth behind his joke escaped most people. Adam was too stunned to pick up the nuances, Veronica too insensitive, and Aunt Prue was out of hearing stacking up the concentrates. But Hugo caught Mattie's brief wince of pain and her furtive glance at Flo. It wasn't the time, he decided, to ask where they'd got the money from.

'I sold the milk quota,' Francis told him, guessing Hugo's thoughts.

'Good for you,' congratulated Hugo, knowing it would be nothing like enough to cover the investment. 'So what's the idea here?'

Flo could feel Hugo's dark eyes glance in her direction, but when she looked up he was listening to her uncle with polite consideration. Thank heavens he had the sensitivity not to mention money.

'We've got great plans,' enthused Francis. 'Lambing pens here, handling shed over there, stables for Shetlands to give rides to school children, piggery for a few rare breeds, and then, eventually, a gift shop; oh, and a tea-room.' Uncle Francis turned to his admiring audience of Harry and Alf. 'You see, lads,' he propounded with the air of a seasoned expert, 'there's three things you need if you want to make a go of a visitor attraction: something to see, something to buy and something to eat.'

Harry and Alf nodded in agreement as if this was something they'd always suspected. This time Flo couldn't avoid Hugo's glance. He was smiling. Clearly Uncle Francis had omitted to remember that it was Hugo who had supplied this nugget of business acumen in the first place.

'So,' Adam bore down on her, shirt slashed to the waist, revealing even more of his golden tan than usual, 'you haven't forgotten the Young Farmers' bash you promised to come to?'

'It's etched on my heart. What do you wear to Young Farmers' bashes?'

'Wellies and leopardskin knickers would do,' Adam quipped.

'But a long dress or a cocktail frock is more usual,' Hugo advised.

'Have you phoned Flo's friend Miranda, Huge?' Adam hinted, hoping he'd go and do it now. 'You promised to take her, remember?'

'So I did.' He didn't mention, Flo noticed, that he'd already asked Miranda to stay. Maybe he thought Adam would suspect him of stealing a march in the married-by-Michaelmas stakes.

'When are the sheep due to arrive?' Adam asked.

'As soon as we can get a sheep transporter and drive over to Firmingham,' replied Francis. 'The top field's ready and we'll keep them there for the moment. We'll need to hire the transporter though.'

'Don't worry about that. I'll fetch them in ours,' Adam insisted. 'On one condition. That Flo comes and helps. When do you want to go?'

'Well . . .' Uncle Francis shrugged. 'We're ready now.'

'No time like the present then,' Adam grinned. 'I happen to have a free evening. Are you up for it, Flo?'

'No. Yes. I suppose so.' Flo wasn't quite sure exactly what Adam was asking if she was up for. Though she had a good idea. 'Yes. Of course. That's kind of you.'

'Kind isn't the word that immediately springs to mind,' murmured Hugo as he watched Adam and Flo head back to Moreton Farm to get the transporter.

It was a thirty-minute drive through winding lanes to Mrs Williams' place near Firmingham Beacon. She was surprised and grateful to see them. 'The new tenant's arriving next week. I was wondering when you'd want them.'

It took several journeys to get all the nervous sheep back to Hunting Farm. 'When you've finished I've got a surprise for you,' Mrs Williams smiled.

'Don't tell me,' Adam whispered loudly. 'A lifetime supply of mint sauce.'

It was just beginning to get dark when they returned to Mrs Williams' for the final time. The old lady led them to the huge tithe barn and flung open the gates. Inside was a freshly painted shepherd's hut on wheels. 'My father's shepherd lived in it all winter. It's got a wood burning stove and a bed and everything.' Adam and Flo surveyed the bare wooden interior. 'Mind you,' Mrs Williams conceded, 'people were tougher in those days.'

'Are you implying I'm a cissy who can only survive with central heating and fitted carpets?' demanded Adam, laughing. 'I could get by for a few nights in that,' his gaze settled on Flo, 'especially if I wasn't entirely alone.'

'Get on with you,' Mrs Williams flicked him with her ancient tweed hat, 'you wouldn't have been alone. You'd have had five hundred sheep to talk to. Now, do you want to tow it with the tractor or shall I harness up one of the horses?'

'Horses, please. I think we'll go back the pretty way,' Adam replied without hesitation. 'Across the tops and down Bredden Valley.'

'That's a long route,' Mrs Williams grinned as she harnessed Paddy, her ancient mare. 'Are you sure you won't get lost along the way?'

'Of course not. I grew up in these hills. Come on Paddy.' He clicked his tongue and the old horse obediently set off, pulling the shepherd's hut behind it.

'Thanks for everything, Mrs Williams,' shouted Flo.

'I'll get one of the farm hands to return the horse and pick up the transporter tomorrow,' Adam added, waving.

Mrs Williams stood waving until they were out of sight. For a second she imagined jogging along over the hills in the moonlight with someone as devastatingly handsome as Adam and felt quite flustered. Then she thought of the countless heroines of fiction, from Hardy's Tess to the irritating Hetty Sorrel in *Adam Bede*, who'd succumbed, with varying degrees of willingness, to the charms of handsome young men like Adam Moreton.

At least these days they ended up not with a hangman's gibbet like poor Tess, but a council flat. And a jolly good thing too.

In the far distance Mrs Williams could just hear the clip-clop of Paddy's hooves departing along the flinty lane.

Oh to be young and eager and able to convince yourself that passion was more important than common sense.

Chapter 11

It was an utterly glorious night. Even at almost ten o'clock, it was dusk rather than darkness that enveloped them in its velvety veil as they trotted along.

'It feels amazingly timeless,' breathed Flo. They'd been travelling for over an hour and had not seen a single other person. 'Almost as if we could be here in this little hut, on this hill, at any moment in history.'

Gently Adam pulled back the reins and Paddy came to a halt on the brow of the hill. Beneath them the valley was spread out, with only the occasional wink of a light to remind them that they weren't the only people on the planet. Adam turned to face her. 'Perhaps we'd better make the most of it then.'

'Make the most of what?' Flo asked, though she knew the answer.

'Of this. Of now. Of being alive.' Above them a sliver of moon appeared from behind a cloud and shone down on them. Slowly, with the moonlight buffing his ludicrously handsome features to silvered perfection, Adam began to undo the buttons of her shirt.

Flo gazed into his eyes, all her city girl certainty deserting her. Was he finally, after so many disasters, the man for her?

Adam reached up a hand and smoothed away the lines of uncertainty on her brow. '"Had we but world enough, and time,"' he murmured into her neck, '"This coyness lady were no crime . . ."'

'Marvell,' Flo murmured back, astonished, remembering her abandoned A-levels. 'I didn't know you liked poetry.'

Adam undid the last of her buttons. A ghost of a smile whispered on his lips. 'Perhaps I have hidden depths. Or heights.' He took her hand and placed it on the tentpole that appeared to be holding up his trousers. Together they fell backwards, their breath panting, oblivious of anything except the primeval urge, call it lust or hope, that had got so many of their predecessors into so much trouble, perhaps on this very hillside.

Afterwards, Flo looked into Adam's eyes, and he ran a hand through her ruffled dark hair. 'Well, Miss Flora Parker,' he said suddenly, twisting his body round until it was he who looked down at her, 'I know this may sound sudden, but I wonder if you would do me the honour of becoming my wife?'

Flo laughed, until she caught the wounded expression in his glorious pale green eyes. 'You're serious aren't you?'

'Of course I'm bloody serious.' His tone was all wounded baby bird.

Flo stroked his ruffled feathers. 'Look, Adam, you're sure this isn't about the bet?'

The wounded look came back again. 'Is that what you think? That I'm trying to bag you before my brother finds someone and gets the manor?'

'Sibling rivalry runs deep. And you love Moreton House.'

'And the fact that you're sassy and sexy and kind and clever wouldn't be enough on its own?'

Underneath her devil-may-care exterior, Flo realized she was as insecure as ever, never knowing if she was loved for herself. 'I suppose it might,' she said dubiously.

'Good. Because that's why I'm asking you, not because of any stupid bet.'

'I'd be a hopeless farmer's wife. I can't even cook, let alone bake or pickle.'

'Pickling isn't part of the job description.' He grinned wickedly. 'How are your blow-jobs? A much more useful skill if you ask me.'

Flo swatted him. 'You'll just have to make a leap in the dark on the blow-job front. Anyway, I thought you'd want to play the field. After all, you're famous for it.'

'Look.' Adam was suddenly serious, brusque even. 'I've played the field. Now I want someone to smile whenever she sees me. I want to smile back, whenever the thought of her comes into my head.' He stroked Flo's short dark hair tenderly. 'And I want a crop of children with names like Reuben and Hepzibah who do what I tell them most of the time without arguing, and occasionally – very occasionally, mind – take the piss. Does that sort of thing appeal to you?'

Flora was stunned how utterly, entirely, blissfully the

picture he painted of their life together did appeal to her. She'd belong at last. No longer would she be a guest, an outsider looking for a lost dream. 'Could we have an Ethan?'

'More Hollywood than New Testament, I'd say. But one Ethan among the Balthazars should be acceptable.'

This was it. Make your mind up time. She could marry Adam and make her life here, have rows of tow-haired children, and a home of her own rather than sharing her aunt and uncle's.

Flo closed her eyes. It was such a vital decision and her history didn't exactly prepare her for it. She'd seen too many unhappy marriages to underestimate the importance of getting it right.

Adam was fun, breezy and easy-going, but was he someone she wanted to be with for the rest of her life?

A memory of Adam coming to fetch Mattie on his quad bike flashed into her mind. He'd been kind to Mattie when everyone else ignored her. It had been Adam who'd first brought a smile to the child's pinched, worried face even before Flo had arrived. It had always been Flo's theory that people who treated children well were trustworthy.

But what if she'd got Adam wrong? What if, despite his protestations, his proposal was partly out of self-interest? And then there were the other women in Adam's life. Would he be prepared to forget them all?

'Adam,' she said finally. 'Remember, I've had reasons to distrust love. Could you be patient and let me think about it? Just spend some time together. After all, it really hasn't been long. For both our sakes?'

A look Flo found hard to read flashed across Adam's face.

'Of course. No girl should have to agree to the holy state of matrimony without her clothes on anyway. Let's get dressed, go home and give you time to consider my faults before you commit yourself.' He touched her face lightly. 'And if you want a really balanced view, ask my mother.'

Flo giggled. 'Would words like perfect, divine, god-like feature?'

'That's about the size of it. Right. Shall we go back? The sooner you get to know me better, the sooner I'll get an answer. When shall we start?'

They dressed with a slight embarrassment coming between them, feeling like Adam and Eve after the Fall. They didn't talk much on the way back, just stared at the stars and leaned against each other. When they finally reached Hunting Farm, Adam jumped down first, 'One thing,' he said, suddenly serious. 'If you did accept me, I promise I'd try to be a really good husband.'

Flo felt a tiny catch in her heart. She stroked his face with featherlight fingers. 'And I'd try to be a really good wife.'

The next morning Flo woke early, before the rest of the household was up. She jumped out of bed and padded across the pale pine boards, savouring the feel of sun on old wood.

Over by the window the texture of an old rag rug tickled her toes. She bent down and inspected it. Even though it was a humble object, it had probably been made at least a hundred years ago. Maybe Prue's aunt or grandmother had created it, sewing together small pieces of clothes that had probably been worn by child after child before being handed over for one more turn of duty as a rug.

'This would be the beginning of a whole new life,' she told herself. 'I'd be here, near my family and I'd have a family of my own.' The sense of yearning was almost overwhelming, the longing to be part of something, frustrated in her for so many years. 'I wish you were here, Mum, to help me decide.'

But it was Mattie's small face that appeared round the door.

'You're awake early,' Mattie smiled, springing across the floor and into Flo's pretty iron bed.

'If you were looking for a husband,' she asked Mattie, 'I mean purely hypothetically . . .'

'It'd have to be pretty hypothetical since I'm only twelve.'

'What qualities would you look for?'

'Three things,' Mattie answered without hesitating. 'I'd want him to be kind. And I'd want him to be kind. Oh, and did I mention, I'd want him to be kind.'

'Why is kindness so important?'

'Because everything else follows.'

'What about looks, charm, wit, passion?'

'Sheer surface gloss.'

'And do you happen to know anyone who fulfils this demanding bill?'

Mattie grinned and looked up at Flo. 'Adam Moreton does. He's the kindest person I know.'

Flo leaned down and kissed her on the nose. 'Thanks, Matilda. You've been a real help.'

She felt unexpectedly nervous when she saw Adam later that day, but he had wisely decided to leave the matter in the lap of the gods and make himself helpful to her uncle instead.

'Anything I can do to help, Mr Rawlings?' he asked so many times that Uncle Francis began to get a hounded look.

'What's come over Adam Moreton all of a sudden?' he asked a few days later. 'He's there every time I look round. He seems to have given up farming at Moreton Farm altogether.'

'The power of love,' teased Mattie. 'He wants to be near Flo.'

After a few more days Francis stopped questioning his motives and took him up on his offers.

'Why don't we make a start on the tea-room?' Adam offered one day. 'The foundations are already down, aren't they?'

'Brilliant idea except that our brickie can't start for weeks.'

'Then I'll do it. Flo here can be my hod-carrier. Come on Flo, time you learned some skills you *didn't* pick up in London.'

The extraordinary thing was how much she enjoyed herself. At first she kept up a stream of jokes about her own incompetence then, realizing how annoying it was, she stopped and listened and did what Adam did. She had, she found, an undiscovered skill at laying the fillets of cement. She didn't admit this, but it reminded her of making mud pies when she was younger. Being an only child, she'd spent a long time doing that.

She could hardly believe it when Ivy rang the gong for lunch. Four hours had passed in a wink. And the afternoon disappeared just as quickly. She was touched too that Adam was prepared to give up so much time. 'Won't they miss you up at the farm?'

'Hugo'll manage. Time he took off his suit and did some real work. Actually, he quite likes having things to himself. Bit of a control freak, my brother.'

Flo thought how differently building the tea-room would feel if she were doing it with Hugo. His sardonic glances would make her clumsy and she'd sense his impatience and get clumsier still. Adam, on the other hand, couldn't be more helpful. At the end of the day they'd completed a whole wall. Flo stood back and admired it, amazed that she and Adam had constructed something so solid.

'And tomorrow we'll do the next wall,' Adam promised, 'unless you've got something better on.'

'It'd be a pleasure.'

By the end of the week the shell of the tea-room was finished. It might, to the expert eye, be a simple concrete structure, consisting of breeze blocks cemented together, more bomb shelter than Charles Rennie Mackintosh, but to Flo it was indescribably beautiful. She could hardly remember ever feeling such intense satisfaction.

'And this could be just the beginning . . .' Adam whispered into her ear, then apologized, looking like a naughty schoolboy. 'I'm sorry. I didn't mean to bring it up. I'm not trying to pressure you.'

But Flo knew that more than breeze blocks had been bonded this week. She slept better that night than she had for weeks. The next morning she caught him before anyone else had arrived. 'Adam Moreton, if you still want me to, I would be honoured to be your wife.'

Adam dropped his trowel and swung her round in a perfect arc of happiness. 'Thank God for that,' he grinned. 'Now we won't have to start on the loos. When shall we tell people?'

'Let's keep it to ourselves, so we can enjoy it without anyone knowing except us, just for a day or two. How about next week?'

'All right,' he conceded, obviously disappointed. 'If I can keep it to myself that long.'

And, ignoring India-Jane's beady gaze from the kitchen window, he lifted Flo up and kissed her until she was breathless and dizzy with relief and happiness.

'Flora! Flora!' Mattie yelled to her a day or two later, 'Vee says you've promised to decorate the village hall for the Young Farmers' dance tonight. Can I help?'

In the excitement of Adam's proposal, Flo had forgotten this rather rash promise – delivered in order to avoid helping Veronica with endless batches of sausage rolls – and in fact the party had slipped from her mind altogether.

'To be honest,' Mattie confided, 'I think Vee only asked you because she knew you wouldn't do it as well as she did last year. She transformed it into a Kansas haybarn.'

'Did she now? To tell you the truth,' Flo mused, 'I'm in rather a romantic mood today. Let's see what we can dream up between us.'

It was just as well the garden at Hunting Farm was bursting with all kinds of summer flowers, and that Aunt Prue was only too delighted for Flo to help herself to them for such a good cause. 'We never have time to sit down and admire them anyway,' she smiled as Flo disappeared with her third wheelbarrow-full. 'But what exactly are you doing? Starting a rival to Covent Garden Flower Market?'

'Come at six and have a look.' Flo tapped her nose and she and Mattie scooted back towards the tiny village hall.

'Right.' Flo surveyed the empty space, which was bare and whitewashed, with paintings of ploughmen and their teams on each wall, but had a rather chilly atmosphere. 'When I was little I went to a *fête-champêtre* in France with my parents and it was the prettiest sight. We'll put bales of hay all round for seating, with little posies here and there. You start on the posies while I bring in the bales.'

Mattie sat obediently down and wrapped raffia round sweet peas and cornflowers.

'Now, what shall we put on the tables? I don't suppose,' Flo winked at Mattie, remembering her unusually detailed familiarity with the inside of the airing cupboard, 'Aunt Prue's got anything we could borrow hidden away, has she?'

Mattie giggled. It was a lovely sound. 'Six white table-cloths. Wedding presents. Virtually never used.'

'Perfect! Mattie, you're a star. Now, how about going and wheedling them out of her? Tell her the flowers from her garden will look stunning against the dazzling white of her table linen.'

Half an hour later Mattie came back so laden she could only just see over the top of a vast pile of table-cloths the size and colour of Mont Blanc. Behind her, with a white napkin in her mouth, Snowy trotted help-fully.

'Fantastic!' greeted Flo, taking the bundle out of Mattie's arms before she dropped it.

'Shall I put one on?' Mattie asked.

Flo smiled and reached for one of a mound of hideous old blankets she'd found in the cellar and cut to table-top size. 'Old Parker family tip. Put a blanket under the cloth first.' She smoothed the blanket and with Mattie's help laid the dazzling white table cloth on top. There was something in the action that brought memories flooding back to Flo. This was what her mother had done for her dinner parties, in the early days, when everything had been happy. It had been Flo's job to help lay the table. She suddenly saw herself, aged six or seven, in her rabbit pyjamas, putting a bread roll on each guest's plate, almost bursting with pride and excitement. Later she'd been allowed to hand out crisps and olives. Had that happiness already soured, like ancient vinegar, when her mother got ill?

She turned away, feeling her chest close up painfully as if a weight had been put on it. Why did human beings go on believing life would turn out for the best when the truth was so blatantly the opposite?

'Are you all right, Flo?' Mattie's small hand crept into hers. Flo squeezed it.

'I am now. Just a bit of a sad memory.'

Mattie picked up one of the small bunches of sweet peas she'd made. 'Why don't we dedicate these to your mum?'

Flo felt unbearably touched. She put the bunch of pale pink and lilac sweet pea blooms, by some incredible stroke of luck her mother's favourite flowers, in the middle of the table. 'She'd have adored those. Thanks, Mattie.'

'I'm sure she loved you lots and lots,' offered Mattie. 'We all do.'

Flo had to wipe away a tear, but this time for a different reason. At last she meant something to someone. 'Come on, Mattie, time's passing. We're going to make a display that'll knock their wellies off.'

Together they quickly covered the other tables in cloths, and put a vase of flowers in the middle of each. Then Flo announced she would need Mattie's total concentration for their *pièce de résistance*.

'Gosh, Flo.' Mattie stood back to admire their handiwork several hours later. 'It's amazing!'

In front of them stood a seven-foot arch of summer flowers, ingeniously woven round chicken wire stuffed with oasis and supported by a garden trellis.

'Not bad, eh? We'll have them doing the Floral Dance before the night's out, you wait.'

In the end, Flo only had ten minutes to get home

and change, which suited her just fine. Except that she realized a party frock was one thing she'd forgotten to bring from London.

'You could always borrow something of Vee's . . .' Mattie offered doubtfully, 'if she weren't . . .' She paused, searching for the right description. '. . . built like a brick shithouse!'

'Mattie!'

'All right,' Mattie conceded. 'India's too small, Mum's too frumpy, it's going to have to be the dressing-up box for you!'

Flo did look a trifle unusual, she had to admit, dressed as Bo Peep, from a previous village pantomime, but it would have to do.

'Very pastoral,' Flo pronounced, glancing at herself in the mirror. 'I know, why don't we borrow a couple of the sheep? At least then I'll look deliberate.'

Together they selected Rowley and three other particularly pretty ewes, whose appearance Mattie perfected with pink ribbons. 'Just leave them in the pen till we go to the party,' Flo advised. 'Let's go and see who's ready.'

To their joint amazement, Veronica didn't even notice Flo's curious outfit. She kept glancing anxiously at her watch and peering out of the window.

'Your friend Miranda's arrived,' announced India-Jane. 'She's getting changed in Mum's room,' India's ten-year-old tones rose scornfully, 'into the *weirdest* outfit of denim and patchwork, with fringes all over the place and daisies in her hair.'

Miranda chose that moment to make her entrance. Her appearance was indeed Woodstock, circa 1967, with the unusual addition of a black wig divided into two ponytails dotted with huge flowers.

'Great outfit,' Flo congratulated. At least it made her own seem more normal. 'Are you presenting a new gardening programme?'

'Actually,' Miranda replied, 'it's Stella McCartney. Very Hippy Chick.' She eyed Flo's curious ensemble. 'Where's yours from?'

'The Dressing-Up Box.'

'Never heard of it.' Miranda looked miffed. She liked to be on top of new trends and hip shops. 'Must be new.'

Mattie and Flo suppressed a giggle.

'Anyway, I thought you were staying over with the nobs.'

'I am. I wanted to keep my outfit a surprise.'

'I can see why.'

'Till the party. For maximum impact.'

The doorbell rang and Veronica rushed to answer it. But Aunt Prue got there first. 'Hugo,' she greeted, 'how lovely to see you.'

Veronica's face plummeted.

'Good heavens,' Hugo's eyebrows shot up at the sight of the two girls, 'is it supposed to be fancy dress?'

'You've obviously no idea, Hugo,' India informed him witheringly. 'Miranda's is Stella McCartney and Flo's is from a smart shop called The Dressing-Up Box. You're obviously out of touch.'

'Is it indeed?' Hugo caught Flo's eye. 'I thought I recognized it from last year's panto.'

Flo forced herself not to react. Look at him, for God's sake. His dark hair was footballer long and his blue jeans looked as if they'd been ironed. What loser would iron their jeans?

'Nice jeans,' she commented before she could stop herself.

'Yes. If only my mother would stop ironing them.'

Come to think of it, Flo mentally amended, what loser's *mother* would iron their jeans? After all, it was pretty pathetic to be living at home when you were pushing twenty-eight.

The fact that Adam also lived at home, at almost thirty, temporarily escaped Flo's attention. She studied Hugo crossly. For God's sake, his shirt even matched his eyes. How vain was that?

'Shall we set out then?' Hugo asked, pathetically unaware that his shirt colour was being subjected to such brutal scrutiny. 'It'll take us all of two minutes to walk.'

'What about Adam?' Flo demanded loyally.

'Gone into Witch Beauchamp with Uncle Kingsley. Joan rang to say a new pair of Asics MC Plus had landed.'

'Why couldn't Uncle Kingsley drive himself?'

'He'd been sampling Alf's nettle champagne all afternoon. Adam said he'd catch us up.'

Hugo and the three women set off for the party with Aunt Prue, Mattie and India all waving enthusiastically at the garden gate.

A few guests were arriving as they walked up the sunny lane towards the hall and they could hear a band tuning up from inside. 'At least they're here,' Vee commented. 'Last year they got stuck in the pub and arrived halfway through the evening.' She disappeared towards the small kitchen attached to the hall to inspect the progress of the sausage rolls.

'Good God,' Hugo exclaimed as they trooped inside, 'it's like the Chelsea Flower Show in here. I wonder where they got all those flowers from.'

'Aunt Prue's garden,' confessed Flo. 'I pinched so many that I left it looking like Telly Savalas' head.'

'Did you do all this?' Hugo asked, amazed.

Flo shrugged. 'It's a bit over the top, I know.'

'It's fantastic. All it needs is a Fragonard swing. Pity no one's getting married.'

The band, Flo noticed, had taken their cue from their surroundings and launched into a folk-rock version of 'As I Walked Out One Midsummer Morning'.

'Why is it?' Miranda bore down on them, deciding Flo and Hugo had been talking for quite long enough, 'Why is it,' she demanded, 'that ninety-nine per cent of folk songs are about men fucking off and leaving maidens in distress?'

'I suppose,' Hugo mused, his blue eyes narrowing, 'that in the golden age of English folk song, maidens hadn't yet acquired the economic power to be the ones doing the fucking off.'

'Thank God they have now,' breathed Miranda.

The hall was filling up fast as brawny young men jostled their way to the makeshift bar and their girlfriends settled down on bales of hay to gossip. Veronica, still looking at her watch, circled with the sausage rolls.

A sudden commotion at the far end of the hall broke into the chatter. Flo burst out laughing at the sight of

Adam leading Rowley the Ram and his three ewes. 'Bo Peep forgot her sheep, apparently. Mattie insisted I bring them, so here they are carrying their tails behind them.'

'As a matter of fact,' Flo whispered, 'Bo Peep changed her mind and abandoned them. Thanks all the same. I'll stick them behind the stage. At least they won't get trodden on there.'

She led the sheep up on stage past the astonished folk band and created a makeshift pen out of spare hay bales. 'At least you won't get hungry,' she consoled them. 'And later on, if you're good sheep, I'll slip you some sausage rolls.'

Rowley the Ram eyed her as if this were a threat rather than a promise.

'Have a glass of punch, Flora,' Veronica offered, avoiding her eye as she rejoined the throng, 'it's as harmless as mother's milk.' Vee demonstrated by taking a large slug herself. Her rigidly sprayed hairstyle slipped a little.

'Who's Veronica waiting for?' India-Jane, who had somehow wangled an invitation, asked. 'She still keeps looking at her watch every ten seconds.'

'No idea. Maybe some strapping young farmer who wants to keep her on her toes.'

'Come on,' Adam insisted, grabbing Flo's wrist, 'now that you've parked your sheep we can at least have a dance.' He whizzed her round the floor to the increasingly frenetic fiddling. Even though the party was noisily under way, more guests were still arriving. 'Look, there's your mother with Uncle Kingsley and Joan.'

Uncle Kingsley rubbed his hands and headed straight for the bar. Either because of his stature in the village or due to the fact that he wore a white dinner jacket, silk cravat and his new trainers, thereby resembling an escaped psycho disguised as Noel Coward, a swathe opened up in front of him and he achieved his goal of a pint of Theakston's Old Peculier in thirty seconds flat.

Pamela, dressed in several rare goats' worth of cashmere, stopped to greet them. When she noticed the focus of Adam's attention her smile could have frozen over the Med.

'How very pretty it looks in here,' she produced finally, in her best patrician voice. 'Your aunt told me you were doing the flowers. Are they real or artificial?'

Flo sensed this was a trick question but didn't know the trick answer. 'Real. They're from my aunt's garden.'

'I always think silk flowers are so much more sensible. Then the real ones can stay in the ground for everyone to enjoy.'

'Come on, Ma,' Adam rounded on her. 'You usually say silk flowers remind you of Bournemouth boarding houses.'

'That's because Pamela's a roaring snob, aren't you Pam?' pitched in Joan, winking at her outrageously.

Adam laughed. His mother, he knew, absolutely loathed being called Pam. It rhymed too closely with Spam and had just about as much class and sophistication.

'Let's get a drink, shall we?' Pamela swept on.

The band struck up 'Strip the Willow' and Adam whisked Flo back on the dance floor where everyone else seemed to be careering rather drunkenly into each other.

'I love all this traditional stuff, don't you?' Adam shouted, just as Miranda and Hugo pirouetted past them and Hugo managed to tread on Flo's foot.

'Ouch!' Flo screeched. 'Lovely. If people knew what they were actually doing.'

The music stopped and, without warning, Adam jumped on to the stage. Pushing his blond hair out of his eyes, and grinning broadly, he grabbed the microphone from the startled singer.

For some reason Flo's heart jumped into her throat and tried to choke her.

'Before we stop for nosh,' Adam insisted, 'I've got a rather romantic announcement to make. I know she'll kill me because she wanted it to be a secret for a day or two, but I just can't do it. I just have to share some brilliant news with you all here tonight. Last night, after building a concrete structure together . . .'

'That's right, get her working!' heckled someone from the back.

Adam ignored him. 'Last night in the farmyard of Hunting Farm, under the beady gaze of Miss India-Jane Rawlings, I became engaged to the lovely Flora Parker!' He pulled Flo on to the stage beside him and held her tightly at his side. 'With whom I hope to spend a long and happy life and build many more lasting structures!'

Before Flo had time to open her mouth a commotion of squealing and grunting behind them made Adam cut short his speech and pull back the curtain.

Behind it, in full view of the two hundred assembled guests, Rowley the Ram was enthusiastically tupping the prettiest of the three ewes.

At the far end of the hall the door opened and a sudden gust of wind made people turn to see who it was.

Framed by the open door, his eyes narrowed menacingly in his fleshy, indulgent face, stood Miles.

Chapter 12

'I should bloody well think so!' came a delighted bellow from somewhere near the bar. 'You've certainly taken your time about it.' Uncle Kingsley's moustache seemed in such high spirits it almost danced. 'And two months ahead of deadline too! I was beginning to think I was backing the wrong runner. Well done, Adam boy!' He turned to his sister. 'Come on, Pamela, get off your high horse before your arse starts hurting and say hello to your future daughter-in-law.'

Flo climbed down off the stage, surrounded by people clapping, yelling and hallooing, not to mention the band breaking out into 'For She's A Jolly Good Fellow'. Pamela, smiling faintly, stretched out a hand which felt as if it had just been dug up in Antarctica. 'Congratulations, Flora. You must come over and I'll show you round the house. After all, it'll be yours soon.'

'Don't worry, Ma,' Adam grinned, 'we'll find you a nice cottage within easy interfering distance.' On seeing her expression he added quickly, 'Not that we'd expect you to move out anyway, would we Flo?'

Flo, who had never even considered any of these ramifications, smiled nervously.

She was rescued by Miranda instantly whooping down on her and folding her into an enthusiastic embrace. 'I think it's wonderful! So fantastically romantic! You and Adam will have rows and rows of babies just like runner beans!'

And leave you free to scoop up Hugo, Flo thought, before she could stop herself.

'I hope you're both very happy,' added Vee, surprisingly. To Flo's amazement Veronica's wishes seemed entirely genuine, despite the fact that she'd been plotting to hook Adam ever since Flo had arrived in Maiden Moreton. Instead, Vee was bursting with excitement of her own. She seemed to be lit from within. The happy halo of her smile moved from Flo and Adam to somewhere just behind them.

Flo turned curiously to discover its real source. There, three feet away, stood Miles, scowling at her.

'He came!' Vee breathed ecstatically. 'I didn't think he'd ever remember!'

'Despite the fourteen messages you left on my answering machine?' His tone, Flo noticed, was remarkably soft for Miles. Could he be falling for Vee's bossy Women's Institute ways?

Pamela somehow managed to detach her pride and joy from Flo's arm and lead him off to be congratulated alone.

'You'll be bored out of your brain, you know.' Flo

knew those Kaa-like tones and turned to face Miles.

'Actually, I've never been less bored in my life. Country life suits me.'

'I don't mean with the country,' Miles added softly, 'with your fiancé. No subtlety. Action Man without the batteries.'

'Unlike you, you mean? If you're subtle, give me the obvious any day. At least I'll know where I am.'

'You'll be phoning me up in three months, desperate for some intrigue.' He looked across the room at where Uncle Kingsley was toasting Adam in a yard of ale. 'No, make that two months.'

'You are so unutterably vain, it takes my breath away,' Flo replied.

'And does your husband-to-be know about the coming advertising campaign? That you're about to appear on billboards the length and breadth of the land.'

Flo faltered for a second. It had all been so sudden she hadn't actually mentioned it to Adam. 'I'm sure he'll be extremely proud.'

Miles followed the direction of her eyes. 'I wouldn't count on it. Perhaps there are some things he wouldn't stand for.' There was such a strong threat implied in his voice that Flo stepped backwards, not wanting to breathe the same air. 'What are you getting at exactly?'

'All in good time,' he taunted, obviously enjoying himself.

'Just fuck off, why don't you Miles?' Flo enunciated in a steely tone just at the moment the folk-rock band chose to finish their trademark version of

'Greensleeves', so that it could be heard throughout the hall. 'I'm not letting you try and ruin my life for the second time. You were the reason I came here in the first place.'

She looked round to find herself staring into the appraising cool blue eyes of Hugo.

'It seems congratulations are in order,' Hugo said in a tone curiously empty of all emotion. 'My brother's a very lucky man. Am I to presume the wedding will be before Michaelmas?'

Flo's breath suspended on a thread. She'd just recovered from the venom of Miles and here was Hugo with his particular brand of disapproval. She waited a beat to be sure he'd actually said it, the crude inference that she had said yes to Adam to make sure they got the house. And then, without any more thought, she tossed the contents of her glass into Hugo's face.

Next morning Flo woke up to a knock on her door, followed by a grinning Mattie, carrying a tray of tea and toast with Snowy in tow. 'Even Ivy says it's okay to spoil you now you're officially engaged!' she announced proudly, plonking the tray down.

Flo laughed and pulled herself up on her pillows. 'I do declare I feel like Scarlett O'Hara, being waited on hand and foot.'

India-Jane appeared in Mattie's wake, carrying the morning paper. 'And Donna from the pub probably feels like Suellen, what with you pinching her beau from under her nose, or rather from under her duvet.'

Flo ignored her.

'And, by the way, Mattie,' India added maliciously, 'you've forgotten the milk and the butter.'

Mattie's face fell.

'Don't worry, Mattie,' Flo reassured. 'Butter's incredibly fattening and I prefer my tea black.'

Mattie sat down gingerly on the bed. 'Do you really like your tea black?' she asked as India disappeared to look for someone else to annoy.

'Absolutely,' Flo nodded.

'I'm really pleased about you and Adam. He's always kind to me.'

'I'd noticed. In fact, it was one of the first things I warmed to in Adam. He's obviously an excellent judge of character.' Mattie glowed as pink and pleased as the roses on Flo's pillow case.

'And I wouldn't listen to any of the gossip. It's only people who're jealous because Adam didn't fancy *them*.'

'Which reminds me,' Flo said quickly, deliberately not asking what the gossip was. She wasn't sure she liked this line of argument. Everyone always seemed to mention Adam and sex in the same breath. 'How is Vee taking it?'

'She hardly seems to have noticed.'

Flo wondered if this was because of Miles and whether she owed it to Vee to tell her what he was really like. The trouble was, Vee might just react by liking him twice as much.

Mattie had only just left, and Flo was contemplating a challenging choice between reading a glossy magazine and having a bath, when Aunt Prue put her head round the door, her eyes shining with happiness.

'Flora! You're awake! I didn't want to come till I could get you on your own. It's wonderful news. I've known Adam since he was a baby.'

'Don't tell me. All the little girl babies were in love with him too!'

Prue detected a certain weariness in her niece's voice where this theme was concerned. 'I always think that sort of thing's more in the mind of the parents, don't you?'

Thank God for the voice of sanity at last. 'Aunt Prue, are you the one woman on earth who's immune from Adam's charms?'

'I think there's more than one of us. Adam's a very nice young man. Though I was a little bit surprised, I must say, that he was your choice.'

'Why's that?' Flo faltered, feeling a little flutter of panic. She so wanted Prue to approve.

'Just that Adam lives life on the surface whereas I'd say you have some very deep pools.'

'That's why I like him! I think enough for both of us. If I married someone deep we'd never be able to make a decision to get out of bed in the mornings.'

'There is a mid-way, I'd have thought, but forget all this. Are you really happy?' Her aunt sat on the bed and reached for her hand.

'Yes. I'm really happy. I was a bit uncertain at first. How on earth *do* you know if someone's The One and you'll love them for ever and ever? But this week, I know it sounds mad, but building the tea-room together was, don't laugh . . .'

'I wouldn't laugh at you, Flora. Ever.'

'Well, it felt like building the foundations of something important. It felt symbolic somehow.'

'I'm so glad.' There was a catch in her aunt's voice as
she pressed Flo's hand. 'You're a really precious girl,
you know. You need someone who'll appreciate just
how precious. It hasn't been easy for you, till now. I do
so want someone who'll see that and cherish you properly.'

'Adam will cherish me, don't worry.'

'Have you fixed a day?'

'No. Not yet. I'll have to talk to Adam about it.'

'And we'll have to get in touch with your father.' She
squeezed Flo's hand. 'To give you away.'

Flo's chest tightened. She was so used to living her
life and making her own decisions without ever consulting her father. Would he even want to come?

'Of course he'll come,' Aunt Prue read her thoughts.
'Everything's going to be all right. I can feel it.'

'Do you really think so?' Flo's voice was suddenly so
soft Prue could hardly hear it. Her large eyes glistened
with unshed tears.

'Yes, I'm sure he will. I can feel it in my bones.' Aunt
Prue smiled. 'At least it's that or osteoporosis.'

A smile floated up through Flo's pain. She'd never
heard her aunt make a joke before. It sounded like a
good omen.

'I think maybe it's time I got up,' Flo announced, 'and
stopped acting like the Lady of the Manor – at least until
I am one!'

Flo was half-dressed when the phone rang downstairs
and Ivy shouted up that someone called Fizz was on

the phone for her. She hopped down the stairs on to the chilly flagstones of the farmhouse hall. Even in July the stones were as cold as an icy well. In her still-bare feet she had to sit cross-legged on the chair by the phone to keep them from freezing.

'Hello, Flora, it's Buzz here from the agency. I've got some good news.' Flo wondered whether to tell Buzz her own good news. She'd expected to feel a bit silly about saying she was engaged but instead she found she wanted to tell anyone and everyone. 'Are you ready for this?' Buzz had sped on in her high-octane London manner. 'They want to shoot in ten days' time. Are you up for that?'

Miles's words flashed into her mind about how Adam would react to her sudden exposure, but she was sure he was wrong about him. Adam wouldn't care. She'd just tell him she was doing it for Rowley the Ram. And Rowley was practically a soulmate.

As it turned out, she had the perfect opportunity to tell him later that morning when Adam arrived with a dinner invitation from his mother plus an offer of a lift into town. Flo watched him through her open window as he walked up to the door, his blond hair glinting in the summer sunshine. He stopped to throw a stick for Snowy, then held it up for the little dog, higher and higher, until Snowy jumped twice her height into the air. There was something endearingly boyish about Adam. He still had that capacity so many adults lose, of being totally absorbed in whatever he was doing. He didn't clutter himself up with looking back or forward. Flo envied him.

He caught sight of her watching him and shouted up to her. 'How's my brand new fiancée this morning?'

'Happy as a lark,' she smiled, and meant it.

'Not regretting saying "yes" to a country bumpkin and burying yourself in the sticks when you could be running back to the bright lights instead?' he asked, when she'd come downstairs.

She shook her head. 'Give me the sticks any day.' She remembered Buzz's call and that she must tell him about the campaign. 'Though I do have to dash up to London for a few days next week.'

'Good,' he pulled her to him. 'You can look at wedding dresses. And not from the dressing-up box this time.' He blushed suddenly and dipped his hand into the pocket of his combats. 'I thought maybe something like this.' It was a crumpled page torn from *Farmer's Weekly*, featuring a bride in a diaphanous strapless dress which clung revealingly to her voluptuous curves. The model leaned against a haystack chewing a piece of straw. 'Come hither' was an understatement.

'Lovely,' Flo murmured, 'though I'm not sure your mother would approve.' Maybe that was part of its appeal. She was beginning to see that shocking his mother gave Adam rather a thrill.

He helped her up next to him on the quad bike which he'd left in the drive. 'So, why are you off to London then? Hugo'd give you a lift. He still goes up once a week.'

'No, thanks.' She didn't feel like explaining to Hugo exactly what she was doing. 'I've been asked to appear in an advertising campaign for Blackmills Whiskey, and they've offered me quite a lot of money.'

'Good for you,' Adam congratulated as if she'd just told him she'd been given a free tumbler with her petrol.

'It'll be on television and some posters. I need to go and shoot it for a few days in London.'

'Wow,' Adam marvelled, 'I didn't even know you liked whiskey.'

'Can't stand the stuff.'

'Isn't that a bit dishonest then?'

Flo rested her head on his back as they bumped along, closing her eyes. He was so innocent in a lot of ways. 'I don't think they really care if I like it or not – as long as I don't go round slagging it off. It's my challenging image they're after, so they say. Anyway, you don't mind that I'll be plastered all over billboards for a little while?'

'Why should I? I'm proud of you.' She felt like kissing him. He was sweet and generous to a fault.

'I wonder what Pamela will say?'

'Who cares?' Adam shouted and revved up the throttle as they approached a narrow hump-backed bridge. The quad bike roared across, jumping a foot in the air. A posse of ramblers jumped off the road ahead and watched them with disdain. 'Bloody rural yobs,' shouted one.

'Bloody townie ramblers!' Adam yelled back.

'How do you know they're townies?' shouted Flo.

'Real country people are too busy to go rambling. They work their guts out then slump in front of the telly. They don't ponce about with little maps in plastic bags. They know where they're going.' Adam slowed down the bike as they came into Witch Beauchamp. 'Will here suit you?'

'I'd rather go somewhere in the village. Near the pub maybe.'

Flo thought he looked a little shifty.

'Want to come and help me with the harvesting?' Flo was touched that he wanted to include her in his work. She'd seen what happened with her aunt and uncle when the wife got excluded all the time.

'Absolutely.'

'Good. Don't forget to wear trousers with elastic round the bottom. You don't want to get rats up them.'

'There aren't really rats are there?'

'Not really. Though farm workers really did tie string round to stop them. These days the rats are spoilt. They stick with dustbins. There are mice though. And rabbits. You're not squeamish, I hope. Don't want no Lunnon ways here, as Ivy would say. So you don't want a lift from Hugo then?'

'No, thanks. I expect they'll send a cab.'

'All the way to Westshire?' He pulled up outside the pub, deliberately avoiding glancing at the upstairs window.

Flo kissed him briefly. 'Well, they are townies.'

'Mugs more like. See you at our house later?'

'I'll try and dress the part.'

'I shouldn't bother. My mother'd really like me to marry someone who dresses exactly like her.'

'I don't suppose there are enough goats on the planet.'

Adam looked puzzled.

'To produce all that cashmere.'

Behind them the sash of a window creaked, but neither noticed. Upstairs, behind the closed curtains, Donna picked up her copy of the Next Directory. There was a dress she'd noticed somewhere towards the back. It was short, with a scoop neck in fuchsia. And the fabric was cashmere.

'What's eating you, Ma?' Hugo asked. As if he didn't know. Adam had always been Pamela's favourite son. While pretending to disapprove of his frank sexuality she'd actually revelled in it. It wouldn't have surprised Hugo if, somewhere upstairs in the depths of her cupboard, among the Pringle jumpers and Hermès scarves, his mother kept Adam's old condoms.

He could also see why the news of Adam's engagement would particularly upset his mother. Despite Flo's vulnerability and the sadness of her lonely teenage years, or maybe even because of it, Flo had a core of strength Pamela herself lacked. Pamela needed to see herself reflected in other people's eyes. Even if they were scared of her, that was fine. But Flo wasn't scared of her. It seemed that if you'd been hurt as deeply as Flo, no minor cuts and grazes such as Pamela could inflict really had much effect. And Pamela knew this. So she called Flo hard.

'So who would you like him to have picked?' Hugo quizzed her. 'Veronica Rawlings? She'd lino the house and put in more silk flowers than Interflora. The vicar's daughter? She'd move in her entire family of happy clappy Christians. Flo will leave the house as you've had it. She's got other things to be getting on with.'

'Like what?' Pamela continued to deftly wrap string round small lamb chops, inserting a sprig of fresh rosemary and stuffing made of apricot and freshly grated breadcrumbs into each. It always amazed Hugo that his mother, when she felt like it, could cook delicious food while wearing expensive knitwear and not even seem to untidy the kitchen. By contrast his own culinary efforts wreaked mayhem amongst the kitchen implements.

'Helping her uncle run this Sheep Centre. She's very good with people and bursting with design ideas.'

'If she's such a paragon,' Pamela snapped crossly, annoyed at her grande dame civility being exposed for the sham it was, 'why didn't you snap her up yourself? Then you'd have been the one who got the house.'

Pamela regretted her words at once. Real pain streaked across Hugo's face like a cloud across a sunny hillside. Good God, Hugo liked the wretched girl too!

'There you are, Pamela!' Uncle Kingsley seemed to be permanently beaming now that the engagement had been announced. 'Do you know where my Brooks Radius IV's have got to?'

'Where they usually are, in your dressing room, I washed the laces. You appear to have dragged them through a mire.'

'Aren't I lucky to have your mother to look after me?' smiled Uncle Kingsley.

Hugo squinted at him, trying to work out if he was being ironic, but irony wasn't his uncle's strong point.

'Funny way you have of showing it,' Pamela sniffed. 'Handing our house over to Adam and Flora.'

'It's far too big for us. It needs to be filled with children and dogs and gum boots.'

Behind them, Hugo's knife slipped as he carved some beef for a sandwich. 'Blast!' he swore suddenly as the blade nicked his finger. 'Oh well,' he laughed, avoiding his mother's searching glance, 'I always did like my beef bloody.'

Dinner that night wasn't the most relaxed of occasions. Pamela had pulled out all the stops in terms of grandeur. A snowy tablecloth with lacy napkins, the best china, crystal glasses, and a huge centrepiece full of exotic fruits, so tall it was difficult to see the person opposite. Ivy had been drafted in to help at table.

'Are you sure this is a good idea, Ma?' Hugo had asked when he realized how far his mother was going. 'You're expecting your future daughter-in-law, not the Queen Mother. She might be a bit daunted. Think you were trying to scare her off.'

Pamela avoided his glance. 'I'm just trying to show her what a wonderful house this is. With its perfect Georgian proportions. Perfect for parties.'

'Except that we haven't had one in twenty years,' Hugo pointed out. 'You were always too nervous of the china being broken or any of the glasses getting smashed.'

Flo realized the moment she walked in that she'd seriously under-dressed. How silly of her to think that because it was an ordinary Wednesday it would be a kitchen supper.

'I was just saying to Hugo,' Pamela announced before Flo was even seated, 'what a wonderful house this is for parties. Perfect for your wedding. Of course you'll have it here.' The fact that there was no question in Pamela's tone began to infuriate Flo. 'I thought perhaps halfway through September, say the fifteenth,' Pamela went on, not even pausing for Flo's reaction. 'That would give us time to do the organising.'

'Just in time for Michaelmas,' Hugo pointed out.

Flo ignored him.

'Now, Flora,' Pamela beamed in on her, 'we know your aunt and uncle, obviously, but tell us all about the rest of your family.'

'There's not much to tell. My mother was a housewife who died of cancer when I was eighteen. My father's a businessman, a banker, who jets around the world. I don't see much of him. He's mostly based in America these days.'

'Did he marry again?' asked Pamela.

'Not that I know of,' Flo replied ironically, then realized how strange this must sound.

'But he will be flying over for the wedding? To give you away?'

Flo could have died of shame when, instead of answering in words, the reply came out as halfway between a choke and a sob.

Adam patted her and took her off for a glass of water while Hugo angrily cleared the table. 'Congratulations, Ma. That was the soul of tact.'

'And how was I to know, exactly, that her mother was dead and her father had disappeared to live in America?

It sounds as if she never even sees him. I don't suppose *he'll* be contributing much to the wedding, banker or no banker. And the Rawlingses haven't got a penny.'

Flo came back into the room just in time to hear Pamela's comment. Very deliberately she pushed her chair into its place instead of sitting down again. 'As a matter of fact, Pamela, you needn't worry about who picks up the bill. I'll be paying for my own wedding.'

'But surely,' Pamela began, 'it'd be too much? The marquee, music, dinner and dancing, the bridesmaids' outfits, not to mention the flowers alone . . .'

'I'm sure I'll manage. Especially as I don't want a marquee. Just a party in the village hall like we had the other night. The sunflowers will be out, so I'll decorate it with some from my aunt's garden. And I'll find a dress at Oxfam in Witch Beauchamp. And I don't think we'll need a sit-down dinner. My cousin Veronica is a dab hand at sausage rolls.' Flo's eyes flashed with hurt and anger. 'After all, as you just pointed out, I don't have any family anyway.'

She picked up her handbag, just as Uncle Kingsley bumbled back in.

'There wasn't any champagne,' he announced, unaware of the mire he'd just jumped into, 'so I brought some of Alf's elderflower cordial. Excellent if you happen to be driving. And also, so Alf says, a cure for constipation, flatulence, insomnia and tactlessness, or do I mean tachycardia?'

'If it's the former,' Hugo insisted angrily, 'then you'd better give some to Ma. She certainly needs it.'

'Let me walk you home,' offered Adam even though

Moreton House was only minutes away from Hunting Farm.

'No, thanks,' Flo insisted. 'I wouldn't mind being alone for a bit. I might stroll down by the river and get some air.'

'I'm really sorry about Ma,' Adam whispered as he saw her out. 'If it's any consolation, she didn't mean any harm by it.'

'I'm sure you're right. But I wouldn't like to see her when she does.'

It was a beautiful night. The warmth of the day had evaporated into a cold clear sky the colour of midnight blue velvet, adorned extravagantly with millions of stars. It was funny that when she'd lived in the city she'd never even noticed the stars, yet they must have been there, glinting like diamonds, while Flo and all the other city-dwellers ignored them.

She paused a moment, leaning on the five-bar gate into Long Meadow. How was it that as soon as she felt she might finally fit in, something happened to ruin it all?

'Flora . . .'

The quiet voice behind made her jump. It was Hugo of all people.

'Sorry to intrude on your thoughts. I saw you leaning on the gate as I was going up to bed. I just wanted to apologize for my mother. She of all people ought to understand about the pain of absent fathers. Maybe that's why she's so crass.'

Flo wasn't sure she wanted to talk about her father but there was something so genuine in Hugo's tone, she couldn't just brush him off. 'Why, what happened in your family?'

'My parents divorced very bitterly. My father ran off with another woman and from then on, despite his best efforts, my mother did everything she could to stop him seeing us.'

Flo heard the pain in Hugo's voice echoing down the years.

'How old were you?'

'Adam was nine and I was seven.'

'Couldn't the courts help him?'

Hugo laughed hollowly. 'In principle, yes. But my mother, as you may have noticed, is an expert at moral blackmail. She made it so fraught that in the end he just gave up.'

'Do you ever see him?'

Hugo looked away. 'He had another family, much younger than us. I suppose it was easier to lavish his love on them.'

Flo reached out a hand in the dark. 'I'm so sorry. It must have been awful.'

'Yes,' Hugo's voice stumbled slightly. 'Yes, it was. That's why I wanted to apologize. And explain. But what about you?'

Now it was Flo's turn to gaze into the dark distance. 'My father was always absent. On business, flying round the world. It didn't really matter till my mother got ill. And then, after she died, he disappeared altogether. He still sends Christmas cards, of course.'

'How old were you?'

'Eighteen. Old enough to bear the pain. Not like you

and Adam. At least that's what my father probably thought.'

'Except that you're never old enough to bear that kind of pain, are you?'

They both stared at the stars for a moment, lost in their individual painful memories. It struck Flo that she wished it were Adam standing next to her, and yet Adam wouldn't deal with loss in this way. He would swallow it and get on with life, which was why she was drawn to him, wasn't it?

'What's his name?'

'Martin,' the word caught in her mouth, so that she could hardly say it. 'Martin Parker.'

'You really miss him, don't you?' Hugo asked gently. 'Will he come to the wedding, do you think?'

Flo tried to reel all her suffering and loss back into her being; all the closeness she yearned for, the sense of belonging she'd never felt, her love for her mother, the father who'd never loved her despite all her efforts. If she wasn't careful the feelings would overwhelm her and she'd be lost. 'Yes, I miss him, but unfortunately he doesn't miss me.'

'You have invited him though?'

Flo closed her eyes. 'Not yet, no.'

'You must, you know. You'd regret it otherwise.' Flo realized that Hugo understood. He understood the temptation she felt to leave her father out of it altogether, to wound him and reject him as he'd rejected her. Except that it wouldn't work because he probably didn't care anyway, and she'd be the one left with the regret.

'Yes,' she said quietly, 'I expect you're right.'

Their eyes locked for the briefest of instants before Hugo turned abruptly away. 'Time to go in, I think.'

'Yes,' Flo answered flatly. 'Yes, it's getting cold.' She shivered slightly. 'Thanks for telling me all this.'

Hugo hesitated. 'I don't suppose it's any consolation, but it's your father who's losing out by not knowing you.'

Flo tried to smile. This was a side of Hugo she hadn't seen before. 'Yes. Well. Good night, Huge.' The use of his brother's name for him brought Adam back into their consciousness almost with a shock.

Flo turned towards Hunting Farm while Hugo leaned on the gate for a moment longer, looking up at the stars as if they might conceivably have some advice to give him.

Flo crept into the farmhouse, not wanting to be caught by her aunt who would want a step-by-step replay of the evening from hell. Instead she took off her shoes and slipped upstairs in stockinged feet.

Finally alone in her room, she got out her pad of writing paper and her favourite italic pen, which she'd had since boarding school days.

'Dear Dad,' she wrote. 'This may surprise you a little (*though it should surprise you a lot, you bastard*, she wanted to add) but I'm finally getting married. On September 15th in Maiden Moreton Village Church. And I would really love for you to give me away. I know you're busy, but it's the one thing I'll ever ask of you. Love Flora.'

She sealed the envelope and hunted for a stamp.

It was no good, he'd never do it. He'd left because he

couldn't go on living here. He'd had to leave and start a new life. And she wasn't part of it.

It struck her like a blow that she didn't even have his address. She'd have to write to her own father care of his place of work. The tears started again and this time she wiped her eyes with the sleeve of her sweatshirt. But not before one fell on to the envelope, disfiguring the lettering of her bold italic hand.

Chapter 13

'I've brought you a nice cup of tea.'

Her aunt's words penetrated the restless depths of Flo's sleep. What was her aunt doing bringing her a cup of tea, that great British panacea for everything from death to divorce, in the middle of the night?

Aunt Prue gently pulled back the curtains to reveal a dazzlingly sunny morning. 'Half-past eleven. I thought you might like to help your uncle release the sheep into their pens, seeing as this excitement is all down to you. I haven't seen Francis this motivated in years.'

Flo pulled herself up and sat back on the flowery cotton pillows, willing herself to put last night's encounter with Pamela behind her and slough off the tempting embrace of self-pity.

'Here's your tea. Nice and strong, none of that mimsy-wimsy Earl Grey as your mother used to say.'

The mention of her mother was Flo's undoing. She tried to turn her face away so that her aunt didn't see.

'Flora, darling girl . . .' Prue removed the shaky

teacup from the counterpane, forcing herself to ignore the dark brown tea that was spreading there. This was no time for getting out the stain-removing spray. 'What's upsetting you? Is it something to do with the engagement?' A sudden suspicion hit her. 'That snob Pamela hasn't been having a go, has she? The things I could tell you about her. Her husband left her because she was such a cold fish. He couldn't stand that superior manner of hers. Kingsley only puts up with it because he's so idle. She's no right to go upsetting you.'

Flo tried to smile at her aunt's sudden tiger-like qualities. She'd have made an excellent memsahib, sorting out the colonies and frightening the natives with her fierce protectiveness.

'No, it wasn't that. I can deal with all that. I'm pretty strong, you know. I didn't mind her comments about my lack of family.'

'Lack of family? When she couldn't even hold on to her husband!' Flo found herself relishing the attack on posh Pamela. She'd never heard her aunt utter a bitchy word before.

'And what about us?' Prue continued. 'Aren't we family, not to mention their closest neighbours? Anyway, how sensitive is that, given what happened to my darling Mary? I could kill that wretched woman – in fact, I might just go round there now.'

'Don't, Aunt Prue, though it makes me feel a hundred per cent better having you spring to my defence. It wasn't really what she said that upset me, she's just got a bit of an empty life and she's utterly obsessed with Adam. He can do no wrong – except by choosing me as a wife. It was the fact that she asked me if my father would be giving me away.'

This time it was no use. No matter how much willpower Flo tried to summon it couldn't defend her against the tidal wave of pain that flooded over her, filling her lungs and her mouth and her nostrils until she could no longer breathe.

'Why does he hate me so much? It wasn't my fault Mum died. I loved her too.'

Her niece's anguish tore at Prue. 'I've asked myself that a thousand times.' She stroked Flo's hair rhythmically, rocking her own body back and forth as if she needed to be comforted herself. 'The only answer I can find is that Martin wasn't a natural candidate for fatherhood. He wanted the high life. Big business. Big cars. First class flights and five-star hotels. Children didn't really fit into that vision.'

'But Mum wasn't like that at all. She didn't even like flying when we went on holiday.'

'Mary couldn't have been more different. They say people choose a partner who has the things they lack and with Martin that seemed incredibly true. Martin had some self-knowledge. He knew his life was driven and potentially empty. Mary supplied all the softness and the emotion. And he did love her very much.'

'She couldn't have had much of a life if he was always jetting off somewhere. Even if it was first class.'

'I think she hoped having you would change him.' Prue looked up, her eyes suddenly focused on Martin's face, which she hadn't remembered for years. Handsome. Demanding. Determined to have his own way.

At first Prue had been jealous of her sister. Mary had always been the pretty one, the one with a social life. And after the first flush of happiness Francis hadn't been a piece of cake as a husband.

'Why on earth did he have me if he hated children so much?' Flo demanded, suddenly furious at the events which still affected her life so much, twenty-eight years on.

'Because Mary longed for you. It took her years to persuade him to have a child. He was one of those men who wanted his wife all to himself.'

'And the only thing that got her all to itself was cancer.' The dead thump of Flo's voice echoed in the still room. 'But why blame *me*?'

'He got this ludicrous notion that having children late brought on the breast cancer.'

'And did it?'

'God knows. A thousand things can bring on breast cancer and we don't know half of them. I don't think he was strong enough to face his grief. You reminded him too much of Mary, so he just took up his old life as if you didn't exist. He did pay your bills, though.'

'Guilt money!' accused Flo. 'If he did that, he could tell himself he hadn't totally shirked his responsibility.' She turned her head away and buried it in her pillow. 'I've written to tell him about the wedding,' she mumbled into the downy depths. 'I've asked him to come and give me away. Fat chance.'

Prue Rawlings had never felt at such a loss in her life. She hated her brother-in-law for what he'd done to this poor child, and yet part of her felt sorry for him too.

She'd never seen anyone as devastated by death as Martin Parker had been. But if grief could be selfish, then Martin's had been exactly that.

Outside in the bright summer sun a cacophony of baa-ing broke out. 'Come on. Get up and help. Sheep are a lot easier to understand than people.'

'You're probably right.' She took her aunt's hand. 'It's all been so much better since I came here, you know. I know it sounds silly but I feel I belong at last. And I'll belong even more when I marry Adam. Think, Aunt Prue, I'll be next door! I'll be able to see you all, watch Mattie and India grow up. It's going to be so brilliant.'

Her aunt smiled, wondering how much this dream of Flo's had influenced her in accepting Adam.

Ten minutes later Flo grabbed her frayed jeans and an ancient tee-shirt and hobbled downstairs, shoving a trainer on each foot, out of the front door and into the farmyard.

Hundreds of sheep of differing shapes and sizes stood as if all patiently waiting for the same train.

'What breeds are they?' Flo asked her uncle. 'I know!' She excitedly pointed out a solid-looking sheep with a thick-set build and a broad, square face, which stood out from the others. It seemed to be half sheep, half stuffed toy. 'That's a Southdown, isn't it?'

'Ten out of ten,' beamed her uncle. 'They were everywhere when I grew up in Sussex. They ate snails from the downs and it gave them a flavour all of their own. People find them too fatty now.'

'And what's that one?'

'A British milksheep.'

'I don't think I even knew you *could* milk sheep.'

'Of course you can. Wensleydale cheese used to be made from sheep's milk. But this breed does have one problem. They have four lambs and only two teats. So you have to bottlefeed their lambs or try and persuade other ewes, who've lost their lambs, to feed them.'

'And how do you do that?' Flo found herself being butted and looked round to find Rowley the Ram sticking his head out of the pen opposite.

'You have to put the skin of a dead lamb round one of the live ones, then she'll adopt it.'

'That sounds pretty Biblical.'

'It works, though.'

Flo blinked against the bright sun. Pity she couldn't have tried something like that on her father to trick him into accepting her.

'Here, have a handful of concentrates.' Uncle Francis dipped into a bright yellow bag. 'You'll soon have friends then.'

Suddenly Flo found herself almost flattened by a stampede of enthusiastic ewes.

'I like that one.' She pointed to one at the back.

'So do I. Dorset Horn. Only sheep that breeds all year.'

'When do the others breed?'

'In the old days Bonfire Night was always tupping night. Old Rowley here would have served about a hundred ewes then. His favourite night of the year.'

'Didn't all the bangs put him off his stroke?'

'A volcano erupting wouldn't put Rowley off his stroke. Only one problem though.'

'Rowley couldn't stand the pace?'

Rowley baa-ed indignantly. 'Rowley'd serve two hundred, happily, wouldn't you, you randy beggar, if you got the chance. No. It meant all the lambs arrived on the same day. Can you imagine getting up in the night to a hundred babies? Exactly the same.'

At the far end of the farmyard, at a safe distance from the sheep, India-Jane stood with her small nose wrinkled in distaste. 'God they pong,' she announced. 'Flora, there's someone on the phone for you. I *think*,' India's face expressed deep scorn at the idea of such a revelation, 'she said her name was Buzz.'

'Back in a minute,' Flo promised, realizing that the session with the sheep had effected the miracle of chasing her blues away.

'Flora, sorry to drag you away from all the cowpat-flinging or whatever it is you jolly country folk get up to,' Buzz apologized.

'I think they only do that at fêtes. And I promise the cowpats are dry.'

'Thank God for that. Bit of a shock, I'm afraid. We can only have the location we want this weekend, starting Thursday. Would you be up for that? You'd need to zip straight up to London, without the cowpats, for a fitting, say, the day after tomorrow?'

Flo took a deep breath. London seemed on another planet from Hunting Farm, and not necessarily a friendly planet at that. 'I expect they'll spare me.'

'I'll send a car then.'

A wicked smile lit up Flo's face. She'd sort out posh Pamela. 'Buzz, could you do me a favour? Send a limo.'

'You're not going all It girl-ish on me? Arriving drunk

and disorderly? Running up vast expenses with your coke dealer?'

Flo laughed. 'I'm a reformed character. No. It's just that there's someone I want to impress.'

'I'd better make it a stretch then. Don't tell the leading man or he'll want one. Be ready at eight. And you'd better stay for a few days. We could be shooting all weekend, maybe into next week too.'

As Flo sorted out what she'd need for her trip, she remembered that this weekend she'd promised to go harvesting with Adam. She doubted he really needed her help, but the gesture had touched her. She wanted to get involved in all the different areas of his life. If she was going to be a farmer's wife she didn't want to be like Aunt Prue, doing all the caring and catering, but not actually involved in the business of farming. She wanted to get stuck in properly.

Laughing at the wonders of modern technology, she rang Adam on his mobile phone. He answered from the tractor.

'We're up at Long Meadow. Why don't you come up and join us? I'll show you how the baler works now.'

Flo decided to walk the short distance between Hunting Farm and Long Meadow. It was a fantastic day. By early afternoon there was still a faint mist hanging over the valley which gave it a magical look. She crossed several fields, one of them newly planted with seedlings. Once she might have strode through the middle but now she'd learned to respect the growing crops. Her route then took her over Snaws' Hill, a stiff climb with an incredible view over three counties from its highest point. Laughing at the sheer physical pleasure of being young, alive and just engaged to someone who offered her a solid and secure life among people she loved, Flo ran down the far side of the hill like a child, with her arms spread wide. Then, making sure no one was looking, she dropped on to her back and rolled the final fifty feet, the world twirling and twisting, blue sky and green grass together, until she came to a halt in a breathless heap, laughing.

'You're a mad girl, Flora Parker,' Adam's voice greeted her. He stood between her and the sky, his face full of sunshine and tenderness.

'I thought you were supposed to be on the tractor,' she accused.

'I was until I saw you acting about six, rolling down here, so I got Dickey to take over. Couldn't miss all the fun, could I?'

'It's just such a beautiful day. And I was so happy.'

'You don't have to apologize. You're allowed to behave like a six-year-old whenever you want.'

'Thanks. But actually I really do want to learn how to work a baler.'

'Come on then.' He held a hand out to help her up.

'I hate to show my total ignorance,' Flo said shyly as they walked towards Long Meadow, 'but what actually happens at harvest-time?'

Adam didn't bat an eyelid. 'The combine cuts the wheat and separates it into grain, which is stored here.' He pointed to the vast metal attachment. 'The straw's then rolled into round bales and fixed with twine, and then the tractor comes along and picks up the bales and takes them to be stored, or sometimes leaves them in the field. Want to have a go on the baler?'

Flo climbed up. It was a wonderful feeling, creating giant swiss rolls out of straw. She loved sitting here, actually driving the baler with Adam quietly beside her, the sun creating a heat haze on the meadow all round them.

'Look,' Adam smiled, 'you're all covered in dust, just like me.' She looked down to find a fine coating of chaff all over her arms.

'I'm not sure you could sell whiskey looking like that,' he teased. 'You look more like Worzel Gummidge.'

Flo threw back her head and laughed. Somehow the image appealed to her far more than the old Flo's had.

They spent the whole afternoon making bales, stopping only for a brief drink and bite in the shade of an elm tree. It was almost seven before they'd collected all the bales and taken them back to Moreton Farm. Flo could hardly ever remember feeling more tired as they parked the baler in the barn. Or happier. It was just the same as when they'd built the tea-room.

'This is the life,' Adam announced. 'When we're married I'll just retire to the kitchen with the racing pages and you can do all the real work.'

'Not likely. Or rather, only if you're looking after Hepzibah and Ethan and all their little brothers and sisters.'

Adam pulled her to him. 'I hope they all have your spirit,' he whispered.

'And your looks,' Flo replied.

'Perhaps we'd better not waste any time.' Adam's

green eyes took on a wicked glint. 'Dickey and Ted have gone already. It's just you and me.'

Flo remembered their last encounter. 'What about Hugo?'

'In London.'

'In that case . . .' Together they sank into the mounds of hay that were intended to feed the winter cattle, but which could serve other more immediate purposes first. Flo was sure the cattle would allow them that.

As Flo packed her bag, she realized how much she hated the idea of going back to London. The fun she'd had with Adam made it even more of a wrench. And, stupid though it might be, she had a sense of premonition about the shoot. Perhaps it was the association with Miles, but she knew she didn't want to do it.

Still, she reminded herself, it was only a few days and the Sheep Centre wouldn't be happening if it weren't for Blackmills Whiskey. She ought to be toasting it, not complaining.

'I'll drink to that,' she said out loud, shoving her make-up, unused for the last few months, her leather coat and her five-inch Jimmy Choos into her bag. 'Time for the old Flora Parker to come out of her box.'

Mattie was wide-eyed and disbelieving when the endless white limousine arrived in their lane the next morning. 'Maybe it's Elvis Presley looking for a country home,' she breathed.

'I think you'll find he's already got one,' corrected India-Jane, pretending not to be impressed by the car, 'up in heaven. Who on earth could it be for?'

'Actually, it's mine,' grinned Flo. 'Want a ride to the end of the lane? One thing, though, we're taking a detour via Moreton House and you have to be very, very quiet.'

Flo whispered her instruction to the driver and he turned the great monster of a car, just missing one of the stone griffins adorning the gateposts at the top of Moreton House's driveway. They all climbed into the back, and the immense car glided silently, apart from the occasional muffled giggle, up the drive to the elegant Queen Anne facade of Moreton House.

Pamela was already standing outside, pretending to deadhead the roses.

'That's Alf's job,' Mattie whispered, 'Pamela never normally bothers.'

'Excuse me,' the driver pushed the button to lower his electronically controlled tinted window, 'can you tell me where I could find a Miss Flora Parker?'

'She's staying next door at Hunting Farm,' Pamela informed him, chilliness fighting with curiosity.

The limo slid soundlessly away just as someone else joined Pamela in the courtyard.

'Who on earth's that?' asked Hugo.

'God knows,' Pamela lied. 'Hope it's not some frightful pop star hoping to move in to the village and lower the tone.'

'You should listen to yourself occasionally, Ma. Sometimes you sound like the most crashing snob.'

'I'll second that,' whispered Flo, peeping out through the darkened glass at a retreating pair of ironed jeans containing Hugo Moreton. Hugo really was a lot more likeable than she'd imagined.

At the bottom of the drive, in full view of Pamela and Hugo, the car stopped and Mattie and India climbed out. Flo lowered her window and waved regally.

'Bye Flo!' shouted Mattie, running along beside the limo for as long as she possibly could. 'When will you be home?'

'As soon as I can. I'll give you a ring.' As the car sped off, she saw that Pamela had disappeared but Hugo still stood outside, smiling to himself. Mattie had used the word 'home'. And for the first time she could ever remember, it felt exactly right.

Buzz was waiting for her at the agency to take her to the costume designer and on to the wigmaker's.

Flo had forgotten how very pleasant it was to have people fussing around you, pampering you, washing and cutting your hair, offering you constant cappuccinos and generally trying to anticipate your every whim.

'Anything I can get you?' Buzz winked as the wig-maker combed her short hair even flatter against her skull so that she resembled a tailor's dummy in a Miss Selfridge window. 'Sandwich? Toy boy?'

Flo shook her head. 'Neither thank you. My love life's complicated enough.'

Flo caught sight of her eerie reflection in the window. Scary. Why had she said that about her love life being complicated? It wasn't really, apart from the shadow of Miles which still leered up at her occasionally. It was quite simple. She was engaged to Adam. She would be married by Michaelmas. She was happy.

That night they put her up in the Portobello Hotel. Flo

wondered vaguely where the room was in which Johnny Depp had run a bath of champagne for Kate Moss, before the maid unsuspectingly ran it out. The bar was full of the kind of people she'd mixed with all the time. Funny how phoney and skin-deep they seemed now.

From the middle of the loudest, most glittering group a black-haired figure, looking distinctly puffy and over-weight, detached itself and came towards her.

'Hello, Flo. I didn't know you were back in town.'

'Hello Miles. Only very briefly.'

Miles fixed her with a malevolent gaze. Over-fed animals were supposed to be less dangerous, but there had to be exceptions. 'Just long enough to shoot a TV campaign, perhaps?'

'Goodnight, Miles.' Flo cursed herself for not asking to stay in an anonymous hotel chain. Miles would hardly be lurking in the bar of the Forte Post House. Still, she wouldn't worry about him. He'd probably decided to cut his losses and get on with life.

Unfortunately, Miles wasn't the forgetting type.

Miles watched Flo walk towards the lift then change her mind and go for the stairs. In this gathering of models and film types she was hardly noticeable at all, he decided with satisfaction. A little country mouse.

Except that she was noticeable by not being notice-able. Her obvious insouciance and the fact that she seemed immensely unimpressed by her surroundings gave her a patina of real stardom. Damn her.

After she'd gone he tapped a number on his mobile and retreated behind a pillar away from his noisy friends to have a brief conversation.

Five minutes later he emerged in possession of the exact details of where tomorrow's shoot would be happening.

He smiled expansively. 'Waiter, bring another bottle, would you? I'm in the mood to celebrate.'

The advertising agency had decided to reject the gentleman's club in favour of a laddish winebar in the City called Fizz.

Fizz's recipe for success was simple: in a bull market where every trader was taking home an annual bonus bigger than the sum total of what his father had earned across an entire working life, the clientele would pay the earth for any crappy old stuff as long as it was labelled Champagne. Consequently that was all Fizz sold. If you wanted something more *recherché* like designer beer with a slice of lime, you had to head for the Puke and Parrot round the corner.

'Welcome to hell,' announced the director's assistant, a nice young man with a goatee beard. 'We just wanted you to have a look at how the place would feel with real punters in it. We're about to clear it and bring in the actors while you're getting made up. We've taken over that office-block over there.' He pointed to a glass-fronted insurance company. 'Wardrobe and make-up are on the third floor with the hairdresser and wigmaker. We'll just wheel you across when we're set up. Are you clear what you're doing?'

A copy of the shooting script had been delivered to Flo in the car. She only had one line to actually speak, but there were complex moves to master. The director had decided to shoot the entire commercial on one shot, like something he'd seen in a movie.

'Just your luck,' breathed the assistant, 'to get some-one who thinks he's Scorsese shooting a bloody whiskey commercial. Still, I'm sure you'll be fabulous.'

Flo trotted along through the crowded winebar behind the PA, a pretty blonde in a tiny, handkerchief-point Hippy Chick skirt and tight black bodice, which clearly brought out the Neanderthal instinct in the male drinkers. The competition to buy them both a drink was so intense Flo thought any moment a fight might break out.

'Is it always like this?' she shouted to the barmaid over the noise of slow handclaps, popping corks, and noisy bursts of laddish laughter.

'Yes,' bellowed the girl in confident Australian tones, 'except on Fridays. Then it's worse!'

Flo was deeply grateful when the Goatee reappeared and led her back to the calm of the office block to get her costume sorted out.

The transformation was amazing. When Flo looked in the mirror an hour later it was the old version of her-self, the one she thought she'd left behind, who stared back at her. Long blonde hair, skintight snakeskin leather jacket and tarty snakeskin shoes. 'Don't think about how many cobras gave up their lives for your outfit,' suggested the stylist. 'I'm sure they died happy. I must say,' he stood back to admire his handiwork, 'you do look sensational. Bois de Boulogne tart with just a touch of transsexual. How on earth did they come up with this look?'

'Do you mind?' Flo laughed. 'This is how I used to dress.' She was amazed that underneath the tarty exterior they'd put her in a dead simple Jasper Conran shift, which reeked of cocktails in the Ritz just as the top garments reeked of sangria in Stringfellows. When she whipped off her jacket and wig, the transformation would be amazing.

'All right, folks,' announced the stylist finally, 'I think we're ready to start.'

The sight that awaited Flo at the location took her breath away. It was a modern Hogarth. The genuine drinkers had been replaced by actors who seemed even drunker and leerier than the originals. A vast army of scuttling people stood around her, some with clipboards, others toting sound gear or carrying film and video cameras, a stills photographer with a huge chrome equipment case, the director, his assistant, and several gofer types in baseball hats. The whole scene was lit by giant lights as if it were a football match or Cinderella on Ice.

The entire street was taken up by huge vehicles. Crowds of commuters diverted their journeys to take in the excitement of a film crew, several policemen pretended to keep charge while secretly clocking every detail, and finally a location catering van dished out doughnuts and hot chocolate. 'That's because we're shooting through the night,' the PA whispered. 'I can recommend the maple syrup latte. If you feel peckish just ask.'

Peckish was the last thing Flo felt. Terrified maybe. Her stomach was quietly liquefying with fright at the sight of all these people, spending all this money, depending on her, Flora Parker, to get it right. When she'd agreed to do the commercial, she hadn't foreseen the scale of the thing, or that there would be this much pressure on her.

All that she could manage was a glass of water to calm her nerves, but the PA had disappeared. Trying not to attract any attention, Flo made her way to the catering van.

'Hi,' greeted the caterer, a chubby man in his fifties, with a friendly smile, 'what can I do you for? Cappuccino? Double Espresso? Hot choc?'

'Just water please.'

'Still or sparkling?'

Flo's brain went to mush. How on earth was she going to remember what to do on the set in front of all those critical eyes if she couldn't decide on which water she wanted? Then the most weird thing happened to her: she, who considered herself to have the constitution of several rhinos, felt her breath speed up, her palms begin to run with sweat, and her knees start to buckle under her. Just as blackness beckoned the caterer leaped out from his van and caught her. 'Here,' he said kindly, 'a glass of tap water. You don't want that mineral muck when you're feeling under the weather. God knows what they put in it.'

Flo took three sips and started to feel better.

'You sit down here on the steps for a bit,' offered the man, 'till you feel all right again.'

Next to her two lighting technicians were tucking into a mound of doughnuts the size of K2. 'What do you think of the catering?' one asked the other.

'Not as good as the Toilet Duck shoot last week. They had smoked salmon bagels. So, what do you reckon on this bird they're using for the shoot?'

'Bit of an amateur, I heard. Got her tits out in the paper, Bill says. That's enough qualification these days. Probably can't act to save her life. What with the director wanting an Oscar, could be a long night.'

Anger revved up in Flo, dispelling any fear of a blackout. She jumped up off the steps and pulled her blonde wig firmly into place. 'I'll tell you one thing,' she snarled at the astonished pair, 'if it's a long night, it won't be because of me but your crappy lighting.'

As they watched, open mouthed, Flo strode off, raring to prove she could do it in one take.

Behind her the catering man chuckled. 'More doughnuts, lads? Or have you lost your appetite all of a sudden?'

For the rest of the night Flo operated on auto-pilot. The director took her through her moves, which seemed reasonably straightforward at first. As the night wore on, however, she realized how wrong she was. To her amazement, though, it wasn't her who got things wrong but the other actors. As they started again for the twentieth time she began to see why everyone so resented the director wanting to shoot the scene in one shot. In a normal shoot if someone cocked up they could just restart that section and edit it in afterwards, but in this case they had to go right back to the beginning.

It was well after midnight by the time they finally got it right.

'Okay,' yelled the assistant, relief lighting up his exhausted features, 'that was good.'

Not good enough for the director, though. He insisted on three more versions before he allowed the set to be struck. 'Back tomorrow, same time,' he instructed. 'And learn your bloody moves.'

Flo and the PA trudged back to the office over the road.

'You were great,' congratulated the girl. 'I've seen famous actors fluff ten times more often than you.'

Through her exhaustion, Flo felt a buzz of elation and relief. She hadn't let anyone down.

Back in Wardrobe, she quickly stripped off the Jasper Conran dress and handed it to the stylist to be bagged up and labelled for tomorrow. 'How many more times do you think we'll do it?' she asked the stylist.

'Hard to tell. Some directors are fussier than others and Alan's the fussiest of them all. Just lie back and think of the money. Do you want a shower? The managing director's got his own. We're allowed to use it if we want.'

Suddenly the thought of hot water battering her skin was irresistible. 'Maybe I will. Is anyone else around?'

'Only you and me. The others have all scarpered, lucky sods. Don't worry, I'll keep a lookout.' She began bagging and labelling the other actors' clothes, whistling as she did.

The shower was glorious. The MD of Goldsworth Insurance clearly liked to pamper himself. Flo helped herself to his Crabtree & Evelyn Shower Gel for Gentlemen and lathered it liberally over her breasts, breathing in the heady, aromatic blend of chypre and spice. She closed her eyes, letting the exhaustion and anxiety of the day steam away.

Suddenly her body tensed. She'd heard a sound, tiny but entirely distinct. Like the click of a camera. She snapped open her eyes but there was no one there.

The tiredness must be getting to her. She was imagining things. Dismissing her paranoia, she stepped out of the shower and dried herself with the managing director's monogrammed towels.

She said goodbye to the stylist and eased herself gratefully into the cab waiting for her downstairs. Back at the hotel the bar was quiet, empty of Miles and his freeloading cronies.

In another ten minutes she was in bed with the light out, her limbs beginning to ache with tiredness and the aftermath of tension. She tried to remember yesterday with Adam on the baler, all the sheep baa-ing excitedly at Hunting Farm and Uncle Francis brimming over with good humour. She reminded herself how lucky she was to be able to help them by doing something that cost her so little.

But the vision that filled her mind as she finally drifted off to sleep wasn't remotely gentle or pastoral. It was of Rowley the Ram in full priapic flood, tupping one of the prettiest ewes. And his cruel and greedy expression was extraordinarily like that of Miles.

Chapter 14

They finally finished shooting at ten the next evening. Flo never wanted to see a glass of whiskey – or the inside of a laddish winebar – ever again. She longed to get back to Maiden Moreton as fast as the hired limousine would carry her. She turned down the offer of another expensive hotel room and instead was driven through the night, so that she could wake up in the familiar iron bedstead at her aunt and uncle's home.

Next morning, when Snowy and Mattie jumped on her, as they always did, it felt like months rather than days since she'd last seen them. 'I've missed you both so much. What's been going on while I was away?' She was far more riveted, Flo realized, by the gossip from the village than anything featured in *Hello!* magazine.

'Oh, the usual, you know. Dad and Harry have been decorating the tea-room you and Adam built, Ivy's started on the scones though no one'll want them for weeks, if at all. Mum keeps humming and looking happy; she's even started picking flowers which she hasn't done for years. Every jug, vase and toothmug is full of them so no one can even brush their teeth. Adam says Pamela's fallen out with Joan because Uncle Kingsley's been paying her too much attention. Pamela suspects this trainer thing's all a cover, apparently, for something more sinister. Or at least so Adam tells me.'

'I can imagine that would get up Pamela's nose. Down-to-earth Joan would never put up with Pamela's snobby manner.'

Flo couldn't help grinning. Every detail enthralled her, no matter how trivial.

'India's being beastly about your trip to London. She says advertising's the manifestation of a dying capitalist society. But that's only because she's jealous you're making all this money.'

'She's absolutely right, of course. That's why it pays so well.'

The sound of a horn persistently beeping finally persuaded Flo out of bed. Down in the farmyard, where the sheep were now neatly penned into enclosures according to breed, Adam and Hugo sat on the quad bike, dark hair contrasting with blond. 'Come on, you lazy Slugabed,' shouted Adam, 'time for part two of Practical Farming Skills.'

He blew her a kiss and Flo's heart zinged at how handsome he was, how easy and charming his smile, how it brought answering smiles in everyone who came under his spell.

'I'll be right down. Just looking for my wellies.'

She appeared moments later in jeans, a checked over-shirt and her Lady Northampton boots.

'You know,' Adam told her with a grin, 'you almost look the part.'

She climbed on to the back of the quad bike next to Rory the red setter and they took off over the hill behind the farm, sheep skittering out of their way as they passed. Snowy made a brave attempt to follow until Mattie caught her and scooped her up, waving.

It was a heart-stopping scene: rolling green fields running parallel to a small river, where several swans paddled in the watermeadows and a heron lazily lifted his wings, with a line of elm trees sloping towards the horizon and the gentle contour of the downs behind. A perfect English landscape.

They stopped for a moment in a small gully. 'God, it's beautiful here,' Flo sighed.

'Not for long,' Hugo replied, a tinge of bitterness in his tone. 'This is all farmland. In ten years it'll have gone. Or been turned into vast agribusinesses. Look at the difference between here and northern France. Enjoy it while you can.'

'Good old gloomy Hugo,' Adam teased. 'It's only land, old man. What does it matter if it's divided into big bits or little bits?'

Flo surveyed them both. They were so different. Adam so light-hearted and easygoing, like a river whose smooth surface was never ruffled by swirling currents. Hugo, darker and more intense, with sudden swirls of anger that broke through his English exterior.

'It makes all the difference in the world,' Hugo persisted. 'Small farms are what keep the countryside looking the way it does. Besides, each small farm belongs to a small farmer. It's a way of life.'

'So, what's so great about being a small farmer anyway?' Adam asked, only half teasing. 'Everyone hates your guts. They all think you drive round in a Range Rover and fiddle the subsidies when actually you work bloody hard for no return. Remind me again of the attractions of being a small farmer.'

'How can you ask that?' Hugo brushed back his hair with irritation. 'Making things grow. Being close to the land. Watching the seasons. Having something worthwhile to hand on to your children.'

Suddenly Hugo flushed as red as the poppies in the field behind them. 'Well, it's you two who'll hand it over to your children, seeing as you're the ones who're getting married.' He stumbled to a halt. 'That is, I mean, if you want children . . .'

'I expect we will one day,' Flo rescued him. 'Adam wants rows of them, don't you?' She reached out to stroke his hair.

Adam grinned like a cat stretching in the sun. 'I need to get respect from someone. I certainly don't get it from my brother. He thinks I'm just a pretty face.'

'I respect you,' Flo smiled.

'Right.' His smile was pure invitation. 'Let's move on to those wifely skills, shall we?'

If they'd been alone she'd have quipped back that her blow-job technique was fine, thank you, but she remembered Hugo's presence just in time. He already thought she had the morals of a seasoned-up hyena. 'So what are these wifely skills you have in mind?'

'Driving a grain trailer at harvest,' Adam began the list. 'Bottle-feeding lambs whose mothers have abandoned them. Minding the calves. Keeping the books. Feeding the sheep in winter. Making sure my overalls are clean. You know, nothing too demanding.'

'Hang on. How am I going to look after Ethan and Hepzibah and all their little brothers and sisters and do all that too?'

'You fit it in around your other chores, woman. You'll be fine. Oh, and I forgot one more thing . . .' Ignoring Hugo, he pulled her close so that she could feel the heat of his skin against hers. 'The farmer's wife is the one who has to cut off the bullock's bollocks.'

'Excuse me?'

'Entirely traditional. Even our mother tried. You put a ring round them and they drop off. Only Ma bottled out after only one side, and the poor bullock had to go around at half-cock.'

Flo began to feel distinctly queasy. Even the thought of posh Pamela putting rings on bulls' privates couldn't quite convince her she was cut out for some aspects of the farmer's life.

'What were those rewards you were mentioning again, Hugo?' she asked faintly.

But Hugo had jumped down and found a gate that apparently needed attention, though it looked fine to Flo.

'I'll see you at home later,' he shouted. 'Don't be late for lunch. Ma's cooking something special. And Flora, don't believe Adam if he tells you there's only one way to see if the corn's ready to cut.'

'Don't tell me,' she shook her head lovingly. 'You have to lie down on it?'

Adam laughed. 'It's worked in the past.'

'Well, things are going to be different in the future, my lad,' she warned.

'Then you'll just have to keep me happy at home, won't you?' The look he gave her almost set the cornfield alight.

'I'll do my best.'

Behind them the gate banged noisily shut.

She spent the next hour being taken round to far-flung corners of the farm. 'When does harvest begin exactly?' Flo asked, slightly ashamed she didn't already know. Her childhood memories were full of golden blazes of corn and combine harvesters. But surely that had been in August?

'Any minute.'

'But it's only July. I thought harvest was in August.'

'You've been reading too much Thomas Hardy. It starts earlier than it used to.'

'And tell me something I really ought to know. I remember when I was a kid that after it was finished all the fields used to be ablaze, burning the stubble.'

'Not allowed any more. The Government's decided it's better for the little birdies if we leave the stubble on the ground all winter and don't plough it in till the fifteenth of February. So that's what we do.'

'That's very ornithologically sound of you.' She heard a skylark swooping above them, its glorious lilting song charting its flightpath like a musical vapour trail. 'I didn't know you were so keen on conservation.'

'As a matter of fact,' Adam confessed, 'we do it because they pay us. And of course,' he added, seeing her disapproving expression, 'because we very much enjoy the song of skylarks.'

'Liar.'

'I have to confess I can't really hear it through my CD of Meatloaf.'

'Philistine!'

They got back to Moreton House at precisely five to one. Flo was impressed that Adam achieved this without even looking at a watch.

'Instinct. Lunch, one o'clock; tea, five o'clock; supper eight, except during harvesting when it's any time up to midnight.'

Flo repressed a slight sense of apprehension at how much structure Adam was used to.

'Don't look so nervous. Ma likes it this way. You can do what you want.' He pulled her to him and kissed her, just as Pamela appeared from the garden.

'Are you two ready for lunch, or is love enough of a diet?'

This time, at least, they were eating in the kitchen. It was a lovely room, the kind that advertisers of expensive kitchens copied and immediately ruined, because they removed all the real clutter of life and replaced it with children in ballet tutus, wellies that had never seen the great outdoors, and piles of fresh figs and daunting-looking aubergines chosen for their shade of sheeny purple.

The charm of Moreton House's kitchen lay in its scrubbed simplicity. A large, square, unfashionable deal table stood, centre stage, in front of a vast inglenook fireplace in which an ancient unfashionably cream Aga was recessed. Above the recess was a mantelpiece adorned with vast pieces of blue-and-white Italian spode china. Serving dishes, carving platters and two huge and beautiful soup tureens.

On the vast built-in dresser was a well-worn trug containing vegetables Alf had brought in from the garden – carrots with pale green fringes, ripe tomatoes, pinky-red raspberries. A string of onions and a plait of garlic were suspended from the Victorian clothes-airer on the ceiling. An ancient refrigerator, almost pre-war in appearance, chugged quietly in the corner.

Despite the welcoming look of the place there was a curious, and not exactly aspirational, aroma which Flo hoped had nothing to do with lunch.

'Hello, Ma,' Adam greeted his mother with a kiss. 'What's that awful pong?'

'She be making fancy fish-water for the cat,' Ivy announced ominously.

'It's a tip Mrs Bourne gave me at bridge last week,' explained Pamela. 'You boil up the bits and bones, then strain it into ice-cube trays. *Voilà*. Then you can defrost a nice drink for Jasper.'

'Blessed animal,' muttered Ivy. 'And what happens if some poor soul wants a gin and tonic and uses it by mistake, I'd like to know? Be in for a nasty shock, won't they?'

'Then anyone helping themselves to a gin and tonic had better ask me first,' replied Pamela meaningfully. She'd often considered marking the gin bottle, which she suspected of falling faster than it should do when Ivy was around.

'Hello darling,' she greeted Adam, her voice melting with tenderness. 'Ivy's come to help. Isn't that nice?'

Flo hadn't realized the word 'nice' could sound so lukewarm.

'Be an angel, Ivy,' Pamela requested, 'and fetch a few of those plums from the tree in the orchard.'

'You mean the plum tree where you let 'em drop last year and rot where they fell?' Ivy asked pointedly. She greatly disapproved of what she saw as Pamela's wasteful habits where nature was concerned. In Ivy's view all fruit and veg, not to mention herbs, berries and sloes, should be preserved, salted, dried, pickled or eaten on the spot.

'Exactly the one,' replied Pamela who was used to Ivy's tactics of old.

Ivy reappeared a moment later with a pudding basin full of ripe fruit.

'Peel and slice them, would you, so we can have a nice plum crumble?' Pamela requested.

'They don't be plums,' Ivy announced as if there were no hope of Pamela ever getting the hang of country ways, even after forty years.

'Fine. Sloes then,' Pamela raised her eyes to heaven.

'They don't be sloes neither.'

'What do they be?' Pamela asked in exasperation. 'I mean,' she corrected herself as Flo tried to suppress a giggle, 'what are they, then?'

'They be bullaces,' Ivy stated as if this fact were entirely obvious to anyone with half a brain.

'Fine.' Pamela struggled to keep her patience. For once Flo sympathized. Ivy was laying on the rural one-upmanship a bit thick. 'Then we can have a lovely bullace crumble, can't we, Ivy dear?'

When the lunch was finally ready they all sat down round the kitchen table. 'Now.' Pamela wasted no time before getting to the point. 'Hugo says I've been bullying you. That I should let you choose where you want the wedding. Perhaps you'd like it at your aunt and uncle's house?' Pamela tried to repress a shudder at the thought.

Flo thought about it for a moment, realizing it would probably be impractical now the sheep were there. As India would point out. Too much of a pong.

Pamela pounced on her hesitation.

'Of course Moreton *is* rather a lovely house and it might be a nice way of handing it over to you and Adam.'

The realization of what Kingsley's bet would actually mean to Pamela struck Flo for the first time with sudden force. 'You really don't have to move, you know,' she said, wondering if she might regret these impulsive words. 'This place is so huge. There's room for all of us.'

'The last thing a bride wants,' Pamela insisted in a martyred tone, 'is her mother-in-law hanging around. I'm afraid I've spoiled Adam a bit. I couldn't help having a soft spot for him.'

'Neither could every other woman in the county, from what I can gather.'

'So you'd consider having the wedding here, after all?'

In the absence of Hugo, Flo could sense she was on her own. 'Provided my aunt and uncle were genuinely involved, yes.'

Adam looked at the kitchen clock. 'Ma, I've got to make a start on Maiden Field or we'll never even be harvested by Michaelmas.'

'Half an hour won't make any difference,' insisted Pamela. 'You can stay out later tonight.'

'Thanks a lot, Ma. Ted and Dickey will really appreciate that.'

'Hugo'll help when he's back. He's only nipped into Witch Beauchamp to pick up your uncle's new trainers. They're the ones from Japan he's been waiting for. To be honest, I think he was glad to get away from all this wedding talk.'

Flo knew what he meant.

'He's just jealous,' Adam announced with satisfaction.

'Now, where would you like the marquee?' Pamela, with pad in hand, turned back to Adam and Flo. 'And would you mind very much if I did the flowers myself? It's a bit of a hobby of mine.'

'Of course not,' Flo replied, trying to shake off the sense of unreality that kept enveloping her. The event they were discussing was her own wedding. And it would be taking place in less than two months' time.

'We've got so much to do,' beamed Pamela. 'Banns, menus, music – and what about your vows, are you going to go with the traditional version and promise to obey?'

'Seems an excellent idea,' grinned Adam. His hand

crept meaningfully across her thigh. 'Then you'd have to do whatever I tell you, wouldn't you?'

'I don't think the wedding vows encompass most of your suggestions,' Flo teased. 'So we'll scrub that one then, shall we?'

It was true that Hugo Moreton was happy to have an excuse to get away.

It was market day in Witch Beauchamp, one of the few small towns in the county which still held cattle auctions. Most farmers now sold straight from the hoof to the supermarket or abattoir, but every fourth Wednesday in Witch Beauchamp a few old boys still gathered to stare up cow's backsides and listen to the auctioneer rattle off his mantra of cattle prices, before repairing to the Angel for a consolatory pint and a moan about tumbling farm prices. Long before the licensing laws had been relaxed throughout the country, Witch Beauchamp's pubs had stayed open all market day.

Hugo slipped in to look for Dickey, who could never resist the lure of extended opening hours and the chance to have a really lengthy whinge, to remind him he was needed on the combine.

'Through there,' pointed out Donna, leaning provocatively on the bar so that Hugo was treated to the full Grand Canyon of her cleavage. 'Putting the world to rights with Alf.'

'Thanks.' He didn't ask how she'd guessed he was looking for Dickey. Donna knew everything that happened in a ten-mile radius. He glanced at her again.

There was something different about her today. Perhaps it was a new addition to her extensive line of nose-studs? Or another provocative tattoo to join the bluebirds fluttering above one breast. Donna, he knew, was rumoured to have a tattoo in a place where only the privileged few could see it.

'How's your brother?' she asked, cat's eyes narrowing in the pub's smoky gloom.

'Deep in wedding plans.'

'So he gets it all instead of you.'

'If he gets married first, yes.'

'So why let him? You could get married too.'

'Not just to get the farm.'

'Why not?' Donna's smoky gaze pinned him to the spot. There was something witchy about Donna.

'Because I believe marriage is about something else, I suppose. Not just a bet.' Hugo was conscious he sounded pompous. He should have answered with a joke. And anyway, it sounded as if he thought Adam was marrying simply to get the farm, whereas it was obvious he was besotted with Flora.

'Marriage is always a bet,' Donna countered. 'Usually a bad one. I see enough of 'em in here to know that.'

'So you'd never get married then?'

Donna tilted her head to one side. 'I'm not saying that. If the right man came along . . .' her voice purred with honeyed invitation. 'But he'd have to be pretty special.'

Suddenly Hugo realized what the change was. Donna had cut her hair into a style that was gamine and feathery, a carbon copy of Flo's.

'You should, you know,' Donna said softly.

'Should what?'

'Get married. Adam doesn't really want the farm. He says it's bloody hard work for no return. A mug's game, he says.'

'Farmers all say that.'

'Adam means it.'

'I'd better get Dickey now.' Hugo suddenly wanted to get away from Donna, and her tacky allure and uncomfortable revelations. Surely Adam would never really sell up? Donna just wanted to get back at Adam because he'd dumped her for Flo, proving, no doubt to Donna's fury, the old adage that there was one kind of girl you went to bed with and another kind you married.

When she woke up next morning with the sun pouring in through the gap in her curtains, Flo realized she was happy. She wasn't sure how this miracle had come about, but it had. The wedding was beginning to seem less terrifying, and more a pleasure to look forward to. The longer she spent with Adam, the more any lingering doubts evaporated.

Even Pamela was unbending, Veronica had accepted it with reasonable grace, and Mattie had been thrilled when Flo had asked her to be a bridesmaid.

'Silly outmoded institution,' India-Jane had mumbled, eavesdropping.

'So you don't want to be one too?' Flo had teased.

'Will I get white satin shoes?'

'I'll order them today.'

'All right then,' India conceded, 'if you really, really want me to.'

The next few weeks were the happiest Flo could remember. In the day she helped Adam on the tractor, harvesting oats and barley, making silage, learning how to test the ears of wheat for moisture content. In the evenings she and Pamela made lists and wrote out invitations. For the last few days Aunt Prue had buried her resentment and joined them, which gave Flo enormous pleasure.

If only the Montagues and the Capulets could have got to the canapé-choosing stage, what a different scenario it might have been, Flo reflected.

Auntie Prue, hitherto the most practical down-to-earth of people, seemed to be engulfed in a tulle and organza fantasy and had started sewing individual wedding favours, designing place settings and drying rose petals to make real confetti.

'Harvest's almost over. Why don't we have a Harvest Picnic like we did as children?' Aunt Prue suggested. 'I'll make up something nice.'

The next afternoon Flo and her aunt strode through the prickly stubble of Maiden Acre towards the small knot of men in the far corner. Noticing her basket, Adam's face lit up. 'See yon goddess who approacheth with nectar and ambrosia for her hungry swain.'

'I don't want no rice pudden,' Dickey muttered. 'No matter what they eat in Lunnon.'

'Actually,' Flo shook her head, laughing, 'it's Aunt Prue's home-made pork pie, Ivy's rock cakes and Veronica's sent some . . .'

'. . . sausage rolls . . .' cut in Adam and Hugo together.

'Here you are, Dickey,' Hugo opened the tupperware container, 'just for you. Nice, plain, non-ambrosial sausage rolls.'

'That's more like it,' Dickey agreed, not realizing the others were laughing at him. 'I likes a nice sausage roll.'

Adam grabbed a couple of bales of straw from the baler to lean on and Flo spread the rug. 'Very nice,' approved Adam. 'See, you're going to make a wonderful farmer's wife.'

'I've been taking lessons from my aunt,' smiled Flo.

'Who's deeply grateful she doesn't have to worry about the price of wheat or hygiene regulations in the dairy any more, only listen to the gentle baa-ing of sheep,' countered Prue.

'You won't feel so cheery about it in winter,' chipped in Dickey. 'When you got ninety lambs a-born in one night and half they's mothers rejecting 'em.'

'No, probably not,' agreed Aunt Prue, 'but it's glorious summer now and I actually see my husband occasionally during daylight hours, which is a major miracle.'

'I'm glad to hear it's all going so well.' Hugo helped himself to some more pork pie, pushing up the sleeves of his shirt to reveal a plimsoll line of tanned skin changing abruptly to pale. How, Flo wondered, did Adam manage to avoid that?

'Early days yet,' Prue smiled. 'We've still got a long way to go, but Francis is a different man.'

It struck Hugo, looking at Prue Rawlings, that she was a different woman too. A light dusting of freckles had appeared across her cheeks and nose which gave her an almost girlish look, and she'd let her hair out of its usual unflattering ponytail. It was the colour of warm walnuts. He'd never noticed before. There was even, as she leaned forward to press more pie on him, the suggestion of perfume. The only real question that troubled Hugo was how the hell they'd got the money for the venture. He hoped to God they hadn't borrowed from some unscrupulous source who would wring them for every penny they made.

His eyes strayed to Flo. Had she been the one who'd encouraged them to make this leap in the dark? If so, he hoped she knew what she was doing.

Flo's eyes were, as usual, fixed firmly on his brother. Adam had stood up, declaring that it was too damn hot, and had stripped down to reveal cut-off shorts. The sun was so bright now that you had to shade your eyes. It had built up steadily through the day to a stifling intensity.

Adam's body, streaked with sweat and dust, caught the setting rays, making him look, even to his own brother's eyes, like some young god. It was a pity looks were so much more powerful than minds.

Repressing a sudden stab of jealousy, he turned again to Prue, who had just asked him if he was exhausted after the harvest.

'The summer's always the busiest time for us. Still, I can't complain, I'm bunking off for a week or two once the harvest's over.'

'Where to?'

'The States. I advise a couple of banks on agricultural investment.'

A sudden thought occurred to Hugo. It was outrageous but not impossible. He wouldn't mention it to Flora, though. She'd be too disappointed if it didn't work out.

Chapter 15

'Have you thought about who you'll ask to be your best man?' Flo cleared a path through the sweat and dust on Adam's chest with a loving finger. They were lying in an island of flattened corn in the last of Moreton's fields, the distant hum of the combine in the background. The sun battered down on them without a single cloud to relieve its intensity. Flo could feel the sweat gathering in the recess at the top of her collarbone. She couldn't remember feeling this hot since holidays in Greek islands, but then she'd had the cool waters of the Aegean to jump into. Here, even the dewponds had dried up in the sudden heatwave.

'Give us some of that barley water, would you?' Adam shielded his eyes from the glare while Flo rolled over to get the basket, revealing an inviting flash of knicker.

Adam wasn't a man who could resist such temptation, or indeed any temptation at all. With one hand he began to caress her buttock, while the other crept round towards her zip, at the same time pulling her towards him. Flo felt her breath quicken, even though her more modest instincts would have told her that a field, in the middle of harvest, with the drone of a combine harvester only a few yards away, was not the most sensible of erotic locations.

Before they could get any further, Flo felt a cold nose stick itself in her ear, and she shot up into a sitting position.

'Snowy!' she yelped, 'what are you doing here? You might have been killed by the combine.'

'It's okay,' Mattie's voice reassured her from beyond their hide-out, 'I wouldn't have let her near the combine. Gosh, what are you doing in here, where no one can see you? Are you making a den to hide in? I used to make dens all the time when I was little.'

'Yes, Adam,' Hugo's voice seconded, a couple of paces behind Mattie, 'what *are* you doing in there where no one can see you?'

Flo, pulling down her skirt and rearranging her clothing primly, found herself looking up into the challenging gaze of Hugo, and blushed unaccountably. Why should she be embarrassed about kissing her own fiancé?

'They were looking for you up in the Five Acre. You're needed to help with the grain hopper. Unless,' he paused and added with the faintest veil of hostility, 'you're too busy showing off your threshing machine.'

'Don't worry,' Adam picked up the challenge in Hugo's tone instantly, 'it's in great working order, thanks.'

'I'm sure it is,' Hugo's eyes narrowed in the sun, 'it certainly gets plenty of practice.'

'I don't suppose, Huge old chap,' Adam leaned back

on the rug again, his tone silky smooth, 'you'd consider being my best man?'

That shut Hugo up. After only a beat of hesitation he replied. 'Of course. Naturally I'd be delighted.'

After Adam had gone off to do his duty with the grain hopper, Flo headed back through the prickly stubble with Mattie and Snowy towards Hunting Farm. The stubble, newly cut, was sharp as razors and Flo, whose feet and ankles were starting to bleed, realized how stupid she'd been to wear sandals.

'Why don't we go by the lane instead?' Mattie offered thoughtfully. 'The stubble's probably bad for Snowy's paws.'

'And my silly London legs, you mean.' Flo climbed over the stile into the sun-dappled lane. Ahead, an arch of trees created a temptingly shadowy tunnel. It was like having a heavy weight lifted off your shoulders. 'Aaah,' said Flo, 'feel that breeze. Is it usually this hot?'

'The farmers love it. It means they don't have to dry the grain. If it rains it costs them a fortune. Flo?'

'Yes.'

'Why was Hugo so cross back there?'

'Was he cross?'

'Couldn't you tell? He wasn't like Hugo at all.'

'Perhaps he thought Adam ought to have been pulling his weight, not picnicking with me. You know how it is between siblings – look at you and India-Jane.'

'I suppose. It's just that he's much grumpier lately. Maybe it's because of the farm. I heard Hugo telling Joan in the shoe shop that Adam would probably sell it and bugger off to London with you once you were married.'

Flo bent down, pretending to remove a stone from her sandal, a sudden rush of panic blitzing through her. She and Adam hadn't really discussed the future, except that they both wanted children. She'd assumed they'd always live on the farm. She realized with a shock how much the idea of Adam and the farm were linked in her mind. Was it Adam she cared most about or the lifestyle he offered? Somehow, the idea of Adam in London seemed all wrong.

'Anyway, poor Hugo. Joan says if he weren't such a decent chap he might have tried to rush to the altar before you. He really needs a nice girl, Joan says.'

'And I know where to find one. I've just decided who to ask as my maid of honour.'

'Maid of honour!' squeaked Miranda, falling about with laughter when Flo asked her if she'd do it. 'I'm not sure I'd pass as Maid of Anything. Still, as long as there's no virginity test, I'd be thrilled.'

'Great, and I've got another good idea. Why don't you call up the best man and invite him out to dinner? All in the cause of family harmony, natch.'

'Do you know,' Miranda purred, mentally rifling through her wardrobe for something demure and Maid-of-Honour-to-be-ish. 'I might just do that. By the way, how did the shoot go for the Blackmills ad?'

Flo felt a weird sensation at the mention of Blackmills, as if a cold shadow had suddenly flitted across the safe, cosy room she was sitting in at Hunting Farm, with its ripening fruit on the window-ledge and a fly buzzing lazily against the closed window. The world of London and ad agencies seemed entirely alien. 'It was fine. Actually, I rather enjoyed it. Gwyneth Paltrow, I wasn't. But I wasn't *too* appalling. At least I remembered my one line.'

'And when will we be seeing this masterpiece on our screens and hoardings?'

'To tell you the truth, I'm not really sure.'

'Why don't you find out? If it's bang up against the wedding maybe you ought to prepare Adam for having a famous wife.'

'I'll hardly be famous.'

'Want to bet?'

'Everything all right?' Aunt Prue asked a minute later, seeing Flo perched on the window seat, lost in contemplation of the garden. 'Nothing worrying you? No cold feet or anything?'

Flo braced her shoulders, chasing away her momentary worry. 'Feet warmer than toast,' she reassured. 'Though I suppose I'd better do something about getting a dress.'

'I did have a thought about that . . .' Prue hesitated.

'Tell me,' begged Flo. 'I threatened Pamela I'd get it at Oxfam, but that was just to annoy her. And I don't think I can face London and the bridal boutiques with salesgirls fussing all over me, telling me I look beautiful in tulle when really I look like a reject from *Gone With the Wind*. So what's the idea?'

'Come up to our room.'

Flo followed her aunt up the polished wood stairs with the red Turkey runner, distinctly threadbare in parts but all the more beautiful for it. Flo could distinctly remember bumping down the stairs on this carpet at the age of five or six.

Her aunt and uncle's room was on the first floor with wonderful views overlooking rolling farmland towards the distant river. Sun dappled its polished floorboards, there was a faint smell of beeswax, and outside the wide open windows a thrush was singing in the bushes.

'It's so lovely here,' Flo sighed, leaning out of the window.

'And it's thanks to you we can stay,' came her aunt's muffled reply as she delved beneath the depths of their four-poster bed. She emerged triumphantly with an enormous flower-patterned hat-box. 'I got it down from the loft yesterday, but I didn't know whether I was interfering.'

'You're the least interfering person I know,' Flo reassured her. 'So what is it? The hat you're planning to wear to the wedding? It looks big enough for the Ascot Opening Race.'

'Open it and see.'

Intrigued, Flo undid the pink ribbon that tied the box up, revealing a snowy ocean of tissue paper inside. Gingerly, feeling as if she was undoing something infinitely precious, she lifted out the liquid gold of a satin wedding gown. 'Oh my God,' Flo breathed. 'What a fabulous dress. Was it yours?'

Flo took it out and held it up against herself. Its huge train unfolded around her like molten caramel.

Prue's hands fell to her side and she tried to turn away to hide the fact that her eyes were full of tears. 'No. It was your mother's. Why don't you try it on?'

Her hands shaking, Flo undressed and slipped the satin confection gently over her head.

Prue helped her ease it down over her body and smoothed out the hem, arranging the train all round her. 'It fits exactly,' Prue whispered, studying her niece in the mirror, 'except that it's too tight over the bust on the left side.'

'They didn't call me Amazon for nothing.' Flo's eyes were fixed on her aunt's.

'You look beautiful.' The words sounded as if they'd been wrung out of her, letter by painful letter. 'Flora, she'd have been so proud of you.'

Flo turned and, forgetting the dress, clung to her aunt for dear life. 'I know.'

'Have you heard from your father yet?'

Flo stiffened, determined not to show how much she cared. 'He won't come. Though I'm sure he'll have an excellent excuse. Still,' Flo forced herself to smile, 'I've got you and Uncle Francis and no one could ask for more than that. I'd love to wear my mother's dress. It'll make my day.'

'Here, I'll hang it up for you.' Aunt Prue produced a padded ivory silk hanger, adorned with tiny pansies. 'I couldn't resist buying this. I knew how perfect it'd be.'

She helped Flo out of the dress and hung it up. Outside there was an outbreak of furious baa-ing in the farmyard. 'I wonder if Rowley's got out. You'd better go and warn Francis before we have a rash of February lambs being born.'

When Flo had disappeared downstairs, Prue took one last look at the dress.

'Bloody Martin,' she said with sudden, uncharacteristic fury. 'Can't you see how incredibly sodding selfish you're being?'

Hugo Moreton quite enjoyed the dual aspects of his life; farming took up most of his time but he also got a kick from giving advice to investors. He was even looking forward to the upcoming business trip. Weddings had a habit of occupying every waking moment of the participants. His mother had already withdrawn under a veil of net and tulle, and Adam went round with a permanently smug smile that Hugo would have found hard to tolerate even if he hadn't been jealous.

Besides, after the wedding the farm would be Adam's and he would have to think about an entirely different future of his own. One without farming. He could, of course, take on the tenancy of another farm – with farming doing so badly there were plenty available – but it didn't feel the same to flog your guts out if the land didn't actually belong to you.

There was a message on his machine from Miranda, informing him she was to be the Maid of Honour and that there were things they needed to talk about. Why didn't they meet over dinner?

His hand hesitated inches from the phone, before he willed himself to make the call. Flora Parker was in love with his brother and in less than two months would be Adam's wife. It was time he forgot about her and started to find a life of his own.

Miranda was already waiting for him the next night at the restaurant she'd suggested, installed confidently on a raspberry-coloured banquette, nursing a raspberry-coloured cocktail. He wondered if this were for deliberate effect.

'I'd go for a purple drink next time, or at a pinch orange – I think the contrast would work for you.' He smiled teasingly as he slid in next to her.

For a good half-second Miranda looked mutinous, before offering him one of her flirtatious grins. 'You found me out.' She summoned the waiter to order his drink. 'Maybe you aren't all so out of touch in the country.'

Hugo smiled slowly. 'That depends what with. There are some things we know more about than you do.'

Miranda laughed her dirtiest laugh. 'I'll bet you do. You know, I think this best man and bridesmaid thing has definite possibilities. As a matter of fact, I bought myself a little book on wedding etiquette.' She reached into her bag and extracted a slim volume decorated garishly with a three-tiered cake, two gold rings and a plastic bride and groom. 'And it says here that one of the best man's vital duties is to sleep with the bridesmaids.'

'Fine,' Hugo responded, his tone deadpan. 'But aren't Mattie and India-Jane a little young?'

Forgetting all her Londoner's sophistication, Miranda picked up the slice of orange adorning the side of her glass and threw it at him.

'I'll make you pay for that,' she said boldly. 'Later on.'

'Tell me,' he responded, raising his glass to his lips, 'is that a threat or a promise?'

Chapter 16

'How about these ivory ones with the feathers on the front?' Joan brandished the wedding shoe catalogue she'd just obtained for Flo, 'or these glorious things with little beads on? Even Cinderella wouldn't have lost a shoe if she'd had these on.'

Joan's two assistants tried to sneak a look and were sent off to tidy the stockroom. Fortunately, for a Thursday morning in August, the shop was quiet and Joan was able to devote herself to Flo's needs with undivided passion. In all her thirty years in Witch Beauchamp she'd never shod a bride before. Not even, she admitted with a sigh, herself.

Flo shook her head. 'I'll leave the feathers to the birds, but I really like the plain satin mules.'

'What do *you* think, Kingsley? Shouldn't she go for the feathers? *I* would if I were a bride.'

'Ah,' Kingsley teased, 'but then nobody's asked you, have they? Anyway,' he added in the tones of a eunuch being consulted on advanced sexual technique, 'why should I have an opinion about wedding shoes?'

'Because the whole thing's your blessed fault, that's why.'

Kingsley retreated behind the new season's Nike brochure. 'Besides, I've got to decide what I'm wearing on my own feet.'

'And who's going to notice, I'd like to know, apart from Flo's dog and she'll probably wee on you.'

'All right, if you twist my arm, I suppose the ones with the feathers are rather fetching.'

'There you are,' Joan crowed, delighted.

'All right,' Flo caved in, 'the feathers it is. I'd quite like one of those feathered head-dresses as a matter of fact.'

'What,' asked Uncle Kingsley in alarm, 'like Hiawatha?'

'She means the kind that are a bit like a hairband with a couple of ostrich plumes attached, don't you Flo?'

'Something like that,' Flo agreed.

'They've got some lovely ones in the hat shop in Salisbury,' confided Joan.

'So you've been shopping as well, have you?' Kingsley quizzed Joan.

'Had to get my outfit too, you know.'

'What's it like?' demanded Kingsley. 'Not mutton dressed as lamb, I hope?'

'It's a coat-dress,' one of Joan's assistants chipped in, having returned from the stockroom only to ignore the customer who was trying to attract her attention.

'In fuchsia silk,' added the other.

'With a matching pillbox hat.'

'And matching shoes.'

'Sounds very pink,' winced Kingsley.

'At least I won't look like a gentleman of the road, like some people I could mention.'

'Being a true gentleman comes from within,' Kingsley insisted disdainfully.

'Then you'll fall short there too,' laughed Joan.

'Come on, Flora Parker, let me give you a lift home and take you away from all these menopausal harpies,' said Kingsley.

'Less of the menopausal,' Joan insisted tetchily. 'I had the change of life years ago. And don't tell me it suits me.'

'It doesn't.'

'Get out of my shop,' Joan insisted, shooing him to the door, smiling tenderly.

'I'm your landlord, I'll kindly remind you,' Kingsley tried to summon up his dignity.

'Then I'd better serve some customers to pay your extortionate rent.'

'Really,' Kingsley muttered with exasperated affection as he left, 'that woman gets worse and worse.' But when Flo glanced across at him, she saw he was smiling.

When Uncle Kingsley dropped her off she found Hunting Farm in complete chaos, getting ready for its official grand opening in two weeks' time.

Vee had turned out to have an unexpected flair in the decoration of tea-rooms, and had taken the basic breeze-block structure Adam and Flo had built and transformed it with white paint, green shutters and a green front door.

But the real surprise was how she'd decorated the inside. What had been a chilly space with bare walls and a concrete floor was now a lovely Shaker-style interior.

Instead of the chintz-on-chintz look that tea-shops usually favoured, with dried flowers that looked as if they'd been picked in the First World War adorning every table and wheelback chairs in cheap veneered wood, Vee had opted for a simple duck-egg blue colour-scheme with scrubbed pine furniture and occasional sculptures made of driftwood. The centrepiece was a glorious heron which reminded Flo of the one she watched down by the river. On each table there were handpicked bunches of garden flowers, each tied with duck-egg blue ribbon.

'It's fantastic, Vee,' Flo congratulated warmly, 'you really have a gift for this.'

Vee looked like a parrot being given a prize for elocution.

'It does look quite nice,' she conceded with mock modesty.

No one could accuse life in the country of being dull. The opening of the Sheep Centre followed by the wedding was more than enough excitement for the moment.

But Flo was wrong about that. She'd hardly walked into the farmhouse than Prue handed her the phone. 'Someone called Buzz. Very urgent, apparently.'

Flo carried the phone out into the sunny farmyard. 'Buzz, hello, how's it all going?'

'Brilliantly.' Buzz's high-energy tones lit up the wires between London and Maiden Moreton. 'In fact, so good we've decided to bring the schedule forward and re-launch this week. Blackmills's PR people have booked the Passion Cafe for Thursday. You will be there, won't you?'

'Well, I . . .' Flo could think of a thousand places she'd rather be than London with a bunch of journalists.

'Come on, Flora, it's in the contract. Think of all that lovely money. There may be press to do, too. Just close your eyes and remember all those shaggy sheep you've got to pay for. You're going to be hot news.'

Flo's heart sank. She just wanted to immerse herself in a healthy obsession with bridal magazines and place settings. 'And when will the TV ad be going out?'

'From this week too.'

'Bloody hell.'

'I must say, Flora Parker,' Buzz's acerbic tones held an edge of frustration, 'for an It girl you're a very reluctant celebrity.'

'An ex-It girl who's about to become a country wife.'

'And does your lucky fiancé know what's round the corner?'

'I'm not sure he realises what's involved,' Flo admitted.

'Then I think you'd better tell him, don't you?'

Buzz, of course, was absolutely right. Flo decided to get it over with and tell him now.

'Flora!' Pamela descended on her as if she were bearing manna in the desert, 'just the person I wanted. Do you think we want a pink and blue country garden look for the flowers or just stick to traditional white?'

Flo had a brainwave. 'Why don't you talk to Veronica?'

'Veronica?'

'She's over at the new tea-room for the Sheep Centre. It looks completely brilliant. She's got a real feel for decoration.'

Pamela, in her usual fashion, completely ignored this suggestion. Advice from Veronica was clearly not on her agenda. 'You don't think the pink and blue? Delphiniums will be so lovely.'

Flo took a deep breath. 'Delphiniums would be glorious. Do you know where Adam is?'

'Harvesting somewhere.'

This was brilliant. Moreton Farm was enormous.

'Here,' offered Pamela, 'try the mobile.'

In the end she found him in the middle of the big field on the other side of the ridge. He mimed that he'd be twenty minutes and she sat down on the stile watching the huge machine cut the wheat, store the grain behind it and chuck out the chaff. By the side of the field she could see rustling in the grass where the harvest mice looked for shelter from the giant monster that had chomped up their nests.

Eventually Adam jumped from the cab and called to Dickey to take over as he strode across the flattened gold of the field. It was an extraordinary image. Adam, golden haired and golden skinned, wearing only his old shorts and desert boots, framed by bright blue sky and golden chaff. It was the kind of look Calvin Klein paid millions trying to achieve. Adam possessed it naturally.

'This is a nice surprise. Don't tell me. You've had enough of wedding plans and want to elope this afternoon?'

Flo laughed. 'If only. No, actually I'm enjoying it all more than I expected. It's just that I've got to go to London this week. The whiskey commercial I made is about to be launched. I might have to do some interviews. The advertising agency's expecting a lot of interest. I'm really sorry about the timing.'

Adam was supremely unperturbed. Flo didn't know whether it was because his horizons stopped at Witch Beauchamp, or he genuinely didn't mind. Either way it was a huge relief.

The next question was what to wear. In the end she decided that the Jasper Conran outfit she'd been allowed to keep after the shoot would be ideal. It would also mean she wouldn't have to shop. Shoes would be a problem since she'd lived in gum boots and trainers lately. Then she remembered a pair of hot pink Manolo Blahniks she'd slipped into her suitcase. They'd cost too much to throw away. Now they could earn their keep. Fantastic! Add a raspberry wrap and it might even look as if she'd taken endless trouble. How to be a celebrity without spending a penny.

Adam took a break from the combine to drop her at the station on the morning of the launch. 'Wow!' he commented as he picked her up. 'How many girls am I marrying? You look completely different.'

'Don't worry, I'll be back to normal soon.'

'No, I like it. I won't need other girls, will I, since I won't know which Flora I'm coming home to.'

Flo waved goodbye as the train drew out of Witch Beauchamp. The sun was shining in a Delft-blue sky and she was off to launch a campaign she was starring in, only weeks before her wedding. All in all, she had a hell of a lot to be grateful for.

After he'd waved Flo goodbye, Adam headed back to the car, which he'd left open as they ran for the train.

'Hello Adam.' Donna was draped provocatively across the passenger seat. 'What brings you into town?'

Adam reddened. 'I've just seen Flo off. She's starring in some commercial for whiskey.'

'Is she now?' Donna pulled up her already short skirt and uncrossed her rather plump legs. There was a tearing noise as sweaty skin separated from sweaty skin. Adam groaned.

'So then, Adam,' Donna's voice was pure invitation, spiced with deliberate devilment, 'how are you going to cope with having a wife who's more successful than you are?'

The Passion Cafe was the newest of London's trendy haunts. The name, it struck Flo, was curiously unsuitable. It had an asexual minimalist air, with waitresses dressed in black combats and black vests carrying canapés on corrugated iron trays decorated with what looked like plumbing supplies.

It was funny, Flo thought, how for so many years she'd loved being the centre of attention, for ever doing something even wilder and more outrageous, and now she absolutely hated it. It was a trial to keep smiling and answering question after question about her change of image, and the worst thing was that Buzz had let slip to the PRs about the wedding. Now all of the journalists wanted to know about Adam. She told them as little as she possibly could and kept changing the subject to Blackmills Whiskey, which made the Blackmills people adore her and the journalists roll their eyes in boredom.

'Would you say,' asked one persistently, 'that the advertisement is another example of Girlpower?'

Flo tried not to laugh. 'Absolutely not,' she shook her head vehemently, realizing that if she played them at their own game they'd let her escape sooner. 'What I'd say,' she said with sudden intensity borne of wanting to get away, 'is that it's more important than that. It's an example of an entirely new genre: Post-Girlpower.'

That had them all scribbling furiously. Across the other side of the room Buzz treated her to an approving wink.

Flo began to enjoy herself. It was rather nice to have every word you said treated with such respect, without anyone shouting, 'The Emperor isn't wearing any clothes!'

'And how precisely,' cut in a voice from the back, 'would you define "Post-Girlpower"?'

Trying not to panic Flo searched for the questioner among the sea of faces in the crowd.

It was Miles. But she had no time to wonder how he'd got himself invited. He was doing his best to humiliate her and she had to get out of the hole he'd deliberately dug for her.

'What I mean,' Flo paused, racking her brains for any inspiration, 'what I mean is that Girlpower was all about proving something. We're better than men. The world belongs to us. What post-Girlpower is about . . .' she looked Miles straight in the eye, 'is to say, "Look, we don't have to prove anything to anyone. We're here. And we'll behave exactly the way we want. Not madonnas or whores or angels. Just us."'

Buzz led the round of applause while the Blackmills executives beamed as if they'd thought up the concept themselves. Flo found herself whisked off for another round of interviews. She scanned the room for Miles, to see if he was planning any more acts of sabotage, but he seemed to have disappeared.

And then he was at her back. 'How's Action Man? Started to bore you yet? I hope he isn't in for too much of a shock? Rather narrow-minded those country types.'

'Miles,' Flo tried to calm herself down. This was just Miles stirring. There wasn't anything he could really do to wreck her wedding. 'What the hell are you on about?'

'Wait and see. I've got a lovely surprise for your wedding present.'

Flo shivered slightly. There was nothing nice about Miles or his presents, she was sure of that.

It was an enormous relief when the launch was over and Buzz drove her to the station. 'You were fantastic. They'll all be off to their hot little word-processors with a brand new concept. Blackmills have certainly had their money's worth.'

'Did you see who it was who asked the question though?'

'Your ex-representative,' Buzz replied.

'And I noticed another thing. He was really pissed off when I didn't fall apart.'

'They always are, men like him. I wonder what the bastard's up to.'

'All I know is that he seems particularly pleased with himself.' It wasn't an encouraging thought.

When she got back she'd never been so glad to see Maiden Moreton and Adam. Thank God Adam was a million miles from the cynical manipulativeness of a Miles. She'd fallen for Adam for his sunny straightfor-wardness. Life wasn't the fraught and angst-ridden business for Adam that it was for most people. He didn't fall into hidden snake-pits full of venomous cobras because he didn't notice they were there. And she loved him for it.

'Hello, gorgeous,' she greeted him when he came to meet her, 'you don't know how lovely it is to be back.'

'Hello star, how was the smoke? Did they all worship at your feet?'

'They did actually.' She surveyed her own personal Greek god. His skin looked even yummier than usual and she couldn't resist nuzzling into his neck. To her astonishment, Adam pulled gently away, hastily doing up the top button on his shirt.

'Aren't you sweltering with your buttons like that?'

'You'd be surprised,' Adam insisted, 'how sharp the breeze can be up on the top meadow.'

'Right,' Flo repeated, 'I suppose it is quite high.' She looked out of the car window at the heat haze that hung over the countryside, distorting every horizon so that it looked like a Saharan mirage. On the road outside the car tyres squelched in the melting tarmac.

When Adam dropped her off at Hunting Farm the house was empty. Everyone must be outside preparing for the grand opening in a few days' time. The whole family had been living and breathing sheep for days. Soon they'd know if all their efforts had paid off.

She stepped over the mat, littered with post. A lot of the letters looked like replies to their wedding invitation. She picked them up and shuffled through the pile. The last was a smart white typed envelope with a US postmark.

Flo's heart somersaulted and her palms began to sweat as she slid her aunt's paper-opener carefully under the flap, terrified to see what was inside.

It was a formal letter from her father's secretary telling her that he was away on business at present but she had forwarded the invitation on.

Flo sat down heavily on the bottom of the stairs. Why, after all these years of disappointment, did she let herself care so much?

The ringing of the phone only a few feet away rescued her from the edge of tears.

'Flo! I can't get away from you!' It was Miranda. 'Honestly, everywhere I go, there you are. You're even at my local cinema. It must be so exciting.'

'Sorry, Miranda,' her mind was still focused on that short impersonal note from the States. 'What are you on about?'

'Your picture! It's everywhere!'

'Is it? They had a launch for it and do you know who pitched up and asked a bastard of a question? Miles.'

'He's probably still annoyed with you for cutting him out of the deal.'

'I cut him out because I can't stand him and I don't trust him. Besides, I gave him a share of the money.'

'I expect he'll get over it,' Miranda tried to reassure her. 'I mean, what can he really do to hurt you, after all? But look, that isn't really why I rang. I rang to say thanks a zillion.' Flo could hear her friend fizzing like an Alka Seltzer.

'What for?'

'For pushing Hugo in my direction. It finally happened.'

'What finally happened?'

Miranda became uncharacteristically coy. 'You know.'

'You mean you and Hugo went to bed together?'

'You don't have to tell the whole of Westshire. Yes. We did. And it was fantastic. He's a real dark horse. What that man can do with his . . .'

'Miranda,' Flo interrupted, feeling the sudden need to cover her ears, 'Let's just leave it to the imagination, shall we?'

'Speaking of which,' Miranda sounded disgustingly fulfilled, 'he's got plenty of that too.'

'I'm very happy for you. Now, I've got to go and muck out some sheep.'

'Oh.' Miranda sounded disappointed. 'So you don't want any more gory details?'

'Not just at the moment thanks.'

'But you're not jealous?'

Flo finally let her exasperation show. 'Why on earth should I be jealous? I'm getting married to his brother in four weeks' time.'

'Well, that's all right then. I'll save the best bit till I see you in person.'

'I'll live for the moment.'

Flo shrugged and pulled on her gum boots to go in search of the others. She'd just been told so much about Hugo Moreton's unexpected sexual prowess that it was hard to imagine what the best bit might be.

Chapter 17

'I declare the Hunting Farm Rare Breeds Sheep Centre duly open!'

Flo cut the baby pink ribbon attached to two surprisingly patient Dorset Longhorns, while the crowd of assorted locals, school children and Witch Beauchamp worthies clapped loudly.

Flo hadn't been sure she was the right person to do it, but Aunt Prue had insisted. She was the nearest thing they had to a celebrity.

'Besides, you're fairy godmother to these beasts. If it weren't for you they'd all be best end of neck by now.'

Flo smiled at the gloriously pastoral scene in front of her. Adam and Hugo were giving tractor rides in the paddock to twenty children at a time, all packed into the trailer which they'd covered in green crêpe paper for the occasion. Alf had a flower and plant stall, mostly pinched, Flo suspected, from Aunt Prue or Uncle Kingsley's gardens, but for such a good cause who cared? Prue had a row of children milking one of the ancient ewes, who seemed as tolerant of twenty pairs of small hands as she had been of her countless lambs butting at her over the years. Vee was showing another interested gaggle how to make sheep's cheese.

'Disgusting muck,' commented one surly-looking man.

'Stick to cheddar then,' quipped back Vee, 'thick, bland and tasteless – just like you!'

But the surprising *pièce de résistance* was Ivy sitting on the steps of the shepherd's hut spinning spellbinding tales of how her father had been a shepherd and lived in a hut just like this one each winter.

'He started working for the squire when he were sixteen, looked after five hundred sheep. He didn't need no schooling. Just had to be able to carry six hurdles on his back.' She pointed to the heavy panels of woven twigs. 'They used hurdles for everything then, making sheep pens and lambing pens. He stayed the whole winter in that hut, even come snow six feet high. He tied sacks round hisself to keep warm, everyone did that, rubbed goosegrease on his chest, and waited till lambing were finished.'

Wide-eyed, the children took in this stark contrast to their own comfortably central-heated, fitted-carpet existence.

'Didn't he pong an awful lot?' asked one doubtfully.

'He ponged a lot anyway,' Ivy replied to general mirth. 'But then everyone ponged then. No bathrooms in those days. No inside lavvies. Most people hummed a bit. The clean ones were the unfortunate ones, acause they noticed!'

Flo glanced round. To her amazement Donna, of all

people, stood waiting with a posse of twenty or so children, her row of ear piercings glinting in the morning sun like the war jewels of a post-modern Amazon princess.

'Hello, Donna. I didn't expect to see you here.' Flo tried to sound more welcoming, but she'd never liked the girl since the incident over Uncle Francis's drinking.

'Just helping out with the kiddies for the day.'

Donna certainly didn't look like a kindergarten teacher with her nose studs and a diamond winking in her belly button.

Donna treated Flo to an appraising stare. 'You've got the same job as me these days, I hear. Flogging booze. Though I bet you get paid better for it.'

For some ridiculous reason Flo wanted to say she'd given the money to the Sheep Centre, but why should she feel so defensive? It was nothing to do with Donna anyway.

'Nice work if you can get it,' Donna taunted.

Flo knew she should rise above this, but couldn't help herself. 'Yes. And I was damn good at it too. Excuse me, I think my aunt may need some help with the milking.'

Flo could feel the power of Donna's dislike pursue her across the farmyard. Three hundred years ago the girl would have made a highly sought-after witch. Wringing chickens' necks for pleasure and putting curses on people would have been right up her street. On the other hand, if she'd managed to get an education, instead of working in a pub, she'd probably be running a multinational company by now.

The raffle was drawn, the tea was over, and it was

time for the highlight of the afternoon, Uncle Francis's sheepshearing demonstration. Sixty children sat in neat rows watching the glinting flash of his shearing tool, a lethal piece of metal that looked like flattened-out tongs but was as sharp as a razor.

'Please miss, what are those two sheep in there doing?' prompted an inquisitive six-year-old.

Rowley, who could always be relied on to let the side down, was attempting one last bid for sexual gratification, undeterred by the fact that his companion was (a) entirely disinterested and (b) male.

'They're just having a cuddle,' attempted the village schoolmistress discouragingly.

'No, they're not,' corrected a piping voice from the front row. 'They're having a shag. Is it true, miss,' demanded the voice, which probably belonged to a relation of Donna's, 'that farmers shag their sheep?'

There was a sharp intake of breath from their teacher.

'Only the pretty ones,' answered Donna before the schoolmistress had a chance to change the subject.

Eager to get away from Donna, Flo went to look for Adam at the tractor rides but there was no sign of him. Alf and Dickey had taken over, with Ivy standing by handing out advice.

'Have you seen Mr Moreton anywhere, Ivy?'

Ivy gave her a strange look, as if she didn't want to know, then shrugged. 'I did see 'im round by duckpond earlier.'

Flo followed in the direction Ivy had indicated. As she approached she could hear a child howling piteously, then, just as suddenly, the sound stopped.

Round the corner, in the part of the farmyard nearest the pond, Hugo Moreton sat on the wall with a small child, pretending to extract coins from its ears. The child, mesmerized by its own capacities as a mini-mint, sat in silent amazement.

'He was beside himself because he dropped his money in the pond. I'm showing him how he can make his own.' For the second time in a week Flo was taken aback by the gentleness of Hugo's manner.

She felt almost guilty asking if he'd seen Adam.

Hugo's reaction reminded her of Ivy's. There was a pause before he replied. 'Sorry. Haven't seen him for a while now. Perhaps he's in the tea-room.'

Together they walked back, the little boy between them, holding on to both their hands. The sudden intimacy of the moment struck them both. They looked, for all the world, like parents. A shy smile passed between them.

'There you are Paul!' Donna scolded the little boy when she caught sight of him. 'I've been looking for you everywhere.'

At that moment Mattie appeared, her face crumpled up in distress. 'Dad, come and have a look, the sheep in the end pen's got something wrong with it.'

'Oh, dearie me,' Donna drawled as they all rushed to see. 'I hope it ain't scrapie.' She leaned down conspiratorially. 'Now, children, listen to me, don't tell any of your parents that the sheep's not well, will you? We wouldn't want them to have to worry about you lot coming into contact with something nasty.'

You bitch, thought Flo furiously, instantly

understanding Donna's tactics. This was the one way she could be sure they *would* tell their parents.

'What's the matter?' Aunt Prue abandoned her milking and ran across the farmyard to join them. 'Is one of the sheep ill?' She leaned over the edge of the pen. The sheep was lying on its side in the clean straw, its stomach distended, obviously struggling for breath.

'It's nothing I recognize,' Uncle Francis said gravely. 'But I think we ought to call the vet.'

The drama, not to mention the live sex show, over, the schoolchildren filed away, loaded down with balloons, prizes, plants, and some of them with faces painted by Vee in the form of different farm animals.

'It's been a big success,' Flo smiled at her aunt.

'Except for that sheep,' Prue replied anxiously.

Donna and her little party were almost the last to leave. It struck Flo that the wretched girl was waiting for something. And then she saw what. Adam and Hugo were removing the last of the crêpe paper from the trailer.

'Hello, Adam.' Donna leaned boldly against the farmyard gate. 'You look very buttoned-up in that shirt. Why don't you let a little sunshine on your skin then?'

She reached up as if to undo his top button.

Adam turned abruptly away just as he had the other day when Flo had asked the same question.

Snowy chose that moment to start barking fiercely so Flo missed the look of guilty complicity that passed between them.

But Hugo didn't.

'Miranda!' Flo yelled at the vision of urban inappropriateness walking towards them through the farmyard. No one would guess that Miranda, in her delicate flower-buttoned cardigan, flirty pink silk skirt and pink ponyskin mules, had intended to visit the opening of a Sheep Centre, but this was in fact the case. 'What on earth are you doing here?'

'Hugo told me about it, and I know how much it means to you, so I thought I'd come along. Have I missed all the fun?'

If Flo knew her friend, Miranda had probably fine-tuned her arrival to miss all the fun deliberately.

'Sadly, you have. Though we do have a case of a sheep with the shits we'd welcome your advice on, as a farmer's daughter.'

Miranda looked appalled. 'Is that a tea-room over there?' she enquired, managing to put her pink ponyksin mule in the one puddle in the entire farmyard. 'Oh, dear, I've got my shoes all wet. Could I lean on you, Hugo?'

Hugo, who knew as well as Flo that underneath all this girly performance Miranda was steelier than Mrs Thatcher, proffered his arm.

Watching them laugh together as they went in search of one of Ivy's fruit scones, Flo tried not to think about Miranda's bedroom revelations. No doubt Miranda had embellished the story somewhat. She always made a mountain out of a medium-sized member.

Instead Flo turned her attention to her uncle. 'So, how do you think it went? There were at least a hundred and fifty visitors, I'd guess. Imagine if it were like that every day!'

'One hundred and thirty actually,' he smiled, looking faintly embarrassed about the antique farmer's smock Prue had kitted him up in, 'but it was pretty good.' His face clouded over briefly. 'Except for that Southdown ewe. She seems pretty poorly. The vet's coming later.'

'Do you want to stay the night?' Flo asked Miranda when she went to find her in the tea-room. 'I'm sure Aunt Prue would be delighted.'

Her friend looked faintly embarrassed, so unusual an occurrence in Miranda that she didn't quite know how to arrange her features. 'Actually, I'm staying at Moreton House. Hugo says I ought to get to know his mother, that we'd get on like a house on fire.'

Flo blinked.

In her estimation Pamela and Miranda would get on roughly as well as Queen Elizabeth I and Mary Queen of Scots. One of them would end up minus their head. 'Fine. Presumably you're having dinner there too?'

'Why don't you and Adam join us?' Hugo suggested quickly. He looked round for his brother, but Adam had disappeared. It was no surprise, Hugo noted furiously, that Donna had too. Her small posse of schoolchildren were standing around looking bored. 'Right.' Hugo hoped Flo hadn't noticed. 'Who wants a ride back to the village on the trailer?'

They whooped with glee while Miranda pretended to look enthusiastic too, only giving herself away by the moue of distaste as she climbed on board at the thought of what any traces of farmyard manure would do to her new silk skirt.

Fortunately, when the vet arrived he decreed that the

ailing ewe had probably only a minor infection and after three days of antiobiotics she'd be as right as rain.

'Thank God for that,' breathed Uncle Francis. Flo noticed for the first time how pale and sweaty he was looking. 'That would have been all we needed, when we've opened up officially at last.'

'Don't worry,' Flo reassured, trying to forget the ominous gleam in Donna's eye. 'I'm sure everything's going to be fine. Now, I'd better go and change out of these mucky jeans. I'm going over to Moreton House to join them for dinner and I'm not sure Pamela would go for the smell of sheep shit.'

Watching Miranda and Pamela pretend to get on with each other that night, Flo found, was better than a soap opera.

Pamela, having declared how much she liked Miranda, probably in order to annoy Flo, had to stick with it, even though she clearly found Miranda's loud laughter and habit of confessing all her indiscretions hard to stomach. Once or twice, Flo noticed Hugo smiling to himself as his mother pretended to laugh at one of Miranda's more outrageous revelations.

'Tell you what, Flo,' Miranda hissed to her, as they both showed willing by carrying dirty plates to the kitchen, 'she's not nearly such an old bat as you said.'

A cough behind them signalled that Pamela had joined them. So much for winning over Adam's tricky mother.

Adam, by contrast, was unusually quiet.

'Are you all right, darling?' Pamela asked, in a tone that would have made Oedipus blush.

'You'll have a lot to live up to there,' hissed Miranda. 'She sounds like she's in love with him herself.'

The next day Flo was to be in charge of the tea-room, as Veronica had an appointment. It was another glorious day. She skipped down to breakfast to find her aunt and uncle going over the day's bookings. 'Two school parties this afternoon. That makes a hundred children, plus a pensioners' outing from The Cedars. They'll head straight for the tea-room and the loo.'

'Or the loo then the tea-room in that order. Do you think we should bake some extra scones?'

'Ivy's already on the case. Two dozen plain and two dozen Ivy specials.'

'They'll *certainly* need the loo then,' said Uncle Francis.

It was fantastic to see him happy, even cracking terrible jokes. They were all laughing when the phone rang. He came back a moment later, looking whiter than Ivy's dough. 'It was the local education authority,' he said, his voice ringing through the room, 'they're cancelling the two school visits. Apparently they received a complaint from a visitor yesterday, and with all this BSE and scrapie around they can't afford to be too careful.'

Uncle Francis looked as if a truck had run over him. 'School visits were going to be our mainstay,' he said bitterly.

'Don't worry,' Flo tried to cheer her aunt and uncle up, 'it'll blow over.' She willed herself to sound more optimistic than she felt. 'Meanwhile, we'll just have to develop something else to be our mainstay. What about concentrating on the pensioners? We could get them to tell us their memories of farm life. I could do a poster for the old people's homes. There are plenty around.'

'Flora,' her uncle smiled back at her, 'what did we do before you came to stay?'

Flora felt a gulp of emotion rising in her throat. She squeezed his hand affectionately. When the phone rang again they both stiffened.

Flo moved first. 'I'll answer it.'

It was hard to put an optimistic gloss on the second call. It was the warden of The Cedars. They'd had a call from a concerned visitor too.

The sense of gloom that descended on the Sheep Centre was so thick it was almost visible. Each of them, every single family member, from India-Jane to Ivy, had contributed to the mad rush of the final days before the opening. It had been a real family venture, fired by the shared sense of optimism and the sight of Francis and Prue's excitement.

It had seemed to be the perfect answer: a modest income but one that would keep them on their farm, and deliver them from the anxieties of their previous life. Her uncle hadn't even been to the pub for weeks, Flo was sure of it.

Flo spent most of the morning on the phone to various officials at the local education authority, explaining in words of one syllable that there was zero risk of a child being in contact with scrapie and the affected sheep had simply had bronchitis. It was no good. A child in the neighbouring county had fallen ill after a farm visit, so the deputy education officer explained, and the authorities were walking on eggshells at the moment.

'Oh for God's sake!' Flo remembered her own childhood visits here, mucking out cows and horses, her hands eternally filthy. 'Does that mean we have to keep three million other children wrapped in cotton wool, never allowed to see what a real farm's like?' She felt like pointing out the recent research she'd read that modern children were too clean for their own good, which was why they picked up so many infections in the first place.

The tragic thing was that she remembered the case from the newspapers. The farm involved had been sloppy in their hygiene standards, whereas after so many years dealing with the demanding milk regulations, Uncle Francis had always made sure Hunting Farm was spotless.

She had made one final desperate phone call and was debating whether it would work when Mattie and Snowy appeared. Mattie's small face was pinched with anxiety and even the little dog had stopped manically wagging her tail. It was funny, Flo realized, how she'd started seeing Snowy as Mattie's dog.

'Flo, what are we going to do? There aren't any visitors at all except Dickey, who felt so sorry for us he's just paid one pound fifty for a ticket.'

Flo put her arms round Mattie and tried to hug away the worry.

On the other side of the farmyard, Uncle Francis appeared, his cap pulled down over his eyes and his shoulders drooping.

'Just nipping into Witch Beauchamp for an hour,' he called.

Prue had followed him, a look of deepening anxiety in her eyes. She glanced at Flo and their gaze locked for a second in mutual understanding. Uncle Francis was paying a visit to The Sign of the Angel.

A vast flame of fury began to blaze in Flo. They'd all tried so hard and now it was ruined. And she knew whose door to lay the blame at. Now her uncle intended to get blind drunk and they would all be back where they started.

'I'll see you later, Mats. I've got an errand to run too,' she announced.

Who would get there first, the Beetle or Uncle Francis's ancient Land Rover? Then Flo remembered the quad bike. It could go across fields in half the time. But maybe Adam or one of the farmhands was using it. And she didn't actually know how to operate the thing.

She was out of breath from running and had a painful stitch in her side by the time she got to the barn at Moreton where the quad bike was kept. The place was deserted. Pamela must have gone off on some wedding quest and Kingsley had probably driven her.

Flo forced herself across the last few yards to the barn.

There it was. The keys were kept in a wooden box on the wall behind the bales of hay with those to the rest of the farm equipment. She sighed with relief. They were hanging up on the third hook.

Surely it was like starting a motor bike, not that she'd ever started a motor bike. Gingerly, Flo put the key in the ignition and held her breath as the powerful machine shot forward. She braked suddenly, throwing it into a skid. 'Right,' she told herself, trying not to shake, 'you've just given yourself a lesson in how *not* to ride this thing.'

The farmyard was still empty when she edged out over the nearest field towards the ridge and, beyond that, the river. Driving straight across country it should only take about ten minutes to Witch Beauchamp. She wished to God she'd paid more attention in geography lessons, so that she could recognize contours and ordnance survey signs. Then she remembered, if she stuck to the river it would take a couple of minutes longer but at least she wouldn't get lost.

She finally nosed her way, windswept and elated, into Witch Beauchamp. Thank God, there was no sign of the Land Rover.

It was early and the pub hadn't been open for long. The landlady was down at the end of the bar polishing glasses. 'Morning. What can I do for you? You don't look like an eleven o'clock drinker. You're Flora, aren't you? The girl who's getting married to Adam Moreton?' There was an unexpected sympathy in her tone.

'That's right. Actually I'm looking for someone. Could you tell me where Donna is?'

The landlady raised an eyebrow. 'In her bed, I expect.'

'No, I'm not,' corrected a voice behind her.

Donna appeared in a white vest top and cut-off shorts. Her skin was glowing like a ripe plum. Her eyes shone with triumph.

'Could I speak to Donna in private for a moment?' Flo asked evenly, though she'd have liked to strangle the girl with the studded choker she was wearing for causing so much pain.

'I'll go and see to the new barrels,' the landlady consented.

'Does your employer know you've been making anonymous calls to cause trouble for her customers?' Flo asked, in a low but furious voice. 'Because if she doesn't I'll very much enjoy telling her.'

'Maybe I won't be needing my job much longer,' Donna challenged.

Flo decided to ignore the bravado. 'Four months ago after he'd been drinking here, my uncle tried to shoot himself.'

Donna didn't flinch. 'Times are tough in farming. It happens all over.'

'Except that he was drinking solidly here for hours beforehand. You must have known how worried he was about the farm. He gave up drinking altogether when he bought the Sheep Centre. He's been busy and motivated. But now you've ruined that too.'

'Says who?' Donna challenged.

'The warden of The Cedars old people's home. He tried to ring the caller back on 1471. It was the pub's number.'

'Right, Donna,' the landlady's voice fizzed threateningly out of the gloom like the touchpaper on a lethal firework. 'You had better go up to your room and stay there till I come and talk to you. How dare you implicate us in your nasty doings?'

Before Donna could answer the door to the snug opened and Uncle Francis appeared.

Flo stepped back into the darkness of the scullery next to the bar, praying he hadn't seen her.

'Morning, Mr Rawlings,' the landlady said with deceptive brightness.

At the sight of the two women Uncle Francis looked slightly abashed. 'Good morning. I'd like a pint of Guinness please, Mrs Simms, and a large whiskey chaser.'

'I'm awfully sorry, Mr Rawlings,' replied the landlady, avoiding Donna's eye. 'But I'm afraid we're closed today. We've been having problems with our staff. You just can't get them these days, can you?'

'Thanks a million, Mrs Simms,' Flo breathed when her uncle had left. 'At least there aren't any other pubs in Witch Beauchamp.'

'If I was you,' Mrs Simms advised, 'I'd nip over to Victoria Wine and make sure he doesn't get himself a take-away. I recognize the signs.'

Flo smiled her thanks and dashed out the side entrance. If she remembered rightly there was a back alley, known in Westshire as a 'wynd', that came out near the off-licence.

This time she was too late. Uncle Francis was already in the shop.

Fortunately there was a dithery old dear in front of them, counting out the pennies for her bottle of sweet sherry.

'Hello, Uncle Francis,' Flo greeted him with cheerfulness she didn't feel, 'fancy seeing you here. I just popped in for a nice bottle of wine for dinner tonight. I thought we could all do with cheering up.'

Her uncle looked at her as if she were an avenging angel wielding a fiery sword, sent down expressly by the Lord to keep him from the one thing he needed.

'And did I tell you?' Flo added brightly. 'I think I've found an independent expert who'll come and do a report we can send to the local education committee.'

'Flora Parker,' her uncle's gaunt, weatherbeaten face softened into a smile of unexpected tenderness, 'how come, every time I'm about to do something bloody stupid, there you are, standing next to me?'

'Search me,' smiled Flora, suspecting he'd guessed about the unscheduled pub closure. 'Now, shall we get back and book in that expert?'

Now that things were looking up, at least a little, at the Sheep Centre, Flo could begin to think more about her wedding.

'What do you want to say in these vows of ours?' she asked Adam next morning, wrapping herself in a sheet to protect her modesty. They were in Adam's bedroom, fortunately situated over the stable block and therefore out of ear-shot of Pamela and the rest of the family. Adam, who had no such compunction about being naked, was sprawled on top of the covers next to her. At least he'd stopped going round in buttoned-up shirts and was back to normal.

He leaned down and blew in her ear. 'I always liked the bit about "With my body I thee worship".'

Flo swatted him playfully. 'You would. But do you want the Book of Common Prayer version or something up to date?'

'God no!' Adam looked appalled. 'Give me a few thee's and thou's any day. This isn't a shopping list in Tesco's we're going to recite.'

'Without the obey, though.'

Adam sat up doggy-fashion. 'But I want to obey.'

'Well, I don't.' She pushed him over, and as he fell he pulled her down with him.

'Okay, no obeying,' Adam conceded. 'But I would like to plight my troth, if that's all right with you.'

Flo grinned. 'You can plight your troth with me any time you fancy.'

The sound of Pamela calling to them put a sudden end to any unofficial troth-plighting.

'Hell, it's Ma. I'm going to sneak out the side way before she gives me some appalling task or other.'

'I'd better go back to the guest room.' Flo had been allocated a room of her own for the nights she stayed over at Moreton House. Pamela knew Flo didn't stay in it but pretended she did. Honour was thus satisfied all round.

Unfortunately, neither of them had remembered that this was the day the vicar was coming to talk to them about the important step they were on the point of making.

'Where *is* Adam?' Pamela demanded crossly when Flo appeared from the guest room. 'The vicar will be here in ten minutes. Doesn't he realize he's getting married in three weeks and you still haven't agreed on your vows or any of the readings?'

'We have, as a matter of fact. We want to stick to the traditional vows, but without the obey bit.'

'What about scripture readings?'

'I don't think choosing extracts from the Bible is Adam's strong point,' Hugo pointed out. 'He only used to read the racy bits at school. You don't fancy Susannah and the Elders or the chap who lay with the wrong sister, do you?'

Miranda giggled.

'Well, you'd better go and fetch him, Hugo. The vicar's a very busy man.'

'And we're not?' Hugo replied caustically. 'All right, I'll go and get him.'

'You're in the dog-house,' he informed Adam when he eventually tracked him down. 'The vicar's due to discuss the service.'

Adam said nothing as they walked back across the fields. The heat of August had waned and there was already a sense of autumn in the air.

'You are all right, aren't you?' Hugo asked sharply after they'd been walking for several minutes in silence.

'Why shouldn't I be?'

'You don't seem exactly ecstatic, that's all, for a bride-groom-to-be. You could still change your mind, you know.'

'And lose the farm?'

For a split second Adam thought his brother might hit him.

'Anyway, why should I change my mind?'

Hugo fixed him with a furious gaze. 'Maybe I should ask the barmaid at the Angel that.'

Adam retaliated, his eyes glinting with answering anger.

'What's any of it got to do with you?'

'I like Flora. She's had a tough life despite her glamour girl image. She's brave and fun and she deserves better than to be screwed around by you. If you aren't a hundred per cent committed, get out now.'

'You always were holier than thou. Just because you went to bloody college.'

'You could have if you'd wanted,' Hugo snapped back.

'And who would have run the farm? Someone needed to be hands on while you were poncing away being a student. Anyway, if you think so much of Flora, why didn't you go after her?'

'Because, like ninety-nine per cent of womankind, God help them, it's *you* she fancies. But if you go into this just to get your hands on the farm, I'll bloody kill you.'

'It's not just for the farm,' Adam insisted. 'I like her too. It's just that . . .'

'It's just that you're a boy who can't say no, who wants all the candies in the sweet shop. Grow up, Adam. Or give up on this wedding idea now.'

'It's too late. You'll just have to stand up on the day and object.'

'How would that help anyone?' Hugo demanded. They'd arrived at the gate to the farmyard. 'Look, you'd better go and see the bloody vicar. I'll stay out here.'

Adam leaped over the gate and strolled, whistling, towards the house. If only he weren't so good-looking, Hugo thought bitterly, he wouldn't get away with the way he behaved. Beauty was such a powerful thing and yet it didn't bring happiness, especially for people who fell for it in others.

As he went in the front door of the farmhouse, Adam noticed a handwritten parcel addressed to him. Maybe it was an early wedding present. He was puzzled to find it was a men's magazine called *Upfront*. He was about to put it down and flick through it later when he noticed the headline and a small photograph of Flo.

'There you are Adam!' Pamela fussed, noticing him standing in the porch. 'The vicar's here. He's been waiting ten minutes already.'

But Adam didn't hear her. He was too busy tearing off the transparent wrapper and flicking through the pages.

'Really, Adam,' complained his mother, 'this is hardly the time . . .'

'For Christ's sake, Flo,' Adam demanded, ignoring his mother and the vicar, 'what the bloody hell possessed you to do this?'

There, across a double page spread under the heading The Blackmills Babe as You've Never Seen Her, was a close up of Flo, entirely naked, soaping herself in the shower.

'Oh my God,' Flo whispered, her heart pounding so hard it hurt, 'that was what Miles was talking about.'

'Good heavens,' Pamela stuttered.

'I think I'd better go,' offered the vicar. 'Another time, perhaps . . .'

'Bloody Miles.' Flo had to fight back the tears of humiliation. 'I *knew* he was up to something. Adam, I'm really, really sorry. I had absolutely no idea this photograph was being taken.'

All eyes in the room were fixed on Adam. But Adam did the unexpected. Instead of ranting and raving he put his arms round her. 'Don't worry. As you say, you didn't know the photograph was being taken.' He took the magazine and chucked it, with perfect aim, into the wastepaper basket. 'Now, vicar, shall we go through the order of service?'

Half an hour later, after the vicar had disappeared, Flo made her excuses and ran back to Hunting Farm. She desperately needed some time to herself in the safety of her uncle and aunt's home.

'What did you make of that?' Miranda whispered to Hugo as she left.

'I haven't the slightest idea,' Hugo confessed.

It was the truth. If Adam had any doubts about going ahead, surely here was the perfect excuse to cancel the wedding? No one would even blame him. He couldn't want the farm so much that he'd put up with any humiliation? Or maybe this new-found tolerance was a sign of how he intended to conduct his married life. With both of them doing exactly what they wanted, with whomever they wanted. Hugo shivered at the thought. He would lay odds that that wasn't the kind of marriage Flo wanted.

'Kingsley,' Pamela commanded, still reeling, when her brother returned from his latest spree in Witch Beauchamp, 'fetch me that magazine from the waste-bin.'

Pamela leafed through until she found the offending page. 'I don't understand my son. His fiancée appears in a lurid magazine with no clothes on just before their wedding day. If it were me, I'd call the whole thing off. But what does he do? He hardly reacts at all. What possible explanation, Kingsley, can you offer for that?'

Kingsley studied the page of the magazine with great attention. 'Well, she does have very nice . . .'

'*Kingsley!*' erupted his sister furiously, 'give me that copy of the magazine. *Now!*'

'I think I'd better go after Flo and see if she's all right,' Miranda offered.

Miranda found Flo sitting in the farmhouse garden on the swinging chair.

'Are you all right, Flo?' she asked gently.

'*Bloody Miles!*' Flo muttered, breaking a stick she'd picked up from the grass. 'Bloody, sodding Miles!'

'Oh dear,' commented India-Jane, who had come to see what all the commotion was about. 'Poor Vee. She's decided she's in love with him. She always was a bad picker. I'd rise above it if I were you,' India offered with all the accumulated wisdom of her ten years. 'After all, there are worse things than taking your clothes off.'

'Name them.'

'Dropping mustard gas, bombing Dresden.' India had just been doing the World Wars in History.

'I suppose on that scale it's small potatoes, but it was still an invasion of my privacy. Not to mention probably illegal. And it could have wrecked my wedding.'

'And Adam's,' Mattie pointed out. 'Everyone thinks Adam's just a pretty face, but he's kind too. Of all the grown-ups it's Adam who always comes and asks me to go and help him on the farm. And, let's face it, he can't really need my help, can he? He's just being nice.'

Flo was touched by this reminder of Adam's small acts of kindness to the child everyone else overlooked.

When they had a family of their own, he would be a great father.

'I know,' agreed Flo warmly, 'and he's been terrific over this business of the magazine. Some men would have broken it all off.'

'Mmmm,' agreed Miranda, 'I wonder why he didn't.'

Chapter 18

Flo angrily broke the head off a Japanese anemone and threw the delicate petals on the lawn. How had Miles got away with this? Surely reputable magazines couldn't print candid photographs without the subject's permission?

She'd have to get in touch with the magazine and find out how they'd got it. She certainly wasn't going back to retrieve it from Moreton House and she was damned if she'd buy one. Hugo, she remembered, had a copy of the *Press Directory* in his office, which would list the magazine's details. She could go now and have a look. She just hoped Hugo wouldn't be there, and that he didn't keep the door locked.

'I'll see you later, Miranda. There's something I need to do.'

'All right.' The one thing Miranda hated about country life was that people always seemed to have something to do. They never just lay around on rugs or stayed in bed all morning.

Luckily for Flo, Hugo hadn't locked his office. She sat

at his desk and leafed though the *Mims Press Directory* until she found *Upfront*. It was very new, and the name of the editor was unfamiliar. She wrote the number down anyway.

'Would you mind telling me what you're doing in here?' She looked up to find Hugo standing furiously over her. 'You may not respect your own property or your body . . .'

'*How dare you!*' Flo's voice was cold as polished steel.

But Hugo wasn't listening. 'You just can't resist it, can you? Taking your clothes off. Couldn't you make it as a proper model, that you had to resort to this?'

'How dare you disapprove of me when you don't know anything about it. As a matter of fact, I didn't know that photograph was being taken. I'm trying to work out what I can do about it.'

She could see he wasn't convinced. She stood up, wishing there were something heavy she could throw at him. All she had was the press directory. It would have to do. She lobbed it at him just as Mattie arrived to look for her.

For once, Flo didn't stop to greet the child but ran past her. 'What on earth's the matter with Flo?'

Hugo looked shifty. 'I simply voiced my disapproval that she should appear naked in a magazine when she's about to marry Adam.'

'If she did,' Mattie defended hotly, 'then she probably did it for us. She's paying for the Sheep Centre with the money she's making from the advert. Every single penny came from Flo. You should be ashamed of yourself, Hugo Moreton. Flo is a good person and if you can't see that, you're the one with the problem!' Mattie picked up the press directory and threw it back at him. 'Maybe you'd better ask yourself why you're quite so angry, Hugo. Is it really on behalf of Adam? Or are you the one who really minds the most?'

This time he caught the press directory and put it down. It fell open at the page Flo had been consulting. *Upfront* magazine was listed in one corner.

Flo had been telling the truth.

A wave of guilt lashed over Hugo. Who the fuck did he think he was, passing judgement on Flo without even knowing the story?

Mattie was right. He was jealous.

He, who had always prided himself on his liberal principles, hated and loathed the thought of thousands of punters buying *Upfront* magazine and drooling over Flo's body.

Flo obviously wanted to know who was behind this. The one thing he could do, to apologize to her, was to find out.

He wrote down the address of *Upfront*. He had a business meeting in London tomorrow and afterwards he would make a point of calling on them. Maybe then she'd forgive him.

Hugo found the offices easily enough the next day. They were tucked away in Soho, above a Chinese restaurant in a small street near Chinatown. Even though the magazine looked glossy, the enterprise was clearly run on a shoestring.

Hugo rang the bell and waited, feeling like a punter

about to be summoned by a Czech hooker. Eventually a young man in a tracksuit and bicycle clips appeared, more closely resembling a boy scout than a purveyor of almost-porn. 'I'd like to see the editor, please.' Hugo smiled his most engaging smile.

'Does he know you're coming?'

'Not yet. But perhaps you could tell him I've got a shit-hot idea for a money column that will appeal to wannabe Porsche-owners.'

'I'll see what I can do,' promised the youth. 'You'd better come up.'

Once inside, the offices of *Upfront* were a surprise. They could as easily – give or take the odd pin-up on the wall – have been the home of *Cycling Weekly*. Hugo wasn't sure what he'd imagined, but certainly something sleazier and smokier than this bright airy space with its brightly coloured furniture and faint whiff of air freshener and hard work.

Even the editor was unexpected, a public schoolboy called Henry.

'I like the sound of your idea.' Henry offered him a bright pink chair. 'I've often thought now we're a share-owning democracy we ought to have a money column. Provided it was angled right. To the young male spender, that is, who probably wants a fast buck rather than a nice safe pension.'

'Absolutely,' Hugo nodded. If he wasn't careful he'd end up writing the thing. The fact that he knew nothing about it clearly wouldn't bother Henry.

'You just have to keep reminding yourself who readers are.' Henry was getting really fired up now. 'They're

"Live Now, Save Later" types. They don't want to be sensible like their dads. Look, why don't you give it a crack? No guarantees, but I'll pay you if I like it. You're on e-mail, I assume.'

'Absolutely,' Hugo reassured.

'Can I tell you anything? About the magazine. Would you like our current issue?' Henry handed a copy over.

Hugo pretended to flick through. 'As a matter of fact, there was something I wanted to ask you. This photograph.' He stopped at the shot of Flo. It really was very erotic. 'How did you come by it?'

Henry stiffened visibly. 'Why do you want to know?'

'As a matter of fact,' Hugo decided honesty would be the best policy, 'she's my brother's fiancée. And she says the photograph was taken without her knowledge or consent.'

'Bloody hell. She's not going to sue us is she?' Henry lost his public school affability.

'Depends if she can find out who took it. She'd rather sue them.'

Henry switched on his computer and keyed something in.

He leaned back in his chair and studied Hugo. 'You're not really going to write a City column for us, are you?'

'Probably not.'

'Will you if I tell you where we got that shot?'

'Possibly.'

'I have a hunch you could do it. Have a go. We got the photograph from someone called Miles Panton.'

'Did you? That's very interesting indeed.' Flo had been telling the truth. He memorized the contact number that had appeared on Henry's screen next to Miles's name. 'Thanks very much.'

Henry winked. 'Just don't tell Miles I told you. He's not a very nice person.'

'So I gather. Thanks for your help. And who knows? I might bung you a few columns after all.'

Outside the offices of *Upfront*, Hugo stood under the pagoda arch in Chinatown and dialled Miles's number.

He was out. Instead there was a useful message addressed to whomever he was due to meet, announcing that Miles would see him at the Soho House at one o'clock.

How very convenient. The Soho House was no more than four streets away. It was three-thirty already, but Hugo had a feeling Miles would be a long luncher.

'Mr Panton, please,' Hugo smiled, with such charm that the waitress, even though she was tired and longing for the end of her shift, found herself smiling back as she consulted her list. 'He's upstairs on the second floor.'

Hugo climbed the two floors with the spring and grace of an athlete. He recognized Miles at once. Miles was sitting at the far end of the restaurant next to an elegant full-length window. His fleshy, decadent face made Hugo think of a spoiled boy who thought he always deserved the biggest slice.

As Miles watched Hugo cross the floor, a spark of understanding dawned on him just seconds before Hugo's punch connected.

With unexpected stoicism, Miles neither cried out nor flinched, but merely dabbed at the blood trickling from his mouth with a pink linen table-napkin.

'She'll hurt you too, you know,' he announced, then returned to his brandy and cigar.

Every time she went out in the next few days, Flo wore sunglasses, terrified that some laddish reader of *Upfront* would have seen the photograph, or that local gossip would have rocketed its sales in Witch Beauchamp. But no one raised an eyebrow.

All that happened was that Buzz called to sympathize and to see if she wanted to try and sue. Blackmills, she explained, were pretending to be shocked, but had declared the photos 'tasteful', by which they meant they generated masses of free publicity.

Flo decided to take Mattie's advice and 'rise above it'. She had plenty to do at the Sheep Centre. It would soon be forgotten, she told herself. At least they'd had some good news there. The local education committee, pending a favourable report from the independent expert Flo had hired, had agreed to let school parties back to Hunting Farm.

Adam said no more about the magazine and had started coming to get Flo on the quad bike again. When she wasn't there one morning, he took Mattie instead. 'Want to come and help find a heifer who's hurt her foot? She trod on a flint and now it's got infected. We need to bring her in for treatment.' He smiled his most winning smile. 'I could do with a bit of company.'

Mattie jumped off the gate post where she was pretending to be a statue and climbed up next to Adam, glowing with importance.

They found the missing cow in the highest field,

leaning against a dry-stone wall, looking sorry for herself. 'Here, girl,' Adam crooned, his tone gentle and reassuring, 'let's have a look at that foot.' Like all female beings, the heifer surrendered herself to Adam instantly.

'You're a wise little thing,' Adam said, so unexpectedly that Mattie didn't know whether he was talking to her or the cow. 'Give me some advice. If you'd done something really stupid, would you tell the woman you were about to marry, even if she might break off the engagement?'

Mattie considered this proposition. She'd guessed there was something not quite right between Flo and Adam. 'I would if the woman I was engaged to had done something silly too, and thought *I* might be the one who did the breaking off.'

'Do you know what,' confided Adam to the heifer, 'Mattie Rawlings may only be twelve years old but she's got more horse sense, sorry make that cow sense, than any adult I know.'

Mattie's small face glowed from amber to red. She was helping two people she loved. 'Glad to be of service. Consult the oracle any time.'

'Actually,' Adam grinned, 'we have Ceefax.'

The best thing about Adam, Mattie decided, was that you never knew when he was joking.

'Where shall I put this?' demanded Ivy grumpily, as she and Alf lugged a vast package between them. With only two weeks to go before the wedding, the presents were beginning to take over the dining room. 'Good Gawd,' Ivy complained, 'this gift must weigh more than I do.'

Alf unceremoniously put down the package and

picked up his wife. 'It does 'n all.' He cawed with laughter as Ivy struggled to regain her dignity.

Dying to know what was inside, Flo unpacked the giant present, finally unveiling, from beneath a shroud of bubblewrap, a three-foot silver statue.

'Gosh.' Flo raised an enquiring eyebrow at Adam. 'This definitely wasn't on the list. I wonder who it's from.'

' 'Ere, Ivy,' Alf inspected the new arrival from every angle, 'I reckon it's the surprise Dickey's been saving up for from his catalogue. He's been smug as a garden gnome for weeks. I wonder why 'un chose this?'

Flo knelt down to inspect the lettering on the plinth.

'I must say,' Adam scratched his head, 'it's perfectly . . .' he floundered around for the right word.

'. . . gorgeous,' Flo supplied firmly. 'Adam, look at this.' Flo felt a sudden catch of emotion that the down-to-earth Dickey, who rarely even spoke unless about the quality of the soil or the likelihood of rain, had secretly saved up for this extravagant flight of fancy. 'It's Flora, the Roman goddess of flowers. How incredibly thoughtful of Dickey. I feel really honoured.'

'Is that what 'un is?' Alf commented laconically. 'To me 'un looks like one of they Daleks.'

'That's 'acause you be about as cultured as a length of garden hose,' Ivy stated, pleased at getting her revenge.

'Please tell Dickey how thrilled we are,' Flo asked Ivy. 'Until we get the chance to tell him ourselves.'

'I'd bury 'im if I was you,' Alf advised. 'Say 'e got lost in the post, like.'

'My goodness,' Pamela exclaimed, looking as happy

as a young bride herself and bearing a vast checklist, with different coloured copies containing lists of tasks for the key wedding participants, 'whatever's that?'

'A lovely present from Dickey,' Flo said firmly. 'It's Flora, my namesake. Isn't that incredibly kind?'

Although nothing further had been said on the matter of the magazine picture, Pamela had decided to overlook Flo's feet of clay, not to mention any other part of her anatomy that had been on display, in the greater cause of achieving a smooth-running wedding day.

'How lovely,' said Pamela, in a tone divided between shock and horror. 'Now, I've got a few tasks I need to delegate to you.'

Ivy groaned audibly.

'Alf, I want you to go and pick up the oasis.'

'What, the rock band?' piped up India-Jane, who'd been sent by her mother to see if any of the Rawlingses could be useful. 'Are Noel and Liam coming?'

Pamela ignored her. 'I mean florist's foam. We'll need enough for ten centrepieces, plus hanging arrangements and two or three really large urns. The florist will help you.'

Alf looked glum. Then he remembered that today was market day in Witch Beauchamp and the pubs would be open. He could get a few pints of Morley's in and ogle the barmaid at the Angel. Brassy piece. But then Alf liked brassy pieces. They livened life up. 'Okay, missus, us'll be off, shall us?' He began to head for the door.

'Hang on a minute, Alf,' Pamela commanded. 'Ivy, I've ordered three dozen boxes of sugared almonds from the stores.'

'What you going to do with them, then?' Ivy enquired.

'They're for the wedding favours.'

'I thought he only got them on the wedding night when everyone's gone home,' cackled Alf.

'Thank you, Alf,' Pamela sniffed. 'They're little bags tied with ribbon that you put at each person's place setting. Pick them up will you, Ivy, there's a dear? Alf will wait for you, won't you Alf?'

Alf sighed. No Morley's Best for him. And not a hint of Donna's forbidden fruit neither.

'Thank you, Ivy. Oh, I forgot. Could you also pick up the organza from Material Girl? Then, perhaps you could run up the bags this afternoon. I'll do you a pattern.'

Ivy's chin went up. She knew Alf would want to nip into the pub and lust after that loose piece behind the bar and she'd promised herself the revenge of eyeing up the tasty young man in the butcher's. Watching him chine a chop brought her out in goosebumps. Now Pamela was demanding she slaved over a hot sewing machine.

As if scenting mutiny among the troops, Pamela treated them all to her most ingratiating smile. 'I know I speak for Adam and Flora when I say how much we really appreciate your help. This wedding couldn't go ahead without it.'

'How about us?' Flo chipped in. 'Shouldn't Adam and I be doing something to help too?'

'You just relax,' cooed Pamela. 'You'll be busy enough next week.'

'Come on,' whispered Adam, putting on a clipped RAF voice. 'Let's make a break for it. There's a whole world out there where people are free and happy and no one talks about weddings.'

'Right,' Flo grinned and they both slipped away, laughing and feeling a bit mean, while Pamela, in check-list heaven, went off to find Uncle Kingsley in case he might be sitting idly enjoying himself.

'So,' Flo entwined her fingers with Adam's, 'where do you want to go? A quiet drink somewhere?'

Adam's fingers tensed in hers. 'No. Not a drink. I'd just like to have you to myself for a change. There's something I wanted to talk to you about.'

'Let's walk down to the river. I'll show you my heron.'

She led him down the narrow path behind Moreton House, over a gentle incline where sheep were peacefully grazing. Now that harvest was over, the bones of the landscape were appearing again. The brown of the ploughed fields was rich and voluptuous, almost like the pile of brown velvet. In the distance they could see Dickey on the tractor, encircled by a cloud of gulls who were searching for worms in the newly turned earth. Down by the river there was at first no sign of Flo's heron but then suddenly he rose up out of the water-meadow, his heavy wings beating.

'Amazing, isn't he?' Flo asked.

'Not as amazing as you,' Adam answered. 'I take all this stuff for granted. You notice every detail.'

'Only because I'm a city girl. It's all new to me.'

'How are you feeling, city girl? Excited?'

Flo nodded. 'And terrified.'

'Flora . . .' Adam began. 'I said I had something I need to talk about . . .' He stopped and looked away as if choosing his words carefully, winding up his courage for some important revelation. She could see how hard he found it. Adam was a man of action not words.

But before he got the chance Miranda and Hugo appeared round a bend in the river, feeding each other blackberries.

'We found them over there,' Miranda laughed, not noticing that she'd interrupted something. 'Huge as plums and absolutely delicious.'

'You know why, don't you,' Adam pointed out, relief unclouding his clear green eyes that he wasn't, after all, going to have to make an act of confession. 'It's because that clump of bushes is over the cess-pit.'

Miranda spat out the giant blackberry and squealed.

'Nothing wrong with that.' Hugo helped himself to a particularly juicy specimen. 'Shit makes the world go round.'

'Are you two up for a quick drink?' Miranda asked.

Flo's eyes raked Adam's face. 'Wasn't there something you wanted to tell me?' she prompted.

'Oh hell, trust us to go and interrupt!' laughed Miranda, looking entirely unrepentant.

Flo registered the proprietorial 'us' of coupledom and glanced at Hugo. He didn't seem to have even noticed.

'Don't worry.' Adam jumped up and pulled Flo after him. 'Nothing that won't keep. After all, we'll be married next week and everyone knows that's when you run out of conversation.'

They stopped at a tiny pub on the river, more like a

front room than an inn, and lazed on the bank for an hour watching a family of swans, before heading back to Moreton and the farm.

'Adam! You're back, thank heaven.' Pamela descended on him the moment he opened the door. 'There's been a bit of a crisis. Alf's van broke down and he needs you to go and fetch him and Ivy.'

Adam took a deep breath. 'Fine.'

'See you later.' Flo reached up and kissed Adam.

'Aaah!' sighed Miranda, snuggling up into Hugo's shoulder. 'Isn't that sweet?'

'Fuck off, Miranda,' Flo replied. 'And stop doing all this Ickle Girl number on Hugo. It's making the rest of us puke.'

'Who's suffering from a nasty case of PBB then?' Miranda replied sweetly.

'What the hell is PBB?'

'Pre-Bridal Bitchiness. Don't worry. I expect it's perfectly natural. Like getting thrush on your honeymoon.'

Market day was the only day of the week that Witch Beauchamp became a metropolis. The car parks filled up with tractors, horseboxes and cattle transporters from early morning and anyone unconnected with the cattle auction had to walk for miles or park on double yellow lines.

Adam swore. There was no sign of Ivy and Alf. He'd hoped they would be standing by the Exchange building. Then he spotted Ivy, surrounded by large bags of oasis, by the bus shelter. He shoved the bags in the boot and helped Ivy into the back of the car. 'Where's Alf got to?'

Ivy raised a disdainful eyebrow.

'Let me guess. The Angel?'

'Where else?'

The Angel was the one place in Witch Beauchamp Adam didn't want to go. 'Ivy, you wouldn't just . . .'

'Me, go into that den of temptation, full of liquor and Jezebels? "The Lips that Touch Liquor,"' she quoted loftily and clearly inaccurately since Alf liked his pint, '"Shall Never Touch Mine."'

Maybe Donna wouldn't be behind the bar today. He racked his brains for her day off, then his spirits plummeted. Whatever it was, it wouldn't be market day. Market day in Witch Beauchamp was the rough equivalent to harvest at Moreton. All hands were required on deck.

The saloon bar was so packed and dark it was impossible to see who was in it. The only light came from a vast fire which crackled away unnecessarily, ignoring the fact that it was glorious September, the best month of all in Westshire. The cigarette and pipe smoke gave the room an air of being seen through dirty glass. Farm workers, who risked themselves against the elements daily, and got very badly paid for it, were not going to sacrifice smoking, one of their few pleasures, for the piffling reason that it might kill them.

Adam tried to pick out Alf without being spotted himself. It didn't work.

'Hello, there, my lover.' Adam felt a pair of golden arms, plump and sheeny in the firelight, slip round his waist and pull him into a small scullery. Even though he didn't want to, even though he knew this was the last thing he should do, Adam felt himself begin to stiffen in response.

'Hang on a minute,' Donna laughed, stroking the evidence of her power over him, watching it grow in her hand, 'before there's any question of that, I've got something to tell you. Congratulations, young squire, sir, you're going to be a daddy.'

Chapter 19

Aunt Prue was in her dressing gown when she heard a loud tap on the kitchen door. It was Hugo, carrying a large bunch of flowers. 'Could you give these to Flora with my apologies? I'm afraid I behaved outrageously.'

'So Mattie tells me. She says you accused Flo of never keeping her clothes on.' Prue would have smiled, but there was an intensity about Hugo that forbade it.

'Worse. I accused her of posing for a sexy photograph when she didn't even know it was being taken.'

'And would it have been so terrible if she had posed?' Aunt Prue shocked herself at the question. 'Isn't it rather up to her what she does with her body?'

'But she didn't. She was telling the truth. I went to see the editor of the magazine.'

'You did *what*?' thundered Flo's voice behind them. They both turned to find Flo, in a baggy tee-shirt and bed socks, her hair standing up like a cockerel's. 'How dare you? It's got absolutely nothing to do with you. How *dare* you interfere in my life like that? I'm perfectly capable of fighting my own battles. What if I'd wanted to sue? You could have screwed the whole thing up for me. And the thing is – *it's nothing to do with you*. You're not even my fiancé!'

'So, you were just going to let Miles Panton get away with it, were you?' Hugo was beginning to sound as angry as she was. 'You'd have let him just sit there with his self-satisfied smile and his ponyskin shoes.'

A thought struck her. 'You didn't go and find Miles too, by any chance.'

Aunt Prue bit her lip. Hugo was flushing uncomfortably.

'You didn't hit him, by any chance?'

'Just the once,' Hugo admitted.

'And I suppose that satisfied your male sense of injustice, did it? You felt your property was protected, even if it was actually your brother's property.'

Hugo stiffened. 'Don't worry. You won't have to stand my Neanderthal values any longer. I'm going away. On business. I won't be back till just before the wedding.'

'Thank God for that,' Flo snapped. 'Now I'd better put some clothes on before you accuse me of trying to seduce you.'

'In those socks?' Hugo attempted a smile. 'Hardly.'

'I think you'd better go. And you can take your flowers with you.' She flounced back upstairs.

After Hugo and his flowers had left, Auntie Prue and Mattie looked at each other. 'I wonder what's got into Hugo,' said Prue.

'As if we didn't know,' said Mattie.

Walking back to Moreton House, Hugo told himself that he must stop, that the whole thing was ridiculous. Everything Flora had said was right. It was just that there was one thing he could still do for her which, if he pulled it off, would be the best present he could ever give her. On the other hand, he might screw it up and her fury with him today would be nothing compared to her fury then. Maybe he should leave well alone.

On the other hand, leaving well alone was one thing he'd never been very good at doing.

Half an hour later, Prue knocked on her niece's door. 'D-Day minus seven. And the weather's looking great.'

Flo leaped off her bed. 'I don't want it great today. It might shine itself out by the wedding. The very expensive forecast we got from the Met Office is pretty iffy.'

'Nonsense. Ivy says the swallows and martins are flying high above the river.'

'And what does that tell us exactly?'

'It means it'll be fine, you see. When it's good weather the swallows and martins fly high to eat the midges. The midges stay down by the river when it's going to rain. That's when you see the swallows swoop.'

'So no swooping swallows spells good weather?'

'Exactly.'

'Do the Met Office know this? They could save millions on satellites. Has Hugo gone?'

'Yes.'

'Good.'

'Aren't you a little bit pleased?'

'What? That Hugo's gone? Thrilled.'

'That he hit the odious Miles.'

'He was just being Neanderthal. Like he said.'

'Hugo Moreton is the least Neanderthal young man I know.'

'You've got a soft spot for him, haven't you, Aunt Prue?'

'I've always liked dark looks and there's something thrilling about clever men who get physical.'

'But he behaved outrageously.'

'Yes.'

'It was nothing whatsoever to do with him.'

'No.'

'If anyone was going to hit Miles it should have been Adam.'

'But Adam didn't. Hugo did.'

'And are you saying there's some deep significance in this?'

'I'm saying I'd think about it if I were you.' She smoothed the ruff of dark hair that Flo had been sleeping on. 'Look at you, you look about six in those socks.' She turned away suddenly, wiping a tear. 'I wish your mother were here.'

Flo put her arms round Prue's neck. 'We both do. We know that. There's something about weddings that needs mothers and fathers of the bride. Still, I have a wonderful aunt and uncle instead.'

'Your uncle is looking more sheepish than a flock of Southdowns, terrified at making his speech.'

'Just tell him to keep it short, and no jokes about pretty ewes.'

'Not having second thoughts? No cold feet or pre-wedding jitters?'

'Nothing a furry hot water bottle couldn't cure. I suppose, if I'm honest I do have one worry.'

'What's that?' Her aunt tried not to look alarmed.

'I'll hate to leave Hunting Farm. It's become like home to me.'

'But you won't be leaving,' Prue smiled through the gloss of tears that had welled up, making her feel very foolish indeed. 'You'll be practically next door.'

'I know. Isn't it amazing?' Flo's voice rang with pleasure. 'All my life I've wanted a family. Now I'll have you and Uncle Francis and Mattie and India-Jane and Vee, not to mention Ethan and Hepzibah and all their little brothers and sisters.'

'Flora,' Prue broke in, her tone more serious, 'I know you've longed for a family of your own, but are you sure life on a farm is what you really want? It's a very seductive fantasy but real life is very different.'

'I know. I've seen your worries up close, remember.'

'Of course you have. Even how farming drove Francis to drink and very nearly to suicide. We owe you a lot, Flora.'

'Not as much as I owe you.'

'Which is why I thought I ought to talk to you.' Prue looked away, took a deep gulp of air, and plunged in. 'You don't seem, I don't know, quite as happy as a bride-to-be should be. Of course, it might just be wedding nerves. But what if it isn't? The reason Francis and I have come through in the end is because we love each other. Are you sure you love Adam for himself, not the idea of being a farmer's wife in a gorgeous farmhouse?'

Flo ran her hand through her hair, hurt and angry. 'If

anyone else asked me that, I'd sock them one. Surely you haven't been listening to Pamela? Do you assume, like she does, that it's really Moreton House I'm after?'

'Not Moreton House, no. But maybe a kind of corn on the cob lifestyle? I suppose what I mean is,' her aunt's eyes held real anguish, 'I know you long for the family life you never had, but is it Adam you love, or the way of life he represents? Because if it isn't really Adam, no amount of smiling children on quad bikes will make you really happy. Or him for that matter.'

Aunt Prue got slowly to her feet. 'End of lecture. I'm sorry. I'll go now. If I'm imagining this, all you need to do is tell me so.'

'Aunt Prue.' Flo looked her steadily in the eye, pushing any residual doubts firmly out of her mind. 'It's all in your imagination. I love Adam for himself.'

'Fine.' Her aunt's smile, the smile Flo had been seeing so much more of lately, was firmly back. 'Okay, now the lecture's over we can start really enjoying ourselves. What are you doing about a hen night?'

'I hadn't thought. But I know just the person to organize it.'

Miranda was thrilled to be asked. With Hugo away she had no real reason not to go back to London and work. Flo's request had two advantages. First, she could phone in sick and stay on in Maiden Moreton. Then she could proceed to drink so much at the hen night she actually *deserved* a sick note.

The nice thing about being out of London was that they could forget any attempt at sophistication.

Miranda discovered a naff nightclub in Chippenham, complete with dayglo cocktails and male strippers. Flo hadn't, until that night, imagined herself as the kind of girl who'd anoint a bodybuilder with baby oil and stick a daisy up his bum.

She was wrong.

But Pamela had been the real revelation. After inviting herself, drinking three cocktails in a row and giving a surprise rendition of 'Roll Me Over In the Clover', including several particularly rude verses no one else had heard, she was sick out of the minibus window on the way home. Flo suspected she wouldn't be doing any more wedding planning the day after.

'You look terrible,' India-Jane greeted them all the next morning. 'How can it possibly be called fun to get totally drunk, throw up in the flower bed, and feel this bad the next morning?'

'Why indeed?' asked Miranda, clutching her head. 'And anyway, who was so drunk they threw up in the flower bed?'

All eyes turned accusingly to Flo. 'Of course,' Miranda conceded, 'that was after you'd performed an indecent act on the male stripper.'

Flo paled and threw her head into her hands. 'I didn't!'

'No. You didn't. To be fair you'd have needed jaws the size of Tower Bridge to attempt it.'

Flo nervously glanced at India-Jane.

'Don't worry,' India reassured her, 'we've done all that stuff in PHSE.'

'Oh, God.' Miranda clutched her head. 'I wish Hugo

were here. He's got this amazing hangover cure that involves Ribena and Dioralyte.'

'I didn't know Hugo went in for hangovers,' Flo commented. 'He always seems so responsible and disapproving.'

'You'd be surprised. There's a lot you don't know about Hugo.' Miranda smiled to herself. 'I wish he'd hurry back.'

Flo felt a pang of, what? Envy at the obvious affection in her friend's tone? How ridiculous. She'd deliberately thrown them together. She could hardly object that the plan had worked.

'Right, only two more days to go. What do you fancy doing? Helping your prospective mother-in-law in a highly responsible way or bunking off to the beauty salon to get our nails done?'

'No contest, I'd say.'

'Plus, an aromatherapy massage might bring us back to the living.'

'That would be bliss.'

'Just avoid the Reflexologist. She'll tweak your toes and charge you twenty quid to tell you you've got the mother of all hangovers, which you could have told her in the first place.'

'So, where shall we go?'

Flo racked her brains. Neglecting her health and beauty regime had been one of the joys of country life. No more eight glasses of spring water a day, eating nothing but lettuce leaves and weighing yourself every ten minutes. In Westshire mud was something you got on your boots, not paid to have smothered on your face.

Within five minutes Miranda had located the only really expensive beauty salon in three counties.

They spent a blissful day wrapped in fluffy white towels, indulging in facials, having their nails done, and being stroked and pummelled. 'Right,' Miranda demanded halfway through the day, 'how's your bikini line? A girl's got to think about such things on her wedding day. How about getting Lesley here to sculpt your pubes into a nice heart shape? You don't want sex to be predictable, now do you?'

Miranda sat up, so fired with enthusiasm she nearly dropped her glass of passion fruit juice. 'I know. You could have a tattoo. With a letter A for Adam and an arrow pointing to the crucial part.'

'Miranda,' Flo giggled, 'for God's sake calm down. That's one set of directions Adam *doesn't* need.'

It was four in the afternoon before they finally left, minus a large dent in their Visa cards, or rather Miranda's because she'd insisted on paying for the treat as a wedding gift.

'What utter bliss,' Miranda sighed with satisfaction, 'I haven't felt so satisfactorily plucked and pummelled in a long time.'

'You are a brilliant friend,' Flo thanked her, linking arms with her as they went in search of the Beetle. 'I finally feel like a bride-to-be.'

'Just as well.' Miranda threw her bag in the back of the ancient, open-topped VW. 'Since it's less than forty-eight hours till your wedding.'

Back at Moreton House everything was chaos.

'Oh, there you are!' Pamela swooped down on Flo

like an elegant dove with its feathers ruffled. 'Thank heavens!'

'What's the matter Pamela? You didn't think she'd changed her mind and run off to disco in Ibiza, did you?' Miranda asked.

Pamela ignored her. 'The vicar wants you and Adam to rehearse in the church. He'll be here in half an hour. Could you go and pull Adam off his wretched tractor?'

For once Adam wasn't on his tractor.

'He'd be up beyond the river, looking at the winter wheat,' shouted Dickey.

'Thanks, Dickey. And thank you for your beautiful statue. I'll find a good place for it in the garden when all the fuss dies down.'

Dickey grinned, his weathered face disappearing into wrinkles as deep as a gnarled oak tree. 'That should annoy Her LadyBitch. Not quite her style. Though happen she won't be up at the house much longer. Day after tomorrow, *you'll* be new Lady of the Manor.'

Flo waved goodbye, Dickey's words reverberating in her head. Perhaps one reason Pamela was organising their wedding with such mad energy was to put off the thought that, if not now, then at some time soon custom decreed that she move out of Moreton House. It would now belong to Adam and his new wife. Her.

'Bye, Dickey,' she called. 'And make me one promise.'

'What be that?'

'That when I'm living at Moreton House you won't call me Her LadyBitch.'

'Ah,' conceded Dickey, 'I'm making no promises. But I doubt you'll behave like 'un.'

Adam was kneeling down when she found him, over to the far left-hand corner of the field near the river, examining the tiny seedlings.

Flo knelt down beside him. 'Your mother wants us,' she smiled. 'Time for the run-through in church.'

'Fine,' Adam nodded. 'Look at these seedlings. They've only been in the ground a week and already they've put down roots. They'll hang on in there now through snow or drought, growing every day until we harvest it. Just like a baby taking root in the womb.' There was a curious catch in his voice she'd never heard before. 'Amazing, isn't it, the cycle of life?'

Flo touched his cheek. It wasn't like Adam to be philosophical. 'Yes it is. And we're about to be part of it. Are you ready now?'

Adam stood up. 'Yes, I'm ready.'

'Let's go and make your mother happy then.'

Maiden Moreton church had originally been built for the exclusive use of the family and retainers. It was a small stone structure, more of a chapel, and not as dark as a medieval version would be, with more room for pews.

Even without the flowers that would soon adorn it for the wedding, it had its own peace and beauty, and a kind of whitewashed simplicity that spoke of continuity and a reassuring timelessness. Standing here, before God and a hundred of your closest friends, you could indeed believe that you were part of life's rich tapestry.

Uncle Francis was already standing up at the front. 'To think,' he whispered, patting her hand, 'I'll have to go through this three more times.'

'You'll be an expert by then. And remember – at least this time you're not paying.'

'Have you agreed on the vows?' asked the vicar.

'Yes,' Adam nodded, 'we're dropping the obey bit.' His eyes strayed to the long side window, too late architecturally for stained glass, but giving a magnificent view of the churchyard.

A figure appeared to be standing at the lych-gate, watching the proceedings. Perhaps it was a passer-by. Everyone in villages loved a wedding.

Then there was a click, as if someone had opened the outer door of the church, but no one came in.

'Right,' proceeded the vicar, eager to get home to his wife's shepherd's pie and tonight's episode of *Countdown*. 'Where's the best man?'

'Still away on business, I'm afraid,' apologized Pamela. 'But I'm sure he'll be back in good time.'

'One certainly hopes so,' tutted the vicar. This was turning into a very unpredictable union.

'When *is* Hugo due back, Ma?' Adam asked.

'I'm not really sure. I was expecting him back already.'

'He is coming though?'

'For heaven's sake, Adam. Hugo wouldn't dream of missing your wedding for the world.'

'Then I wonder what the bloody hell's keeping him.'

The vicar gave Adam a quelling look.

'He's certainly cutting it a bit fine,' Uncle Francis endorsed. 'There's not long to go.'

Flo squeezed her uncle's arm tighter. Soon she'd be married to Adam. Soon she'd have her very own family.

When the rehearsal was over they filed out of the church together.

In the porch, sitting on the ancient weathered bench in a nest of bright red tissue paper were a brand new pair of baby bootees.

'Funny,' said Pamela, picking them up. 'I could have sworn they weren't there when we came in.'

'Probably something to do with a christening,' suggested the vicar. Only two minutes now till his programme started. 'I'll pop them over to the vicarage till someone comes and claims them.'

'Good heavens,' Pamela blurted, suddenly struck by the symbolism, 'You don't think this is some kind of rural ritual do you? Like that thing they did in *The Mayor of Casterbridge*.'

'The Skimmity-ride? That was to expose people who were having an affair, wasn't it?' Flo tried to recall the details from her English Literature days.

'Exactly. So this could be someone implying you're having a shotgun wedding.'

'Really, Pamela.' Uncle Francis came to the rescue. 'What an extraordinary turn of mind you have. I'm with the vicar on this one. Probably just a mislaid christening gift. Now,' he clapped a white-faced Adam on the back, 'who's joining me for a quick G&T?'

Chapter 20

'Break-faaast in bed! Break-faaast in bed! We say Happy Wedding Day with break-faaast in bed!'

Flo was woken up by the sound of Mattie, closely pursued by Snowy yapping at her side, carrying a tray with a white cloth, on which croissants, butter, jam and a mug of coffee were beautifully arranged

'Mattie, you are thoughtful! What a lovely way to start my big day.'

She spread the butter and jam onto the croissant and bit into it, almost cracking her tooth in the process. It was hot outside but frozen solid in the middle.

'Nice?' Mattie's serious little face looked at her hopefully.

'Perfect,' lied Flo. 'Is everyone up?'

'Mum's in the kitchen working out a rota for the hairdresser's, Miranda's annoying her by sitting smoking at the kitchen table, Ivy's furious with Alf because he hates weddings and won't come and India's sulking because Dad said he liked my hair like this.'

Mattie had had her hair trimmed the week before,

transforming it from bird's nest to bob, and India-Jane deeply resented the dawning of any interest in looks, no matter how faint, in her sister.

'Sounds pretty average for a wedding day then. Any hot water left?'

'I'll go and see. If there is, you deserve it. I'm sure it's the bride's prerogative not to pong.'

'Thank you, Mattie,' Flo acknowledged faintly.

Fortunately there was plenty of water left and Flo was able to luxuriate in its foamy depths, listening to a CD of 'Music to Marry By' which had come free with *Wedding Day* magazine. She looked out of the small bathroom window, lost in the stately grandeur of Pachelbel's 'Canon', soaping her skin to the thrilling tones of 'The Arrival of the Queen of Sheba', then drying herself to the 'Grand March' from *Aida*. Finally she stood, entirely nude, and tried on her tiara, as the music started on the 'Wedding March'.

Elaine, the hairdresser in Witch Beauchamp, only had two basins, two hairdryers and two stylists, so Flo and Aunt Prue took precedence over Vee, India and Mattie. Ivy had already been, using her 'pensioners half-price on Thursday' offer. Pamela, naturally, wasn't mixing with the hoi polloi and had hired a hairdresser to call at Moreton House. Joan from the shoe shop, Ivy informed them all in a snide tone, had gone all the way to Swindon. 'I wonder what *she* be up to, trying to gild the gingerbread at her age,' muttered Ivy darkly.

'She's not *that* old,' pointed out Prue tartly. 'Certainly under sixty. Anyway, I think you mean gild the lily.'

Prue, Flo noticed, was putting up with a lot less

nonsense from Ivy lately. Before long she'd be telling Ivy what to do instead of being bossed around by her.

'Can't think why she wants to go all that way,' complained Elaine. 'We do her hair usually. Of course, if we aren't good enough . . .'

'Maybe she wants a change of image,' Flo offered diplomatically. It was amazing how diplomacy was a social skill in London but a survival skill in the country.

'Well, I hope they don't go over the top,' muttered Elaine into the mirror. 'Now, how do you want this blessed tiara on?'

'Where *is* Hugo?' demanded Pamela, her voice getting shriller by the moment. 'Have you tried his London number?'

'Yes,' Adam replied testily.

'How about that girl's house? Flora's friend. Melissa?'

'Miranda. She's over at Hunting Farm. She hasn't heard from him either.'

'Then what about the wretched banks he does business for. They must know where he is!'

'It's Saturday, Ma,' Adam replied, his patience wilting by the minute. 'The whole of the City closes down on Saturdays. Besides, I've never really listened when he's talked about them. They could be any banks as far as I'm concerned.'

Pamela dodged a scurrying caterer carrying a trough-sized bowl of salad.

'I can't believe this of Hugo. It's incredibly selfish.'

'Yes, isn't it.' Adam was rather enjoying Hugo being

branded the selfish one for once. Usually Hugo was Mr Responsible. 'I'll never speak to the bastard again if he lets me down.'

'We'll just have to have a contingency plan. Kingsley!' Uncle Kingsley, who was just about to pour himself a stiffener, looked round guiltily. 'It'll have to be you.'

'What will have to be me?'

'You'll have to be Best Man if Hugo doesn't get here in time.'

'I won't have to make a speech?'

'*His speech!*' yelped Pamela. 'Who's going to make the speech?'

'Not quite as vital as the bit in church,' Adam commented. 'I wonder what he did with the rings.'

'Don't worry, I've got them.' Pamela moved out of the way before she was mown down by the florist, who clearly couldn't see out from behind the vast arrangement he was carrying.

Kingsley made the drink he was stealing a double.

'Right, Kingsley, what are you going to wear?'

'I could get out my tails, I suppose.'

'Perfect. And Kingsley?'

'Yes?'

'No trainers.'

'I can't understand it,' Miranda shook her head. 'Hugo seemed such a reliable kind of person. Do you think it's because of me? Is this an over-the-top way of saying he doesn't want to see me again?'

'There would be easier ways of getting out of a relationship than offending your brother and alienating your entire family,' Flo reassured. 'He's probably just stuck in some stacking pattern over Heathrow.'

'There are such things as phones,' Miranda pointed out tartly. She was wearing a skintight black sheath-dress with black and white ponyskin mules.

A huge black feathered hat crouched on the bed like a malevolent crow, waiting to be put on.

'Very Cruella de Vil,' remarked India-Jane, who looked misleadingly sweet and innocent in white organza with pale pink daisies around the hem.

'Actually, I was going to buy it in Schiaparelli pink but I didn't want to upstage the bride.'

'That's not like you,' teased Flo.

Miranda ignored her. 'Adam must be incredibly upset.'

'Let's just keep our fingers crossed. There's still another hour to go.'

Mattie appeared at her elbow. 'How are you doing on the "something borrowed" stuff?' she asked shyly. 'Only, I wondered if you'd like to have this?' She held out a metal medallion of Lisa Simpson. 'She's sort of my idol. She's brave and she always tries to sort things out. Rather like you.' Mattie blushed. 'But you don't have to have it. Really.'

'I'd love it.' Flo held out her arms to the little girl, feeling unbearably touched. 'She's sort of my idol too. Thank you.'

Mattie beamed.

'I've got something blue for you,' India offered, not one to be outdone. It was a flower-shaped ring, from a Christmas cracker, with a flashing blue stone.

'Perfect.' Flo slipped it on. 'Now, all I need is something old.'

'Your dress,' reminded Mattie. 'Mum says it belonged to your mother.'

'Absolutely.' Flo looked away, almost overcome that she could possibly forget.

'And I suppose, unless you want to leave your bridegroom standing at the altar, you'd better put it on.'

With Miranda's help, Flo gently eased herself into her mother's satin dress. 'It's the most amazing fit.'

They both looked at Flo in the mirror. Aunt Prue suddenly appeared with a camera, just as Miranda was fastening the veil to the back of the tiara. 'Smile! Make a wish!'

Flo laughed. 'I thought that came later.'

'Well, you never know. Make one now anyway.'

Flo didn't really have to. Her wish was always the same. 'Is Uncle Francis ready?'

'Yes, and very, very nervous.'

'Ivy's already gone. Wearing an outfit that looks suspiciously like our old bathroom curtains. She couldn't persuade Alf to change his mind. He's gone to put fertilizer on the winter wheat instead.'

'Just like Adam will be doing to Flo later on,' Miranda cackled.

'I hope he doesn't use the same technique,' offered Auntie Prue in a rare joke. 'Alf wears a gas mask and uses a spray gun.'

They tried not to dissolve into giggles when Veronica arrived in the room, with more flowers on her dress than Kew Gardens.

'Watch out, Vee,' offered India-Jane, 'don't bend over or you might get plucked.'

'Not with my luck I won't.' Miles, she remembered with irritation, hadn't even had the courtesy to reply to her invitation.

'Right,' Vee adjusted her hat, which was adorned with even more blooms, 'it's half-past three. Time we all set out for the church, don't you think?'

'I must say, Kingsley, you're a fine figure of a man in tails,' Pamela congratulated. 'You should get dressed up more often.'

Uncle Kingsley adjusted his top hat in the vast gilt of the hall mirror. 'Good. Now where have you put my button hole?'

'*Button holes!*' shrieked Pamela. 'I knew I'd forgotten something! I haven't ordered any sodding button holes!'

Kingsley looked at Pamela in alarm. Swearing, like laughing aloud, or having a good time, was something alien to his fragrant sister.

'Us'll go and pick some roses, shall us?' offered Dickey, who was in charge of driving the car to church in case it was needed.

'Absolutely,' Pamela thanked him, rooting around for safety pins.

Dickey came back with an armful of white rosebuds. 'You're a lifesaver, Dickey. Pin one on yourself while I do Adam and Kingsley. Do you think Alf will be needing one?'

'Alf bain't coming. Says he prefers funerals. At least they're honest. All that nonsense about worshippin' with your body.'

'I must admit,' Adam confessed, holding out his lapel so that Pamela could pin on his rosebud, 'I can't quite see Ivy going in for body-worshipping.'

'Ouch! I've stuck the pin in my finger!' Pamela swore again.

A small trickle of blood appeared, which she wrapped swiftly in a tissue.

'That bain't a very good omen, be it?' Dickey shook his head. 'Blood on a weddin' day. That bodes bad luck right enough.'

'We've already had the bad luck, Dickey,' Adam pointed out irritably. 'There's no sign of my brother Hugo. And he's supposed to be the bloody best man!'

They all trooped out to start the short walk over to the church, leaving the small army of caterers, florists and the string quartet to finish their final preparations.

Dickey hung back for a moment, a few feet from the catering tent. He'd been watching the caterers' comings and goings and had worked out exactly where the brandy was kept. That would sit nicely on the three or four glasses of home-made peach liqueur to which he'd already treated himself, strictly in the honour of the bride and groom.

By the time they got there the church was already three-quarters full. Four of Adam's old school friends who had agreed to be ushers, and various farmhands, were in charge of supervising the car parking in two of the nearby fields.

Despite Dickey's dark predictions, everything seemed to be going well.

The soothing notes of Pachelbel's 'Canon' floated out

into the glorious blue of the September afternoon.

'Ready to take the plunge?' Uncle Kingsley asked Adam gently. 'Better get in there before the bride arrives. Weddings are one time when it isn't Ladies First.'

Pamela turned her son to face her. With his blond hair, golden skin and pale green eyes he was a dazzling bridegroom. Flora Parker was a very lucky girl.

Behind them, a sudden diversion made Pamela turn.

It was Joan. At least they thought it was. Except that her grey hair had miraculously become an elegant silvery blonde, and her rather frumpish clothes had been replaced by something understated but distinctly glamorous from Frank Usher.

My God, thought Pamela furiously, *she looks better than I do!*

The wedding party were all so taken up with Joan's transformation that none of them noticed another guest slip uninvited into the church.

In the interests of camouflage, Donna had abandoned her usual style for something more discreet by Laura Ashley. With the addition of a straw hat from the charity shop, which she'd trimmed with silk flowers, she blended in quite nicely.

'Bride or groom?' asked Adam's oldest prep school friend as Donna walked confidently into the flower-filled church.

'Neither,' she answered in a low fruity voice, 'I'm the other woman.'

Adam's friend laughed at her joke and speculated that, if she wore a bit less eye make-up, she'd clean up really very well.

Five minutes later Adam set off down the aisle, smiling and waving to friends and guests.

When he approached Donna's pew she turned her head and gave him the benefit of her most alluring look.

Everyone in the village had turned out to watch the progress of the bridal party as they strolled the few short yards across the green to the church. One or two of the cottages had put out flags or white streamers, and small children stood on walls, throwing petals in Flo's path.

'Your mother walked the same way,' Prue whispered, then wished she hadn't. Flo's happy smile turned wistful round the edges as the ghosts of the past came and settled among the happy waving villagers.

Outside the church, Uncle Kingsley stood and waved back. 'I'm standing in for Hugo. Not as good looking but at least I'm here.'

'Hasn't he even been in touch?' Flo asked, stunned. Poor Miranda. She'd be so disappointed. And Adam would take it as a deliberate slight, no matter how good the eventual excuse.

'Not a dickie bird. I must say I'm surprised.'

Flo stopped to admire the outside of the church for a moment. All round the entrance, a flower arch had been built, just like the one she'd made for the Young Farmers' dance, bursting with pink roses, alchemilia mollis, cornflowers and Japanese anemones. Inside the church she could glimpse the pew-ends draped in a similar display.

'Aren't the flowers glorious?' Flo squeezed her uncle's

hand. All she had to do was step through the arch and into her new life.

'Will you take my arm?' Uncle Francis offered. 'I think I can hear them starting up the "Wedding March".'

Flo took a deep breath. This was it. The day she'd dreamed of all her life. The day she would finally fit in and have a family of her own.

Somewhere in the distance she could hear the faint sound of shouting, out of place on this happy and harmonious day.

Aunt Prue picked up her train and distributed it among the bridesmaids. Then she straightened her niece's veil and gave her a tender kiss on the cheek. 'You're a truly beautiful bride. I know Mary will be smiling down on you.'

The shouting in the street was getting louder. Flo and her uncle glanced round in time to take in Alf driving his tractor at Grand Prix speed down the village street. Two men were hanging on behind him.

Flo felt her heart plummet like a lift whose shaft has broken. One of them was Hugo Moreton.

And the other was her father.

Chapter 21

'Hello Flora.' Her father spoke the words Flo had fantasized so wildly about hearing. 'I'm sorry this is so last-minute. I've come to give you away.'

A swirl of emotions flooded through her. Anger. Relief. Gratitude. Fury. Love.

Inside the church the 'Wedding March' finished. After no more than a beat, it tactfully started up once more.

For a brief second Flo thought of hitting him with her bouquet or kneeing him in the groin.

Instead she opened her arms and he held her so tight that the satin of her mother's dress was crushed against her. Flo didn't care. She shut her eyes and held on like she had when she was a small girl, before everything had started to go wrong.

When she opened them, her hazel eyes were level with his dark ones and tears blurred her vision. 'I should bloody well think so,' she said after almost a minute of silence had passed between them. 'About time too.'

'Hello Martin.' Prue, usually the most level-headed

of women, heard the crack of emotion in her own voice. 'Welcome back.'

Behind her father, dressed in a morning suit, Flo was aware of Hugo's presence for the first time. 'How on earth did you find him?' she asked.

Hugo smiled. 'It's a long story.'

'What he means,' Martin cut in, 'is that I took a lot of convincing. All that stuff about immovable rocks and irresistible forces. But then Hugo is pretty persuasive. He knew how much it would mean to you if I made it and, I can tell you, he wouldn't give up till I came.' He looked from his daughter to the young man with whom he had spent the last two days and decided to take the risk. 'And he obviously loves you to distraction. So why the hell are you marrying his brother?'

For less than a heartbeat, the world stood still.

Adam hadn't even noticed her father's absence. Hugo had spent days persuading him to come.

'I think we'd better go in,' Uncle Francis said gently. 'That is, if you still want to.'

Flo's gaze darted to her aunt's, but Prue was still struggling with the shock of her prodigal brother-in-law's return. Flo was on her own.

If only Hugo would say something, confirm or deny what her father had just asserted. But he remained obdurately silent. Maybe this was some notion he had of fair play, or maybe her father had just got it all dreadfully wrong.

The vicar suddenly appeared in their midst, fussing about like an anxious old lady. 'Is there something the matter? The bridegroom is looking rather nervous. He's been standing at the altar for twenty minutes now. Could you possibly put him out of his misery?'

All eyes were on Flo. She took her father's arm, her heart still beating wildly. 'Yes,' she said, smoothing the satin of her mother's dress, 'we're just coming now.'

Clutching on to her father as if he were all that kept her from disintegrating into the ether, Flo weighed everything up. She'd chosen Adam because he was so different to her, because he complemented her, and together they made a whole.

As she walked slowly down the aisle to the tune of Mendelssohn's 'Wedding March' it struck her that perhaps this was exactly what her mother had thought, wearing the same dress in the same church. But was her parents' marriage the model she wanted for her own?

As they passed each flower-decorated pew a ripple of recognition spread through the church like a wave. Miranda, huge hat taking up two spaces, caught sight of Hugo and mimed a mock sigh of relief.

Pamela's face was a picture, then she recovered herself and whispered frantically to Kingsley, who stepped away from Adam and prepared to hand over the rings to Hugo.

The next few minutes, when the vicar greeted the congregation and said the opening prayers, passed as if in a dream for Flo. Even the rousing tones of 'Bread of Heaven' couldn't penetrate her shocked and trance-like state.

And then came the moment everyone had gathered to hear.

'Dearly beloved,' intoned the vicar, 'we are gathered

here in the sight of God and in the face of this congregation to join together this man and this woman in holy matrimony.'

Flo's heart began to feel like a trapped bird wildly beating its wings against the cage as if its life depended on it. She glanced desperately round but saw nothing but smiles of love and anticipation. Hugo looked stonily ahead.

Two thirds of the way back, Donna moved to the end of the pew, unnoticed by the main protagonists, pushing past people who gave her furious looks of disapproval.

'I require and charge you both as you will answer at the Day of Judgement,' intoned the vicar with remarkable jollity – he enjoyed this bit – 'that if you know of any impediment why you may not be lawfully joined in matrimony, you do now confess it.'

The silence seemed to last for eternity, although it was only a few seconds.

'Yes,' said a voice, clear and steady, and surprisingly loud. 'I'm afraid I do.'

Chapter 22

Throughout the church people strained forward in their pews, as if waiting for some explanation for this disaster. The organist stopped checking through the music for 'Where Sheep May Safely Graze'. Pamela looked so pale and shaken she had to be steadied by Kingsley. Miranda's crow feathers shook in disbelief. Uncle Francis and Aunt Prue exchanged glances of what could be dismay or relief.

'Oh shit,' muttered India-Jane to Mattie, in a distinctly audible whisper. 'Do you think we can keep the frocks?'

Flo turned to Adam, who stared at her, his face a picture of wounded disbelief.

'I'm so sorry, Adam. This is all my fault. I didn't realize until he asked us that question what a terrible mistake we were making. We'd have only regretted it.'

'This is all to do with Hugo, isn't it?' Adam demanded. 'I knew, you know, but I decided to give you another chance. Don't think if you marry him you'll get the farm. Donna and I will get married first. And she's having my baby, so we've even got Uncle Kingsley his precious heir.'

Adam turned on his heel and strode furiously back up the aisle, grabbing Donna as he passed.

At the end of the pews she turned, giving the congregation a wide smile of triumph.

'Gosh,' whispered Mattie, close to tears. 'Who'd have thought Adam would behave like that?'

'What do we do now?' Flo's father asked, not looking nearly as upset as he ought to for someone who'd come three thousand miles to a cancelled wedding. 'Do you want me to take you home?'

'Hold on a moment,' Hugo spoke for the first time. He turned to the vicar. 'Do you think I could have a word in private? Could you come and help out too, Uncle Kingsley?'

The three of them disappeared into the vestry, with the vicar muttering that it was all most embarrassing, and it had never happened in his church before.

They were only in the vestry for five minutes or so, but to the party still standing at the altar the time seemed infinite. A thousand thoughts crowded into Flo's mind, but she brushed them all away.

With Adam she'd been, as Prue had tried to tell her, pursuing a dream, not a relationship. She could blame Adam for carrying on with Donna, but that wasn't the core reason for her change of heart. The real cause was that until this moment she'd let her fantasies overrule her instincts. Now, this time, she'd follow what they told her, which was that Hugo, not Adam, was her soulmate, the man she could truly love with her whole being.

The organist switched from 'Where Sheep May Safely Graze' to 'Ave Maria' just as Hugo came out of the vestry with the vicar and a smiling Kingsley.

'Ladies and gentlemen,' Hugo announced, his dark hair flopping into his eyes in the way Flo now realized she loved. 'On behalf of our two families I'd like to apologize. You've come for a wedding. And, with any luck, a wedding is what you shall have.'

Flo's heart did a dance. She smoothed the satin of her mother's dress and smiled at her father tenderly. He squeezed her hand in return. Happiness and relief lit up her whole being. It was going to be all right. She hadn't screwed up her entire life. She'd got to the very brink of disaster and found that it was Hugo she really loved, not his brother.

'So, with great thanks to the Reverend Honeywell,' Hugo continued, 'I would like to invite you to celebrate the union of two very special people.' Flo's body leaned forward of its own volition. 'My uncle, Kingsley Moreton, and the woman he has secretly loved for so many years, Miss Joan Little.'

Chapter 23

This time the gasp of the congregation was audible. It was soon drowned out by the cheering and clapping as Joan, glowing with love and happiness in her brand new clothes, made her way to the front of the church and took the hand of a delighted Uncle Kingsley.

'Her LadyBitch won't like that,' whispered Dickey to Bill, who was standing next to him at the back of the church.

'About time too,' muttered Ivy. 'She's been waiting thirty year for him to make an honest woman of her.'

'Thank God for that,' breathed Miranda, directing her most dazzling smile at Hugo.

In the front pew, on the left side, unnoticed by the major participants in the drama, Pamela had to sit down and fan herself.

Rising to the occasion, and with admirable tact, the organist rejected a third rendition of the 'Wedding March' in favour of a rousing version of 'The Arrival of the Queen of Sheba'.

*

The wedding reception had a giddy charm, borne of the unexpected.

The guests drank faster and laughed louder and were more prepared to make fools of themselves on the dancefloor than anyone could remember at a country wedding. Someone remarked that it reminded them of VE Day, after the war had ended.

The catering staff were particularly thrilled, since Pamela took the opportunity to install herself in a chair at the bottom of the garden, hit the Pimm's No 2, and leave them completely alone.

'How did the guv'nor manage that, then?' asked Alf admiringly.

'He's been carrying round a marriage licence for six months now, not daring to pop the question,' said Ivy. 'Mr Hugo was the only one who knew.'

'He's a sly one, then, eh? In't he?'

Flo slipped discreetly back to Hunting Farm and changed out of her wedding dress, folded it carefully back into its sea of tissue paper and placed it gently back in the hatbox.

'Are you all right?' asked a soft voice behind her.

It was her father.

'Yes. I'm fine,' Flo lied.

'No, you're not.' Martin came over and sat on the bed beside her. 'You're aching with hurt. Not just today but from all those years I neglected you.'

Flo had told herself she was going to be strong but the tone in her father's voice melted her resolve like ice in August.

'I thought I could create a family with Adam. Put

down roots. Being so near to Aunt Prue and Uncle Francis made it even better. I'd belong at last. I don't think I really knew Adam or what he wanted.'

'And it was my fault you were so desperate to do it.' In the mirror she saw the bald patch on her father's head. His youth and vigour seemed less convincing up close. 'I loved your mother so much. I suppose all my life I wanted her to myself.'

Flo wasn't sure how she dared say the next words. Maybe she'd already lost too much today to care. 'Prue says it was a selfish love, that you were thinking of you, not her.'

Martin's body shook with one volcanic sob. 'Prue was right.' His voice was low and anguished. 'And how could I not see the miracle of you?'

As the light began to fade from the sky they clung to each other, silently, drawing comfort from each other's presence. Finally, it was her father who spoke.

'I'm sorry about Hugo.' For the first time Flo noticed the transatlantic twang that had settled in his voice. 'I guess I got that young man wrong.'

'Like I did his brother.'

Flo straightened her shoulders and turned to face him. 'I've decided to go back to London. It's been a lovely fantasy here, and they're great people. Especially Prue and Mattie. But I suppose, deep down, I'm a city girl at heart. You can take a girl out of the city . . .' she started.

'. . . but you can't take the city out of the girl,' Martin finished for her. 'You could come to America with me. Make up for some of those lost years.'

She smiled tenderly. 'I'd like to visit. But for now I need to get my life sorted out. If it isn't here, I need to find out where it is.'

The thought of leaving all this – the farm, the Sheep Centre, even Ivy and Alf, and the sense of belonging she'd felt for the first time – was almost too much to bear. But there was no reason for her to stay now.

'Feel like going back to the party?'

'Yes.' She put her hand up to her hair and realized she was still wearing her tiara.'

'You were a beautiful bride. I'd say you will be again but you'd probably kill me.'

'I'd strangle you with my bridal garter. And enjoy every minute.'

'It was your mother's dress, wasn't it?' His voice skipped like a stone on dead water.

'Yes. Prue had kept it.'

'Mary would have loved that.'

'Except for one detail. I didn't actually get married in it.'

'At least you didn't pay good money for it either, as your mother would have said.'

'There is that. We even managed to recycle the reception. I should have guessed about Joan and Kingsley. I'm so happy for them.' She put the tiara in the hatbox with the dress and veil.

'Ready to show 'em you haven't collapsed and turned to the smelling salts?'

'Yes. I'd love to raise a toast to Joan and Kingsley. Let's go.'

The marquee was still thronged with guests, and the

small dancefloor packed with revellers in various stages of insobriety, trying to follow the elaborate movements of the Maccarena.

There was no sign of Hugo and Miranda. Flo tried not to think where they might have got to.

'So,' Uncle Francis appeared beside her, and slipped his arm round her, 'bit of a turn up for the book. Though I'm surprised at Adam. I thought more of him than that. Are you all right, Flora love?'

'It'll be that Donna's influence,' Ivy threw in darkly from the dancefloor. 'They do say she's a witch.'

'I'd say Donna's appeal is strictly earthly,' corrected Flo.

Aunt Prue noticed with delight that Flo and her father seemed to be on intimate terms. Thank God something had worked out for the best. 'Hello Martin,' she greeted him with a friendly smile, trying to forget the times she could have cheerfully beaten him to death. 'Where have you been all this time?'

'Making a terrible mistake. Missing years of Flora's life.'

'Well,' Prue said meaningfully, 'you can make up for that now.'

'Yes. I hope Flo's going to come and visit soon.'

Flo looked round for Pamela. In some ways all this must be hardest on her. Losing a son. Gaining Donna. And now losing her brother as well, with whom she'd spent half her adult life, as well as shared her home. 'Have you seen my almost-mother-in-law anywhere?'

'Come to mention it, no.'

Aunt Prue took her hand. 'I'm so sorry, darling. We

were all deceived by Adam, not just you. If it's any consolation, I don't think he was using you. I think he wanted the farm, certainly, but he was dazzled by you, by your kindness and your warmth and your sophistication.'

'But what he really wanted was Donna.'

'I don't suppose it'll last five minutes.'

'Do you think they'll want to live here?'

Prue shrugged. 'I can't see Donna as a farmer's wife. Though she might like to try out being Lady of the Manor for a while. Just to annoy Pamela and queen it over the locals. Anyway, what I wanted to say was that we've loved having you. You've brought us back the happiness we'd lost. Do stay. You'll always have a place at Hunting Farm.'

Flo fought back a sob. Her dream of finally belonging here had so nearly come true.

'You wouldn't have been happy,' Prue sensed what she was thinking. 'Not if Adam had been carrying on like that.'

'No,' Flo agreed. 'I think I'll just go and look for Pamela.'

There was no sign of Pamela outside in the marquee or the garden so Flo slipped up the impressive staircase.

She finally found Pamela in her bedroom. Her hair had come adrift from its elaborate hairstyle and there were black runnels on her elegant cheeks where the mascara had run. She was stuffing clothes into a huge suitcase on the bed. 'I've decided to go away for a bit. Leave the lovebirds to themselves. I couldn't bear to be here when Adam brings that girl back.'

'No. I'm sorry about all this. You organized a wonderful wedding.'

'Yes. Just not for the right person. It's been a trying day.'

'Where will you go?'

'To a friend in Cornwall, I expect. Till I get a clearer idea.'

'I'm going back to London. For roughly the same reasons.'

Pamela paused in her packing and smiled a small, tired smile. 'Life doesn't turn out the way you expect, does it? If it's any consolation, you would have made a lovely daughter-in-law. Fun, thoughtful and a much better hub of the community than I ever was. You'd have organized the flower festival and the children's Easter egg hunt brilliantly. Ivy and Alf dote on you. I never had the common touch.'

On an impulse, Flo hugged the older woman. She felt Pamela's bony, upright body stiffen then melt for a moment. 'Good luck, Flora.'

'And to you, Pamela.'

Chapter 24

It took Flo a while to make the break.

Disobligingly, the weather turned into an Indian summer and became the most glorious end to September anyone could remember. The sky remained a deep Greek blue, with not even the highest, tiniest clouds to mar its clear vastness. Everyone said it looked more like Montana than Maiden Moreton. The days were cooler, but only pleasantly so, and the sense of approaching autumn gave it a sharper tang. A 'gather ye rosebuds', or in the case of Westshire, gather ye black-berries and sloes, mentality set in.

It was almost as though the countryside was making itself deliberately hard to leave, like a mistress who senses the end of an affair and invests in erotic under-wear.

The worst thing of all was watching Snowy and Mattie together. Mattie had changed more than anyone else during Flo's months there, and part of her blossom-ing into confidence had been down to the little dog, Flo was sure of it. It was hard to imagine Mattie tucked away in an airing cupboard, frightened by the adult anxieties of the world, now. Still, Flo told herself, her aunt and uncle could always get Mattie a dog of her own.

Flo snapped her case shut. It wasn't as full as she'd expected. Life at Hunting Farm hadn't required a vast wardrobe.

Downstairs her aunt and uncle, Vee, India-Jane and Mattie had all assembled to see her off. Even Ivy appeared and pressed a box of scones into her hand. They weighed a ton.

'Goodbye, Flora darling. Come and stay as often as you like. We'll always be here.' Practical Aunt Prue brushed a tear from her eye.

'I will.' Flo struggled to keep the emotion out of her voice. 'I promise.'

'Thanks for everything, Flora,' Uncle Francis said softly. 'You were a lifesaver. Literally.'

It was too much for Flo. This time the tears started and she had to grab Snowy and bury her head in the little dog's soft white fur as she said goodbye to Vee and India and Mattie.

Then the inspiration came to her, agonizing at first, but irresistible in its logic.

'Here, Mattie. You keep Snowy. London's no place for a dog anyway, even one that's half pyjama case, like Snowy. She'll be much happier making a nuisance of herself here with you.'

Mattie's face lit up, then crumpled. 'Flo. I couldn't. She's your dog. You'd miss her dreadfully.'

Flo wiped her face, stroking Snowy's fur, damp from her tears, one last time.

'She'd only pine for you and the open spaces. You keep her. It'll give me all the more reason to visit, won't it?'

Mattie took the little dog and clung on to her. 'Thank you, Flo. We'll e-mail you, won't we Snowy? To tell you how she's getting on.'

'You do that.'

'Goodbye, Vee. Come and visit.'

'I will.'

'Goodbye, India.'

'Adam was all surface dazzle, you know,' India-Jane confided from the vast experience of her ten years. 'I never trust charm. It's a very dubious character trait.'

Flo smiled in spite of herself. 'You should be a writer with that razor perception of yours.'

India looked thrilled. A pink blush stole over her clever nut-brown face. 'I'm writing a short story as a matter of fact. About a city girl who comes to the country and falls in love with it.'

Flo laughed shallowly. 'You would. And does it have a happy ending?'

'I don't know yet. What do you think?'

'I'll tell you when I get back to London.'

She climbed inside and undid the roof of the Beetle.

'See you all soon. It's been the best time.'

Hugo had been staying with Miranda since the wedding.

Miranda, who could never bear to have anyone's

smelly socks in her pink boudoir, found there were exceptions. She even got a kick out of washing Hugo's. And she loved the fact that when he came home before her, he'd make them both a meal. And there was no fuss and no desperate need to be praised for his Herculean achievements.

He bought flowers too. Until Hugo's arrival, Miranda had gone in for a single calla lily, the pretentious person's flower du jour, but Hugo loathed them. He liked corny red roses, for God's sake. And after only a week, their timeless charm was becoming more and more apparent to Miranda.

Hugo had brought a whiff of reality into Miranda's rarefied lifestyle. And she was loving every minute.

Well, not every minute. She didn't love the silences or the habit Hugo had of staring into space then shrugging, as if physically dislodging some powerful image from his mind's eye. As if she didn't know what it was.

At first Miranda's solution was constant activity.

If Hugo didn't get time to sit down, he wouldn't get time for unexpected images settling in his brain.

And then she went and said it. The fatal words, the simple sentence Miranda had willed herself not to utter, with all the enthusiasm of a con man avoiding a lie-detector test.

'You're thinking about Flo, aren't you?' she asked one evening, before she could strangle the question at birth.

The words sat there, bald and shiny and threatening in the cosy nest Miranda had been trying to create.

Hugo shrugged.

Miranda's eyes raked his face like twin lasers. This

was it. Her big chance. Maybe her only chance and she was torpedoing it. She couldn't believe the words were hers.

'You'd better go, then, hadn't you?'

She longed for him to say, 'I don't know what you mean,' or even 'Flo's not interested in me.' Instead he leaped to his feet, kissed her with grateful passion and ran out of the door. 'I know why she chose you as her friend. You're fabulous. Thanks Miranda!'

'Me and my big mouth,' Miranda mumbled and got herself the biggest glass of wine she could pour.

Flo found she could hardly drive for the tears that clouded her vision. Especially when she came across Kingsley and Joan waiting in the drive to wave goodbye. Prue must have phoned them.

'Goodbye Flora.' Kingsley tried to look sad, but he was clearly too blissfully happy to pull it off.

Behind him, a man was up a ladder, banging. Flo's heart stopped when she saw what he was doing. He was putting up an estate agent's For Sale sign.

'Kingsley!' she said urgently. 'You're not selling Moreton House after all this?'

'I'm afraid so. We had a letter from Adam's solicitor. He and Donna have decided to try their luck in Spain. They need some capital.'

'Oh my God, I'm so sorry, Kingsley.'

'It's only a house,' Kingsley shrugged, but she could hear the pain in his voice. 'Do you want to say goodbye? I've got a buyer arriving in five minutes. From the City. Wants something to do with this year's bonus now he's already got the Porsche and the hunter. You've just got time.'

Flo nodded. To think she'd dared to imagine it might all be hers. Its perfect Queen Anne proportions, the lovingly tended herbaceous borders, the walled kitchen garden, and the years of Moreton family history, dating back to the Roundheads and the Royalists. She knew which side the Moretons would have been on. What would some flashy city type make of it? A weekend pad to show off. He'd probably install a multi-gym in the chapel.

'Sad old day, eh, for the master?' Flo jumped at Alf's question. She hadn't seen him digging the large flowerbed. 'But then, he weren't very wise to make that bet in the first place, were he?'

'No, I suppose not. What are those flowers you're digging?'

'Michaelmas daisies. I have to separate 'em or they'll be takin' over the garden.'

Michaelmas.

It was Michaelmas that had started off this crazy situation. To think she hadn't even heard of it before she came here. Like so many other things. Telling herself to stop all this stupid regret, she took a deep breath.

'Hello, Flora.' The sound of another voice rooted her to the spot. 'My uncle said you'd be out here saying goodbye to the house.'

Flo's face flushed redder than a poppy in an August wheatfield. 'Hugo! I thought you'd gone back to London with Miranda.'

Hugo's hair flopped into his eye and he had to brush

it away sheepishly. 'I've been given my marching orders.'

'Oh?'

Behind them, Alf concentrated furiously on his digging.

'Yes. I talk about you all the time, apparently. Miranda said why didn't I just go and tell you that it was you I really wanted.'

Flo felt suddenly lightheaded as if from lack of oxygen. 'And is she right?'

'Of course she is. It's always been you. But you preferred Adam.'

'Until I got to the church.'

'Yes.'

'So why didn't you say anything to me then?'

'You were too upset.'

'I'm not upset now.'

When Uncle Kingsley and his portly buyer appeared round the corner five minutes later they were assailed by an unusual sight.

Flora Parker, locked in a passionate Rodin kiss with Hugo, while behind them, apparently in blissful ignorance, Alf kept on steadily digging.

It was only when Kingsley coughed loudly that they prised themselves apart.

'Good God,' beamed Kingsley. 'I wish you two had thought of this a little earlier. Then things would have been very different.' He looked at the buyer with dislike. 'Unfortunately you've left it too late. I'm legally bound by Michaelmas.'

'Aah,' mused Alf, finally putting down his fork, and

busying himself with the purple daisies, 'but which one? You didn't ever say *which* Michaelmas, as I recalls, did you, squire?'

'What exactly are you getting at?' asked Uncle Kingsley testily. And then it dawned on him exactly what Alf was implying. 'Stap me! You're right, Alf.' Uncle Kingsley looked as if Moses had just come down from the mountain and handed him a tablet of stone. 'I didn't say anything about which Michaelmas.'

'Can someone fill me in?' asked Flo, mystified.

Hugo was suddenly grinning like a gargoyle. 'What Alf means is that there are two Michaelmases. Old Michaelmas Day used to be in October – the eleventh, I think.'

'And new Michaelmas is the end of September,' offered Kingsley.

'What date is it today?' Flo asked, finally catching their drift.

Alf looked at his state-of-the-art digital watch that Dickey had got him from his catalogue. 'It be October the eighth, according to this here watch.'

'Then there's still time!'

Hugo grabbed Flo's hand and started running.

The City buyer stepped backwards out of their path. He'd always found country types rather weird.

'Excuse me, Mr Hugo!' shouted Alf after them. 'But haven't you forgotten something?'

Hugo stopped, momentarily nonplussed. 'What's that?'

'You bain't asked the lady yet. It is custom. Even in these parts, you know.'

Hugo dropped to one knee. 'Flora Parker, would you do me the honour of becoming my wife, mistress of Moreton House and saviour of four-hundred years of history from someone who couldn't give a toss?'

Flo dropped down to the grass next to him. 'I will,' she said loudly and clearly. 'If you put it like that I don't have much choice, do I?'

'No.' Hugo pulled her against him and bent his lips to hers again. 'None whatsoever.'

'Plenty of time for that later,' Uncle Kingsley tutted. 'Now get yourselves down to the register office, will you?'

'Would someone kindly explain to me,' the buyer demanded, finally losing patience as Hugo, Flo and Kingsley tore off across the lawn, 'what the hell is going on?'

'I reckon,' Alf announced, turning back to separating the Michaelmas daisies to hide his glee, 'you can probably conclude that Moreton Manor's no longer up for sale.'

'Then you can all go and fuck yourselves!' retorted the buyer, brushing out his unsuitable linen trousers.

'I think,' Alf grinned to himself, eager to get home and tell Ivy the good news, 'that's more or less what Miss Flora and Mr Hugo's got in mind.'

Acknowledgements

This book has been a pleasure to write thanks to the help given to me by so many people, and because of the love they feel for the rural way of life.

First thanks are to my continual inspiration (not to mention mother-substitute) Anne Norris, farmer's wife and farmer's daughter, and to her husband Noel of Crowham Manor Farm, Westfield, for their friendship and fascinating information about farming past and present.

To Jane and Ray Ellis of Lullington, East Sussex, and their son, Duncan, who not only painted an exceptionally useful picture of the farming year but also took me on a combine!

To Richard and Anne Brown of Clapham Farm, Litlington, who always look the perfect country family on their quad bike, for their very useful input.

To Terry Wigmore of the Seven Sisters Sheep Centre, East Dean, whose grandfather was a shepherd and who keeps the shepherd's craft alive for modern generations.

To Ruth Gasson, former Senior Research Fellow, Centre for European Studies, Wye College, University of London, and active supporter of the Women's Farm & Garden Association.

To Sue Gaisford, countrywoman and writer, for her hilarious vignettes of country living.

To Kitty Mason for first introducing me to my 'place of the heart' and to my great friend Cresta Norris, for suggesting it.

To everyone in the village of Litlington who have made us, the wicked weekenders, so welcome. Nothing could have made our lives – and memory banks – richer than our years here.

To my agent and friend Carole Blake, *not* a country girl, for her support and for the wonderful line that she's always grateful the country's there, as long as she doesn't have to visit it.

To both my editors and friends Imogen Taylor and Barbara Boote and all at Little, Brown who are phenomenally helpful and always bursting with enthusiasm.

To Stella Gibbons for writing the best book that could ever be written about rural life.

To the author (unnamed) of a wonderful leather-bound tome of the 1920s entitled *The Farming Year* which gave me the inspiration for how to resolve my plot.

To my daughters for putting up with my country passions even though, on the whole, they'd rather be shopping in Brent Cross.

To my son, Jimmy, for loving the country still.

And lastly to my new husband, Alex, with whom I tied the knot after seventeen years (and three children) in 2000. I had to have a wedding in this book because I had one in real life too!